MOTION TO KILL

"Who said she needs protection, Counselor?" said Sheriff Kelly Holt.

"Anybody who starts the day with a dead husband needs protection," Lou Mason answered.

"This is an official investigation. I don't need any volunteers."

"I've got an obligation to my partners to find out what happened." Though true, it was the least of Mason's concerns. If Sullivan's death weren't murder, telling Kelly that both his client and his dead partner were crooks would put him on the hit list. "Just tell me what your next step is. Maybe I can help."

She didn't miss a beat. "Was Sullivan working on anything that might make someone want to kill him?"

He expected the question. "The firm has a lot of clients who have a lot of problems and are unhappy about all of them. I can't tell you anything because of the attorney-client privilege."

"Counselor, I spent the last ten years with the Bureau sifting through more double-talk than you can imagine. I'll make this simple. If you withhold information in a murder investigation, I'll lock you up before the ink dries on the warrant."

BOOK YOUR PLACE ON OUR WEBSITE AND MAKE THE READING CONNECTION!

We've created a customized website just for our very special readers, where you can get the inside scoop on everything that's going on with Zebra, Pinnacle and Kensington books.

When you come online, you'll have the exciting opportunity to:

- View covers of upcoming books
- Read sample chapters
- Learn about our future publishing schedule (listed by publication month *and author*)
- Find out when your favorite authors will be visiting a city near you
- Search for and order backlist books from our online catalog
- Check out author bios and background information
- Send e-mail to your favorite authors
- Meet the Kensington staff online
- Join us in weekly chats with authors, readers and other guests
- Get writing guidelines
- AND MUCH MORE!

**Visit our website at
http://www.kensingtonbooks.com**

MOTION TO KILL

Joel Goldman

PINNACLE BOOKS
Kensington Publishing Corp.
http://www.kensingtonbooks.com

PINNACLE BOOKS are published by

Kensington Publishing Corp.
850 Third Avenue
New York, NY 10022

Copyright © 2002 by Joel Goldman

All Kensington Titles, Imprints, and Distributed Lines are available at special quantity discounts for bulk purchases for sales promotions, premiums, fund-raising, and educational or institutional use. Special book excerpts or customized printings can also be created to fit specific needs. For details, write or phone the office of the Kensington special sales manager: Kensington Publishing Corp., 850 Third Avenue, New York, NY 10022, attn: Special Sales Department, Phone: 1-800-221-2647.

Pinnacle and the P logo Reg. U.S. Pat. & TM Off.

First Printing: February 2002
10 9 8 7 6 5 4 3 2 1

Printed in the United States of America

For Hildy, the wife of my life

ACKNOWLEDGMENTS

A number of people were instrumental in helping me with this book. From the beginning, my wife Hildy and my children—Aaron, Danny, and Michele—supported me. Many people, including my sister Susan, my cousin Merilyn, and my friend Dan, read and reread the early drafts, adding their enthusiastic encouragement. My agent, Meredith Bernstein, gave me a chance and became my good friend. Michaela Hamilton and Lucas Mansell helped me round out the book. John Fraise, retired Kansas City Police Department Homicide Detective, provided reality checks. Paul Dinas, Editor in Chief at Kensington Publishing, turned my dream of writing into the joy of authorship. My editor at Kensington, Karen Haas, guided me through the final turns with a steady hand. I am grateful to all who helped make this happen.

Chapter One

A dead partner is bad for business, even if he dies in his sleep. But when he washes ashore on one side of a lake and his boat is found abandoned on the other side, it's worse. When the sheriff tells the coroner to "cut him open and see what we've got," it's time to dust off the résumé. And the ink was barely dry on Lou Mason's.

The time was seven-thirty on Sunday morning, July 12. It was too early for dead bodies, too humid for the smell, and just right for the flies and mosquitoes. And it was rotten for identifying the body of a dead partner. These are the moments to remember.

Mason's dead partner was Richard Sullivan. Senior partner in Sullivan & Christenson, his law firm for the last three months. Sullivan was the firm's rainmaker. He was a sawed-off, in-your-face, thump-your-chest ball buster. His clients and partners had loved the money he'd made for them, but none of them had ever confessed to liking him. Though in his late fifties, he had one of those perpetually mid-forties faces. Except that now he was dead, gray as a Michigan winter and bloated from a night in the water.

Sullivan & Christenson was a Kansas City law firm that employed forty lawyers to merge and acquire clients' assets so they could protect them from taxation before and after death. When bare-knuckled bargaining didn't get the deal done, they'd sue the bastards. Or defend the firm's bastard if he was sued first. Mason's job was to win regardless of which bastard won the race to the courthouse.

The U.S. attorney, Franklin St. John, had been preparing a special invitation to the courthouse for Sullivan's biggest client, a banker named Victor O'Malley. The RSVP would be sent to the grand jury that had been investigating O'Malley for two years. Sullivan had asked Mason to defend O'Malley the day Mason had joined the firm as its twelfth partner. Mason had accepted and Sullivan had spoon-fed him the details of O'Malley's complex business deals. Mason quickly figured out that O'Malley had stolen a lot of money from the bank he owned. He was having a harder time figuring out how to defend O'Malley. Fifty million dollars was a lot to blame on a bookkeeping mistake.

Two days earlier, Sullivan had taken Mason to lunch and, over a couple of grilled chicken Caesar salads, casually inquired what would happen to O'Malley's defense if certain documents disappeared.

"Which documents?" Mason had asked.

Sullivan had studied Mason for a moment before

answering. "Let's assume that there are records that show O'Malley and one of his business associates received favorable treatment from his bank."

Mason hadn't hesitated. "That's what the whole case is about. There are too many of those documents to lose even if I didn't mind going to jail with O'Malley. Which I do."

"Lou," Sullivan had said gently, "I only care about the documents with my name on them. Do you understand?"

Mason had nodded slowly, wiping his hands with a white cloth napkin more than was needed to clean them. "I'm not going to jail for you either," he'd answered evenly. "I'll look at the documents, and we'll figure something out."

Sullivan had given him the pained look of a disappointed parent and changed the subject. Mason knew then that he'd never see the documents. And in the same instant, he'd also known that his career at Sullivan & Christenson was over. He had failed Sullivan's test, but passed his own. He'd decided to think it over during the firm's annual retreat that weekend, but he knew what he would do come Monday morning. Quit.

The retreat was at the Buckhorn resort at the Lake of the Ozarks in southern Missouri. It had been a long weekend of golf, drinking, and leering for the lawyers and staff. Mason had gone for a walk after the Saturday night poker game, stopping at the beach, a kidney-shaped plot filled with sand along a retaining wall at the water's edge. A slight breeze rolled off the water, just enough to push the air around. A young couple was braided together at one end of the beach. He lay down at a discreet distance on the only lounge chair, turned his back to them, and felt the loneliness of the voyeur.

He didn't realize that he'd fallen asleep until a voice interrupted the recurring dream of his last trial before he'd joined Sullivan & Christenson. Tommy Douchant, his client, his best friend, looked up at him from his wheelchair, eyes wild, tears beading on his cheeks, as the jury announced its verdict against them. Mason begged the jury to come back, to listen to him, as they filed out of the courtroom, their faces dissolving as a voice sliced through his dream.

"Excuse me . . . are you Lou Mason?"

Tommy rolled back into Mason's subconscious as he opened his eyes. The voice belonged to a woman standing over him, backlit by the glare of the morning sun. The glistening effect was a mixture of a Madonna-halo and a Star Trek transporter. He thought about asking her to beam him up while he rubbed any leftover drool from his chin stubble.

The best he could do was a slightly sleep-slurred, "Yeah, I'm Mason." Snappy repartee after spending the night on a bed of vinyl was sometimes the beginning and end of his charm.

"I'm Sheriff Kelly Holt. We need to talk."

"It's okay, Officer, I paid for the room." *Drumroll, please,* he silently requested, satisfied that he was really hitting his stride now.

"I'm sure you did, Mr. Mason. I'm more interested in whether you know Richard Sullivan."

Fully awake now, he stood so that he could see her clearly. Khaki uniform, Caribbean-blue eyes, Pope County Sheriff's badge, natural, no sweat beauty, pistol on her hip. A shade shorter than his six-feet, with honey-colored hair that draped the shoulders of a tanned, athletic body. She was a slap-on-the-cuffs dream come true, but her question flattened the fantasy.

"He's my law partner. Is there a problem?"

"I'd appreciate it if you would come with me. I'll meet you in the lobby at six forty-five, that's in ten minutes. You may want to change first."

Mason looked down at his beer-stained T-shirt and gym shorts with a hole where the pocket used to be. He realized he was losing on banter and style points.

Doctors, lawyers, and cops all use the same technique when they give bad news. They tell you a little at a time. Knowledge is power—give it away all at once and the power is gone. Having done the same thing, Mason knew better than to press.

He was ten minutes late, but smelled better and looked better in tan chinos, green polo shirt, and deck shoes. The rest of him fit the clean clothes. Dark, closely trimmed hair, and steel-gray eyes that his aunt Claire always claimed darkened like thunderheads whenever he was angry. An anonymous flying elbow thrown during a muddy rugby scrum had left him with a speed bump on his nose just below eye level. He was clean-shaven at seven, but could expect a five-o'clock shadow an hour early. Good orthodonture bred a sincere smile that juries had found persuasive through ten years of practice in his first firm. It had yet to be tested in his new one.

Mason had had some luck and notable failures—his ex-wife, Kate, being foremost—with women. He knew it wasn't politically correct to immediately appraise Kelly as a social prospect, but it filled the time while he waited for her to tell him what was going on. She showed no more interest in him than in any other out-of-towner she'd awakened on the beach, and she wasn't talking. So Mason took the first shot as they settled into her pickup and pulled away from the resort.

"Listen, we can play twenty questions or you can just tell me what this is all about."

She smoothly shifted gears as she kept her eyes on the curving road that snaked away from the lake. A two-way radio crackled with background static. He rested his head against the butt of a shotgun mounted on the rear window.

Kelly chose questions over answers. "When did you last see Mr. Sullivan?"

Mason rolled the window down and let the truck fill with the muggy morning air. The smell of summer flowers and long grass was a welcome change from midtown traffic.

Sullivan had sat across from Mason at last night's poker game, his first with his future former partners. For a ten-dollar buy-in, he had spent the evening with a good cigar, cold beer, and an open window into their psyches. Mason believed that poker makes you win with your strengths and fold with your weaknesses. Luck always plays a part, but even the luckiest lousy cardplayer will eventually lose it all if he gives the cards enough time. Sullivan was a good cardplayer, but he'd hit a losing streak that could spread to the other partners who depended on the business he brought in.

"Last night around eleven. We'd been playing poker."

"Who else played?"

"Snow White and the seven dwarfs. All the regulars."

"You were better company before you woke up.

Or is this just a phase of your arrested adolescence?''

"Tell me what happened to Sullivan. After that and eight hours of sleep on something besides vinyl, I'll charm your socks off."

She answered without a sideways glance or a hint of humor. "One of the locals found a body this morning. It's been in the water overnight. The ID belongs to your partner. I want you to tell me if the body belongs to the ID."

Her voice was pure matter-of-fact, as if she had told him to check the tires and the oil. He caught a quick dip in her shoulders, as if she was dropping her burden of bad news in his lap. Still, she said it with a practiced weariness that convinced Mason she was used to violent death. He wasn't. He was accustomed to family deaths, natural causes, and ritualized grieving. Floating bodies were not part of Mason's life-cycle résumé.

Barring a freakish case of mistaken identity, Mason knew that Sullivan was dead. The odds of his ID being mismatched with a stranger were slim. Mason didn't know him well enough to grieve honestly. Partners are harder to get to know than spouses or friends. Agendas overlap only on narrow ground.

His emotions were a mixed bag that didn't include grief. He was more relieved than sorry. Mason knew that Sullivan's suggestion that Mason destroy evidence in the O'Malley case would be buried with him. Mason could stay at the firm if he chose. Yet he couldn't muster any enthusiasm for reversing his decision to leave. There was, he realized, no glory in defending Victor O'Malley. His aunt Claire's warning that he wasn't cut out to fight over other people's money, especially when the money was dirty, echoed in his mind. His recurring dream of Tommy Douchant's trial reminded him of unfinished business that he would have to complete on his own. Sullivan's death may have shown him the way out instead of the way back in.

Mason was certain that Sullivan's death wasn't accidental or natural. The sheriff would have told him so, since there would be no reason to withhold that information. The likelihood that Sullivan's murder was tied to the O'Malley case and perhaps to the documents Sullivan had asked him to lose swept through him like a convulsion. He was shaken by the twin possibilities that the killer might want to eliminate O'Malley's other lawyer and that the sheriff might suspect him in the crime if she knew what Sullivan had asked him to do. He felt his color drain and hoped the sheriff would attribute it to the grief he couldn't summon. It occurred to him that he was probably the least likely person to identify Sullivan's body.

"Why did you choose me?" Mason asked her.

At last, she surrendered a small smile. "You weren't my first choice. We found a key to a room at Buckhorn. It belonged to Mr. Sullivan. The hotel manager gave us a list of the rest of the guests from your firm. You were third on the list. The first two checked out at dawn."

"Harlan Christenson and Scot Daniels," he said as she nodded.

Harlan Christenson had sat next to Mason at the poker table. He was a grandfatherly patrician of Kansas City society, opening doors that Sullivan never could have knocked on. Where Sullivan was brusque and kept everyone at arm's length, Harlan touched everyone. He shook their hands warmly and guided them to his office with his arm comfortably around their shoulders. He was widowed and Mason was divorced, so he invited Mason to his farmhouse for dinner every couple of weeks after he'd joined the firm. They cooked out and tossed fishing lines in his pond, never really trying to catch anything. Together Sullivan and Christenson had built a powerful practice. A shock of white hair hung loosely over his forehead, accenting his coal black caterpillar eyebrows. Shaped like a badly stuffed pillow, he had filled his chair to capacity and grunted his bets with a scotch-scratched voice. Only his head and hands had moved as he'd peeled back the corners of his first three cards, praying for aces.

Mason's other best friend and law school classmate, Scot Daniels, had sat on his other side. Scot and Tommy Douchant had flipped a coin to decide which one would be best man at Mason's wedding. Scot had called heads and won. Tommy claimed he'd used a two-headed coin, a charge Scot never denied. Scot had started with the firm when they'd graduated and was now second in command in the business department, which Sullivan ran. Ten years after graduation, he still carried 175 pounds rationed along a swimmer's V-shaped frame that barely stretched to six feet. His eyes were robin's-egg blue with the shell's dull finish. Fine dark blond hair, slicked back, etched an undulating hairline along an angular, sallow-cheeked face. Scot's expressions had broadcast the roller coaster of poker's changing fortunes.

Kelly asked, "Any idea why they left so early?"

"Scot had to get ready for a closing on Monday. Harlan said he had a noon wedding."

"And that left you, Mr. Mason. What were you and your partners doing at the lake?"

"Having our annual retreat. Lawyers, legal assistants, and administrative staff getting away from it all but not each other."

She pulled in at a marina called Jerry's Port. The water rolled with a slight chop stirred by the steady boat traffic of the lake patrol. Mason's chest tightened along with his throat as he wondered if he'd recognize Sullivan's body. He remembered a wrongful death case he'd handled in which the victim had drowned. A body left in water long enough swells up like an inflatable doll, stretching the features into a macabre mask. The pictures of the deceased in that case had led to a rash of tasteless jokes in his office, none of which he could recall.

Mason followed Kelly to a sheriff's department patrol boat. She drove the boat while he hoped the spray off the lake would help him keep his cool. Soon she turned toward shore, aiming at a sign that read CRABTREE COVE. The sides of the cove were lined with private docks. Modest lake homes sat above the docks, away from the water that fed a shallow marsh at the heel of the inlet. Two other patrol boats were anchored across the back of the cove, forming a floating barricade. Cutting the motor to barely above idle, they coasted past the sentries until the bottom of the boat slid noisily into the soft mud.

Knee-high grass had been tramped down into a rough carpet leading from the water's edge to a short, squat, rumpled man wearing dirty brown coveralls. He could have been half man, half stump, sitting on a log next to a tarp-covered shape that was roughly the size of a body.

"Mr. Mason, say hello to Doc Eddy, Pope County coroner," Kelly said.

"Damn shame, Mason, too bad," he said wiping his hands on his pants before pulling back a corner of the tarp.

Sullivan's lifeless eyes stared unblinking into the still rising sun. Heat, water, and death had stolen his attraction and intimidation. Oily engine exhaust mixed with the swampy smell of brackish water and the sickly sweet odor of decomposing flesh. Mason's stomach pitched and yawed as he lost last night's dinner.

He stumbled a few yards away while the aftershocks rocked his belly, and his head slowly stopped spinning. Kelly appeared at his side and pushed a towel into his clammy hand. He was surprised at the softness of her skin when their hands brushed against each other.

"Listen, I'm sorry," she said. "There just isn't an easy way to do this. Is it Sullivan?"

The metamorphosis from "him" to "it" suddenly seemed natural. "Yeah, probably—don't know. You better ask his wife." He was fresh out of smart-ass. Dead bodies, Mason realized, are hell on humor.

"We tried to reach her in Kansas City. No one answered."

"That's because she's here—at the lake. They have a place in Kinchelow Hollow near Shangri-La. We're having brunch over there at eleven this morning."

Kelly turned back toward the others. "Doc, we'll meet you at Listrom's Mortuary in an hour. Tell Malcolm to hold the body for identification. Counselor, you come with me to see Mrs. Sullivan."

Kelly aimed him toward the boat with a slight shove. He didn't need the help, but he got the point.

Chapter Two

The path from Sullivan's private dock to the deck on the back of his house followed a switchback route up a slope landscaped with descending terraces set off by railroad ties and planted with a multihued variety of annuals and perennials. Mason thought to himself that if Matisse had been from the Ozarks instead of France, he'd have painted Sullivan's backyard instead of all those gardens. Kelly and Mason climbed the path while Pamela Sullivan watched them ascend toward her from the protective shade of a moss-green canopy suspended over the deck. Mason had only met her once in the last three months. She was cordial but disinterested, a seemingly well-cared-for woman accustomed to the role of professional wife.

Mason wanted to protect her from the news that Kelly carried, even though there was no avoiding it. Protecting people when they were in trouble. That's what the law is for, his aunt Claire had taught

him. She was his father's sister and the first lawyer,
liberal, and hell-raiser in his family. She'd wielded
the law like a club for her clients, who were usually
poor, disadvantaged, or just outnumbered. "There,
that one," she would tell him when he'd been a
child and she'd read the paper to him about the
day's injustices. Then she'd be off on another mission. She'd raised him after his parents had been
killed in a car wreck when Mason was only three.
She'd tried talking him out of going to law school,
telling him that he wasn't cut out for the only
kind of law worth practicing. Her kind. He'd gone
anyway, silently suspecting that she was right. He'd
enjoyed the battle, but didn't care enough about
the war she'd never stopped fighting. When he'd
graduated, he joined a small firm that specialized
in representing injured people.

"It's the kind of practice where I can do good
and do well at the same time," he'd told her.

"Go sell your slogans to someone else," she'd
answered.

Mason thought of Aunt Claire as the sun rose at
their backs. She would have called Kelly the intru-
sive arm of the law. Investigating, accusing, and
punishing. Aunt Claire had taught him that it's the
lawyer's duty to shield the individual from that
power. It was that duty, she told him, that drew
her to the law. He understood the duty but it had
never held the allure for him that it had for Aunt
Claire. Still, as they reached Pamela, he could hear
Aunt Claire's voice telling him, "There, that one."

When Mason had first met her, Pamela had the
look of a handsome woman who did not miss the
untarnished beauty of her youth. She carried herself with the confident assurance of someone who
understood that age brings its own luster. This

morning her chin-length chestnut hair was held back by a lavender sweatband. Her face was lightly made up, but not enough to cover the glow from a just-finished morning run. A trace of sweat darkened the scoop neckline of the yellow T-shirt that hung over her matching shorts. She stood with her hands on her hips, her full chest rising and falling with still settling breath, giving them a quizzical look as they topped the stairs.

"Oh my, excuse me. It's Lou, isn't it?" she asked him with sudden recognition.

"Yes, Pamela. I'm Lou Mason, one of your husband's partners. We met a couple of months ago."

"Of course. Please excuse me. I wasn't expecting you or the police," she added, turning toward Kelly and extending her hand.

"I'm Pamela Sullivan. But I expect you know that or you wouldn't be here. What can I do for you, Officer?"

Kelly shook her hand quickly and firmly. "Mrs. Sullivan, I'm Sheriff Kelly Holt. Would you mind if we spoke inside?"

Pamela said, "My, this is starting to sound quite official." Kelly didn't reply and Pamela's refined control showed the first sign of fraying as she held her arms folded across her chest. "Yes, it is a bit cool this morning, isn't it."

It wasn't close to being cool, Mason thought. Though he understood Pamela's sudden chill. There was no possible explanation for their visit that could include good news. As if she sensed their purpose, Pamela led them slowly inside to delay the inevitable a few seconds longer.

They followed Pamela through a sliding glass door and into the den. Some lake homes are furnished with city house leftovers and garage sale bargains. Sullivan's was furnished with money. Cream-colored, matching overstuffed sofas sat across from each other, separated by a large, low, square table of burnished wood with an inlaid tile border. Floral-upholstered wingbacked chairs faced each other across the other sides of the table. Accessories dotted appropriate end tables, secretaries, and other furniture with decorator names Mason didn't know. Fresh-cut flowers filled the room with a sweet fragrance. One wall was punctuated with six-foot windows, another opened to a full kitchen, and a third held a well-stocked bar. Pamela gently lowered herself onto the sofa as if she understood the fragility of the moment. Uncertain of his status, Mason stood near the sliding door. Kelly sat on the edge of a chair next to Pamela.

"I'm sorry to intrude on you, Mrs. Sullivan," Kelly began in a soothing voice that quickly gave way to a crisp matter-of-factness. "A man's body was found this morning in a cove not far from here. A wallet was also found with your husband's driver's license and credit cards. The man generally matches your husband's physical description. Mr. Mason thinks it may be your husband."

Pamela held fast, her jaw tightened and her eyes widened at the implications. She shook her head in response to the inevitable question of whether she knew where her husband was. Kelly's request that she identify the body left Pamela mute.

Pamela's reluctance renewed Mason's protective instincts. "Sheriff, I'll bring Mrs. Sullivan, but I would think my identification is sufficient."

Kelly barely acknowledged his offer without taking her eyes from Pamela. "You're welcome to come along, Counselor, but identification has to be made by next of kin if possible." Her soothing tone was reserved for the newly widowed. He was entitled only to her official voice. "You can bring Mrs. Sullivan in her car," she instructed.

"I'm not a native, Sheriff. I'll need directions."

"I'm certain of that," she replied. "Take County Road F to Lake Road 5-47 and pick up Highway 5 south. Go across Hurricane Deck Bridge and take the highway all the way to Starlight. Listrom's Mortuary is on the Square. I've got to return the boat, and I'll meet you there."

Doc Eddy greeted Mason and Pamela at the mortuary. He introduced Malcolm Listrom as the finest mortician in Pope County, able to restore the departed to a grandeur they had never achieved while among the living. So highly did he praise Malcolm's gift that Mason decided the coroner was in for a cut. The sheriff's department, he said in conclusion, had long favored Malcolm with the official business of restoring victims of gruesome deaths to a peaceful final visage.

Malcolm basked in Eddy's praise while emitting appropriate solicitous sounds of sympathy for the bereaved. When Mason told him that the deceased was just passing through and would be buried in Kansas City, he became a waiter trying to turn his table. Kelly arrived a few minutes later and Malcolm led them to the room where he prepared bodies for burial.

Malcolm plied his magic in a ceramic-tiled, circular operating room dominated by two large surgical tables in the center. Glass-covered cabinets filled with unfamiliar solutions and tools lined the walls.

The air was heavy with disinfectant that made their eyes water.

Sullivan was covered in an off-white sheath and adorned with a vanilla toe tag marked *John Doe.*

"I'm afraid I haven't repaired the damage, Mrs. Sullivan," Listrom apologized. "We're not allowed to prepare the body until the authorities approve."

Pamela nodded, but Mason wasn't certain she had really heard him. He stood behind her as Listrom pulled back the sheet.

"No, you bastard, not like this," Pamela said as she slumped into Mason's arms.

Sullivan's eyes were closed. His features were soft under the fluorescent light. Mason pretended he was attending an open casket funeral and forced himself not to flinch.

He half carried Pamela into a waiting room and gently set her onto a sofa beneath a comforting portrait of Jesus, smiling beneficently, hands outstretched. Kelly murmured her condolences to Pamela and motioned Doc Eddy and Mason to an adjoining office.

Mason asked, "Has anyone made a determination of the cause of death?"

"Can't tell yet," Doc Eddy said. "He's got a knot on the back of his head. May have fallen and hit something. Won't know for sure until we give him the canoe treatment."

"Canoe treatment?" Mason wondered out loud.

Eddy laughed. "The incision goes stem to stern. Just like hollowing out a log for a canoe. It's an old coroner's joke."

His crack made Mason punch up his defense of Pamela a notch. "I doubt if Pamela will want an autopsy. She's been through enough."

"An autopsy is required in the case of all suspicious deaths. Doc Eddy will do it this afternoon," Kelly said.

"Wait a minute! You just said he hit his head and fell in. He probably drowned. There's nothing suspicious or unexplained about that. There's no reason to put Pamela through that."

"A ski boat belonging to Sullivan was found tied up at the Buckhorn marina this morning. We found an earring on the boat and your partner doesn't look like the earring type. I doubt if he hit his head, fell in, and the boat drove itself back to the marina. I'm betting someone helped him into the water. I'm sorry if that's hard on Mrs. Sullivan, but that's the way it is."

"If you're going to question her, you'll do it in my presence and you'll stop when I tell you."

He was drawing lines for a client who hadn't retained him. Aunt Claire would have told him he was finally showing some promise. He and Kelly eyed each other, trying to guess when the confrontation that was brewing between them would finally erupt.

"Take her back to her house, and I'll meet you there in an hour. Questioning is always more productive immediately following a death. I've been through this enough times to know that."

"Yeah, Sheriff, I'll bet that the lake is a real hotbed of murder and mayhem."

Her withering stare confirmed that he'd just made an ass of himself. He conceded the moment to her and shepherded Pamela to the car.

They made it back to Sullivan's just before eleven. Diane Farrell, Sullivan's legal assistant for ten years, was sprawled on the doorstep, wearing a Melissa Etheridge T-shirt over baggy jean shorts and rubber thongs. She flicked ashes from her cigarette into clay pots brimming with red, pink, and violet impatiens. She was leaning against a brown grocery bag filled with fresh fruit for the brunch. Pamela walked past her without comment, too dazed to speak.

Diane was plain and thick with a blocky face bolted to a rectangular body. Her hair was a washed-out brown matching the grocery bag. She had dark, wide-set eyes, a nose too small for her broad face, and thin lips on a downturned mouth. Diane wasn't to be underestimated. She promoted and protected Sullivan as if he were her own. Try to go around her or behind her and you'd probably end up just going—to another firm. Office scuttle-butt had her madly in love with Sullivan, though no one could picture them together. Sullivan only played with beautiful women. Ordinary need not apply. But she had job security and a kinship with Pamela, who welcomed her as a link to her wandering husband.

"Mason, what's going on? Where's Sullivan?" she asked.

Mason knew Diane well enough to dislike her, and he disliked her enough not to soften the blow. "He's dead, Diane. Someone found him floating in the lake this morning. Pamela and I just identified the body."

She studied his face for some hint that it wasn't true. Her eyes were like black holes, sucking in everything and emitting no light. When he didn't recant, she went inside, calling for Pamela. Her stoic response made him feel like a heel for smacking her with the news.

Mason spent the next twenty minutes telling his colleagues, as they arrived for brunch, that even though the firm's biggest producer was dead, everything would be fine. They didn't believe it and neither did he, but it was the sort of thing people said and accepted when bad news was too fresh to argue with. Some wanted to stay and help. But there wasn't anything for them to do. He was waiting for the sheriff. Aunt Claire's voice wouldn't let him leave Pamela to be questioned without a lawyer. When the last group drove away, he picked up Diane's fruit and went into the house.

No one was in the den, and he was enough of a stranger not to knock on closed bedroom doors. Diane emerged a few minutes later, dry-eyed with her normal shade of pale.

"How's Pamela?" he asked.

"Her husband is dead, so that's a bummer. Other than that, I don't know."

Diane didn't promise to be a great source of comfort to Pamela. "The sheriff will be here soon to question her. I'll stay for that. You don't have to stick around."

"She expects me to stay, Mason. You play lawyer. I'll take care of Pamela."

One more reason not to envy Pamela, he decided silently.

Kelly arrived at noon. Mason introduced Diane, who barely acknowledged her. Pamela had showered, changed, added fresh makeup, and appeared composed as she returned to the den. She and Kelly took the same seats as before. Mason stood at Pamela's left with Diane on her right. They were a mismatched pair of sentries.

"When did you last see your husband, Mrs. Sullivan?" Kelly began.

"Last night, about seven o'clock. We were supposed to go to Buckhorn for dinner. We had a fight and he left.''

Mason drifted away from Pamela's chair so that he could watch her face for any sign of weakness that would trigger his instruction not to answer any more questions.

Kelly continued. ''What did you fight about?''

''I never remember anymore. We just fight.''

''Where did he go?''

''He took the ski boat. I watched him from the kitchen window.''

''Which way did he go when he left the cove?''

''Toward Turkey Bend.''

''Do you know anyone who lives up that way whom he might have gone to visit?''

''No, we don't have many friends at the lake. We have a lot of visitors, and they either stay with us or at a client's condo.''

''Whose condo is that?''

''One of Richard's clients has a condominium in a cove near here. I don't know who really owns it. Richard never talked about his clients. I only knew that he was able to use it for guests when we entertained at the lake.''

''Did you have guests at the condo this weekend?''

''No.''

''Do you water-ski, Mrs. Sullivan?''

''No, why do you ask?''

''Has anyone else used the ski boat recently other than your husband?''

''No, and he doesn't ski anymore either. He says his knees can't take it anymore. He just uses the boat for transportation.''

''Mrs. Sullivan, the lake patrol found your husband's boat at dawn. It was abandoned. I wonder if you can identify this earring that was found on the boat?''

Kelly removed a single gold hoop earring from an evidence bag. Pamela instinctively reached for her ear and removed one of her own clasp hoops.

"It's not mine, if that's what you mean. I've never pierced my ears," she said.

Kelly's silence told Mason that she knew her business. More could be learned by waiting than by asking.

Pamela let the silence hang for a moment. She pulled herself upright, looked directly at Kelly, and answered with a last shot of dignity.

"The earring probably belongs to someone younger with a flat belly and firm tits and I don't know her name. Now, if you'll excuse me, it's been a long morning." Pamela rose and turned away. Diane padded behind her as they retreated into the bedroom.

"Son of a bitch!" Mason said.

"Seems likely," Kelly added.

"How about a ride back to Buckhorn, Sheriff?"

"Sorry, Counselor. I'm not running a taxi service."

"I wasn't planning on tipping you. You dragged me into this mess. You can't leave me stranded here."

"Yes, I can. Your partner's death isn't neat and tidy, and I like neat and tidy deaths, Counselor. Now, if you don't mind, I've got a lot of work to do."

"Maybe I can help." Her arched eyebrows told him that she didn't think so. "Look, I admit I'm a reflex smart-ass. But I helped identify the body and brought you here. And I was just trying to protect Pamela."

Mason doubted that Sullivan had died of natural causes as any decent asshole would have done. O'Malley's indictment on charges that he'd skimmed money from the bank that he owned was inevitable. Sullivan had practically confessed to helping O'Malley steal the money when he asked Mason to lose documents that incriminated him. Mason knew that Sullivan's only chance to save himself would be to testify against his client. O'Malley couldn't invoke the attorney-client privilege to prevent Sullivan from testifying about their crimes. O'Malley's best defense would be a lawyer that was too dead to testify. Mason was the only other lawyer in the firm who knew what Sullivan knew—or who knew what Sullivan had intimated to him. If Sullivan had been murdered, Mason wanted to know sooner rather than later. His protective instincts were becoming self-centered.

"Who said she needs protection, Counselor?"

"Anybody who starts the day with a dead husband needs protection."

"Diane can take you back to Buckhorn. This is an official investigation. I don't need any volunteers."

"Don't worry. I'm going home today, but I've got an obligation to my partners to find out what happened." Though true, that was the least of his concerns. But it was the only excuse he could use until he knew whether Sullivan had been murdered. If Sullivan's death weren't murder, telling Kelly that both his client and his dead partner were crooks would put him on O'Malley's hit list. "Just tell me what your next step is. Maybe I really can help."

Kelly sighed impatiently, as if he would accept her annoyance as an answer. His silence said not likely.

"Okay," she said finally. "I follow the most logical line of investigation. That means find out where Sullivan went and who he was with before he died. He left his house around seven. Mrs. Sullivan saw him heading toward a client's condo. I want to know where it is and who owns it."

"How will you find it?"

"I'll start with county records of property ownership."

"Perfect. I may recognize a name and save you a lot of trouble."

Kelly looked at him as if she'd just found a stray dog and couldn't decide whether to feed it or take it to the pound.

"I hope you're ready for a long ride home. I've got some stops to make."

"Sheriff, I'm like lunch meat. I'm always ready."

Chapter Three

Kelly dialed her cellular phone as they pulled away in her pickup truck. It was a portable model that plugged into a cradle beneath the radio. A speaker hung from the driver's visor.

"Riley, it's Kelly. Get your lazy ass off your back porch and meet me at the courthouse in half an hour." The playful teasing in her voice told Mason that Riley almost certainly didn't have a lazy ass. He wondered what kind of ass Riley really had that caused Kelly to react that way.

"Listen, little girl. I got you that badge, and I can have it back in a heartbeat. Your daddy never woulda talked that way to me."

Riley's voice came through the speaker with a pleasure that said they'd played this piece many times before. Her laughter was rich, lighting her eyes. Mason was relieved that Riley sounded a generation removed. He was also surprised at his relief.

He had lost track of the different emotional chords Kelly had struck with him in less than half a day.

"Friend of yours?" Mason asked as she hung up.

"Riley Brooks has been the register of deeds since I was a girl. He talked me into taking this job until a new sheriff is elected in November."

"What happened to the other sheriff?"

"He got carried away with strip-searching women who ran stop signs. Someone had to finish out his term."

"Don't tell me you weren't first choice, Sheriff?"

Kelly gave him another annoyed glance. She seemed to have an inexhaustible supply. "I was an FBI agent for ten years. My partner was killed last winter. I quit and came home. End of story. Now tell me about the poker game. When did it start."

Mason didn't blame her for being more interested in figuring out who killed Sullivan than in becoming his new best friend, so he didn't mind changing the subject. "After dinner, about eight."

"Was Sullivan there when the game started?"

"No, he didn't get there until after nine."

"So we've got at least two hours unaccounted for. Give me the names of the players and, this time, leave out your imaginary playmates."

"Scot Daniels, Sandra Connelly, who runs the litigation department, Harlan Christenson, Angela Molina, Phil Rosa, and me."

"Who are Angela and Phil?"

"Angela is the executive director of the firm, chief bean counter, and administrator. Phil Rosa is an associate. One of the rising stars in litigation."

"Was Sullivan alone when he left the card game?"

Mason hesitated because he knew where she was headed. She was interested in more than tracking

Sullivan's movements in the hours before he died. She was making a list, probably a short one, of suspects. Mason didn't know whether she would put his name on that list if she found out that, in order to save himself, Sullivan had asked Mason to commit a crime. He didn't want to find out. All he could do was steer her investigation away from the O'Malley case until he knew if Sullivan had been murdered. If he had been, Mason would tell her everything and put his faith in the system.

Kelly cut through his hesitation. "If you don't tell me, Counselor, someone else will. Someone always sees something and they're always anxious to talk about it."

Mason knew she was right. "Sullivan left with Cara Trent, one of the law school students who work for us during the summer."

"I'll need a list of the names, addresses, and phone numbers of everyone who was at the retreat, especially Cara Trent. I've only got the partners' names so far. Chances are one of them will know where Sullivan was before and after the card game."

"I've got a firm directory at the hotel. You can have it."

"Fine. Let's start with you, Counselor. Where were you last night?"

The color rose in Mason's cheeks as he considered the tone of her question.

"I was in my room before the card game, and I spent the rest of the night on the beach where you found me this morning."

"Alone?"

"Alone. Before and after." Wrong answer.

"Did you talk with anyone? Did anyone see you?"

"I had room service. You can check with the hotel."

"What about when you were on the beach?"

"Just a couple who were too busy with each other to notice me. You better take me in, Sheriff. I confess. The job was too good. I couldn't stand all the money."

"Let's hope everyone else is so helpful, Counselor," she said as the corners of her mouth creased in a neat smile.

Well, even the Berlin Wall eventually came down, Mason thought to himself.

"Was Mr. Sullivan working on anything that might make someone want to kill him?"

He should have expected the question, but her smile had left him flat-footed. He had felt the same way in his last rugby match when a forward got past him with a fake pass. There was a reason that that move was called a dummy. And he was it.

"The firm has a lot of clients, Sheriff. They have a lot of problems, and they are unhappy about all of them."

"Counselor, I spent the last ten years sifting through more double-talk than you can imagine. Make this easy on both of us and tell me if any of those clients might want to kill him."

"I'm not going to speculate about any client. If it turns out that my partner was murdered, I'll tell you everything I can. Until then, I can't tell you anything because of the attorney-client privilege. I'm sure the FBI has heard of that."

"Mr. Mason, I'll make this simple. If you withhold information in a murder investigation, I'll shove your smart mouth right up your smart ass. Are we clear on that?"

"They teach you how to do that at the FBI academy?"

"The first day."

Mason stuck with his "I'm too cute to hate" grin. Kelly countered with her "don't bet on it" glare.

Kelly downshifted as they rolled into the center of the county seat, Starlight, Missouri. The Pope County Courthouse was a classic colonial edifice at least sixty years old. It rose from the center of the town square with Missouri limestone columns guarding the entrances on all four sides. A Civil War cannon stood resolutely on the south quadrangle. Neatly manicured grass, still lush in spite of the midsummer heat, fanned out from the foundation, flanked by concrete sidewalks.

The courthouse reminded Mason of Tommy Douchant's case. It had been his job to do well and do good for Tommy, and he had done neither. His slogan had never proven to be so empty. Afterward, he went over every detail of the trial with his aunt Claire. She had listened closely.

"Do it over again," she had told him when he'd finished.

"I can't get a new trial without new evidence. You know that."

"Then get the evidence and quit feeling sorry for yourself and Tommy. I can't stand pathetic."

He'd promised himself that he would. It had been four months since Tommy's trial and three months since he'd started at Sullivan & Christenson. He'd discussed the case at the first partners' meeting he attended after joining the firm. No one was interested in investing time and money in a case that had already been lost. His promise was gathering dust.

Riley Brooks met them in the office of the regis-

ter of deeds. He was well past six feet, with a skin-
and-bones frame that made him appear even taller.
A ring of gray hair circled his bald head like an
ill-kempt tonsured monk. He wore a one-piece,
short-sleeved lemon jumpsuit that was bright
enough to compete with his beaming smile. He sat
on the edge of a table, his long legs easily reaching
the floor, his high-top sneakers impatiently tapping
the linoleum.

"What'll it be, Kelly? Drug smugglers? Terror-
ists?" he asked, enthusiastically rubbing his hands
together, obviously hoping for both.

Kelly feigned irritation, but her eyes said she was
glad to see him. "Just property ownership records,
Riley. I'll save the bad guys for regular office
hours."

Riley, disappointed but dutiful, dug up the plans
for the coves that included Sullivan's house and
the four coves between it and the dam, which was
the direction Pamela Sullivan had last seen her
husband heading. The legal descriptions enabled
him to print out the names of the owners from the
county's computer system in ten minutes. Warning
Kelly to lock up when they were done, Riley left
them alone in the courthouse.

"If we divide the records, we'll be done faster,"
Mason suggested. Kelly reluctantly tore the printout in half. They studied the printout and the
plans.

"Recognize any names, Counselor?" Kelly asked.

Mason kept his eyes on the printout, not wanting
to meet hers. He recognized one name and wasn't
surprised when he saw it. He was willing to dodge
her other questions but he wouldn't lie to her.

"Just one. It's SOM, Inc."

Her smile returned. "Who or what is that?"

"A company owned by Richard Sullivan and Victor O'Malley."

"I don't suppose O'Malley is one of those dangerously unhappy clients."

"He pays his bills on time."

"Thanks, Counselor. I was beginning to think I'd have to torture you for information."

"Does this mean I get a deputy's badge?"

"Not yet. I don't want the responsibility if you accidentally stick yourself. Let's go see if anyone is home at SOM, Inc."

The computer printout said that SOM, Inc., owned a condominium located two coves away from Sullivan's. The twisting, winding lake roads made it a twenty-minute drive. The condo was part of a "garden style" project with two units on each of three floors. SOM's was on the top floor. No one answered when they knocked. Kelly and Mason walked around to the back and peered through the sliding door on the balcony. They were about to give up when they heard a woman's voice from the other top-floor condo.

"It's about time you people showed up. I've been complaining for months."

The voice belonged to a short woman with the kind of fat that begins at the ankles and ends just below the ears. She was draped in a sundress that billowed from her shoulders like a two-man tent. The alternating electric blue and white diagonal stripes were briefly disorienting.

"I'm Sheriff Holt, ma'am. What have you been complaining about?"

"I know who you are, honey! I read the papers. Who's your boyfriend?" She looked Mason over, shaking her head, and whispered loudly, "Nice looking but soft. Stick to the local talent, Sheriff, they've got better staying power!"

Kelly swallowed her laughter and introduced Mason.

Velma Marie Fouche invited them in for a cup of coffee and conversation, both of which were served in a living room furnished with one of the few remaining knotty pine pit-groups.

"I'm sorry, Velma, but I haven't been told about your complaints. Bring me up to date."

Velma warmed up to Kelly's easy manner. Mason was learning that she had a style for every occasion.

"It's the women. Every week there's a new batch. It's disgusting!"

"Tell me about the women."

"Oh, you know. They're young and pretty and bouncy."

"Who are they with, Velma?"

"Men old enough to be their fathers!"

"Have they bothered you?"

"Nope."

Kelly smiled indulgently. "Then what's the problem?"

"My husband. He sees these sweet young things and gets ideas. Won't leave me alone and I need my rest."

Mason nearly choked on his coffee.

Kelly didn't miss a beat. "I'll see to it that we look into your complaints, Velma. Did you see any of these people last night?"

"Well, I couldn't sleep so I went out on the balcony for some air, and I seen two of 'em walk down to the dock and get in a boat."

"What time was it?"

"Close to midnight."

"What kind of boat?"

"One of them powerboats, like the skiers use. Can't stand 'em—they're too loud and they scare the fish off."

"Can you describe the people you saw?" Kelly asked.

"She was a long-legged blonde. Busty and crawling all over him like ants at a picnic. He was one of the regulars. I couldn't see him too well, but I recognized him from all the times I seen him here. Jockey size and suckin' in his gut trying to look sharp."

"Did they come back?"

"Just her. Maybe an hour later. She was here and gone."

Velma didn't remember anything else. Kelly thanked her for the coffee and her help, gave her a business card, and told her to call if she remembered something more. They tried the rest of the units. No one else had seen the blonde or her jockey-sized companion.

"Sullivan fits the description of the man Velma saw," Kelly said as they drove back to Buckhorn. "Does Cara Trent fit the description of the woman?"

"As much as any good-looking blonde," Mason answered.

"Why was Sullivan staying at the hotel if he and his wife had a house at the lake, and he and O'Malley owned that condo?"

"Easy," Mason explained. "The retreat is supposed to build camaraderie. Can't do that if we don't all stay in the same place."

"Maybe, but so far it doesn't sound like Sullivan

spent much time in his room. Do you suppose that Victor O'Malley knew that Sullivan used their condo to cheat on his wife?"

Mason wasn't surprised that Kelly kept changing the subject. He used the same technique when questioning a witness. It kept the witness from getting too comfortable with the questions. "I don't suppose anything, Sheriff, but O'Malley doesn't strike me as someone who would care."

"So why would O'Malley want Sullivan dead?"

"You don't give up, do you, Sheriff? You can't decide whether to arrest everyone in the firm or everyone the firm represents."

"Counselor, people get killed for a lot of reasons. Including not telling the cops what they need to know soon enough to save themselves."

"I'll keep that in mind," Mason answered.

They drove in silence the rest of the way to the hotel. Kelly parked her truck in the circle drive at the hotel entrance and got out.

"You don't have to come in," Mason told her. "I'll get the firm directory from my room and bring it to you."

"I'm more interested in Sullivan's room," Kelly said. "And I've got the key."

"Don't you need a warrant to search his room?"

"Not if you let me in. Do you want the hotel maids to throw away any firm files Sullivan may have brought with him?"

Mason knew that Kelly could have asked Pamela Sullivan or the hotel manager to let her in. Neither would have refused. His refusal would only add to her suspicion that he was holding back information. He realized that she wanted to see his reaction to anything they found in Sullivan's room. Mason had spent the day reacting to events beyond his

control, hoping to nudge the investigation away
from O'Malley. It was like trying to hold back a
rising river with a single sandbag.

They stopped at his room first, and he gave Kelly
the firm directory. It listed every employee's name,
direct dial number, cell phone number, and e-mail
address.

"Here's your list of suspects, Sheriff," he said
cheerfully.

"Well, I can cross off one name."

"Whose?" Mason said hopefully, wishing that it
was his.

"Sullivan's. I don't think he committed suicide."

"That's very funny for a sheriff," he said.

"Wait until you hear my good material, Counselor."

She almost sounded coy, which utterly confused
Mason. He studied her for a clue. She offered none.
She cycled through the good cop, bad cop routine
so often that he thought she might be schizo-
phrenic. If she was trying to keep him off balance,
she was succeeding. Kelly was smart, attractive, and
gave fleeting suggestions that she liked him—all
of which he could easily succumb to if she gave
him a chance. But he knew that she'd put his head
on a pike outside the village gates if she thought
he was involved in Sullivan's murder.

Kelly led the way to Sullivan's room and handed
Mason the key. They smiled at each other and
Mason fantasized for an instant that they had
checked in for a more pleasant purpose.

"Not in your dreams, Counselor," Kelly told
him, guessing at his thoughts.

"If man doesn't dream, he has nothing," Mason
answered.

"A man whose dreams won't come true still has nothing. Open the door."

Sullivan had a suite instead of the single room Mason had been assigned. A briefcase sat on a desk in one corner of the living room. Mason quickly walked past a sofa and entertainment center and picked up the briefcase while Kelly checked out the bedroom.

Mason popped the latches on the briefcase, mildly surprised that it wasn't locked. Once he saw the contents, he knew why. It was an inventory of insignificance: Friday's *Wall Street Journal,* the agenda for the retreat, a paperback copy of a John Grisham novel, a CD case titled *Johnny Mathis' Greatest Hits,* and a portable CD player with headphones. He left it open for Kelly to see.

"Find anything interesting?" she called from the bedroom.

"Nothing. How about you?"

"Just this," she said as she returned to the front room, gingerly holding a letter-sized sheet of white paper by one corner. She set it down on the desk next to the briefcase. "Don't touch it. Just read it."

It was a typewritten memo from Sullivan to Harlan Christenson dated July 10, two days earlier. Mason read it silently, aware that Kelly was watching each twitch he was fighting to control.

Lou told me today that Victor O'Malley would be convicted unless we lost certain documents that he had found in our files. I told him no. I'm not going to take any chances with him. I'll fire him on Monday after the retreat. There's no reason to ruin the weekend because of one person. If he tries

*to cause any trouble, I'll report him to the state Bar
and he'll probably be disbarred.*

When he finished, he looked up, almost expecting her to have drawn her gun and her
Miranda card at the same time. Instead, he caught a
glimpse of sadness before she resumed her official
tone with a single question.
"Is it true?"

Chapter Four

"I realize that we've only known each other a few hours, but do I look stupid to you?" Mason slammed the briefcase shut, stood straight, arms half-cocked toward her, daring her to say yes.

"A lot of killers look pretty smart. They just do stupid things that get them caught."

"So how am I supposed to prove that I didn't have a conversation with a dead man?"

"Tell me about O'Malley's case and tell me you didn't talk to Sullivan about it."

Mason let out an exasperated breath, clasped his hands behind his head, and did a quick circuit of the room. Kelly stood still, watching him orbit around her, while he decided how much of the truth to tell her. He decided to stick with what had already been reported by the press.

"Victor O'Malley was Sullivan's biggest client. Franklin St. John is about to indict him for bank fraud. I'm defending him."

"That's half an answer. Tell me the rest of it."

Mason didn't care about Sullivan anymore. Sullivan was dead and had set him up with the memo. But O'Malley was still his client and if he told Kelly too much, he would get disbarred. He drew a line only a lawyer could stand on without crossing.

"We had lunch on Friday and talked about the case. The rest of it is bullshit."

"And you won't tell me what you talked about because you're more concerned about attorney-client privilege than going to jail for murder. That memo reads like a good motive. You kill Sullivan and keep your job."

"Give me a break, Sheriff. That memo reads like a good example of libel, which is a motive for a lawsuit, not murder," Mason told her. "The only thing libel and murder have in common is that with each you have to prove that the defendant acted with malice."

"So Sullivan struck first and you struck back. Malice begets malice. Libel to kill."

"That's practically poetic, Sheriff. But, believe me, Sullivan wasn't worth it and the job wasn't worth it. I'd already decided to quit."

"Why? Because of your lunchtime chat with Sullivan?"

Mason stopped pacing. Her last question caught him like a sharply tossed lasso. "That's only part of it. I've got a case that the firm won't take. I'm going out on my own so I can handle it."

"You put on one hell of a defense, Counselor," Kelly answered with unsparing sarcasm.

"I'll tell you what, Sheriff. You subpoena every memo Sullivan ever wrote about O'Malley. This is the only one you'll find, if he even wrote it. I've been through those files. Sullivan got things done.

He didn't write memos about it. And he wouldn't wait to fire me or his mother because of the damn retreat."

"So why did he write the memo?"

"To set me up."

"Why wouldn't he just get rid of the documents himself? And why would he need to set you up?"

Mason didn't answer. He sat on the arm of the sofa and let her think out loud, nodding as she said it.

"If you get rid of the documents and get caught, the memo gives him plausible deniability. If you refused, he could get rid of the evidence and still blame you if anyone ever found out. In the meantime, you're gone. The documents probably incriminated him and O'Malley."

"Now you, Sheriff," Mason told her as he got up. "You put on one hell of a defense." He offered her his best smile and his right hand.

She declined both. "Then show me the documents."

His hand and smile went limp at the same time. "I can't."

"Counselor, you've got to get over this privilege stuff. This is a murder investigation until the coroner tells me differently, and you're working your way up the suspect list."

"It's not just the privilege," he told her. "I've been through those files. I don't know what documents he's talking about. Let me know when the coroner makes up his mind. I'm going home."

She handed him Sullivan's briefcase. "I'll let you return this to Mrs. Sullivan. Drive safely," she said as he left.

He hoped that she meant it.

* * *

Straight, flat roads are hard to find in the Ozarks. Two-lane county roads and state highways bob and weave like a punch-drunk fighter across and around the hilly countryside. Mason worked the clutch on his seven-year-old Saab as he slipped in and out of small packs of slow-moving cars headed back to the city. Each time he crossed the yellow line to pass someone else, the Saab's engine revved and whined against his demand for more speed. The engine was never as enthusiastic as Mason was, but it got the job done.

The air-conditioning had quit the week before and Mason hadn't had time to get it fixed. The hang-on July heat punished him for letting it go. He left the windows down and compensated for the hot, noisy wind by cranking up Santana's newest CD. He hung his left arm out the window and drummed his hand impatiently against the door while he waited for a chance to pass another driver who didn't care when he got home.

Mason took Highway 52 west through Eldon and on to the junction with Highway 5, where he headed north, hoping to leave the plodding traffic behind. Soon he saw a black Ford Explorer pulling up behind him, its driver in a bigger hurry than Mason. He waved the driver to pass him and waved again as the car went by. No one waved back. At least not that he could see through the tinted side windows of the Explorer. Mason let the Explorer open up a quarter-mile lead and then held the distance between them at a steady sixty-five miles an hour.

Ten minutes later the distance between them started to shrink. Mason drew within a couple of car lengths and slowed to fifty-five miles an hour, matching the reduced speed of the Explorer. Mason grew impatient with the Explorer as they rode in tandem, up and down the rolling grade. The highway was little more than a country road that intersected with unpaved farm roads. The next junction was a good fifteen miles north. Mason waited until they reached a reasonably level stretch of road before deciding it was time to take the lead.

He pulled out to pass, accelerated to catch the Explorer, and started to ease in front when the Explorer suddenly sped up, keeping pace with him. Mason gave the Saab more gas and glanced over at the Explorer's opaque windows. The late afternoon sun bounced off the tinted glass, obscuring any image of the driver.

Mason pushed the Saab harder, unable to gain any ground and unwilling to drop back. He was hot enough, tired enough, and annoyed enough to keep pushing the Saab to pass the Explorer and not to notice that the road had bottomed out like the trough of a wave. As they started back up the next hill, an airhorn bellowed from a flatbed tractor-trailer loaded with hay bales bearing down on Mason from the crest of the hill.

Mason answered with a squeal from his own horn, but neither driver changed course. At their combined speeds, he guessed the truck would be in his lap before he could finish passing the Explorer. Mason hit his brakes, intending to swerve back into his lane behind the Explorer, only to see the Explorer slow down with him. Mason couldn't believe that the driver of the Explorer was hanging him out in the wrong lane, threatening to turn him into a hood ornament for the truck. But there was no other explanation for the trap Mason had stumbled into.

The truck was close enough that Mason could see the driver, mouth opened wide, screaming at him and waving his hand sideways, telling Mason to get out of the way. Mason screamed back, unable to hear his own voice over the wind, the road, and their dueling horns. He stole a glance at his speedometer. Though his speed had dropped to forty-five, he still felt as if he were flying. He knew he would be when the truck hit him.

A thin strip of gravel separated the paved road from the tall grass alongside it. Barbed wire strung between steel fence posts marked the outer boundary of a farm. Cows on the captive side of the fence looked up as if they sensed that something was about to happen that even they couldn't ignore.

Mason pounded on his horn, screamed again at the driver of the truck and the driver of the Explorer. His hands slid around the wheel, greased by the sweat pouring off of him faster than the wind could dry. The Explorer kept pace, cutting off any retreat. The truck was slowing, causing the trailer to shimmy and its load to rock sideways. But it couldn't slow down quickly enough. Mason saw the certainty of the impending crash in the stricken eyes of the truck driver, who had pushed himself as far back into his seat as he could, arms extended to his own steering wheel.

Without thinking, Mason spun the steering wheel hard to his left and jammed the gas pedal to the floor. The Saab bolted off the road and shuddered in the wake left by the truck as it blew past. The ground dropped off slightly from the road. In the next instant, Mason was flying—not on the hood of the truck, but right at the cows. The Saab landed hard and fishtailed clockwise. Mason fought the wheel, found the brakes, and rode out the spin until the car bounced to a stop against the barbed wire.

The shoulder harness held him in a fierce embrace. The jolt from the car landing was no worse than the countless hits he'd absorbed in rugby matches since he began playing in college. He'd played long enough and kept in shape well enough to take a punch or kick in the middle of a maul. Those blows were thrown in sport. This was a coldly calculated attempt to put him on the shelf—permanently.

Mason climbed out of the Saab, shaking as much from adrenaline as anxiety. Dodging eighteen-wheelers in an airborne car gave new meaning to flying by the seat of his pants. He walked around the car, checking for damage. The barbed wire had etched an abstract pattern in the paint on the passenger side but the car was otherwise unscathed.

Mason leaned against the hood, waited for his heart rate to slow down to suborbital speed, and tried to put the day's events into perspective. Richard Sullivan was dead, probably murdered. He was last seen with an attractive blonde, not his wife, at a condo he owned with Victor O'Malley. Mason was defending O'Malley against criminal charges the feds were about to file. Sullivan had set up Mason as the fall guy in a scheme to get rid of evidence that probably incriminated both Sullivan and O'Malley. And someone had just tried to kill him and make his death look like the result of his own reckless driving.

It wasn't hard to connect the dots. The picture just didn't make any sense. He realized that he'd have to take a closer look at the O'Malley files in the morning. If he lived that long.

Chapter Five

Mason's house was on 56th Street, between Ward Parkway and Wornall Road, just one block south of Loose Park, a sprawling green space perfect for walking with your girlfriend or running with your dog. Mason hadn't had a girlfriend or a dog since he and Kate had divorced a year ago. Kate took the dog, Tuffy, who was a mixed breed with German shepherd and collie parents.

"She's tougher than she looks. That's why I named her Tuffy," Kate had explained when they'd rescued the dog from the pound not long after they were married.

Mason spoiled Tuffy like an only child and the dog returned his affection. Custody of the dog was the last battle they'd fought in the divorce. Kate won when she'd simply taken Tuffy and dared Mason to complain to the judge. He settled for visitation, feeling only slightly less foolish.

The neighborhood was thick with large houses

built during and just after World War II. The area was a magnet that held on to older people with old money and attracted boomers with new money. A fixer-upper easily ran half a million.

The house had belonged to his aunt Claire until she'd given it to Mason when he'd graduated from law school. She had lived in it for twenty-six years before she had inherited him.

"I'm fifty years old," she told him. "It's time for a fresh start. I bought a loft in a rehabbed warehouse downtown. It's in the garment district. The building is filled with artists and tech geeks. The whole place is alive."

Kate had winced at the condition of the interior when she'd moved in. "You've got Ethan Allen, futons, chrome and glass Scandinavian, oriental rugs so threadbare a moth wouldn't use them for a snack, Grateful Dead posters, and pictures of dead immigrants."

"Think of it as multigeneration chic," Mason told her. "And the dead immigrants are my great-grandparents."

The good news was that the mud-colored brick aged better than people did, so the two-story Colonial exterior had held up well. As long as you didn't look too closely at the weather-beaten white shutters or stick your fingers in the spongy, wood-rotted window frames.

Mason paid a guy to mow the lawn, rake the leaves, and shovel the snow, which he considered a fair contribution to urban gentrification. Still, most of the neighbors averted their eyes when they walked by, and he swore that a few crossed the street to avoid a close encounter. Maybe it was the untrimmed oak trees whose low-hanging, heavy branches scraped the yard. Or maybe it was the blue floodlight he'd used to replace the burnt-out porch light. Go figure.

The only exception was Anna Karelson, who lived across the street. Anna and Mason were "wave and hello" neighbors. He waved and she said "hello" whenever they saw each other coming or going. Occasionally, she trapped him on the sidewalk and pumped him about his personal life, letting him know that hers was an unhappy marriage. She and her husband had recently filed for divorce.

When Mason pulled into the driveway of the house he had lived in for thirty-two of his thirty-five years at a little after eight o'clock, Scot Daniels was pacing the sidewalk in front. Scot and Mason had met during the first week of law school when they were assigned to the same study group. Mason was amazed that Scot had already outlined the assignments for the first two weeks of class. Scot was amazed that Mason understood the material after a single reading. Scot mastered the details and Mason painted the big picture. The combination got them through law school in the top ten of their class. They shared an apartment in Kansas City after graduation until Scot got married. Mason was his best man, a favor Scot returned at Mason's wedding.

"I was at the office getting ready for my closing when Harlan called about Sullivan," Scot said as he followed Mason into the house from the garage. "Harlan has called a partners' meeting for eight o'clock tomorrow morning."

Mason dropped his bag on the kitchen floor, grabbed two bottles of Bud Light from the refrigerator, and led Scot onto the redbrick patio.

He said, "I helped Pamela identify the body. I can go a long time without doing that again." The memory was fresh enough to make his stomach do a quick back flip. He settled into a lounge chair and set his beer next to the cordless phone on a glass-topped, black, wrought-iron end table.

Scot alternated between pacing back and forth and doing laps around the patio with a folder tucked under his arm. He nodded appreciation for the beer and took a long pull on the bottle without missing a step.

"Sullivan really knows how to screw up a good retreat."

"Better yet," Lou said, "the sheriff thinks he was murdered."

Scot stopped cold, his beer bottle dangling from his hand. "Get out!"

"She can't prove it, yet. But his body was found in a cove on one side of the lake, and his boat was found at Buckhorn's marina. She also found a gold earring on the boat, and Pamela says it isn't hers."

"That sounds more like adultery than murder," Scot said. "Who does he suspect?"

"I said 'she.' Her name is Kelly Holt. And she suspects everyone who hated Sullivan or stood to gain from his death. It's what cops do."

Scot finished his beer with another long pull and wiped his mouth with the back of his hand. "Well, if that's the test, I'll make her list."

Mason looked at him, wide-eyed. "Is that a confession?"

"Yeah, right. But you know that I hated the son of a bitch, and I'll inherit his clients. Sullivan was a total shit to work for. Nothing was ever right or good enough."

"Scot, that's not news. You've been complaining

about Sullivan since the day you started. But you never complained about the money."

"Because I'm smart enough to know that I'm a good lawyer, but a lousy salesman. I did all the work while he played golf. And I don't play golf. I guess I'll have to learn if I want to hold on to his clients."

Mason had listened to Scot complain for years. It was the one thing that had made him hesitate about joining the firm. He finally decided that Scot's grousing was just his way of dealing with the stress of his practice. Sullivan's death, however, added an unsettling context to those complaints. Kelly would definitely add Scot to her list of suspects. Mason didn't want to be a witness against him, so he changed the subject.

"What happens to the firm without Sullivan?"

"Nothing good. You remember the death benefit I told you about?"

"Sure. If a partner dies, the firm has to buy out his ownership interest."

"Right. The firm bought life insurance on each of the partners to pay for the buyout."

"So the insurance pays off Sullivan's wife."

"That's the problem. Sullivan never took the physical exam the insurance company required. His death was uninsured."

"So the partners owe Pamela the money?"

"Exactly one million dollars," Scot answered. "And the firm doesn't have it."

"Well, that's great. What's the good news?"

"I think we can work out a deal with Pamela. I've done their estate work. She doesn't need the money. The real problem is what Sullivan didn't tell us about him and O'Malley. This afternoon when I was getting ready for my closing, I was in

Sullivan's office looking for his copy of the contracts. I found this."

Scot handed him a subpoena demanding that Sullivan & Christenson produce all of its files on O'Malley before the Federal Grand Jury at 9:00 A.M. on July 17th.

Mason said, "That's this Friday. I'm defending O'Malley. Sullivan didn't tell me about this."

"It looks like Sullivan didn't tell anyone."

Mason shifted into defense counsel mode. "St. John is getting ready to indict O'Malley. That's not a secret. The subpoena is just his way of putting on pressure. We'll claim attorney-client privilege. The judge will throw the subpoena out."

"Don't be so sure," Scot said. "St. John isn't just coming after O'Malley. He wants Sullivan and the firm."

Scot handed Mason a letter to Sullivan from Franklin St. John dated June 1. In a very polite fashion, the letter informed Sullivan that both he and the firm were targets of the grand jury investigation.

"That means the grand jury is probably going to indict Sullivan and the firm," Mason said. "Sullivan knew St. John was gunning for us and didn't bother to mention it! That no-good prick! No wonder he was trying to set me up!"

Scot asked, "Set you up? How?"

"We had lunch on Friday. Sullivan asked me to destroy documents that would incriminate him. I told him no. Then he wrote a memo to Harlan claiming that I had made the suggestion to him and that he was going to fire me on Monday."

"How did you find out about that?"

"The sheriff found the memo in Sullivan's room at Buckhorn."

"Welcome to the list of top ten suspects," Scot said hollowly.

"Yeah, the sheriff thinks I killed Sullivan instead of suing him for libel. Don't worry, though. I've got a terrific defense," Mason responded.

"What's that?"

"Someone tried to kill me on the way back from the lake," Mason said neutrally, as if that would make it sound less threatening.

Scot dropped his empty beer bottle. The glass shattered on the brick patio. "You're shitting me!"

"Maybe. I don't know for certain. I was trying to pass someone on Highway 5. The driver held me out in the other lane until I was about to hit a truck head-on. I swerved off the road at the last second, or there would be two openings at the firm."

"You think there was a connection?"

"If Sullivan was murdered, his death is probably linked to O'Malley. At least I can't think of anything else that could get him killed. I'm defending O'Malley. Sullivan tried to get me to destroy incriminating evidence. I refused. Sullivan set me up. Someone tried to kill me and make my death look like an accident. It makes as much sense as anything else."

"Did you report it to the cops?"

"Not yet. I'll tell the sheriff, but she'll probably think I'm making it up. I didn't get the license number of the guy who hung me out in the wrong lane. I can't prove it even happened."

Scot listened, nodding without agreeing. "I know this sounds trivial in comparison, but if St. John really wants to put pressure on the firm, he'll ask the court to freeze all our assets. They don't need a conviction to do that."

"You're right," Mason said. "I remember a firm that got caught in the savings and loan scandal. The feds claimed that they were liable for the failure of the S and L and got an order freezing their assets. The firm disappeared overnight. Last one out the door turned off the lights. Any suggestions?" he asked.

"We've got to get out in front on this. Harlan will be overly cautious, too protective. Most of the other eight partners are goddamn sheep. We need someone to investigate the firm's exposure and get St. John to back off until we figure out what's going on."

Mason knew that Scot was right. Harlan was perfect for recruiting clients, but he was a conscientious objector to trench warfare. If St. John was coming after the firm, it would be a bloody fight.

"That'll require outside counsel," Mason advised.

"Bad choice. We'd never be able to control it. You've got to do it. You're new enough to the firm that you'll have credibility with St. John. You can offer St. John the dear, departed Sullivan and save the rest of our asses."

Mason wondered if the bottom of his beer bottle could explain how a simple weekend at the lake had managed to turn into such a nightmare. He was definitely the wrong choice. This battle required someone totally committed to the firm. He wasn't.

"Listen, I hate to pile on the bad news, but I don't plan to be around long enough to handle this case."

Scot stared at Mason, eyes narrowed in a "now what?" glare. "What the hell is that supposed to mean?"

"It means that I decided to quit when Sullivan asked me to destroy evidence."

"So what! Sullivan's dead, and you didn't destroy any evidence. That's bullshit!"

"Not to me. O'Malley's case is a tar baby that I'm not going to get stuck with. Besides, I'm going to try to get Tommy Douchant a new trial. The firm already turned that case down. I've got to do that on my own."

"Lou, Tommy's case is a loser. You already lost it once. Don't waste more time on it."

Mason bristled at Scot's slam, uncertain whether it was intentional. "It's not a loser if I dig up evidence that will get Tommy a new trial. I owe him that much."

"What about what you owe me, Lou? I got you this job. You've got a year to file a motion for a new trial. It's been, what, four months since Tommy's trial? You've got eight months left. I need you now."

"You need someone from outside the firm. Someone who's objective. Someone who won't be a suspect if it turns out that Sullivan was murdered."

"Wrong. I need someone I can trust. If Sullivan was killed, who's going to work harder to clear your name and mine? You or some hired gun that's got a dozen other cases he's got to keep track of? Besides, I'll make certain the firm lets you reopen Tommy's case."

Mason sometimes made poor choices when people made him feel like a badly needed, ungrateful shit. The last one had required a divorce to correct it.

"Okay. Let's see what happens in the morning," Mason hedged. It was a half promise Scot would make him honor.

He walked Scot to the front door and said good night. Closing it behind him, he stood in the front hall and looked to his right at the portraits of his great-grandparents—Aunt Claire's grandparents—on the dining room wall. Tobiah and Hinda Sackheim had immigrated to the United States from Lithuania in 1871. Tobiah, ignorant of English, couldn't tell the immigration official his name. Somehow, he explained that he was a stonemason and the Sackheims of Lithuania became the Masons of Ellis Island.

From their perch on the wall, they guarded the silver candlesticks they had brought with them to America. Aunt Claire had always kept the candlesticks on the dining room table and, when Mason was little, she lighted them each year at Passover and told him the story of the Jews' Exodus from Egypt. Both stories, one of his people and one of his family, fed her passion for justice and had once fired his own. The flame still burned brightly for Aunt Claire, but was little more than a flicker for him. Mason stared at the candlesticks and replayed the memories, searching for a spark he didn't find.

He returned to the patio, picked up the pieces of Scot's broken bottle, and lay back down in the lounge chair. He watched the moon rise as his eyelids fell, wondering if continually sleeping on patio furniture was a sign of the early onset of dementia. He was jolted awake by the cordless telephone. Blinking, he focused on his watch. It was nearly midnight.

"Yeah?" he said thickly.

"Sorry if I woke you." Kelly Holt sounded too cheerful for the end of a long day.

"That's all right, I had to get up to answer the phone anyway."

Long pause. He couldn't believe his evil twin, the high school freshman, invaded his body every time he talked to this woman.

"Will you be in your office tomorrow? There are a few things I need to ask you about." She was all business and clearly not interested in bonding through teenage humor.

"Sure. We've got a partners' meeting at eight that may go all morning. The afternoon will be crazy talking with clients. How about five o'clock— my office?"

"Fine."

"Any news?"

"Just one thing. Your partner was murdered."

Chapter Six

Mason had quit his old firm, Forrest, Mason & Goldberg, a week after Tommy Douchant's trial ended. Tommy had worked construction until one sun-drenched spring morning when the hook on his safety belt broke, bouncing him off steel I-beams onto the pavement two stories below. Paraplegics don't work construction. Mason sued the safety belt manufacturer, Philpott Safety Systems, and lost.

Tommy's case should have been settled, but he turned down two million dollars the day before the trial started. Mason told him to take it. He found out the day after the trial that his partner, Stephen Forrest, had met secretly with Tommy and convinced him to turn the offer down. Forrest didn't care that Mason had a tough case. He wanted to ride Tommy's broken back to a bigger payday and his share of a fatter fee.

Tommy's case wasn't the first one Forrest had

sabotaged. Mason told him that he wasn't quitting because of the money, it was the lack of trust. It was like coming home and finding his wife in bed with someone else—again. It was the "again" part that Mason couldn't handle.

Mason called Scot and a week later he was the new gun in Sullivan & Christenson's litigation department.

His old firm was a six-person shop specializing in representing injured people.

"It's half a practice," Aunt Claire had told him.

"How can you say that?" he'd asked. "We help the little guy, the person who can't afford to take on the big corporations on their own."

"Yes, you help the outnumbered," she'd conceded. "But it's all about the money, not noble causes. Every time I see a plaintiff's lawyer in a thousand-dollar suit driving a hundred-thousand-dollar car and living in a million-dollar house, I want to kick him right in his jackpot."

She'd been no fonder of Sullivan & Christenson. "That kind of firm has more rules than people," she'd cautioned Mason when he told her he was changing firms. "You're not cut out to join the army. Anybody can do what they do. Besides, there's no honor in stealing one thief's money back from another."

"Even a heartless corporation deserves a good lawyer," Mason had said.

"But you're wrong for the job. You're not heartless. And that's the brutal truth." Aunt Claire had claimed all her truths were brutal or they weren't worth believing.

Mason had tried convincing himself that he took the job with Sullivan & Christenson for the change of scenery. The brutal truth was that he took it because he thought it was safer. He could live with stealing one thief's money back from another more easily than he could live with another Tommy Douchant. In the last three days he'd discovered that there was nothing safe and easy at Sullivan & Christenson. Aunt Claire had been right.

As Mason cinched his red tie beneath the collar of his white shirt and slipped on his gray suit, he wondered how much of the firm's business for heartless corporations would be left after Sullivan's death. The Monday morning uniform. Appropriate for partners' meetings, funerals, and circumcision ceremonies. Today promised to roll elements of all three into one festive occasion.

Scot Daniels and Harlan Christenson were waiting for him in his office.

"Harlan and I want to go over a few things with you before the meeting," Scot said.

Harlan's face sagged under his silence. He had the connections that got the firm started. Sullivan had the backbone that made it a powerhouse. Without Sullivan, Harlan was lost.

"Before we get to that," Mason said, "the sheriff investigating Sullivan's death called me late last night. She said Sullivan was murdered."

Harlan muttered, "Dear God," and shrank farther into his chair. "How?" It was all he could manage.

Mason answered, "She didn't say."

"What's next?" Scot asked.

"She's coming here this afternoon to ask me some more questions. That's all I know."

"Why is she so interested in you?" Scot asked.

"How should I know? Either she thinks I did it, or she can't resist my boyish charms," Mason answered irritably.

Scot studied him for a moment. "Then we'd better focus on what we do know. I came in early this morning to get a look at the files the grand jury subpoenaed. Quintex Land Corporation was at the top of the list."

Mason said, "I thought Quintex was the company O'Malley used for his real estate deals. St. John is after him for bank fraud, not real estate fraud. What's the connection?"

"I don't know. Quintex has been around a long time and a lot of assets have passed through it," Scot answered.

"Did O'Malley use Quintex for anything else?" Mason asked.

"A few years ago, he started using it for other investments," Scot said.

"Were the deals clean?"

"Sullivan handled the real estate deals. I don't know about them. I handled the investments. They were all cash deals. No banks involved. St. John can't be interested in those."

"Maybe one of the other partners knows something that might explain some of this," Mason suggested.

"We have to tell them about the subpoena, but I don't think we should put the details on the table yet. For now, we'd better keep this among ourselves. Harlan agrees with me," Scot responded.

Steady breathing was Harlan's way of saying yes.

The eleven remaining partners of Sullivan & Christenson assembled in the firm's south conference room on the thirty-second floor of the Grand Street Pavilion, an O'Malley Development Co. project, financed by O'Malley's Mid-States Savings & Loan and managed by O'Malley Properties. Sullivan insisted that the firm not exceed the developer's allowance for tenant improvements. "Wallpaper won't make you money," was his explanation. In this case he was right. Leasing from the firm's biggest client at market rates kept O'Malley happy by filling his building. There was no need to add to the expense.

The conference room, like the rest of the two floors the firm occupied, was finished in a nondescript blend of taupe, mauve, and teal hues woven through the carpet, woodwork, and grass-cloth wallpaper. Equally generic art decorated space that could be quickly vacated for new tenants. Twelve chairs surrounded the conference table, five to a side and one at each end.

Lawyers are pack animals who have a clear pecking order reflected in office assignments and seats at conference tables. Mason had inherited a seat on the side with a view out the windows. Harlan took his customary seat at the far end of the table. Mason wondered if anyone would adjust the pecking order by claiming Sullivan's vacant chair at the head of the table opposite Harlan. Grabbing it too soon could send someone to the back of the pack.

Scot was the last to arrive and, without breaking stride, landed in Sullivan's chair, dropped a sheaf of papers in front of him, looked around the table, and said, "Okay, Harlan, the day's gonna be a bitch, so let's get started."

Harlan described what was known of Sullivan's death, omitting that he had been murdered. Mason attributed the omission to Harlan's innate avoidance of unpleasant news. Harlan spoke of his shock, his sympathy for Pamela, announced that the funeral would be Wednesday at 1:00 P.M. at the Ward Parkway Episcopal Church, and turned the meeting over to Scot. The partners swiveled their heads in unison back to the other end of the table.

"Harlan and I will contact Sullivan's clients and reassure them that their matters are being taken care of. Call any of your key clients who should be personally informed. Everyone else will receive a letter that should go out by the end of the day."

Mason was surprised that Scot didn't disclose that Sullivan had been murdered. He wondered if Scot and Harlan would rather that the partners read about it in the newspaper.

"Has anyone spoken to O'Malley?" asked one of the partners.

"He'll be here at eleven to meet with me, Scot, and Lou," answered Harlan.

Scot pressed ahead before Mason could remind him that he hadn't agreed to stick around and help sort out this mess.

"That's going to be a tough meeting," Scot added. "I found out yesterday that Sullivan and the firm are now targets of the grand jury investigation into O'Malley. The firm's files have been subpoenaed for this Friday."

"How did you find out, Scot? Was that the surprise in your box of Cracker Jacks?" Sandra Connelly asked.

Sandra had joined the firm as a partner a year before Mason did and was the chair of the litigation department. She had been less than enthusiastic about hiring him. Scot told Mason that Sandra didn't think an ambulance-chasing lawyer was corporate boardroom material. Scot told Mason not to worry about her opposition. She had the title, he said, but none of the power. Besides, he claimed she just didn't want the competition. She took her frustration out on Mason by alternating verbal jabs with a sterile indifference accentuated by her insistence on calling him "Louis." No one had called him Louis since the third grade.

Sandra blended hard edges and soft touches. Her shoulder-length hair was the color of maple leaves in the fall. She had hazel eyes, impossibly high porcelain cheeks, and "you know how to whistle, don't you?" lips with a body to match. She'd made more than a few opposing lawyers want to thank her for slicing open their jugular. Mason had invited her to lunch during his first week at the firm. It was like the Arab-Israeli peace talks. No one spoke the same language. Scot told him that she'd never been married, didn't need the money she made, and was lethal in the courtroom. Mason and Sandra hadn't worked on any cases together. He wanted to break through her refrigerated demeanor just to make her stop calling him Louis and because he considered her hostility a challenge to his natural charm.

Scot answered Sandra without looking at her. "I found a target letter from Franklin St. John and the subpoena in Sullivan's desk."

"You mean Sullivan kept this secret from the rest of us but just happened to leave the subpoena and St. John's letter lying around on his desk for the cleaning crew to read?" Sandra snapped.

"Sorry to disappoint you, Sandra," he answered, now looking directly at her. "I was looking for Sullivan's drafts of my closing documents when I ran across them. Now one of us has to deal with the U.S. attorney. Lou will be seen as the least tainted since he's only been here a few months. I think he should handle it. Harlan, what do you think?"

"Excuse me," Sandra interjected. "His name is

Lou Mason, not Perry Mason. Would you like to know what the head of the litigation department thinks about putting the future of this firm into the hands of a lawyer whose idea of a courtroom victory is selling a rear-end collision whiplash sob story? To say nothing of the verdict he got for his best friend in his last trial."

Mason felt everyone's eyes burning holes into him while waiting to see if he got up off the mat after Sandra's body slam. His were on her. She didn't flinch. Trouble was, angry as he was—she wasn't wrong. Vicious—yes. Wrong—probably not. That was the nature of brutal truth. Had she known Mason was quitting, she would have thrown him out the window.

Scot saved him from having to respond. "As a matter of fact, Sandra, what you think is not the subject of this discussion. The people who built this firm will make these decisions. Lou is the right choice."

"Sound judgment, Scot," Harlan helpfully added. "Lou, get started today. Sandra will cover your docket and reassign anything that's in need of immediate attention. You'll have our complete cooperation. Just get it done."

Bugging out now was not an option. Mason wouldn't let Scot down and give Sandra the satisfaction of thinking she was right. "Not a problem. I'll take care of my other cases. That's why I get the middle money. But I'll need help on this," he said.

"Sure, Lou. I'll back you up on the technical side," Scot responded.

"You'll have to stay out of it. You were too close to Sullivan. I don't want St. John to focus on you now that Sullivan is dead. I want Sandra and two associates, one from litigation and one from corporate. Sandra, let's talk after the meeting and make our choices."

Mason couldn't tell whether Scot or Sandra let out a more surprised breath.

"Look, Sandra," Mason continued. "I know you don't like me and you don't think I know what I'm doing. I can't help the first problem but you might be right about the second problem. If we work together on this, at least you can keep me from screwing it up."

Mason was already feeling as though he was in over his head. Putting Sandra on the team gave him a chance to solve both problems. Though it may not have been a good idea to ask someone to hold his safety net who would be just as happy to see him fall off the high wire.

Scot caught his breath and tried to change Mason's mind. "Lou, I think we should try to keep this within as small a circle as possible . . ." he began.

Mason cut him off. "Look, Scot, the stakes have gone up." Mason slowly looked around the table, making eye contact with each of his partners. "Richard Sullivan was murdered. The sheriff investigating his death called me last night. She'll be here this afternoon."

He let the words sink in, watching the reaction of each partner. Most looked away as if to duck from Mason's announcement. A couple of them covered their hearts with their hands as if they'd been struck. Only Sandra, Scot, and Harlan held his gaze.

Mason continued. "This isn't about a partner who died in his sleep. It's about a murder investigation going on in the middle of a criminal investigation of this firm. If I'm going to run this show, then I'm going to make the staffing decisions. I'll lose my credibility if I lose my independence."

Scot swallowed hard. "You're right, of course. You won't get anywhere with St. John if he thinks you're shilling for Sullivan. Meeting adjourned."

Sandra Connelly followed Mason into his office and closed the door. "Nicely done, Louis. I didn't think you had the balls."

"Thanks for the endorsement. I need you. You cut through the crap and get to the bottom line. I don't care if you like me. That's not required. Now, which of the associates do you think we should use?"

She folded her arms and gave him an appraising look as if she'd never seen him before. Mason wondered if she really thought he'd been ballsy or whether he put her on the team as a prelude to surrendering to her.

"Phil Rosa is the best litigation associate we've got. He's a workhorse and he never misses anything in his research. Maggie Boylan is the top corporate associate."

"Sounds good. Assemble all of the O'Malley files, including personal files from everyone's offices, in the thirty-first-floor conference room. Lock the door. Skip Sullivan's office. We'll do that together. There'll be no more solo searches."

"You may have some pretty big balls after all," she said on her way out.

Mason pounded down the internal staircase to the thirty-first-floor office of Angela Molina, the firm's executive administrator. Angela could figure more angles than Rubik's cube had and she used them to squeeze every penny of profit out of the practice and into the partners' pockets. Together with a legendary office intelligence system, she kept things on an even keel. Angela had jet-black, wavy hair, olive skin, and a fiery disposition. She was attractive, divorced, and in her mid-forties. Office gossip linked her with Sullivan. But that story followed most women who worked for the firm.

She and Mason hadn't gotten off on the right foot when he insisted on bringing his custom-made furniture that had to be bolted to the wall. Angela objected because it limited her options for future office assignments, one of her chief patronage plums. The initial chill between them had barely thawed over the last three months.

"Angela, I need your help. This is absolutely confidential. The firm has—"

"—been named a target of the grand jury's investigation into O'Malley, and you're in charge of the cleanup." Molina completed the sentence. "What do you have left to tell me, Lou?"

Her instant intelligence bothered him but he'd learned a long time ago that there are no secrets in a law office, especially one managed by Angela Molina.

"Change the locks on Sullivan's office and the thirty-first-floor conference room. Sandra Connelly and I get the only keys. Don't have the property manager do it. I don't want any pass keys floating around."

"O'Malley's property managers won't like it if they can't get into that office to clean, and they'll complain about security."

"Your job is to make them like it, Angela, and I know you have the charm to do it. I want the locks changed by noon. Send out a memo that those rooms are off-limits except to authorized personnel."

"Who are?"

"Sandra Connelly, Phil Rosa, Maggie Boylan, and me. Anyone objects, tell them to talk to me."

Halfway out the door, he told her to send him copies of all the O'Malley bills for the last five years, including the most current, plus work-in-progress.

Mason's next stop was Scot's office. He was on the phone, but waved him in with a signal that said to close the door. He hung up and unloaded.

"Lou, I thought we had a deal on how we would handle this. The last thing in the world I want is for that bitch, Sandra, to be involved. How could you pull a bonehead stunt like that?"

"St. John would rather have a live target than a dead one. You and Sullivan were joined at the hip, which means that you're available. I'm your friend. Sandra wouldn't piss on you if you were on fire. If she believes you're not involved, she'll have more credibility with St. John than I will."

"You're acting like you think I'm in trouble. That worries me, Lou."

"We're all probably in trouble, Scot. We've got to put some distance between you and our investigation. You and Harlan shouldn't be at the meeting with O'Malley except to make the introductions."

"Sounds like you've got it figured out." His shoulders drooped as if Mason had let the air out of him.

"Not even close, my friend, not even close."

Chapter Seven

Mason was ten minutes late to the meeting with Victor O'Malley. Scot Daniels and Harlan Christenson were huddled at the far end of the conference room with O'Malley, a dark-suited trio talking in hushed voices to add weight to their words. Sandra Connelly was seated at the center of the conference table, her back to the door. Her sleeveless ivory-colored dress accented finely muscled upper arms, delicate wrists, and well-manicured hands. Mason recognized O'Malley's son, Vic Jr., leaning over Sandra, trying to make conversation while he stole a glance down the front of her dress. When she didn't respond, he wandered back toward his father, who kept his back to him, barring Vic Jr. from his inner circle. Vic Jr. pretended not to notice by picking microscopic lint off his black silk shirt.

Mason cleared his throat. "Sorry I'm late."

O'Malley turned toward him, waving off any possible offense. "Quite all right, Lou," he said, extending his hand as he walked toward him. "I was just telling Scot and Harlan how much I'm going to miss Richard. I depended on him very much. I don't know how to replace him."

O'Malley's two-handed greeting swallowed Mason's hand, though he struggled to return the intensity of his grip. At six-five, O'Malley took up a lot of space. His equally oversize ego filled the rest of the room. He wore a dark navy suit with a white shirt and light blue geometric-patterned tie. A heavy gold ring with the Marine Corps insignia flashed off his right hand.

"It won't be easy," Mason answered, "but I'm sure Scot and Harlan will take good care of you."

"Of course, of course they will. So long as you keep me out of jail." He said it without smiling, and Mason didn't respond.

O'Malley had a face like an inflated punctuation mark. A few silver strands were laced above his lined forehead. A scarred, bulbous nose was testament to some of the hard knocks he'd taken. He had crisp eyes that missed nothing and a hale-fellow-well-met style that drew people toward him. Mason knew his story from the news clippings in his file. O'Malley was awarded the Silver Star in Vietnam when he led his platoon in a successful bloody attack on a hill controlled by heavily entrenched Viet Cong. That's when he'd learned the importance of location, he often was quoted as saying years later after he had built a banking and real estate empire in Kansas City. And, he would add, the importance of being willing to risk everything if necessary to survive.

Vic Jr., on the other hand, had not climbed out of his father's gene pool. He was round-shouldered with a powdery complexion, a sharp nose, and close-set eyes. He had a nocturnal look, as though he preferred foraging at night to sitting in the conference room. He was a shadow alongside his father for whom he'd worked since graduating from college a few years earlier. Mason had met them once before. O'Malley had done the talking. Vic Jr. had done all the whining.

Harlan put his arms around Mason and O'Malley, forming a new circle. "Lou, I've told Victor that you and Sandra need to talk with him about the government's case and the subpoena for our records. Take good care of him, Lou. Victor has been very good to us."

They all laughed more than Harlan's comment deserved. Mason closed the door as Harlan and Scot left the conference room and sat down next to Sandra. Father and son took seats opposite them.

Mason led off. "Victor, did you know that Richard Sullivan and the firm were targets of the grand jury investigation?"

"Cut to the chase, eh? I like that, young man. Yes. Richard told me. He said it was a sign that St. John was desperate but that I didn't have anything to worry about. He said that you told him I was in the clear."

Mason studied O'Malley for some indication that O'Malley expected him to believe that story. O'Malley's face was a pool of calm water.

"We both know that's bullshit," Mason told him. "You're smart enough to know how much trouble you're in. The U.S. attorney doesn't go after the defendant's lawyers unless he thinks he can squeeze them to turn on their client to save their own hides."

O'Malley didn't flinch. "Then suppose you tell me how much trouble I'm in."

"Here's what I know," Mason began. "Your bank loaned money to real estate partnerships you controlled that were in financial trouble. The bank never should have loaned the money because the partnerships couldn't pay the money back. You knew it and the bank knew it. The loans cost the bank fifty million. The government says that was criminal fraud."

"And my lawyer advised me that the loans were reasonable business investments that turned sour," O'Malley countered. "That's not a crime."

"And I'm not the jury. Did your lawyer get any of that money before he turned up dead?"

"I'm sure Richard charged for his services and was paid."

"Did he collect for anything other than his legal fees?"

O'Malley offered a patient smile. "I didn't write the checks. You'd have to ask him."

"You begin to see the problem here, Victor. Richard Sullivan is dead. You haven't forgotten, have you?"

O'Malley's eyes narrowed and his congenial veneer evaporated. "No, I haven't, young man. My friendship with Richard was the only reason I stuck with this firm and didn't hire a Wall Street heavyweight. I may have to rethink that now that he's gone."

"You may need a Wall Street firm sooner than you think. If the firm is indicted, we'll claim that we didn't know the true nature of your actions because you concealed them. The court will waive your attorney-client privilege, and we can fight over the movie rights.'' Mason wanted him to understand that he was not O'Malley's butt boy.

O'Malley nodded. ''All right, Lou. You've made your point. Better to hang together than separately. What else do you want to know?''

''St. John has subpoenaed our files on Quintex Land Corporation. I want to know why.''

O'Malley sat up straight, adjusted his tie, and looked directly at Mason. ''I don't know. The bank didn't loan any money to Quintex.''

''What does Quintex do?''

''I used it to buy and sell land.''

''Scot said that Sullivan handled the real estate deals but that the company has made other investments besides real estate.''

''Look, Lou, Richard set up more corporations for me than I could keep track of. I certainly can't remember every deal that I ever did. You've got the records. You figure it out and tell me if I've got another problem besides the loans.''

Mason shook his head, realizing the struggle that lay ahead. O'Malley wasn't going to tell him anything he didn't have to. Mason couldn't really blame him. They had only met once before. The lawyer O'Malley trusted was dead and he hadn't decided whether he could trust Mason. Mason and Sandra spent the next two hours hammering him on Quintex, but they didn't know enough to ask the right questions. They realized that they would need at least a week to plow through all the material and scheduled another meeting for the following Monday afternoon.

''Well, what do you think?'' Mason asked Sandra after O'Malley and his son left.

''No jury will ever believe that someone that successful could know so little about how he made all that money. He's not going to help us more than he has to."

"Doesn't he realize that the harder he makes our job, the more likely it is that he gets convicted?"

"Maybe," Sandra answered. "Unless he's more worried about what the government doesn't know than what it does know. We better buy some time from St. John."

"Our appointment is at ten tomorrow morning. Let's have a look at Sullivan's office."

The locksmith was just finishing under Angela's watchful eye. She gave them the Girl Scout salute, handed each of them a key, and posted the NO ADMITTANCE sign on the door.

"The office is secure, so let's leave it until tomorrow. Maybe we'll have a better idea of what we're looking for after we meet with St. John," Sandra said.

When Mason returned to his office, he found six banker's boxes stacked against one wall. Each box was labeled *Douchant v. Philpott Safety Systems.* There was a note from Scot taped to one of the boxes. It read *A deal is a deal. Save the firm and take care of Tommy. Then take the rest of the day off.*

Mason ran his hand over the boxes, deciding whether to open them. He knew that when he did, he'd have no more excuses to quit the firm or to blame the result in Tommy's trial on fickle courtroom gods. He used the letter opener Scot had given him for being best man in his wedding to cut the tape that held the lids on each box.

The first thing he saw was Tommy's safety belt. The Philpott Safety System logo was embossed on the back of the belt. The belt was actually a harness that Tommy had wrapped around his waist and between his legs. A six-foot rope called a lanyard was attached to the belt. A hook shaped like a giant safety pin was attached to the other end of the rope. Tommy had been on a scaffold finishing cement on an elevator tower the day he'd been hurt. He had hooked the lanyard to a steel loop that had been driven into the cement. While he was reaching far to his right, the hook slipped out of the bolt and he fell. There were no witnesses. Mason picked up the belt, worked the action on the safety hook just as he had in front of the jury, and wondered again what he could have done differently to win Tommy's case.

Tommy's employer had given the belt to Warren Philpott, the owner of Philpott Safety Systems, to examine it for defects. Not surprisingly, Philpott claimed there was nothing wrong with it. Mason didn't get to see the belt until after he'd filed the lawsuit several months later. The expert safety engineer Mason had hired said there was nothing wrong with the way it was made. It worked as it was supposed to. But the expert said the design was defective because it didn't have a lock to prevent the hook from opening and separating from whatever it was connected to.

Mason's lawsuit against Philpott was based on the unsafe design. A tough case to win since Philpott's experts said the lock wasn't necessary if the hook was used properly. Philpott had sold hundreds of thousands of the hooks. When a hook failed and Philpott was sued, he usually settled and always won the cases that went to trial.

Philpott's lawyers claimed the accident was Tommy's fault because he did a lousy job of securing his hook. They offered the settlement because they were afraid that the jury would be sympathetic to

Tommy's injury—especially with his wife testifying about life with a paraplegic.

"Two million bucks is a lot of money," Mason had told Tommy the day before the trial. "After attorneys' fees and case expenses, you'll net close to a million-two. You can earn at least a hundred grand a year on the money—more than you ever made working construction."

Tommy didn't hesitate with his bitter answer. "It's not enough, Lou. Not after what those bastards did to me."

"Those bastards aren't going to pay you anyway. Philpott's insurance company is going to pay. This isn't about revenge, Tommy. It's about taking care of your family. You can't take the chance that the jury will send you home empty-handed."

Tommy glared at Mason from his wheelchair. "I'm willing to take that chance, Lou. If you don't have the guts, get one of your partners to try the case."

Mason stiffened at his friend's challenge. "Tommy, this isn't double-dare like when we were kids. It's not about my guts. It's about your brains. Take the money."

"Screw the money. Just try my damn case, Lou."

Tommy didn't tell Mason that Stephen Forrest had secretly convinced him to roll the dice for a bigger payday. LeAnn, Tommy's wife, silently wheeled him out of the courtroom after the trial. They hadn't spoken since. Tommy was living on social security and worker's compensation. Mason was reliving the trial in his dreams. But the verdict never changed.

Mason put the safety belt back in the box and sat down at his computer. Although it had only been four months since the trial, he wanted to find out if there had been anything new in the press about Philpott Safety Systems. He logged on to the Internet and searched for any articles published in the last four months about the company. The only hit was an article in the *Kansas City Star* about the trial.

Mason tried again with a search using Warren Philpott's name. Again there was only one hit. It too was an article published a week ago in the *Kansas City Star*. Only the *Star*'s gossip columnist, not the legal affairs reporter, had written the article. The columnist reported that the police had been called to the Philpotts' home after Ellen Philpott threw her husband's belongings out the second-story window. It was, she explained, her response to the divorce petition he had filed. Mrs. Philpott's spring-cleaning had taken place during a thunderstorm, which had the desired effect of ruining all of her husband's clothes. The neighbors objected to the unsightly appearance of clothing scattered across the lawn. Mrs. Philpott avoided further scandal by collecting the clothes on her patio, where she allowed them to mildew and rot out of the view of her neighbors, courtesy of the six-foot privacy fence that surrounded her yard. Mr. Philpott declined comment.

Mason remembered Ellen Philpott, sitting in the courtroom for five days, first row behind the rail, far side from the jury box, a flexed smile fixed on the back of her husband's neck. Her own neck, thin-skinned and thick-veined, bobbing and weaving with the testimony. Nodding conspiratorially at Mason each morning as they assembled, as if they shared a secret. Mason had wanted to ask her what the secret was, but knew that Philpott's lawyer wouldn't let him talk with her. That was then. Mason decided to work a visit to Ellen into his schedule.

He spent the rest of the day talking to clients. His secretary called at five-fifteen to tell him that Kelly Holt was waiting to see him.

"Sorry, I'm late," she said as she sat down across from him.

"No problem. I couldn't stand another sympathy call. Your timing was perfect."

Mason couldn't decide if she looked better in or out of uniform. She was wearing an indigo suit, an open-necked, lime blouse, and a ruby and jade striped scarf. A gold clip held her hair snugly in back. It was a toss-up. Happily, she wasn't wearing a gold band to match her gold earrings and choker chain.

"I apologize for acting like a jerk yesterday. It's not every day that I get to identify my senior partner's body."

"Forget it. I never get used to the bodies either."

"Last night you said that Sullivan was murdered. How do you know?"

"Sorry, Counselor. It's my turn to claim confidentiality."

"Why? Am I still a suspect?"

"What do you think?"

"That everybody's a suspect until you catch the killer."

"Exactly. You can either confess or tell me who did it."

"I can't do either. But I doubt that someone would try to kill me if I was the killer." Mason told her about his drive back from the lake. "I'm parked in space number 110 in the parking garage. You can check the damage to my car and I can show you the place where I went off the road."

"I'll do that. Why would Sullivan's killer want to kill you?"

"Maybe the killer thinks I know something that would identify him or her. Or maybe the killer thinks Sullivan told me something he doesn't want anyone else to know. Or maybe it was just road rage."

Kelly answered with professional neutrality. "I can't protect you up here. Do you want me to ask the local cops to put somebody here and at your house?"

Mason didn't know whether to be pleased or frightened that she made the offer. If she believed him, she might not suspect him. But if she thought he needed protection, he might be in real danger. He was used to fighting through a pile of muddy rugby players battling over a slippery football. But he'd never played against a killer, and the prospect now didn't seem real. And he didn't like asking someone to take care of him.

"Not yet," he hedged. "I'm defending O'Malley. I've got to deal with a difficult client and a U.S. attorney who wants to put us out of business. I won't have credibility with either if I've got a bodyguard following me around. Do you have any better suggestions?"

"Just one. This is not amateur hour. Get someone else to represent O'Malley and someone else to represent your firm. I don't want to pick up the paper and read that you've been fished out of the lake or sent up the river."

Before Mason could respond, Cara Trent

opened his door as she knocked, carrying O'Malley's bills in one hand and a coffee mug in the other. Cara was a lighter blonde than Kelly, soft where Kelly was sinewy, fragile where Kelly was tough.

"Oh, sorry, Lou, I didn't know you had anyone in here. Angela said you wanted these. She had to leave and I'm right behind her."

"Thanks, Cara. Say hello to Kelly Holt. She's the sheriff from the lake who's looking into Sullivan's death."

Cara took a deep breath as she set her coffee mug on Mason's desk and shook Kelly's hand. To her credit, it was the only part of her that was shaking.

"It's terrible. I didn't know him well, but he seemed like such a fine man," Cara managed to say.

"Yes, well, I'm certain it was terrible for all of you," Kelly answered. "I hope to visit with you about it in the next few days," she added.

Cara looked away from Kelly's steady gaze. "Sure. I'll be around," she said and left.

Kelly watched her leave, giving no clues as to her impressions of Cara. Mason assumed that Cara had known Sullivan a lot better than she would admit. He figured Kelly made the same assumption after he told her they had left the poker game together, but Kelly gave her no cause to suspect that. Kelly picked up Cara's coffee mug by the handle, poured the contents into Mason's trash can, slipped it into the paper bag his lunch had come in, and dropped it into her purse.

"Mind if I borrow this for a few days?"

"Is that the way you take fingerprints in the

Ozarks? What do you use for mug shots? Home movies?"

"Very funny. If Cara were at the lake, I'd ask her to come in and give me a set of elimination prints." Mason furrowed his brow at her explanation. Kelly continued. "I'd tell Cara that we found prints on the boat and at the condo and that we need her prints to eliminate hers from those we found. Since I doubt that she's going back to the lake anytime soon, this cup will have to do."

"Be my guest," Mason said.

She was gone before he could use one of his "how about a drink?" lines.

Chapter Eight

Tommy Douchant had bloodied Mason's nose when Mason asked Douchant's girlfriend to double-skate at the roller rink. Crawling under his table near the concession stand, Mason had tied the laces of Tommy's skates together while blood dripped from his nose. They were ten. Neither of them got the girl. Friendships are born in strange ways.

Tommy was Catholic. Mason was Jewish. Tommy was hotheaded. Mason was sneaky. Tommy joined his father's union. Mason went to college. Tommy broke his back. Mason lost his case. Friendships die in strange ways.

Mason thought about the parts of their lives that intersected and the parts that ran parallel to one another as he sat in his car in front of Tommy's house, engine running, a six-pack of Bud on the seat next to him. Tommy lived with his wife, LeAnn, and their five-year-old twins in a small, two-story

Cape Cod in Prairie Village, a suburb just on the Kansas side of the state line. The community had been built immediately after World War II, funded by low-rate mortgages for veterans.

The house was originally a one-story ranch. Tommy had finished the attic into a second floor, added dormers, and turned the ranch into a Cape Cod. Since then, Mason had watched him paint the inside and the outside, pour a new driveway, and rewire the house.

"Got a new project," Tommy announced with a kid's enthusiasm the week before his accident. "Gonna put up a basketball goal that I can raise and lower so the kids can use it. Wanna give me a hand?"

They were eating ribs and drinking beer at Bryant's Barbecue before catching an early season baseball game. Tommy always asked Mason if he wanted to help and Mason always turned him down.

"You remember those skills tests we took in junior high school?" Mason asked him.

"Yeah. What about 'em?"

"You remember the section titled 'Works Well With His Hands'? My results came back 'has no hands.' "

"Then bring the beer and watch. You can't screw that up."

Mason studied the outside of the house, as if it would tell what had happened to the family who lived inside. Fresh lawn mower tracks partitioned the small front yard into neat twenty-one-inch slices. Mason assumed that a neighborhood kid got the credit. Day lilies, their blossoms leaning over like bowed heads, struggled in the heat beneath the dining room and living room windows on either side of the front door. Flowers were LeAnn's annual project. A pink ball the size of a large grapefruit lay against the base of the basketball goal. Mason looked at his watch. It was eight o'clock. LeAnn was probably giving the kids a bath. The wheelchair ramp from the front stoop to the driveway was the only clue that things were different inside this house.

The front door opened. Tommy sat in his wheelchair, hands on the wheels, gently rolling forward and back over the threshold, as if he couldn't decide whether to stay in or come out. They looked at each other, neither waving, just looking. Mason sighed deeply, turned off the car, and got out, carrying the six-pack of Bud. Tommy rolled his wheelchair over the threshold, onto the front stoop, and down the ramp. They met in the driveway.

Mason didn't know what to say. He couldn't bring himself to tell Tommy that he looked good, though his upper body was still strong, the muscles in his arms still rippled against his T-shirt. But his legs were out of place, muscles wasted, skin pasty. So Mason wouldn't tell Tommy that he looked good. Instead, he scanned the outside of the house again, stopping at the basketball goal. "The kids must like shooting hoops."

"Gives 'em something to do."

"That's good." Mason wanted to get to the point, skip the awkward small talk. But it was easier to talk about anything other than what they had to talk about.

"I built that ramp," Tommy told him, motioning over his shoulder.

"Get out! Why didn't you call me? I could have helped," Mason asked.

"Remember those skills tests we took in junior high school?"

"Right. I brought the beer if it's not too late."

"Never too late, Lou. As long as the beer's cold."

Mason set the six-pack on the driveway after they each took a bottle. They drank in silence, the awkwardness still lingering.

"You really built that ramp?" Mason finally asked.

"Yeah. The workers' compensation people sent somebody out to put one in while I was still in the hospital. There wasn't anything wrong with it. I just don't like other people working on my house."

Mason remembered that Tommy's workshop was in the basement. "How did you get down to your shop?"

"Didn't have to. LeAnn moved my workbench into the garage. I cut the legs down so I could reach everything from my chair. When I finished cutting the boards for the ramp to size, she got me one of those little carts mechanics lay on to slide under cars and I just sat out here scooting around and hammering nails."

"It looks great," Mason congratulated him.

"It looks like shit, but I built it. It's not much, but it's a start."

"What about vocational rehab? I thought workers' comp was going to retrain you."

"They tried. Told me computers was what I should learn. So far, I'm better at ramp building, but I don't know that there's much demand for crippled carpenters," Tommy said without a trace of the bitterness he'd shown at the trial.

Mason was struck by Tommy's matter-of-factness. He sounded more realistic than resigned.

Mason finished his beer as the last shadows of the day crept over them. "I'm sorry about the trial—about the way everything turned out," he finally said. Given enough time, Mason knew he would probably apologize for every disaster of the twentieth century.

Tommy shook his head and waved off Mason's apology. "I should have listened to you and taken the money."

"I should have done a better job."

"Quit kicking yourself," Tommy answered impatiently. "I was the one who screwed up. Your partner told me that Philpott would pay a lot more once the trial got started. I believed him because I was so mad about everything. You were right. All I cared about was getting even. It's too late now."

"Maybe not," Mason said.

"What's that supposed to mean?" Tommy asked, looking up at Mason.

"I want to reopen your case. But I've got to find evidence to convince the judge to give you a new trial."

"How are you going to do that?"

"Philpott and his wife just got divorced. I'll start with her. After that, I don't know. I can't promise you anything. Don't get your hopes up." Mason cautioned himself as well as Tommy.

"Any hope is more than we've had for a while now. Do what you can, Lou."

Tommy reached down, pulled the six-pack up into his lap, and rolled his wheelchair back up the ramp, his arms and shoulders flexing with the climb. When he reached the top, Tommy turned and gave Mason a slight wave. *Not even breathing hard,* Mason thought to himself. He returned the wave.

Kate was sitting on Mason's front step, scratching Tuffy behind her ears, when Mason pulled into his driveway. Scot had been waiting for him the night before. He couldn't wait to see who would show up tomorrow. He didn't see Kate's car, which meant that she and the dog had walked from her apartment on the Plaza, about a mile away.

Tuffy liked to have the back of her ears scratched and, once the scratching started, the dog devoted herself entirely to the sensation, refusing every distraction except for one—Mason. The dog was infatuated with him, which, Mason knew, infuriated Kate. It was, Mason was certain, the reason Kate had stolen her when they'd split up. All of which he remembered with jealous clarity when he stepped from the car, clapped his hands twice, and caught Tuffy when she bounded into his arms.

"Never doubt a dog's devotion," Kate said with a spare smile as she joined them on the driveway. She was wearing a short-sleeved, bright orange cotton shirt, buttoned down the middle, untucked, over black capri pants. The colors highlighted her fine-china skin and fiercely black hair. The clothes clung to her slender frame, stretched at the right places. Mason had the same reaction each time he saw her. He'd do it again. Probably even if he couldn't make it come out differently.

Tuffy finished licking Mason's chin and moved on to sniffing his shoes, pants, and crotch to confirm her master's identity. A squirrel jumped from a tree onto the driveway, daring Tuffy to give chase. Tuffy didn't disappoint.

"She a very faithful bitch," Mason answered.

Kate shrugged off Mason's comment. He marveled at her ability to shrug off things and people. He attributed it to her disengagement gene. It was never more apparent than on the day she'd left the divorce papers on top of the sports section. Mason had tracked her down at her office where she ran an Internet media start-up company.

"What the hell is this?" he'd demanded, slapping the papers on her desk.

She'd looked up at him from her desk, her perfect black eyebrows arched over her luminous blue eyes. They were the same eyes he'd been drawn to the night they met. They were an arresting blue that had taken him into custody on the spot. Then they'd seemed electric. Now they were ice.

"I'm done. That's all."

"Excuse me. You're done? Don't I get a vote?"

Kate had pushed back in her chair, folded her arms, and shook her head like a teacher whose student just didn't get it. "No, Lou. You don't get a vote. Love isn't an election. You're either in or you're out and I'm out. Out of love with you and out of the marriage." She said it without rancor. It was the way it was. She had disengaged.

It may have been simple to her, but not to him. They had been married three years. The first had been erotic and ecstatic. The second had been quiet and comfortable. The third had been dead and boring. Mason called it a slump. Kate declared it a dead end.

Afterward, he read an article by a marriage

expert who said that successful couples developed rituals that helped bind them together. They had none. But he knew they had needed more than a few minutes spent lingering over coffee to trade stories of the day. After the passion, there wasn't enough purpose, he decided. Still, he had been wracked by the breakup. She seemed to have dismissed it. That was the part he never got. When she'd snatched the dog, he'd wondered if it was really just so much water off a duck's back.

"I need for you to keep the dog for a while," she told him as they watched Tuffy tree the squirrel. A moment later, Tuffy lost interest when Anna Karelson whistled at her from her front yard and held a dog biscuit in the air. Tuffy flew across the street. Anna's husband, Jack, had run off with a nineteen-year-old file clerk in his office and then resurfaced, begging her to take him back. She changed the locks. Worst of all, she wouldn't let him have his TR-6, which she kept locked in the garage. Anna waved at Mason as Tuffy bounded back to his side.

He scratched her behind the ears. "Not that I'm complaining, but why?"

"I'll be out of town for a month on a road show."

"You gave up the New Economy for show business?"

Kate gave him an exasperated smirk. "My company is very hot right now. We're one of the best in our space but we need more capital. We're going to San Francisco and New York to meet with venture capitalists. It's called a road show."

"Umm. Sounds thrilling. Better take the money

before you lose interest and move on to something else."

"Keep drinking from that bitter cup, Lou, and you'll give yourself an ulcer. I'll pick up Tuffy when I get back." She walked away without a backward glance, arms swinging with the purposeful stride of an entrepreneur hunting money.

"Not if I see you first," he said when she was out of earshot.

Chapter Nine

At ten o'clock Tuesday morning, Mason and Sandra Connelly emptied their pockets for the deputy marshals guarding the federal courthouse before heading to Franklin St. John's sixth-floor office. The marshals confiscated Mason's calculator and Dictaphone so that he couldn't use them to detonate a bomb in St. John's office. Mason did a double take when the marshal gave Sandra a claim check for the three-inch knife she carried in her purse.

"I collect sharp things," she said in response. "It's a hobby."

"Ever hear of stamps?"

"No edge to it," she said with a shrug as they walked to the elevator.

Franklin St. John was a small, spare man, vain enough to comb the few remaining filaments of hair across his bald head. A high, shiny forehead dropped off to a narrow, long nose, thin lips, and a pointed chin. His upper lip curled into a sneer as he greeted them with a smile. Mason couldn't tell if it was intentional or a cruel trick played by involuntary facial muscles. He didn't look like a nice man, and Mason bet his face was not a disappointment to those who knew him. St. John was a career prosecutor from a political family whose connections reached to the White House. Originally from Kansas City, he'd been an assistant U.S. attorney in Chicago. When the U.S. attorney position opened up in Kansas City, he got the job.

He stood behind a massive desk, flanked by the seal of the United States and the official picture of the president. Tall, brightly lit floor lamps behind his desk cast an artificial aura behind him. Mason was certain the effect was intentional.

St. John introduced them to Gene McNamara, the FBI agent who was his chief investigator. McNamara dressed as if saving tax dollars on his clothing allowance. His tan suit grabbed at the armpits and across his broad shoulders. His face was beefy, with a drinker's hazy red-veined pattern across his nose and cheeks. He nodded perfunctorily at them and took up station at the end of the sofa opposite St. John's desk, his coat opened casually enough to expose the service revolver holstered under his right arm.

"We're all terribly sorry about Mr. Sullivan's death," St. John oozed.

Mason oozed back. "Thank you. We appreciate you seeing us on such short notice. We need your help in sorting out several matters that Sullivan neglected to tell his partners about."

Mason decided that the best approach was to make nice, put his cards on the table, and convince St. John that he wanted to cooperate.

"My office is always pleased to cooperate, Mr. Mason. What did you have in mind?"

"We just found out that you've subpoenaed the firm's files on Victor O'Malley for this Friday and that Sullivan and the firm are targets of your investigation. We need some idea of what you're looking for and time to figure out what the hell is going on."

St. John peered across the desk at Mason as if he'd told him a squirrel had come in his window and eaten his homework.

"Mr. Mason, your late partner was O'Malley's gatekeeper, and we've been banging on the gate for two years. Did you really think you could charge him all those fees and not step in his crap?"

Mason couldn't resist the bait. "We don't have the luxury of sitting around dreaming up conspiracies while sucking on the public tit. If Sullivan stepped on his dick, we'll deal with it." Mason was always good at making nice.

"Stepping on his dick or your own, as you put it, Mr. Mason, may be the least of your concerns. Have the documents here by five o'clock on Friday."

"Why don't we just go see the judge and ask him if he thinks an extension is appropriate since the person you served is dead?"

St. John knew the judge would give them more time to respond and that he wouldn't win any points for being a hard-ass.

"Very well, Mr. Mason, how much time do you want?"

"Thirty days."

"Will that be all?"

"I want to know if you're tapping our phones. Once the press gets hold of this, I want to reassure our clients that their communications remain confidential."

"You're not entitled to that information, Mr. Mason, and you know that. But, in the spirit of cooperation—Agent McNamara, what's the status of our intercepts?"

"Holt handled the last round just before her partner was killed. Our authorizations expired after she quit. We don't have anything in their offices."

Holt's name made no sense.

"Kelly Holt?" Mason practically blurted out the question.

"Yeah, why?" McNamara asked.

"She's the sheriff investigating Sullivan's death."

"I wasn't aware that she stayed in law enforcement," St. John said as he glared at McNamara, reprimanding him for his oversight. "The paper said that Sullivan drowned."

Mason's spirit of cooperation was evaporating.

"He died during our firm retreat. I helped identify the body. That's all I know. We'll have a response to the subpoena in a month."

Mason was silent on the walk back to the office, trying to piece together fragments that didn't match. Sandra obviously knew better than to interrupt his thoughts until they were in the conference room, surrounded by the O'Malley files.

"Are you going to tell me what Kelly Holt has to do with Sullivan's death or do I have to use my knife?" Sandra asked when they'd returned to the office.

No response.

"Lou, it's a very sharp knife."

"Do you believe in coincidences?" he asked.

"No. I believe in chaos."

"O'Malley, Sullivan, and the firm are being investigated by the FBI. Sullivan dies and the sheriff who is investigating his death just happens to be an ex-FBI agent who just happened to be in charge of wiretapping O'Malley. Coincidence or chaos?" He didn't add that the sheriff didn't tell him she'd been involved in the investigation. He hadn't had time to sort through that piece.

"Chaos—the rule of unintended consequences. Seemingly unconnected events run headlong into each other. It's like God is using people to play bumper cars. Sullivan drowned. Where's the connection?"

"Sullivan was murdered. That's not what I would call an unintended consequence."

Maggie Boylan and Phil Rosa pushed the door open before Sandra could respond. They wheeled in a portable workstation carrying a PC, laser printer, paper, legal pads, calculators, and a lifetime supply of Post-its.

"Do you have any idea how many trees will die before we're done with the paper in this case?" Rosa asked.

Mason didn't care. "If you finish reviewing the O'Malley files by Sunday night, you can figure that out. I want an analysis of all of the transactions we've handled for O'Malley. I want to know what each deal involved, who financed it, what changed hands, and the names of all past and present Sullivan and Christenson attorneys who worked on them."

"We could really use a legal assistant to set up a database for all that information. We've got the software to sort the data, but we need someone who uses it all the time if we're going to be ready for O'Malley on Monday,'' Maggie Boylan said.

She expected Mason to agree with such a commonsense suggestion and was surprised when he turned her down flatly.

"Sorry, we've got to keep this team as small as possible. I can't take the chance of leaks."

"Lou, you know she's right. There are thousands of documents to review. Diane Farrell was Sullivan's paralegal. There can't be anything in these files she doesn't already know," Sandra said.

Phil stiffened at the suggestion. "That woman is the biggest pain in the ass in four states," he said. "If she wasn't screwing Sullivan, she had him by the short hairs some other way. Sullivan let her get away with murder. No one can stand to work with her."

"For Christ's sake, Phil," said Maggie, "can't we wait until the body's cold before we start shitting all over the grave? She knows this stuff inside and out. Besides, I'd rather have her where I can watch her than wonder what she's doing to get even for being left out."

Mason reluctantly gave in. "All right, I'm convinced by this underwhelming endorsement. Bring her in, but tell her she's out of a job if she can't keep her mouth shut. Sandra and I will be in Sullivan's office."

A Kelly green carpet with a gold border lay beneath an oak wraparound desk that dominated Sullivan's office. A matching wall-length unit with bookshelves above and cabinets below filled the wall opposite the bank of windows, which opened to the south. A pair of side chairs and matching sofa upholstered in a gold-on-green abstract print completed the eye-popping picture.

Mason tackled the wall unit and Sandra poked through the desk. An hour later they were finished and no closer to any answers. Sullivan kept firm records and a few client files in his office. There was nothing pertaining to O'Malley or St. John's subpoena.

"Where are his files on O'Malley?" Sandra asked.

"Maybe he didn't keep separate files," Mason suggested.

"Or maybe somebody got here ahead of us," she answered. "He probably has an office at home. We should have a look after the funeral. I did find this CD, but it's not labeled."

She handed Mason an unmarked plastic CD case. He removed the glistening disc, booted up Sullivan's desktop PC, and inserted the disc into the CD/DVD drive.

"Man oh Manishevitz," Mason said, whistling. "It's a DVD orgy."

They watched as a half dozen naked men and women mixed and matched parts as if they were playing a deviant version of Mr. Potato Head.

"Look at those angles. I better take some notes," Sandra said.

"That's all the excitement I can stand," Mason announced self-consciously. His face was flushed as he punched the movie disc out of the computer and returned it to its case.

"What's the matter?" Sandra teased. "Afraid to walk down the hall with Johnny Rocket ready for liftoff?" She made a show of letting her eyes slide down his chest to his zipper.

"You are brutal. You know that? But watching a porno flick together is not my idea of bonding with you."

Sandra wouldn't let up. "You sure those big boys aren't making you insecure?"

"Of all people, Sandra, I thought you would know."

"Know what?" she asked.

"It ain't the meat, honey. It's the motion." Mason enjoyed Sandra's silent, red-faced response. "Let's go," he added, grabbing the DVD. "I think I'll keep this so it doesn't show up in the stuff we turn over to St. John."

"Just a minute. Let's try a little reality check with St. John," Sandra said as she unscrewed the mouthpiece of the telephone receiver on Sullivan's desk. "If you liked the movie, you're gonna love this," she said, showing him the miniature microphone attached to the mouthpiece.

Mason ripped the receiver from the phone and fifteen minutes later slammed open St. John's office door with Sandra and St. John's secretary on his heels.

"You really are a piece of work, St. John. Did you really think we wouldn't check for bugs just because you said there weren't any?" He jammed the mouthpiece under St. John's nose.

Two deputy marshals ran into the office, weapons drawn. "Sorry, Mr. St. John, but your secretary pushed the panic button," one of the marshals said.

"They didn't have an appointment, Mr. St. John. They wouldn't even let me buzz you first," his secretary moaned.

"It's quite all right, Paula. You did the right thing. Officers, I'm sorry to trouble you. Mr. Mason and Miss Connelly will be leaving shortly, either with or without your assistance. It makes no difference to me."

Mason pretended not to notice the guards as they advanced toward them. "All I want is some answers, Frank. Why are you bugging our offices?"

He handed Mason the receiver. "Mr. Mason, I'm afraid you may have more problems than either of us thought. Even those of us on the public tit, as you call us, can afford better equipment than this. It's not one of ours. Good day, Counselors."

Chapter Ten

Wilson Bluestone's friends called him "Blues," a name he'd earned playing piano in jazz clubs around Kansas City after he quit his day job as a cop. He and Mason became friends when Mason quit taking piano lessons from him at the conservatory of music. Mason had signed up for lessons a couple of years after he'd graduated from law school and Blues was assigned as his teacher. At his first lesson, Mason had told him that if he could play like Oscar Peterson, he'd think he'd died and gone to heaven. After four lessons, Blues told him to go home, listen to the metronome, and find another way to get to heaven.

Mason got the message and didn't show up for his next lesson. Blues called and demanded to know why he wasn't there. When Mason told him, Blues reminded him that he had paid for the first five lessons and that he ought to get his money's worth.

"Why are you giving up?" he asked when Mason walked into the studio. It was a small, sparse room furnished with an upright piano, bench, and a gray metal folding chair. Posters of Herbie Hancock, Count Basie, and Oscar Peterson covered the center space on three of the walls. As usual, Blues straddled the chair, his arms folded over the back. Mason took the bench, his back to the piano.

He was a bit defensive since he had never thought of himself as a quitter. "Like I told you over the phone. I got your message. I wasn't born to be a genius jazz pianist."

"Why did you sign up in the first place?"

"I love jazz and I think the piano is God's gift to music."

"Yeah, but why did you think you could learn to play?"

Mason hadn't expected this question. "I just assumed anyone who wanted to play could learn to play."

"What do you like about the music?"

"The way it sounds, I guess. What do you want me to say? Is this some kind of exit interview for failing students?"

"That's why you'll never learn to play. It's not what you hear. It's how the music makes you feel. If it doesn't change the way you see the world, you're just in the audience. And the audience doesn't play."

"I guess you're right. I thought learning to play music was like learning a foreign language. First you learn the alphabet, then the grammar, and then you practice speaking. Keep after it, and you've got it mastered."

"I'll bet you don't speak any foreign languages either."

He'd been right, but Mason wouldn't admit it. "Is that all I get for my last lesson?"

"It's more than you got out of the first four."

"So is this all you do? Take people's money to tell them why they shouldn't take lessons from you?"

"Nope. I'm sort of a freelance problem solver."

"What kind of problems?"

"Some like yours. Help people realize that they're better off listening to music than trying to play it. I'm a private investigator. I find people who don't want to be found and I find out things that people want to know. All depends on what needs to be done."

He'd stood up and Mason realized that was the first time he'd seen Blues out of the folding chair. Watching that single movement, Mason began to get an idea of the other kinds of problems he could solve.

Blues was a solid six-three, probably went two-twenty. All of it sleek muscle. But he moved so easily, almost gracefully, that it was clear he had power that didn't depend on size and strength. He had shiny, almost luminescent, straight black hair and a complexion that was somewhere between tan and copper. His face was sharply chiseled with a square chin and dark eyes. The truth was, Mason hadn't paid much attention to who he was or what he looked like until that moment. And he couldn't figure what Blues was. The one thing Mason was certain of, Blues didn't belong to his synagogue.

"Mind if I ask you a question?"

"I'm half Cherokee, half Shawnee. That's what you wanted to know, isn't it? You'd do better not to stare."

"An Indian jazz piano player?" Mason had said it without thinking, almost choking on the question.

"Used to be. Now I'm a Native American jazz piano player. It's not strictly a black thing, you know. And if you've got any more fool questions, don't ask them."

Mason took his advice and didn't ask any more until six months later, when he'd needed help tracking down a drunk driver who had run over a client in an intersection and fled the scene of the accident. He hired Blues to find the driver.

A week later, Blues called to tell Mason that he'd found the driver and asked Mason to meet him at 7th and Pennsylvania on the northwest corner of the downtown. Mason knew the location. Aunt Claire had called it the Lookout when she took him there as a kid to watch airplanes take off and land at the municipal airport. That airport was now limited to small private planes. The commercial airport was Kansas City International, which was twenty miles north of downtown on Interstate 29. The Lookout was on top of a bluff that overlooked the Missouri River, which wound down from the north before turning to the east and heading to its meeting with the Mississippi River in St. Louis. Municipal Airport was cradled into that bend in the Missouri River. It was an odd place for a meeting unless Blues had found the drunk passed out on the bluff.

It was the first week of October and an early cold snap had sucked the last remnants of summer from the air, leaving behind a sharply crisp sky and visible exhaust from the thousands of cars that flew past on the highways that wrapped around the base of the bluff. Mason parked his car and met Blues at the guardrail at the edge of the Lookout.

"Hey, good to see you, Blues," he said, his hand outstretched. It seemed like a friendly gesture. Appropriate for greeting someone he hadn't seen in six months and who had agreed to help him out without even negotiating a fee in advance. Blues was studying the panorama that spread out for miles to the north, west, and east. He didn't look at Mason.

"What are you going to do to him?" Blues asked in reply, without shaking his hand or looking at him.

"Who? The guy who hit my client? I'm going to sue the son of a bitch."

"What do you know about him?"

"Nothing. That's why I wanted you to find him. I need to find out who his insurance company is so I can put them on notice."

Blues turned to Mason and then swept his hand across the view. "What do you see out there?"

Mason started to make a smart-ass remark, like "not the guy you were supposed to find for me"—when he remembered his last piano lesson. There was a message here and he wasn't getting it.

"I don't know. You tell me."

"Over there," he said, pointing to the west. "That's the Kansas River. The Indians called it the Kaw, and that spot, where it pours into the Missouri—right where the Missouri bends to the east—they called that Kawsmouth. Not very original. But it makes the point. Down there, where I-70 cuts across the downtown, that was all bluffs—just like this. Right down to the banks of the Missouri. Back in the 1870s, they dug out those bluffs to make the streets. At first, they just cut the streets out of the bluffs, like gullies. They even called it Gullytown for a while, instead of Kansas City. To

the west, over there, in those old warehouses that
are used for haunted houses at Halloween—that's
the West Bottoms. More hogs and cattle were
slaughtered there than you could ever imagine.
Ten thousand people worked there when the meat-
packing business was booming. Lot of people got
rich. Not one of them an Indian."

"Blues, I know there's a point to this and I do
appreciate the history lesson, but where's my
drunk?"

He made another quarter turn to the southwest.
"Over that way, back into Kansas, you can't really
see it from here, is where the government put the
Shawnee tribe to get them out of the way of all
that progress. They kept moving the tribes farther
west, each time promising them that they could
have those lands forever. 'Course it didn't work
out that way."

"Look, if this is some kind of sensitivity test, let
me know. I'll tell you the story about my Jewish
ancestors sneaking out of their Lithuanian village
in the middle of the night so that they wouldn't
be killed in the monthly pogrom. They ended up
here with a set of candlesticks and nothing else.
My great-grandfather helped cut the stones they
used for those streets and my grandfather slaughtered his share of those animals. Nobody said it
was fair. I don't need for you to know about that
or to give a shit. I just want to know if you found
my drunk."

Blues looked at him with a half smile. "Just
wanted you to know, that's all."

"Know what?"

"I've got more faith in my own system of justice
than in the one you're going to use to squeeze a
settlement out of your drunk's insurance company.

I'll help you when I want to and you'll pay me. I don't like what you're doing or I decide I don't like you—that's it. That's my justice system."

"Fair enough. But if I don't get my drunk, you don't get paid."

"I've got your drunk," he said. "By the way," he added with mock surprise, "I didn't know Mason was a Jewish name."

Mason couldn't hold back his grin. "Yeah? Well, I guess that means we're even since I didn't know there were any Indian piano players."

Their arrangement had worked well over the years. Blues could find just about anyone who didn't want to be found and find out most things that people didn't want someone else to know. And he did it with a confidence and fearlessness that made it difficult for people to resist. When they did, they regretted it.

Blues didn't volunteer much about himself. Eventually Mason strung together enough bits and pieces to know that he'd been married and divorced before he was twenty, served in the army special forces, and spent six years as a cop in Kansas City. He quit the police force after he shot and killed a woman suspected of smothering her baby to stop her from crying. Blues never went into the details except to say that the brass gave him the choice to quit or be fired. He quit being a cop, but kept playing piano and moonlighting as a freelance problem solver. Mason suspected that something more than reading history had shaped Blues's uncompromising solutions for the problems people brought to him. But Mason had yet to turn over that rock. Nor could Mason explain why Blues had agreed to help him with the drunk and the other cases he'd needed help with since he'd quit playing piano. The one time he'd asked, Blues told him it was the only way he could make certain that Mason didn't start playing again.

They met for breakfast Wednesday morning at Nichols Lunch, a midtown diner on the Southwest Trafficway where the upwardly mobile have breakfast and the down-and-out spend hours with a cup of coffee.

"Sounds like you and your pinstriped partners are in deep shit, man," Blues said between mouthfuls of omelet after Mason finished telling him what had happened over the last three days. "You want me to watch your back until this is over?"

"You think my back needs to be watched?"

"Oh, I don't know, Lou," Blues said, drawing out the words with heavy sarcasm. "You've got one dead partner and somebody either wants you to join him or be convicted for killing him."

Mason couldn't ignore the warning in Blues's offer. His willingness to accept it after he'd turned down a similar offer from Kelly was, he recognized, more than a little sexist. He resolved to work on his gender insecurity just as soon as people stopped trying to kill him.

"I've never had someone watch my back before. Is that a hard thing to do?"

"Easier job than teaching you to play the piano."

"Do I get more than one hour a week?"

"I'll be around as much as I can. Most of the time, you won't know it. But I won't have you covered all the time. You'll have to be careful."

"I'll just talk into my collar so the bad guys will think I've got backup around the corner. In the meantime, I don't have a clue who planted the bug. St. John says it's not one of his."

"He's right about that," Blues said as he rolled the minimicrophone in his palm. "Every low-life PI in town has a drawer full of these."

"Sullivan's funeral is at one o'clock today. The office will be closed. Find out if any more of these toys are lying around. Where are you playing tonight?"

"I've got a gig at The Landing."

"I'll see you there around nine."

"Any suggestions if someone decides to skip the funeral to catch up on paperwork?"

"Anyone who's there instead of the funeral will have more explaining to do than you. The elevator to our floors will be locked out and you'll have to use our access code." Mason handed Blues a slip of paper with a series of numbers on it. "Use that sequence on the elevator control panel. It's the only way to get to our floors."

"Why all the cloak-and-dagger stuff?"

"I hate being the last to know what's going on."

"What about your partner who found the bug?"

"Sandra Connelly. We agreed not to say anything to anyone else."

"But you didn't tell her about me, did you, Lou?"

"No, and don't start interrogating me. I'm being careful, just like you told me. See you tonight."

Chapter Eleven

Mason decided to skip the office and visit Ellen Philpott instead. He knew that dropping in on a witness unannounced was better than calling for an appointment. It was easier to hang up than it was to close the door in someone's face.

He had followed the same rule when he met Kate for the first time. He was at a lecture, which was thin cover for a chance to meet women who didn't like getting picked up at bars. He stared at her from the moment she walked in. She was slender and slick, with thick, wavy black hair. And she knew how to move. She didn't walk. She shimmied and shimmered. What she lacked in cover-girl credentials, she made up in mystique. It was a combination of things. The arc of her smile, the promising cup of her hands, the scent that lingered on her very kissable throat. Some of these things he guessed at that night and some he discovered in the fever of their time together.

She didn't notice him that night until after the speaker had shared her life experiences, none of which he could have repeated since he never heard a word the speaker had said. He introduced himself like a thirty-second commercial, politely probed her education, career, and relationship status and immediately asked her out, figuring it was harder to say no in person than over the phone a couple of days later when she'd struggle to remember they'd ever met. When she said yes, he peeled the name tag off of his sweater and stuck it on top of hers, making certain she wouldn't forget his name. Later that night, he looked at himself in the mirror, toothpaste still leaking from the corner of his mouth, and declared that Kate was the woman he would marry.

Ellen didn't surrender as easily. She didn't even come to her door. She summoned Mason from within.

The Philpotts lived in Crystal Lakes, a "gated community" in the suburbs of south Kansas City that offered neither crystal nor a lake. Gated community meant a high-dollar development enclosed by an eight-foot wrought-iron fence to keep out the 99 percent of the economic food chain that weren't admitted to visit or clean. *So much for surprise,* Mason thought.

Each resident's name was engraved on a burnished brass panel mounted on a limestone post outside the automated gate barring the private entrance. A white marble button was provided beneath each name so that a visitor could announce his presence. Mason pressed the button below the Philpott name and waited.

"Speak," a disembodied sharp-toned female voice commanded from the speaker.

"It's Lou Mason to see Mrs. Philpott."

"Of course it is. Third house on the left past the gate. I'm on the patio."

The first house on the left past the gate was Country French stone. The second house on the left was a pale pink Mediterranean stucco with a tiled roof. The third house on the left was a rounded two-story white brick structure that was more industrial than residential. Flower beds were paved with lava rocks. Stainless steel figure eights skirted the high-gloss ebony front door. *Home is where the bunker is,* Mason thought as he walked around to the back and opened the gate to the Philpotts'.

Morning sun baked the inlaid Spanish tiles and red bricks that crisscrossed the patio. Ellen sat on a high-backed, red-lacquered oval stool, her slender shoulders ramrod straight, her wide eyes fixed on a canvas stricken with ill-matched strokes of black and blue acrylic paint, brushes and palette at her feet. Sodden men's clothes, reeking of mildew, were heaped in a pile behind the easel. Mason was glad that the gossip columnist got at least that part of the story right.

"Painting is supposed to soothe me, but I don't want to be soothed," she announced as she brushed her close-cropped auburn hair with both hands. "I'd rather be crazy."

"Go with your strengths," Mason told her.

She laughed so hard she slipped off the stool, stepped on her paints, cursed, and wiped her shoes on an Armani shirt at the edge of the pile. Warren Philpott may have been tough, Mason thought, but he couldn't compete with crazy.

"Now that's real good advice, Mr. Mason," she drawled after catching her breath. Her Missouri twang was just another contradiction. Though he'd not heard her voice during the trial, Mason would have guessed that she was more city than country.

"Thank you for seeing me," Mason began.

"That's not much to thank someone for, Mr. Mason. It doesn't take much effort and the payoff can be kind of skimpy."

"Mrs. Philpott, I'll be honest with you. I'm still working on the case against your husband's company for Tommy Douchant. I know that he's divorcing you. I was hoping you might be able to help me."

"Warren already kicked the snot out of you once. What makes you think I can help you or that I would?"

"I don't know if you can. That's what I'm here to find out. I read the story in the newspaper and thought you might be willing to help me."

She squared up and glared at him, hands on bony hips, elbows flared like a human pelican, the veins in her long neck pulsating. Captain Queeg would make a better witness.

"You must think I'm no better than he is, Mr. Mason. Yes, my husband did me dirty. Shamed me with women no better than twenty-five-dollar whores. And you want me to get my revenge by telling you his secrets. Betray him to get even. Is that what you want me to do, Mr. Mason?"

"Tommy Douchant is my best friend. He's got a wife and two kids who don't eat if the social security check is late. You can call it betrayal or getting even. I call it doing the right thing."

She gave him a calmer, more studied look. "Do you think I'm crazy, Mr. Mason?"

He laughed softly. "No, I don't. I think you're

one powerfully pissed off woman who's trying to figure out what to do with a pile of wet clothes."

"Are you married?"

"Divorced. My wife left me."

"For another man?" she asked. "Or, nowadays I suppose it could be another woman."

"None I ever knew about," Mason answered. "She said she just woke up one day and was out of love with me."

Ellen listened and chewed her lower lip. "I don't know which one would be worse," she finally said. "At least Warren claimed he still had feelings for me. He just wasn't built to be faithful."

"I think the worst one is the one that happens to you," Mason told her.

"You are surely right about that, Mr. Mason." She quietly picked up her palette and brushes. "What would you need to help your friend?"

"The jury decided that there was nothing wrong with the design of the safety hook on Tommy's belt."

"So wouldn't you have to prove that something went wrong when it was manufactured?"

"Exactly."

"So why didn't you do that at the trial?"

"My expert witness said that the hook was made just like the design called for."

"Then you'd have to prove that your own witness was mistaken, wouldn't you, Mr. Mason?"

Ellen Philpott continued to surprise Mason. Her crazy act had evaporated. Her country cousin accent had vanished. And her questions cut to the bottom line. Mason wondered if she was leading him along, hoping he would ask the right question and relieve her of the burden of outright betrayal.

"Not necessarily. Tommy's employer turned the

safety belt over to your husband the day of the accident. I didn't see it until after I filed the lawsuit. If there was something wrong with the hook, he could have switched it for a good one and no one would ever have known."

"Why, Mr. Mason," she said in mock surprise, her drawl fully engaged. "That would be dishonest and deceitful. It would be the act of a man who had no honor."

"Would it be the act of a man who would dishonor a fine woman?" he asked.

Bending over, she reached beneath the pile of clothes and pulled out a metal cash box. "Warren is a collector. He fancies bad women and bad hooks. I suppose a psychiatrist would have a field day tying those two passions together," she said as she handed it to him.

The box contained ten hooks just like the one on Tommy's belt. Mason couldn't tell one from the other. He looked up. She was sitting on the stool, her back to him, adding strong brush strokes of paint to her canvas.

He asked, "Is one of these Tommy's?"

"I don't know," she said, still not looking at him. "Warren used to brag about switching the hooks. He said lawyers weren't very smart. These may not be the only ones."

"Does your husband know you have this box?"

"I doubt it since I found it hidden in his closet. I suspect it's one of those personal things he keeps telling me he wants to stop by and pick up."

"Mind if I keep the hooks?"

"So long as you hang Warren with one," she answered. She turned toward him from her canvas, smiled weakly and wiped a tear from her cheek.

"Damn paint makes my eyes water. Good-bye, Mr. Mason."

On his way to the funeral, Mason stopped at the engineering department at the University of Missouri at Kansas City. Dr. Webb Chapman, the chairman of the department, had been his expert safety engineer at Tommy's trial. He wasn't in, so Mason left him the box of hooks and a note asking him to call.

Chapter Twelve

The Ward Parkway Episcopal Church is a massive limestone cathedral more suited to the Old World than Kansas City. It was filled with several hundred mourners, many of whom were attorneys paying their last respects before picking off Sullivan & Christenson's clients. Somber greetings and heart-felt condolences scarcely hid their burgeoning appetites.

Mason saw his aunt Claire signing the guest book when he walked into the church. She was wearing a trim black suit. Her silver hair was cut short at her chin. She was close to his height and big boned. She considered her size an advantage. There was nothing diminutive about her, either in appearance or demeanor. He caught her eye when she turned around and she nodded in reply, waiting for him to make his way through the line and add his name to the book.

"Thanks for coming," he told her.

"I didn't know the man, but he was your partner, so I decided to show the family flag."

An older woman employed by the firm as a secretary interrupted their conversation and embraced Mason. "He's gone to a better place, to paradise," she told Mason tearfully.

"I never knew a paradise that didn't have a snake in it," Claire said after the woman peeled herself away.

"That's not a heaven-bound theology."

"So what? I'm not heaven bound. Just plant me in the ground and call it a day. If I do enough in this life, I don't much care about the next. And, by the way, next time your senior partner dies, tell me before I read about it in the paper."

"Sorry," he said. "Things have been a little wild."

"The paper said the police are investigating. What's going on?"

Mason leaned into her to muffle his response. "It looks like he was murdered."

"By whom?" she asked in her flat, professional tone.

"The official position is person or persons unknown. Only the living are suspected."

"Including you?" This time the question carried a genuine concern.

"Including me." Mason spotted Sandra Connelly heading for the seats cordoned off for members of the firm. "I'll call you later," he told Aunt Claire, pecking her cheek.

Mason joined Sandra Connelly in the third row, directly behind the family. The Sullivans had no children. Pamela, Diane Farrell at her side, and an array of anonymous siblings, in-laws, and cousins made their black-clothed entrance as the congregation silenced itself. The minister invoked a boilerplate eulogy praising Sullivan's many civic contributions, his devotion to family and church, and the tragic untimeliness of his death. When he left Sullivan only one miracle short of sainthood, Mason figured they'd probably never met. Harlan Christenson spoke briefly but movingly of their years of practice and the brotherly bond that had held them together.

"What a crock!" Sandra whispered to Mason. "Harlan needed Sullivan, but Sullivan would have dropped him like a bad habit if he could have found a way."

Mason turned toward her but his eyes found Kelly Holt slipping into an empty seat across the aisle. She smiled at him as she sat down before looking away. He kept staring.

"My mother always told me it's not polite to flirt at funerals. Who is she?"

"Kelly Holt, the FBI agent who lands in the Ozarks. What in the hell is she doing here?"

"Put your tongue back in your mouth before you ask her."

"No subtlety, huh?"

"Zero. And it doesn't do much for my ego either."

"Remember what your mother told you."

Christenson finished, the organ was playing and the congregation stood as the family followed the casket out of the church. Mason and Sandra left to join the procession to the cemetery and had reached their cars when Kelly caught up with them.

"Hello, Counselor. Got room for one more?"

Sandra stuck out her right hand. "I'm Sandra Connelly, one of Lou's partners. We're running the firm's investigation into Sullivan's death. Lou tells me you're handling the Ozark end of things."

"I wasn't aware of the firm's investigation. Perhaps we can help each other," Kelly answered.

Mason opened the passenger door to his car before their serve and volley moved to the net.

"I'll just follow in my car," Sandra said, slamming her door closed.

"What was all that about?" Kelly asked as he pulled into the funeral procession.

"I don't think she likes you."

"She doesn't even know me. Do you?"

"What? Like you?" Kelly was bright, strong, and attractive. What wasn't to like? She was also direct and Mason usually wasn't, but he liked the question. "You're my favorite former FBI agent turned sheriff."

"Well, you're not my favorite smart-ass lawyer. But I'm getting used to you. Now, what's this about the firm investigating Sullivan's death?"

"I'm not investigating Sullivan's death. I'm trying to figure out how much trouble he left behind, and I'm starting to feel like the guy who follows the elephants around at the circus with a shovel."

"How deep is it?"

"Stop me if I tell you what you already know. Your pal St. John sends his regards. Why didn't you tell me you'd been investigating the firm?"

"Listen, Counselor. After all your talk about privileged information, you should be the last person to complain. But, you may be able to help me."

"With what? You still haven't told me how you know that Sullivan was murdered. Tell me what's going on. Then we'll see who can help who."

"Whom."

"Are you always this annoying, Sheriff?"

"Are you always this insecure, Counselor?"

"You just bring out the best in me."

"Maybe I should have gotten a ride with your partner."

It may not have been Romantic Comedy 101, but the banter was easy and the teasing friendly and promising.

"Okay, that's enough combat for one funeral," Mason said. "Am I still a suspect?"

"I checked the damage to your car. One of my deputies took a report from a farmer who was hauling a truckload of hay down Highway 5 when some idiot tried to pass another car in a no-passing zone going the other way. The farmer said the idiot flew off the road just before he was about to get creamed."

"You see?" Mason told her smugly. "My story checks out."

"Wrong. It doesn't mean your story checks out. Passing in a no-passing zone makes more sense than your story that someone was trying to kill you. I could charge you with reckless driving." She smiled as she said it, which comforted Mason. It wasn't the smile of a woman about to arrest him.

"Why didn't the farmer come back to check on me?"

"He had to go home and change his shorts."

"So I scared the shit out of him. Very cute. Have you been practicing your punch line all day?"

"Just since breakfast. Actually, the farmer does back you up. He said the other driver held you out in the wrong lane. And he did have to change his shorts. Did you?"

"Yeah. And I haven't stopped since. Now what's the story on Sullivan?"

She faced him with a pure cop look that left

no room for negotiation. "I want your complete cooperation."

"Do I get yours?"

"To a point."

"I'll take the same point. Deal?"

Kelly raised her chin and turned up her no-deal look.

Mason continued. "Look, I don't know who killed him or who tried to kill me but nobody wants to find out more than I do. I can't give up a client unless I'm not worried about being wrong. And you're not going to tell me anything about St. John's investigation that could blow his case. So we both know what that point is. We're college graduates. If it gets tricky, we'll work it out. Deal?"

She slipped out of the cop look and put on the punch line smile. "Deal. Sullivan sustained a blow to the back of the head. Probably not enough to kill him or even knock him out. Water in his lungs proves he drowned."

"That's not news. What else do you have?"

"Cause of death was drowning but he had a heart attack first. The coroner says it was probably drug induced. He doesn't have all the lab tests back yet. But he does have one test back. Your partner was HIV-positive."

"AIDS?"

"Not yet. Just HIV-positive. We're not disclosing that information yet. I've got an appointment with the family doctor, Charlie Morgenstern, after the funeral, to examine his medical records."

"Any more surprises—maybe a birthmark that turned up missing?"

"Almost. He had needle marks on the inside of his left arm and the inside of his thighs."

"Don't tell me he was an intravenous drug user too!"

"Intravenous user of something. That's what the lab tests are about."

"HIV explains one thing. Sullivan was stalling on the physical for the life insurance policy to cover his death benefit at the firm. Now I understand why. I wonder who gave him the virus and who he passed it on to."

"Spreading that news would not improve his sex life and might make someone angry enough to get even. The insurance policy is another motive. Who was the beneficiary?"

"Technically, the firm since the money was to be used to buy out his stock. So I guess his wife ends up the real beneficiary. But what difference does that make? He never got the policy."

"Maybe his wife didn't know that. Maybe she only knew he had the death benefit."

"Where do you go with the information on his HIV status?"

"Missouri Department of Public Health. Morgenstern had to report the HIV diagnosis. The state may have tried to track down his sex partners to notify them."

The mental picture of Sullivan listing the names of his sex partners was too much. Mason bet money he asked for extra paper.

"Did you know Sullivan and the firm were targets of St. John's investigation?" Mason asked her.

"No. St. John wanted O'Malley. Naturally, we knew about Sullivan but nothing I saw pointed at him or your firm."

"Well, something changed. St. John sent Sullivan a target letter for him and the firm about six weeks ago. Then he served Sullivan with a subpoena for the firm's records on O'Malley. Sullivan was supposed to turn the files over this Friday.

"How did you find out?"

"Scot Daniels found the target letter and the subpoena in Sullivan's office on Sunday."

"That's convenient."

"Yesterday, Sandra and I met with St. John to buy some time on the subpoena. Your name came up when I asked about wiretaps. St. John said they weren't tapping our phones. Then we found this in Sullivan's office." He handed her the bug.

"Too cheap for the Bureau. This is strictly amateur stuff."

"That's what St. John said. I don't think I'm on his Christmas list anymore."

"Did you find any others?"

"I'll know soon. Is that all I get from you, Sheriff?" he asked as they pulled into the cemetery.

"Maybe. Depends," said Kelly as they stepped out of the car.

"On what? I'll even buy you dinner."

"On what my pal St. John wants," Kelly said. St. John stood alongside his sedan a hundred feet away, motioning her toward his car. "I don't think I'll need a ride back. Dinner sounds great. I'll call you next week."

Mason congratulated himself on getting a date at a funeral and walked toward the gravesite.

Chapter Thirteen

One thing Mason had learned from Blues was to pay more attention to his hometown. After all, he was a fourth-generation resident in a city that at one time had been home to more hogs and whores than just about anyplace in the history of either commodity. Kansas City had been born as the last trading post before the pioneers' leap into the Great American Desert, later known as Kansas. It had survived its adolescence as one of the most wide-open, swinging, corrupt towns of the twenties and thirties and matured into a five-county metroplex straddling the Missouri-Kansas state line with more fountains than Paris and more boulevards than Rome. One recent publication added to its list of honors by naming its citizens the second fattest in the country. It was the kind of award that doesn't make you ask who's number one.

Following the funeral service, friends and family gathered at the Sullivan home in Mission Hills, the

richest of the Kansas-side municipalities that have
grown together into a seamless patchwork of neigh-
borhoods, oblivious to the state line. An out-of-
towner couldn't tell where Jackson County, Missouri, ended and Johnson County, Kansas, began.
But it was easy to tell where the money was and a
lot of it was in Mission Hills. This enclave of the
locally rich and famous was five minutes and a
million dollars west of Mason's house.

Huge homes sat securely on large, heavily treed
lots, along winding streets that oozed an old-
moneyed ambiance. The Sullivan home was a
handsome Tudor set back on an expansive, care-
fully manicured lawn. The circle drive was filled
with cars bearing the Mercedes, BMW, and Lexus
hood ornaments. American-made cars lined the
street.

Two hours of pumping the hands of colleagues
who were planning their pitches to Sullivan's clients was enough for Mason. He found Pamela in
the family room, sitting on a small sofa next to a
stern-faced, dark-haired woman who was holding
Pamela to her breast and stroking Pamela's hair.
The woman looked up at Mason with a defiant
glare. Two half-empty cocktail glasses sat on the
butler's table in front of them. Mason cleared his
throat. Pamela raised her head and sat up. The
woman brushed Pamela's lips with her own while
Pamela brushed imaginary lint from the woman's
breast. This was a post-funeral visitation, not a slum-
ber party, he thought.

"I know this isn't a good time, Pamela, but I'd
like to come back tomorrow morning. Richard may
have left some firm files at home."

Her eyes were slightly glassy. He couldn't tell
whether it was grief, booze, or both. She didn't

introduce her friend, who kept her high-beam glare trained on Mason.

"Certainly, Lou. I should be up and around by ten."

Mason spent the rest of the day and early evening returning calls from clients and answering mail until it was time to meet Blues at The Landing.

The Landing was a piano bar in the northwest corner of the downtown in what used to be the garment district. The five- and six-story buildings that used to turn out dresses and coats had been rehabilitated as offices and lofts. One, however, still ground coffee beans and, when the wind was right, the aroma swept the streets like a runaway Starbucks.

The Landing occupied a three-story, redbrick building on the northeast corner of 8th and Central that felt as if it had always been a saloon. Maybe it was all the beer and whiskey that had been absorbed by the wood plank floors and the bartenders who looked as though they'd heard it all. The food was good and the music was great. The bar was jammed when Mason arrived at nine, slicing his way through the crowd until he found Blues finishing his dinner in the kitchen.

"It's about time you got here, man. I go on in five minutes. I'm gonna play 'Green Dolphin Street' no matter how many times those accountants taking inventory of each other ask me to play the Backstreet Boys' greatest hits."

Blues was not a fan of professional people. In fact, Mason couldn't name many people Blues was a fan of, especially if they wore neckties and counted money for a living.

"How do you know any of them are accountants?" Mason asked.

"You go out there and watch how they move. Only accountants move like that."

Mason didn't want to hear his critique of lawyers. "How'd you make out at my office?"

"I didn't find any more bugs. It looks like somebody cleaned house."

"How could you tell?"

"The bugs have an adhesive backing to hold them in place. Two phones were sticky where they shouldn't be sticky."

"Whose offices?"

"Scot Daniels and Harlan Christenson."

"If someone was bugging all three offices, why leave the one in Sullivan's office?"

"Maybe they wanted to or maybe they didn't have time to pull it out."

"What's the range on these things?"

"Not much. Whoever was listening couldn't have been more than a floor or two away."

"I'm supposed to find out if Sullivan left any dirty laundry behind. It looks like I may be able to open a dry cleaners." Mason left as Blues weaved through the crowd toward his piano.

The next morning, he told Sandra about Blues while they drove to Pamela Sullivan's house. She accused him of being sexist and patronizing for not telling her sooner. Mason told her she was right. Before he could lie and tell her that he was sorry, she told him that he was on his own if he left her out again and that he was invited to her place for dinner Friday night to show that there were no hard feelings. Mason was still trying to remember when she started calling him Lou when they pulled into Sullivan's driveway.

"Pamela, this won't take long," he said as she let them in. "We need to make certain we've got all of Richard's files on client matters."

"Of course, I understand."

"Before I forget," Mason added. "I have your husband's briefcase at the office. There wasn't much in it. Just a book, a newspaper, and a CD. I'll have someone bring it out to you."

"That's not necessary, Lou. I don't have a need for it. Keep it or give it away. Can I offer you a Bloody Mary?" she asked, holding up her own tall glass. "I tried orange juice, but I needed something a little stronger. I'm afraid I'm not very good with death," she apologized.

"Another time," Sandra answered.

Pamela shrugged self-consciously, set her glass down on a narrow table in the entry hall, and led them into a paneled, bookshelf-lined study with overstuffed furniture, a fine Persian rug, and prints of English hunt scenes on the walls. A high-backed chair sat next to a small table adorned with an inkwell and feathered quill. A pearl-handled letter opener lay alongside the antique writing instruments. The desk had six drawers that were devoid of anything related to Sullivan's practice. A credenza behind the desk contained tax returns, financial records, and a locked cabinet.

Sandra asked, "Pamela, do you have the key for this cabinet?"

"Try the desk drawer."

Sandra rifled the desk again with no luck. "Any other suggestions?" she said to Pamela.

"Well, perhaps." Pamela walked over to the bookshelves, reached behind the six-volume Carl

Sandburg biography of Abraham Lincoln, and pulled out a handgun. Before they could move, she calmly fired two rounds into the lock.

"There, that should do it." They gawked first at Pamela and then at the gaping hole in the cabinet and then back to Pamela.

"Richard bought the gun for me after someone broke in last month. He said it might come in handy. He was seldom wrong," she said as she returned the gun to its hiding place.

The cabinet was empty except for an unlabeled CD case. Mason opened it and found a disc labeled *DVD*.

"Do you mind if we take this to the office, Mrs. Sullivan?" Sandra asked her.

"Not at all. But I would appreciate it if you could do a small favor for me."

"You name it, Pamela," Mason said.

"Have someone call me from the office and let me know what to do to collect Richard's death benefit. When Richard told me about it, I never imagined actually getting the money. He didn't seem like the kind of man who would ever die."

She said it with a wistful, sad tone laced with genuine surprise. Her mix of anger and grief since last Sunday made sense to Mason, as did her drinking. Sullivan may have been a son of a bitch, but he was her son of a bitch. It was the way a lot of dead people left their survivors.

Still, her request felt as if she'd just fired another round from her revolver. Mason wasn't ready to tell her that her husband had been diagnosed with HIV and didn't get the life insurance policy to pay for his buyout and that the firm didn't have the money to pay her. He would leave that happy task to Scot after Mason warned him about her gun.

But he did tell Sandra on the drive back to the office.

She looked straight ahead as she muttered through clenched teeth, "That no-good son of a bitch!"

"Seems likely," Mason said. They drove in silence the rest of the way.

The conference room had given birth to a land-fill. It was littered with half-empty coffee cups, Coke cans, wadded paper, and pizza boxes. Phil and Maggie had matching sets of bags under their eyes. Diane Farrell looked fresh, rested, and completely in charge. They had tacked poster board to the walls to keep track of O'Malley's projects. Each was cross-referenced to the other so that assets, ownership, and attorneys could be visualized at a glance. Diane was busily entering data on the computer so they could sort information into end-less combinations.

"Diane, what do you know about these? We found them in Sullivan's offices here and at his house." Mason handed her the two DVD cases.

"You found Richard's porno flicks—big deal." She turned back to her computer monitor. "What do you want—a psychohistory of a man who watched dirty movies on his computer? Give it a rest. Besides, we've got a lot of work to do."

"In case you've forgotten, Diane, you work for me now so unless you want to peddle your bullshit at another firm, cut the crap. Put these on that computer and make sure there's nothing else on them." Mason wasn't certain he could fire Diane but he doubted that anyone would fight to keep her now that Sullivan was gone.

"The king is dead, long live the king. Would now be soon enough, Lou?" For her, it was a surrender speech.

"That would be lovely, Diane."

She inserted each disc into the CD/DVD drive and pulled up a list of the documents on the disc. The only document shown on each was the movie title.

"Satisfied, Boss?"

"How do you know if the list identifies all the documents on the discs?"

"That's what it's for."

"Can you put something on the disc that wouldn't show up on the list, something that you'd have to have a special password to access?"

"I don't know. Programming is not one of my areas. I just run the software on the system."

"All right." Mason turned his attention to Phil and Maggie. "How far have you gotten?"

"Phil and I are about halfway through the files. We should have the raw information compiled in a couple of days. Then we have to figure out what we've gathered. Some trends are starting to appear," Maggie said.

She stopped, waiting for them to ask her to continue. It was the nature of too many young lawyers not to speak unless spoken to, especially if they'd been to the Sullivan school of intimidation.

"Well, Maggie—we're waiting," said Sandra, only too happy to provide the needle to keep her talking.

"The real estate deals handled through Quintex look clean. The property values are backed up by independent appraisals."

"So far, so good. What else?" Mason asked.

"It looks like O'Malley set up a bunch of phony

loans from the bank. The companies are mostly shells with no assets. The money ended up in his pocket.''

"We've known about that for a while. That's what St. John has been pressing him on. Have you found anything else?''

"This may not be a problem yet. There's another set of deals by Quintex that involve the purchase and leaseback of store fixtures. I never worked on those and we haven't sorted them out yet.''

"Fine. Stay after it and, remember, nothing leaves this room. If St. John can tie Sullivan to those loans, he may get the keys to our office as part of the settlement we'll have to make with the government.''

Mason dreaded the stack of mail and messages that he knew would be waiting on his desk. His secretary, Cindy, had divided them into piles marked *junk, I already stalled them until next week,* and *ignore these and die.* Fortunately, the last group was limited to five calls and three letters, which he spent the next two hours answering.

He was starting to review the O'Malley billing memos when Scot walked in and closed the door.

"O'Malley isn't happy.'' Scot's pained expression meant that if O'Malley wasn't happy, he wasn't happy.

"I didn't ask him to be happy—I just told him to tell me the truth. If he can't do that, we've got serious problems.''

"He'll fire us if you don't ease up. He doesn't want you digging up his life. Back off a little, just until things calm down. Let me deal with O'Malley. We can't afford to lose him as a client.''

Mason wondered where Scot stood in all of this. They had been close friends for thirteen years. They had stood up for each other in their weddings and Scot had made a place for him at the firm. But someone had tapped Scot's phone. That had to mean that Scot knew at least some of what had been going on even if he wasn't directly involved. Mason decided to tell him parts of what he knew and let Scot's reaction guide him.

"Kelly Holt says Sullivan was murdered. Someone tried to run me off the road on the way back from the lake. St. John is on us like white on rice. Pamela wants her million bucks. O'Malley is at the center of all of this. I'm not backing off."

"You're making a big mistake, Lou." He slammed the door on the way out just in case Mason missed his punctuation.

Scot's reaction to Mason's catastrophe checklist was near the top of the week's bizarre turns. No questions or comments about the murder of his mentor or the attempt on Mason's life, no concern for his own vulnerability, no solutions for the financial crisis they faced over Pamela's demand for payment. Either Scot didn't care, which Mason didn't want to believe, or trouble with O'Malley was the only thing that really frightened him.

The door had barely stopped vibrating when Harlan Christenson opened it, looking as if he'd just been sent to the principal's office. "St. John has upped the ante. I'm being audited."

"Harlan, lawyers are audited all the time. I doubt if St. John has the clout to single you out. Just give the IRS agent your files and your accountant's phone number and don't worry about it."

"It's not that simple." Harlan picked up a pencil on Mason's desk and rubbed it between his palms.

"How hard can it be? You give the IRS agent your tax returns and answer a few questions."

"If all they wanted was my tax returns, there wouldn't be an audit. I file my taxes on time every year. They've got the returns."

Mason sat up straight, suddenly appreciating the seriousness of Harlan's situation. "Have they asked for any specific records?"

Harlan didn't answer. He gripped the pencil with both hands, studying it as if the answer lay in the dull lead tip. "They want records of my income outside the firm and my business expenses," he said softly.

"Is that a problem?"

Harlan snapped the pencil in half and dropped the pieces onto Mason's desk. A thin trickle of blood dripped from the fat of his palm. He pulled a sliver of pencil from his skin and wiped his hand on his trouser. "Lou, I can't pass the audit. I've been underreporting income and overstating my expenses."

Harlan shrugged his shoulders, stuck his hands in his pockets, and glued his eyes to the floor. He was a child hoping for his father's promise that everything would be all right.

"Who else knows about your tax problems?"

"Scot. I tried talking to him but he just got angry and told me to get out. Said I should have known better." His eyes began to water.

"When's your first meeting with the IRS agent?"

"Monday morning at ten."

"Would you like me to go with you, Harlan?"

Mason offered because he thought Harlan couldn't bring himself to ask. Harlan wasn't strong but he was proud. It was a curiously sympathetic combination. Harlan was in trouble, which meant that Mason couldn't keep his nose out of Harlan's business.

Harlan straightened a bit and shook off the suggestion. "When the day comes that I can't handle some snot-nosed IRS kid, I'd better hang it up."

"That snot-nosed kid can send you away for a long time, Harlan. We've lost one senior partner this week. That's my limit."

"Don't worry. The government will always make a deal for the right price," he said before leaving.

Mason wondered what Harlan had to offer that would be good enough to wipe the slate clean on income tax evasion. He couldn't decide whether the question or the answer bothered him more.

Chapter Fourteen

Sandra Connelly stopped by Mason's office at three o'clock, Friday afternoon. "Eight o'clock okay? Dress casual," she said.

His blank look told her he'd forgotten about their dinner date. Recollection came an instant too late.

"You forgot, didn't you?" He didn't expect the disappointment in her voice. Sandra wasn't someone who let people know they'd hurt her feelings. She just found ways to remind them that paybacks are hell.

"Jesus, Sandra, I'm sorry. This has been a rotten week. I wouldn't be good company anyway. Rain check till next weekend?"

"Sure, no problem. You don't know what you're missing, though."

Her wolfish smile gave Mason a pretty good idea and made him more than a little uncomfortable. Fooling around with a partner, even one as tempting as Sandra, was a low-percentage move. And he couldn't understand her sudden interest since he'd never shown up on her radar before. The worst thing was that part of him didn't object to the image of being taken advantage of by her. Which reminded him of the one and only piece of advice Aunt Claire ever gave him about sex. Think with the big head, not the little head.

Mason finished reviewing the O'Malley billing memos, cross-checking them against the master index of matters Diane Farrell had generated. The firm had been billing O'Malley between $750,000 and $1,000,000 a year for four of the last five years. In the last twelve months, the billings had jumped to $1,500,000. The only problem was that $500,000 in fees had been charged to two matters that didn't exist except in the billing memos. O'Malley had paid half a million dollars for work that had never been done. Nobody could have pulled that off without Angela knowing about it. Mason called her and told her to come to his office to discuss the bills.

"The staff reads all these closed doors like smoke signals," she said as she closed his and sat down. "They figure something big must be happening. It's one of the best sources of office intelligence next to monitoring radio traffic and troop movements."

"Yeah, I know. But, this has been a closed-door kind of week. I've gone over these billing memos, Angela, and I—"

"—figured out that O'Malley was paying for work we didn't do."

"Do you always—"

"—interrupt and complete other people's sentences? Sorry, it's a bad habit. I knew you'd figure it out when you asked for the billing memos. No point in hiding it."

"I appreciate your candor. Why didn't you blow the whistle on Sullivan?"

"It's none of my business what the firm charges its clients."

Mason shook his head. "Angela, I've only been here a few months but the one thing I know is that there's nothing that goes on in this place that you don't consider your business. Try me again."

"You're giving me too much credit. I'm a bean counter. That's all. My job is to make sure clients pay their bills so we can pay ours and that there's money left at the end of the year for my Christmas bonus."

"So you knew that Sullivan was billing O'Malley a half a million dollars for work we didn't do and never once asked him why?"

"I didn't say that. You did."

Mason let out an exasperated sigh. "Okay, Angela. Let's play cross-examination. Did you talk to Sullivan about the bills to O'Malley for work we didn't do?"

She smiled at this frustration. "Isn't it fun to use all that education, Lou? Sure, I talked to him. He was the boss."

"And what did he tell you?"

"To keep my mouth shut . . ." She let her answer dangle, teasing him with the part left unspoken.

"Or else what?"

She eased back in her chair. "Or else he would have me arrested." She said it with sudden resignation, her bravado exhausted. She pulled a cigarette from her shirt pocket and lit it, drew the smoke deeply into her lungs and sent it back out at Mason. It was a gesture that was both an attack and a surrender. "Sullivan was blackmailing me. I had cash flow problems last year and I took an interest-free loan from the firm without asking. He figured it out."

"And if you told the partners about O'Malley, he'd—"

"—go to the police about my loan. I even slept with him, thinking that he might decide to forget about it." Her eyes never left Mason's as she spoke. She'd been caught, but she was tough.

"What happened to the money you borrowed?"

"I paid it back with my bonus at the end of the year."

"Anything else I should know, like why O'Malley would pay us for work we didn't do?"

"Ask O'Malley. He's never given anything away in his life. I'll clean my desk out over the weekend."

"Why?"

"Oh, don't tell me I have to sleep with you too, Mason. You're good-looking enough and all that, but I've lost my appetite for lawyers."

"We need some continuity around here and you're too valuable to lose. Stick around. I'll be straight with you if you'll do the same and let me—"

"—finish your own sentences?"

"Agreed."

Mason's phone rang and Angela excused herself. It was Webb Chapman.

"What am I supposed to do with these hooks? Decorate my Christmas tree?" he asked.

"Something simpler. Figure out which one was on Tommy Douchant's belt."

"Why do you think one of them might have been his?"

Mason said, "Never underestimate a crazy

woman." Webb listened without interruption as he told him about his meeting with Ellen.

"It's an entertaining story, Lou. But it gets you nowhere on identifying Tommy's hook. You'll have to give me a clue where to start."

"Do any of them look like they failed?"

"They all do. That doesn't prove Tommy was using one of them."

"Keep them anyway. I'll see what I can come up with." Mason hung up as he pictured Tommy rolling his wheelchair back and forth across the threshold of his front door. Mason knew he wasn't going back there with more bad news. His problems with St. John and O'Malley were screaming at him louder than Tommy, who would have to wait until Mason got the office under control, or until he dreamt of Tommy's trial again. Whichever came first.

Mason and the other lawyers worked through the weekend. He told Sandra about the phony bills to O'Malley, but they found nothing in the files to explain the fees.

If Sandra was angry with Mason for breaking their date, she kept it to herself. By Sunday night, he and Sandra were the only ones left in the conference room. They had finished reviewing the files on O'Malley's loans from his bank.

"St. John has O'Malley cold," Sandra concluded.

"Ice-cold," Mason agreed. "He convinced the bank to loan money to dummy businesses that he secretly owned. The businesses couldn't pay the money back and had no assets for the bank to foreclose on when the loans went bad."

"Sullivan set up the companies, drafted the loan

documents, sat in on the bank's loan committee meetings, and told everyone the loans were okay," Sandra added.

"So Sullivan was going down too."

"Not necessarily, Lou. Sullivan could claim that he was relying on information provided by O'Malley and that he didn't know the truth."

"Sullivan asked me to destroy documents that would implicate him. There's nothing here that St. John couldn't get from the bank and O'Malley."

Sandra gave him a look sharper than the knife she carried. "These little details slip out of your mouth so frequently. Wouldn't it be just as easy to tell me sooner?"

"Yeah, but it wouldn't be nearly as enjoyable." He recoiled protectively as she smacked him on the arm. "Fine," he told her, trying not to wince. Sandra carried a knife and packed a punch. "We had lunch last Friday. That's when he asked me. I told him no before he could even tell me which documents."

"Why wouldn't he just destroy the documents himself?"

"He may have. But, by asking me, he sets me up to take the fall. If I agree, he owns me. If I refuse—which I did—he claims that it was my idea and uses it to get rid of me. Which he tried to do." Mason told her about the note Kelly Holt had found in Sullivan's suite at the lake.

Sandra said, "Sullivan wouldn't have gone to that much trouble unless somebody else knew about the documents. Otherwise, he'd destroy them and no one would know they ever existed."

"And," Mason added, "we still haven't figured out the fixtures deals with Quintex. But we've got enough to talk to O'Malley about tomorrow."

"What if O'Malley doesn't come clean?"

"We quit and get ready to go to war with him and the feds."

"I don't like the odds," Sandra said. "We're outnumbered and surrounded."

"So we'll have to fight dirty," Mason told her.

Chapter Fifteen

There was a message from Harlan Christenson on Mason's answering machine when he got home just before midnight. The robotic voice on the machine said that the message had been received three hours earlier.

"Lou, it's Harlan. I know it's late, but I was hoping you'd come out to the farm. I need to talk with you about my meeting with the IRS agent. I've got to make a deal. I just don't know how. Call me when you get home. Please." Mason heard fear in Harlan's voice, the icy kind when a car slams on its brakes and shrieks to a stop at the toes of one's shoes.

He dialed Harlan's number and listened to a recorded explanation that the number he had reached was no longer in service or had been disconnected. Thinking he may have misdialed, Mason tried again with the same result.

Harlan's farm was in Stanley, Kansas, twenty

miles south of Mason's house and ten miles west of the state line. The nearest neighbor was a half mile away. He thought of the hours that he and Harlan had spent there, tramping through his fields with a cold beer beneath a clear, spring sky. Congestion and city lights melted away into inky blackness as Mason drove into the country.

The farmhouse stood silently beneath a distant canopy of stars. He was swallowed by the darkness as his headlights faded. He noticed a faint glow leaking through the dining room window as he knocked on the weather-beaten door. A distant train whistle rode the night air, the only answer to his knocking.

Mason squeezed the doorknob with a sweaty palm and cursed as the door swung open. He had never needed to know if he was brave. Pushing himself across the threshold, he realized that bravery and stupidity were first cousins.

Mason called out to Harlan. He didn't answer. The entry hall led straight back to the kitchen and the light he had seen from the porch. The house wasn't air-conditioned and the summer's heat made Mason sluggish. He was suddenly light-headed with heat and fear. The hallway felt like a rope bridge swaying in the wind. Five steps to the kitchen. Between the third and fourth, a shape stepped out from the pantry and filled the darkness in front of him. Mason's head filled with the smell of sour sweat on the man whose shape was all he could see and he heard the shape exhale sharply as he crushed the air out of Mason's lungs with a blunt fist. The shape's powerful hands grabbed Mason by the back of his shirt and threw him headlong onto the kitchen floor.

Mason slid into another shape, soft and silent.

Harlan lay on his side, his head twisted, looking backward over his shoulder, eyes bulging, tongue clenched between his teeth. They lay there together in a deathly spotlight of moonbeams washing through the kitchen window before disappearing into the florescent glare from the open refrigerator.

Mason couldn't find the breath to give sound to his screams. The silence was split by the cough of a grinding engine and tires spitting gravel. He crawled away from Harlan's body, huddled against the front door, shaking, waiting for the nerve to go outside. Finally, he stumbled out the door, slumped weakly into his car, and called 911. He passed the next eight minutes wondering whether to charge the call to the firm. Aunt Claire always told him that humor was the last thread of sanity. He clung to it.

The county cops were politely suspicious. Why was he there? When did he get there? Who hit him? What did he see? What did he hear? Let's start again from the beginning.

Mason sat in the backseat of a stuffy patrol car answering questions in the dark. Every now and then, someone opened the car door, illuminating the spiderweb pattern of cracked upholstery on the back of the front seat. The windows were down but his shirt stuck to his shoulders anyway. The assistant DA who was on call for weekend bodies sat next to him asking the questions. He was young and energetic. Despite the conditions he kept Mason on task, as his teachers used to say. A deputy sheriff was alone in the front seat. He tapped the assistant DA on the shoulder when the paramedics

emerged from the house carrying flashlights and
Harlan, zipped inside a black body bag, laid out on
a stretcher. They watched silently as the paramedics
loaded Harlan into the back of an ambulance and
drove away, the headlights blinding them for an
instant as the vehicle passed by.

The assistant DA said, "One more time, Mr.
Mason. From the top."

Three hours and two detailed interrogations
later, Mason stood under his shower, swearing
never to spend another Sunday with his partners.
Sleep was impossible. Sunrise wasn't far off, and
he went jogging at first light. Another shower and
he headed for the refuge of work. He decided to
wait to announce Harlan's death to the staff until
after he'd talked with Scot.

At eight-thirty he looked up to find Kelly Holt
smiling at him from his doorway, a soft-leather
briefcase in one hand. Mason hadn't seen her since
Sullivan's funeral. He wasn't expecting her, but he
was glad to see her. She was wearing an open-
necked, mauve blouse under a cream jacket with
loden-colored slacks. Her smile didn't last long
when she saw his face.

"Tell me about it."

She closed the door and sat down. It wasn't a
question or a command. It was an invitation, and
Mason gladly took it. She listened and asked questions that he answered dully, having committed
them to memory hours ago.

"Don't try to forget it. You can't. Don't try to
understand it. You won't. Learn not to be afraid
of it, and you'll learn to live with it."

"It's that simple?" Mason asked.

"Nope. The tough stuff never is. The good news is that you owe me for a year's worth of therapy. If it makes you feel any better, I've got more good news."

"I'll take it."

"I know how Sullivan was murdered," she said with a Cheshire Cat grin.

"I don't get cops," he told her. "I'm in the middle of an epidemic of murdered partners and you look like a kid in a candy store."

"Professional pride. I like being smarter than the killer."

"How was he murdered?"

"An overdose of insulin."

"I didn't know he was diabetic."

"He wasn't. I doubt if he would have taken a fatal dose of insulin on purpose. Somebody injected him or duped him into injecting himself. That fits with the needle marks found on his left arm and thighs."

"How do you know it was insulin?"

"Lab tests. And it makes sense with the rest of the evidence so far."

"I thought he drowned."

"He did. The insulin overdose made him sick enough that he couldn't save himself when he hit the water."

"What did it do to him?"

"Probably made him sweaty and nauseated at first. At the end, his heart rate was in overdrive. That's what caused the heart attack. If he hadn't fallen in the lake, that's what would have killed him."

"When do you think it happened?"

"Could have been before or after the card game. The reaction can be fast or take up to a few days."

"What now?"

"I'm going to have a chat with Cara Trent. She was the last person seen with Sullivan."

"Why haven't you talked with her already?"

"I wanted to wait for the lab tests so I'd know what to ask her, and so I'd know when she was lying."

"What makes you think she'll lie?"

"Everyone does at first. Or they leave things out, like you did."

Mason didn't argue since she was right about him. "Mind if I sit in?" He couldn't let one of the firm's employees be questioned about her involvement in a murder without a lawyer present.

"I'd have been disappointed if you didn't insist," she answered.

"Do you think she did it?"

"I don't know. Depends on what their relationship was really like. Murder is a strange business. It attracts the most unlikely people—friends, lovers, spouses—all kinds of partners."

They walked down the hall to Cara's office. She sat behind a wooden desk in her windowless office, twirling a pen absently between her fingers. She jumped slightly when they knocked, as if they'd awakened her. Her face was slack, her eyes puffy. Mason realized she wasn't sleeping and probably hadn't for the last couple of days. Her pale blue sleeveless dress accented her sickly color. Case files were stacked on both sides of her chair. The walls were bare. Her small office got smaller when Kelly showed Cara her badge.

Kelly wasted no time. "Were you with Richard

Sullivan when he died?" she asked. No small talk. Just tee it up.

Cara pulled her chair tightly against her desk, propping herself up. "No." A slight tremor passed along her jawline.

"Mr. Sullivan was murdered, Cara. You were seen leaving the poker game with him on Saturday night. You were the last one seen with him. I'm certain you want to help us find out who killed him."

Cara looked at Mason for confirmation. She was struggling to keep her control as she slowly wadded the edge of her legal pad.

He said, "It's true, Cara. But you don't have to answer any questions. I'm sure you know that."

"No, Cara, you don't have to answer my questions. But I'd have to wonder why you'd refuse to assist in a murder investigation." Kelly said it evenly without taking her eyes off Cara.

"I don't have to answer your questions. You haven't even given me a Miranda warning yet."

"You're half right. But you don't get a Miranda warning until you become a suspect. Are you a suspect, Cara?"

"I don't have to take this. You're not even in your jurisdiction." Cara said it with more whimper than fire and couldn't put enough punch in her argument to convince Kelly to back down.

"I'll make it easy on you, Cara. Neighbors at the condo can ID you. Your fingerprints are all over Sullivan's ski boat. Now be a good girl, and tell me the truth."

"If you've got my fingerprints, you got them illegally. What's the matter, haven't they heard of the Fourth Amendment in the Ozarks?" Cara turned ugly with her last shot, playing lawyer one too many times.

Kelly counterpunched. "Hear, read this." She pulled Sullivan's autopsy report from her briefcase and tossed it onto Cara's desk. "Your boyfriend had a little secret he forgot to tell you about. He was HIV-positive."

Cara turned chalky and started to shake. "You're lying, you goddamn bitch, you're lying!"

"I don't have to lie, Cara. The truth is a lot scarier than any lie I could tell you. Pick it up, Cara. Read it."

Kelly's quiet insistence frightened Cara, who shrank from the report as if it were contagious.

"Pick it up, honey, and read it," Kelly continued, hammering her with a velvet glove. "You probably don't have AIDS yet since it can take ten years to show up. Now read it and tell me what happened."

Cara picked up the report, quivering, tears streaming down her face. "Oh, God, oh my God . . ." she cried and then suddenly doubled over, reached for her trash can, and vomited uncontrollably.

Kelly put her arm around her. Suddenly, she was a soothing big sister helping Cara wipe her face with tissues from a box on the desk.

"Cara, you don't have to say anything else," Mason said. He'd been transfixed by Kelly's performance and almost forgot why he was there. He didn't know much about criminal law, but he knew when someone in Cara's position should keep her mouth shut.

Kelly ignored him and handed Cara the coffee cup she'd been sipping from when they came in.

"It's okay," Cara said between gulps. "I know what I'm doing." Her voice was soft, childlike. "I wanted him to use protection, but he said I was the first one since his wife and I fucking believed him." Anger was taking over. That was a good sign.

"Tell me what happened Saturday night," Kelly said.

"He said he was stuck playing poker with the partners. I was supposed to show up around eleven so he'd have an excuse to leave."

"When did you make your plans?"

"Saturday morning."

"Were you with him earlier in the evening?"

"No."

"Do you know where he was before the card game?"

"I just figured he was having dinner with his wife."

Kelly nodded at her to continue.

"He took me to a condo on the other side of the lake—" She laughed dryly. "He said he felt lousy. He blamed it on his wife. As if that was supposed to make me feel better. Can you believe it?"

Kelly answered in kind, sister to sister. "Yeah, men will really fool you. What happened at the condo?"

"Nothing. He couldn't even get it up."

"Did he have anything to drink?"

"Ice water. He kept saying he was dying of thirst."

"Did he take any medication?"

She took a moment to answer. "No. Not while I was watching."

"Were you in the same room the entire time?"

"Almost. He went to the john just before we left."

"Did you see any syringes anywhere in the condo?"

Cara gave Kelly a quizzical look. "What is that—a trick question?"

"Depends. Did you see any?"

"No. I don't do drugs."

"Are you on any medications?"

"Just the pill."

"How long were you there?"

"Long enough to know there was no helping his limp dick," she said. "On the way back, we stopped in a cove. He must have been feeling better."

"Was he?"

"He asked me to take my top off. He was a real boob man. Then he started shivering and stood up." Her voice rose an octave, and her eyes glazed with the telling of the rest. "He had this funny look, like he was somewhere else, and he was breathing so fast it was freaky."

"Tell me the rest of it, Cara," Kelly said.

"We were standing in the middle of the boat. I reached for him but he fell away from me, backward almost. He hit his head on something. I helped him up." She stopped.

"And then?"

"He took a couple of steps, like he was drunk, and fell in the lake." She shrugged as her voice dropped.

"Did you try to help him?" Kelly asked, the accusation creeping back into her voice.

"I can't swim," she whined, as if that too were someone else's fault. "The water was black—he never came back up."

"Why did you go back to the condo?"

"To look for an earring I'd lost. I was afraid what would happen if people found out about us, especially his wife. The firm would never give me a job when I graduated." Cara looked at both of them, her eyes pleading for a way out. Kelly didn't open any doors.

"I found the earring, Cara. You left it on the boat," Kelly said, concluding the interview.

Mason stayed with Cara after Kelly walked out. He suggested she hire a lawyer and didn't argue with her when she quit. He caught up with Kelly at the elevator.

"Cara resigned. I'll get you her home address. Are you going to charge her?"

"I don't know. Poisoning takes a strong and patient personality. Those don't appear to be her strengths. And she didn't know Sullivan was HIV-positive, so she doesn't seem to have a motive."

"Who did?"

"Look for the person who had the most to gain. Who loved him or hated him too much? Who envied him too much?"

"So many choices and so little time," he said with a half smile.

"Maybe not," she said.

"You've already got a short list of suspects?"

Kelly said, "I'll start with anyone who had access to insulin. You know more of the candidates than I do. Let's kick it around over dinner. How about six-thirty at Brentanos on the plaza?"

"Yeah, sure." And she was gone. Mason started missing her as soon as the elevator doors closed. Maybe it was because he'd been overly celibate lately. Maybe it was because her badge turned him on. He wasn't certain, but he liked missing her.

Mason went back to his office to finish getting ready for O'Malley, who was due in at two o'clock. Scot walked into his office a little after eleven, just as he picked up his phone. Neither of them spoke when he hung up. Mason didn't know where or how to start so he just plunged in.

"That was Pamela. She was just charged with murdering Sullivan, and somebody killed Harlan last night."

Chapter Sixteen

Scot and Mason stared at each other, neither able to speak, until Mason's secretary came in to tell him that Victor O'Malley was holding. "Tell him something's come up and I'll have to reschedule."

Scot said, "Pamela couldn't have killed Sullivan. That's crazy."

"Actually, so far she's only been charged with conspiracy to murder Sullivan. They've taken her to the Johnson County Sheriff's office in Olathe. She wants me to represent her." Aunt Claire would've flown to her side. Mason knew he had to go but he wasn't in as big of a hurry as Aunt Claire would have liked. He had no qualms about defending O'Malley in a white-collar crime case but he was the wrong lawyer to save Pamela from the death penalty.

Scot seemed to have lost interest in Pamela's problems. "Tell me about Harlan," he said, with his gaze on the floor while he shrunk into his chair as if he were trying to crawl inside his three-button suit.

"I got home late last night. Harlan had left a message on my machine asking me to come out to his farmhouse and help him prepare for his meeting this morning with the IRS agent. I called him back but his phone was dead. When I got out there, he was dead too."

"What do the police think happened?" Scot asked quietly, without looking up.

"They didn't confide in me," Mason told him. "They just asked a lot of questions, nodded when I answered, and then asked the same questions again." Mason changed the subject. "Let's send the staff home for the day. We better have another partners' meeting in the morning and figure out how we keep this operation afloat."

Scot agreed and they gathered the staff in the thirty-second-floor lobby and broke the news of Harlan's death. He was a man no one could dislike. Dazed lawyers and staff, many weeping openly, staggered from the office. Angela volunteered for phone duty.

Mason waited until everyone except Angela and Scot were gone before leaving. Victor O'Malley Jr. nearly ran over him as the elevator door opened. Mason was in no mood for O'Malley-lite.

"Sorry, Victor, I wasn't expecting anyone. My secretary told your father that we had to reschedule. We've got a couple of real emergencies."

"We never needed an appointment with Sullivan. He understood how to treat clients."

Weasels were lousy at intimidation, Mason thought. And he was fresh out of client suck-up. "I'll remember that when you're the client. Maybe your father will let you sit in on our next meeting so you can practice.''

Scot rounded the corner in time to hear their exchange. He was redefining pale but managed to welcome Junior with a conciliatory smile.

"Vic, we're all in shock around here," he said in a subdued voice while taking Junior by the arm. "Somebody broke into Harlan's house last night and killed him. The police think it was a burglary that went sour. On top of that, Pamela has been charged with Sullivan's murder. Lou is on his way to the courthouse to see her. I just talked to your father and he understands about the appointment.''

"We've all got problems, Scot, but you and I need to talk about the fixtures deals.''

Scot cast a quick glance at Mason before escorting Victor to his office as Mason stepped onto the elevator. Mason heard a door slam as the elevator silently closed.

He left downtown, heading southwest toward Kansas on the Southwest Trafficway, one of the few freeways in town whose name made sense. Mason called B. J. Moore, a good friend and a better criminal defense lawyer, from his car. He'd first met B. J. when B. J. was representing a man who had embezzled three million dollars from his employer. Mason was already representing the man in a car wreck case. Their mutual client pled guilty to the embezzlement charge and the DA agreed not to charge him with fraud in what turned out to be a phony car wreck claim. Mason left a message on B. J.'s pager and hung up. His car phone rang as he crossed the state line into Kansas on Interstate

35. The Johnson County Courthouse was in Olathe, another once sleepy small town that had grown into a virtual Kansas suburb of Kansas City, even if it was twenty-five miles southwest of downtown. B. J. had just finished an arraignment at the courthouse and said he would wait for Mason.

Thirty minutes later, they were ushered into an interrogation room in the county jail across the street from the courthouse. It was a bleak display of tax dollars at work, off-white walls, white ceiling tiles, and green linoleum, wooden table, four chairs, and no windows. They excused the deputy sheriff who was there to protect them from Pamela and then listened as she declared her innocence and screamed at them to get her out of the "goddamn jail."

"If I'd have wanted to kill that no-good bastard, I'd have shot him with my own goddamn gun!"

The jailhouse clothiers had dressed Pamela in a standard-issue, orange prisoner jumpsuit. She'd gone from upscale, Mission Hills widow to accused murderer in a heartbeat. Jail was a true class equalizer. Her hair was tangled and her makeup was smeared. Her breath and body smelled of stale booze. Pamela was sliding down a rough slope and Mason doubted she would stop before she hit bottom.

Mason tried the voice of calm reason. "Pamela, please—we'll try to get you out of here as soon as we can. To begin with, I can't represent you."

"Why not?" she snapped as she threw herself into one of the metal folding chairs.

"Because you could get the death penalty if you're convicted. So you need a lawyer who knows how to keep you alive. Besides, I could be a witness since I was with you at the lake. You need the best lawyer you can get and that's why B. J. is here."

B. J. was pear-shaped, shaggy-haired, and his suit looked as if he had picked it up where he'd dropped it the night before. Women liked him because he was cuddly. Men liked him because he was without pretense. He had a knack for making people comfortable with him.

"Please don't take offense, Mr. Moore," Pamela said, "but I don't know you, and I'd rather have someone I know."

"Mrs. Sullivan, I'm more interested in how you feel after your case is over. Let me try to answer your questions and figure out if I can get you home for dinner. If you're still here at breakfast, you can hire somebody else."

Moore spoke confidently, always looking into Pamela's eyes. Her hostility softened as he spoke and Mason excused himself.

Kelly was waiting for him when he emerged into the hallway.

Mason asked her, "What's she doing in a Kansas jail for a murder supposedly committed in Missouri? And why was she charged with conspiracy?"

"She lives in Kansas and that's where she was arrested. The DA went for the conspiracy charge because he wanted to grab her and the headlines. It's easier to back off of a conspiracy charge than a murder charge if he can't make the case."

"Doesn't sound too bright to me."

"That's never been an obstacle to elected office before," she answered.

They walked across the street and sat in the shade of the gazebo in the center of the Courthouse Square. The courthouse is quieter during the summer. Mason nodded at the few familiar faces passing by. A groundskeeper rambled away from the gazebo, leaving them alone except for the yellow jackets feasting on the flowers at its base.

"The detective on Harlan's case says it looks like a burglary that went bad. They're trying to find out if anything's missing. Where's his family?" Kelly asked.

"Two kids, one on each coast. His wife died a couple of years ago. Do you really think Pamela murdered Sullivan?"

"I didn't arrest her. The Johnson County DA is up for reelection, and he's grandstanding. That doesn't mean she didn't kill him. I wouldn't have gone for the arrest this quickly."

"I thought it was your case. What happened?"

"I needed a search warrant for Pamela's house. The DA had to get it for me because I'm out of my jurisdiction. We may have found something, and he decided to charge her with conspiracy to commit murder."

"Based on what?"

"We found a syringe and a vial of an unidentified substance. If it turns out to be insulin, he'll claim she planned the murder in Johnson County— which gives him his conspiracy count."

"What happens to the murder charge?"

"The crime was committed at the lake. We'll charge her there and Kansas will extradite her so we can try her on the murder charge first. The DA still looks good when he ships her down to us."

"Which gets me back to my first question—do you think she did it?"

Kelly reviewed the evidence as if she were checking off items on a grocery list. "He was cheating on her and she knew he had exposed her to HIV— not bad for a motive."

"How did she find out that Sullivan was HIV-positive?"

"Sullivan's doctor, Charlie Morgenstern. Sullivan tested positive for HIV last year during his annual physical. Morgenstern told me that he threatened Sullivan that he'd tell Pamela if Sullivan didn't."

Mason swatted away a bee that threatened to land on Kelly's sleeve. "Let's walk," he told her. They brushed shoulders as they stood up, both letting the contact linger for an extra moment. They smiled at each other, each recognizing they'd taken a small step. "Scot told me that Sullivan kept putting off the life insurance physical. Sullivan knew that his personal physician wouldn't disclose his condition to the firm but he must have known that the insurance company would have."

"And," Kelly added, "she had the means. She's been doing hospital volunteer work—helping with home care for elderly people. A couple of them had diabetes. So she probably had access to insulin. We're checking it out."

"And she fed him his last supper—so she had the opportunity," Mason added.

"Maybe," Kelly replied. "That doesn't explain how she would have given him the drug. It was definitely injected. I doubt if she sneaked up on him or talked him into letting her inject him with a fatal dose."

"Did you question her?"

"Nope. She's watched a lot of TV. When we arrested her, she called you and didn't say another word. How is she?"

"She's actually quite well except she says that orange is not a good color on her."

"Okay, I deserved that. Are you really going to represent her?"

"No. That's one case of malpractice I'm not going to commit. She's talking with a friend of mine, B. J. Moore. He's top flight. Why would she keep the most incriminating piece of evidence lying around? She can't be that stupid."

"Lou, the jails are full of stupid criminals. That's why we have so many prisons."

He looked at her for some sign that she'd give him an honest answer to his next question, but he kept getting lost in her eyes.

"Do you have another question, Counselor?" she asked lightly.

"Yeah," he answered, clearing his throat. "What are the odds that both named partners of a law firm under investigation by the Justice Department will be murdered within a week of each other in unrelated crimes?"

"I thought of that, but there's nothing to connect them. Pamela's not strong enough to snap someone's neck, and I don't know of any reason she had to kill Harlan."

"That's exactly my point. Maybe someone had a reason to kill both of them. That would exclude Pamela."

"That's the problem with you amateurs. How do you explain the syringe and the vial we found in her dresser drawer?" She couldn't hold back a satisfied smile.

"How do you explain that there were break-ins at both homes?" He enjoyed her annoyed, tight-lipped response. "That's the problem with you pros—you're too smug. Pamela told me they had a break-in about a month ago."

Their teasing had the familiar ring of a mating

dance just getting started. They didn't know each other well enough for serious emotions. But chemical reactions are as good a place to start as any.

"Don't get cocky," she said. "I'll follow up on the burglaries. If you've got any better suspects, you'd better tell me at dinner. If I don't like them, you buy." The smile turned devious.

"You'd better plan on a lengthy interrogation," he said, abandoning the last remnants of subtlety.

"I warn you, Counselor, I'm a very persuasive interrogator." Kelly gave him a long, promising look before returning to the jail. He rode that look all the way back downtown.

Chapter Seventeen

Angela was planted at the receptionist's desk, reviewing bills between phone calls, when Mason arrived at the office. "How's the radio traffic and troop movements?" he asked.

"Vic Junior left with Scot about ten minutes after you did."

"That kid is like a pimple on your butt. He'd be a lot less irritating if you could just squeeze him until he popped. Where's Sandra?"

"Locked in on thirty-one."

Mason took the stairs two at a time and let himself into the conference room. Sandra was staring out the window while leaning back in a chair, feet up on the table. He settled into a chair next to her and propped his feet alongside hers.

He told her, "Your eyes look fixed and dilated."

She turned to him, frowning. "And you are positively glowing. Hardly the look of a man whose partners are being picked off one by one. Tell me,

Lou, is it her uniform or her handcuffs that have turned you to jelly?''

Mason laughed with none of the nonchalance he wished he had. "I'll let you know when we get past the initial frisking. We're having dinner tonight.''

"Does this mean you're going to stand me up again this weekend? I'll wear a uniform too if that will help.''

He was still trying to figure out Sandra's interest in him. Mason was willing to believe that any woman could be attracted to him, but Sandra wasn't on his list of "Most Likely to Swoon." Maybe a murder investigation was the key to her heart. He enjoyed the attention but Sandra had an air about her that said "look before you leap." Still, the leap was very tempting.

"Come on, Sandra. Things have gotten pretty crazy around here lately. I don't know if I'm coming or going.''

"Well, I definitely recommend coming before going.''

"Yeah, well, that's good advice, but we better sort out this firm scandal before we start on the next one.''

Mason walked behind her, forcing her to change positions to look at him. She made him wait but finally put her feet down and swiveled her chair toward him.

Mason said, "B. J. Moore is going to represent Pamela. I can handle a white-collar criminal like O'Malley but I'm not ready for a capital murder case. Besides, I could end up being a witness anyway.''

"And mooning over the arresting officer in front of the jury would look bad.''

"Okay, okay! My partners are being knocked off like Kewpie dolls on the midway while gorgeous women beat a path to my door. I don't know why the fantasy has to be screwed up by the nightmare."

"Sometimes that's the difference between dreaming the fantasy and living the fantasy."

So, Mason conceded, she was a philosopher and a tease. A combination not found in every law firm. "I like you, Sandra, you're smart, you're tough, and your legs make it very hard to concentrate. But there's only so much I can deal with at one time. Let's stay on track and figure out the rest when this is over."

"Well, I'll consider that a 'not now' instead of a 'no,' " she said. "Fair enough?"

"Fair enough. So, where are we?"

She switched from shameless flirt to killer litigator without breaking stride. "We know that O'Malley has the loan limit problems, but it seems like there should be something else to bring all the feds' firepower down on us."

"I think you're right. Maybe there's some overall picture we've missed. Where are the enlargements of Diane's summaries?"

Diane Farrell had prepared tables that summarized the O'Malley transactions. The tables had been enlarged and coated with a laminate so they could write on them. Sandra picked up the charts, one for each of the seven years, and pinned them to the walls in chronological order. The charts noted the date each transaction closed, the name of the project, a description of the assets involved, and the Sullivan & Christenson lawyer who had handled the deal. Each deal involving Quintex had been highlighted with a yellow marker. They studied them in silence for half an hour.

"Who are the shareholders, officers, and directors of Quintex?" Mason asked.

"Vic Junior is the president, Harlan was secretary, and Scot is treasurer. Father and son are the only shareholders and directors."

He noted her correct usage of the past tense to describe Harlan.

"Were they the original officers?"

"I'll have to check." Sandra began leafing through the Quintex corporate minute book. "The corporation was formed in 1984. Daddy was the sole shareholder, director, and president. Sullivan was the secretary and there were no other officers. Fastforward to 1998 and the current slate is swept into office."

"Now look at the transactions, Sandra. Sullivan is the lawyer on almost all of them until early 1998. Then Scot takes over and Quintex does nothing but the fixtures deals. What the hell are the fixtures deals?"

"Quintex buys fixtures, and leases them back to someone else."

"What kind of fixtures?" Mason asked.

"The lease documents are pretty general. Display racks, countertops, stuff like that."

Sandra handed him another printout that contained summaries of the key deal points in each transaction.

"That explains what but not why or who," he said. "Quintex buys from one corporation and leases back to another. They have alphabet soup names like NKC Corporation and EPT Enterprises."

"I'd say that someone on one end or the other, if not both ends, wanted to make it hard to trace the connection between them," Sandra suggested.

"We're focusing too much on the deals and not enough on who was making them. I want to know who the real players are, and I'll bet the O'Malleys know."

"The two might not have anything to do with each other," Sandra suggested. "Vic Junior may be doing his own deals just to prove to his father that he can make it on his own. Vic Senior may not be involved in or know much about what he's doing."

"Yeah, but Scot and Harlan are obviously involved and they would be a direct pipeline to O'Malley."

"Not necessarily. Scot wants out of Sullivan's orbit. Harlan's slipping further behind Sullivan every year in the amount of business he's generating for the firm. They both need a boost. Maybe they're working with Vic Junior and don't want Sullivan or O'Malley Senior to know what they're doing."

"If you're right, there's no connection between Senior's loan problems and Junior's fixtures deals."

"No intentional connection—but remember chaos?"

"God and bumper cars, right?"

"Exactly. We know St. John is investigating Quintex, but we don't know if it's Sullivan's side or Scot's side or both."

"Meaning anything is possible. Great theory."

"You don't get it, Lou. We're assuming that things are happening for reasons we understand. But we may be completely off base."

"And we don't know what Sullivan knew and we

don't know what Harlan knew since they are both conveniently and permanently unavailable."

"All I'm saying is we have to be willing to look at things a little differently," she said. "We have to look for the unintended connections, not the grand conspiracies."

"Fine, but I'm sticking with what we know and what we don't know. And we don't know enough about the fixtures deals, and I'm going to change that."

Mason called Angela at the receptionist's desk. "Angela, find Diane, Scot, and Maggie. I want them back down here as soon as possible. Tell them to plan on a long night. Then call Victor O'Malley and tell him I'll be in his office in twenty minutes."

He hung up before she had a chance to remind him that she wasn't his secretary, and gave Sandra her instructions. "Tell the troops to peel the onion and find out who owns those corporate layers and what kind of businesses are using those fixtures. I want you to talk with Vic Junior about these deals. We'll compare notes in the morning before the partners' meeting."

"Don't you think we should synchronize our watches, Commander?"

"I'll settle for as close to seven as you can make it. Listen, Sandra, two people are dead already. We may step on the wrong toes with all of this, so please be careful."

"Lou, I'm touched."

"Let's just say that beautiful legs are a terrible thing to waste."

"Don't worry. I can take care of myself. Remember that I carry a knife. See you tomorrow morning."

* * *

Mason walked the few blocks to the Union Energy Building at 14th and Baltimore and took the ancient elevator to O'Malley's twentieth-floor office. It seemed ironic that O'Malley continued to pay rent instead of moving to one of his new office towers. Mason had asked Sullivan about that when he first started working on O'Malley's cases. Sullivan explained that O'Malley had been in the building for twenty years and had the space tied up at rock-bottom rates through a series of long-term options he'd negotiated. O'Malley figured he'd do better by keeping the low-cost space and renting his own properties at market rates.

Victor O'Malley shook Mason's hand with both of his, patted Mason's back, and smiled broadly as they stepped into his office. O'Malley ran his empire from a scraped and scarred desk too small for his frame. The walls were lined with photographs of his projects. There was no room for pictures of his family. The carpet and walls were landlord-finish bland. His windows faced south and west, overlooking the site for the new performing arts center that would be built next year. A fierce battle had been waged in the corridors of City Hall by competing developers, each of whom had invested heavily in pockets of property on the southern fringe of the downtown in the hopes that the city would choose their sites for the project. Millions of dollars had been at stake with each contestant promising to build a world-class facility. O'Malley had characteristically outprepared and outfought the opposition.

Gleaming and buoyant, he quickly drew Mason to the windows to show off his victory. "Goddammit, Lou, just look at that! It's magnificent! Five years ago that land south of the highway was worthless. Half the buildings were abandoned and the few businesses that were left were thrilled to sell and pay their back taxes. You know what their problem was? No vision. No ability to look down the road and see what might happen—and not enough balls to take the risk they might be wrong.''

He put his arm around Mason as they turned from the windows and eased themselves into cane-backed chairs facing each other across a small round conference table opposite his desk.

"I'm still in shock about Harlan," O'Malley said in low tones, slowly shaking his head. "He was a good man, not the brightest lawyer that ever practiced, but good and loyal."

"How did you find out?" Mason asked, surprised at the speed with which the news was spreading.

"The press. It's how I find out everything about myself these days. All I have to do is wait for St. John to leak his latest story and the phone rings off the hook. That's why I was calling you this morning—I figured you'd want to reschedule our meeting."

"Scot said he told you about Pamela's arrest."

"I don't know which is more of a shock, Pamela and Sullivan or poor Harlan. Murder—that's too far beyond me to even seem real. Can I get you something to drink?" he said pleasantly.

"No thanks, Victor. We know that St. John has been focusing on the loans by the bank to companies you controlled. If you're convicted, that can mean anything from civil penalties to jail time. But there are two other problem areas that I need your help to figure out."

O'Malley looked at Mason without expression. "What are they?" he asked evenly.

"Quintex has been investing heavily in a series of sale and leaseback arrangements. The return cash flow was tremendous in comparison to the amount invested. Your son seems to have put those deals together. St. John may be interested in those deals, and we need to know why."

"And the other?" O'Malley prodded.

"Sullivan billed you half a million dollars for work the firm didn't do. You paid it. I want to know why."

"Lou," O'Malley began gently, "with Sullivan and Harlan both gone, I've decided to change counsel. I appreciate all your good efforts, but, under the circumstances, I don't think we should be discussing specifics."

Mason fought the urge to tell O'Malley that he was a no-good slimeball who'd decided to can them because they were too close to figuring out what he was doing. He didn't look forward to telling Scot they'd been fired. The murders of Sullivan and Harlan, an unfunded million-dollar liability to Pamela, the FBI investigation, and the loss of their biggest client would be too much for the firm to handle. Clients would abandon them in droves if the staff didn't beat them to it. Although he was tired of being pushed around, he was ready to start fighting back. He hadn't suddenly fallen in love with the law or the firm. He was just in the mood to step on someone's throat.

"Victor, I understand your concerns, but I thought we'd agreed that we're both better off trying to work through this together. Besides, it'll cost you a fortune to bring someone else up to speed. I don't think this is a good time to make that sort of a decision."

O'Malley's eyes narrowed to cold bands. Bloodless lips spat his reply. "I've made the decision and it's simple enough that even you should understand it. You're fired. I want a final bill on all my matters tomorrow morning, and you'll be paid by noon. Have my files delivered to this office within twenty-four hours."

O'Malley stood to signal the end of the meeting.

Mason remained seated. "You'll have the bills in the morning. If we aren't paid by noon, the lawsuit for our fees will be filed by five o'clock."

Then he got up. O'Malley's face darkened as Mason walked to the door. O'Malley wasn't used to people talking to him the way he talked to them.

"And the files belong to the firm, not you, but you're entitled to copies," Mason added. "It'll probably take a couple of weeks for a job that size, and we'll require payment in advance. Have a nice day." Mason smiled as O'Malley slammed the door in his face.

Mason returned to the office, assembled Angela Molina, Phil Rosa, Maggie Boylan, and Diane Farrell in the conference room and explained what had happened.

"Angela, how many copiers do we have?" he asked.

"Three upstairs and one down."

"That won't be enough. Call one of the copy companies and have them bring over as many portables as they can. Call in as many staff people as you need. I want every scrap of paper in the O'Malley files copied by morning."

"Do you want them bound and organized like the original files?" Diane Farrell asked.

"No. Just stacks of paper in expandable folders with the name of the matter on them. Copy the attorneys' notes and memorandums sections, but don't include them in O'Malley's copies. We'll hold on to those until a court tells us O'Malley is entitled to them."

"Lou, there's no way we can finish that tonight. It's already four o'clock," Angela protested.

"Angela, O'Malley will probably file a lawsuit against us first thing in the morning. We'll give him the copies tomorrow. His new lawyers will spend weeks figuring things out. In the meantime, we can start looking out for our own asses. I'm outta here."

"Where the hell are you going?" demanded Diane. "You leave us with the shit work and head for the nearest bar! No way!"

"Diane, just do your job while you still have it. I have a date with a cop."

Chapter Eighteen

Mason liked the cocky grin in his rearview mirror as he backed out of his garage. His Saab, with its new dents and barbed wire accent stripes, clashed with the overpowering, virile image he'd conjured for himself, but he didn't care. It had been a while since he'd felt the jolt of a new relationship, and he was savoring the sensation as he headed for the Country Club Plaza.

Kansas City grew up with the Plaza, the first outdoor shopping center in the country. The local merchants who once filled the six square blocks of Spanish architecture had been replaced by the national brands that were the flagships of a big city. Shoppers could browse in Saks' windows or admire the European sculpture that dotted the wide sidewalks. The Plaza's success mirrored the prosperity of the city's majority. But that prosperity was more elusive for the minority who lived a mile to the east. Kansas Citians had once separated themselves based on who was pro-slavery and who was an abolitionist. Nineteenth-century prejudices had been replaced by the twentieth-century variety. Mason replayed another one of Blues's history lessons. It was, he told Mason, more proof that the more things changed, the more they stayed the same.

Mason was glad that Kelly had chosen Brentanos, a comfortably sophisticated restaurant with southwestern décor, little pretense, and an attentive but discreet staff. Tables buzzed with conversations that remained private. He found a seat at the bar, positive that the rest of the world was revolving around him. He waved nonchalantly to Kelly when she made her entrance. She hadn't changed from the morning, but still managed to bring the sun inside with her. Mason ordered them each a cold bottle of beer. Raising the bottle to his lips, he winced as a thin stream of brew splashed past his mouth and splattered in a widening stain in his lap. His reign as the king of cool was short-lived. Hope and humility were restored when a laughing Kelly playfully cleaned off his pants with her napkin.

Dinner was the backdrop for the exchange of life stories. Kelly told him about growing up in the Ozarks, in Pope County. Her mother wasn't ready for marriage or motherhood and walked out on her and her father when she was an infant. Her father was killed in a farming accident when she was sixteen. She lived with relatives until she went to college at Southwest Missouri State in Springfield. The FBI recruited her during her third year of law school at the University of Missouri. When she went to Washington, DC, for her training, it was her first trip out of the state. Since then, she had seen the country's underbelly in tours with the organized crime strike-force in New York, the gang strike-force in Los Angeles, and the drug strike-force in Chicago. Her last assignment was Kansas City's financial fraud unit.

"What was your partner's name?" Mason asked.

Kelly paused, looked at the bottom of her glass, and answered softly. "Nick. Nick Theonis."

"Did you ever find out who killed him?"

Kelly's eyes shone with a coldness he didn't expect from her. "It was a drive-by hit. I saw the shooter's face. His left eye was only a slit—like he'd been cut and lost his sight. His smile was the worst. He enjoyed it."

"Could you identify him?"

"Jimmie Camaya. He's from Chicago and started out there working for the Jamaicans as a drug courier and graduated to freelance killer. The mob likes him for high-profile hits because he takes risks nobody else will. The FBI's shrinks say he gets off on it."

"Why hasn't he been arrested?"

Kelly laughed. "You really are a Boy Scout, aren't you, Counselor?"

"I just figured the good guys are supposed to win a few?"

"Yeah, well, we do win a few every now and then. But Camaya stays a step ahead. He goes underground after every hit. No one sees him again until somebody goes down."

"So who hired Camaya to kill your partner?"

"That part's just speculation. We were working in Chicago. Nick was taking bribes to tip off the mob about drug busts. Nobody was suspicious because we nailed enough of the lower-level dealers to keep the bureaucrats happy."

"How'd you find out?"

"After Nick's death, McNamara searched Nick's apartment and found records of the payoffs. He put me on administrative leave until he finished the investigation to make certain I was clean."

"Gene McNamara? St. John's lapdog. Where does he fit in?"

"We were all in Chicago together. The Bureau transferred us to Kansas City when St. John was appointed U.S. attorney. He wanted McNamara to head up his investigation and McNamara wanted Nick and me on the team."

"What did McNamara come up with?"

"Carlo D'lessandro runs the Chicago mob. Nick was on his payroll. Carlo must have gotten worried about Nick's loyalty and had him hit. The Bureau didn't want to hang its dirty laundry out in public. So Nick is dead and Camaya disappears. I quit the day he gave me the report."

"But you were exonerated."

"McNamara told me I was cleared because they couldn't pin anything on me—not because he thought I was innocent. I'd have spent the rest of my career in Alaska."

"Charming guy. Which reminds me. You never told me about your ride with St. John after Sullivan's funeral."

"Vintage St. John. He wanted to know what I knew about Sullivan's death and reminded me in his usual subtle way that I had left under a cloud that could rain on me at any time. He promised me sunny skies if I kept him informed."

"What did you tell him?"

"I suggested that he and McNamara try some anatomically impossible dance steps."

"Did you suspect Nick was moonlighting?"

She played with her spoon, swirling the remnants

of her coffee. "You've got to trust your partner completely or it doesn't work. I'd invested an awful lot into the relationship. It bought a lot of loyalty, maybe the wrong kind."

The mist in her eyes said there were layers of meaning in her words. "Were you in love with him?"

"Sometimes."

"I don't mind."

"Do you always have to be so damn sensitive, Counselor?"

"I'm just not jealous of the dead."

She laughed and swept her hair back. "So much for sensitive. And I just thought you were trying to get in my pants!"

"How am I doing?"

"Well, rehashing old murders is an interesting approach. Does that normally work for you?"

"I never know what works for me. Might as well give it a run."

They left, strolling past the outdoor sculptures, weaving in and out of the crowd that jammed the shop-filled streets. Mason remembered the first night he walked on the Plaza with a girl and tried to hold hands with her. Their fingers accidentally brushed together, and he felt a surge of pride when their sweaty palms joined. Now he got queasy asking a woman when she'd had her last blood test. Times have changed.

Kelly's hand slipped into his like an old friend. It was easy, and it was his turn to talk. Mason told her about life in his aunt Claire's house. When he tried to make excuses for screwing up, Aunt Claire reminded him that life was about causes and not becauses. Being raised by a maiden aunt seemed the most natural thing in the world because it was

all he had ever known. He had all the uncondi-
tional love any two-parent kid could ask for. Aunt
Claire set the bar high and expected him to do
back flips over it. He ended up with a house, great
memories, and a lifetime supply of rules to remember. Mason gave her the highlights on Kate—and
there weren't many—before he switched back to
her.

"Why did you go back home after you quit the
Bureau?"

"I wanted out of city life. I know that the country
isn't pure. But it seemed like all I ever saw in any
city was the dirt that people did to each other. But
with this case, it looks like my exit strategy has a
few holes in it."

They wandered to the eastern edge of the Plaza,
hands intertwined, arms swaying slightly to their
newfound private rhythm. Sitting on the edge of a
fountain, they watched the fading sunlight fracture
through the mist into miniature rainbows. Last
week's heat had marched east, leaving the city host
to a cool front. The air cleared as the temperature
dropped, turning the evening into one that
demanded sleeping under the stars.

Confession exhausted itself. Trivia filled the
space with a stream of consciousness zigzagging
through baseball, modern art, and celebrity look-
alikes.

"So who do you look like?" she asked.

"When I was eighteen, older women said I
looked like Dustin Hoffman. Fifteen years later, a
girl at Baskin-Robbins told me I was a dead ringer
for Tom Cruise. Go figure."

"They saw what they wanted to see. Who do I
remind you of?"

"No one I've ever known."

"Now there's a good approach, Counselor."

First kisses are promises. Hers was moist and soft. Second kisses are offers. His was plain. Third kisses are answers. Hers would have to wait.

"So, who's on your short list of suspects?" she asked, pulling back.

"You really know how to keep a guy's interest."

"I told you I was a tough interrogator. I was just softening you up."

"Soft is not where I was headed."

The fountain lost its magic, and they started walking again—west this time.

"Come on," she said, consoling his hormones. "A deal is a deal. I paid for dinner and now you turn in all your friends."

"Pretty funny for a cop," Mason said. "I don't think Pamela did it. Sullivan wouldn't let her inject him with anything—he wasn't the type."

"So who does that leave?"

"You mean other than the unnumbered women whom he exposed to AIDS?"

"I want the short list, not the long list," she answered.

Mason took a deep breath and jumped in. "Angela Molina says Sullivan was blackmailing her because she embezzled from the firm."

"Angela qualifies."

"Angela also says that Sullivan billed O'Malley half a million bucks for work that was never done— and O'Malley paid for it."

"Add O'Malley to the list. Anyone else?"

Mason hesitated. Scot's name was the next obvious one to add to Kelly's list. He struggled to find a reason not to say his name. Loyalty was the only one. On almost any other day, that would have been reason enough. But Mason's suspicion of Scot was growing like a bad seed. Mason settled his guilt at naming Scot with the hope he was wrong.

"And Scot Daniels. He hated Sullivan and wants me to convince St. John that Sullivan was the only bad guy in the firm."

"Was he?"

"I don't know. Scot handled a series of transactions for O'Malley that we haven't figured out yet. They may not pass the smell test."

"With Cara Trent and Pamela, that's not such a short list. Do any of them have access to insulin?"

"Pamela's the only possibility so far."

"There's always money. What do you know about Sullivan's estate?"

"Not much. Scot wrote the estate plan. He say's Pamela's in good shape, but I haven't seen the will."

"Where is it?"

"Probably in the safe at the office. I'll check with Pamela and B. J. Moore. If they don't object, you can come by tomorrow morning and I'll go over it with you."

"Tell me more about your review of O'Malley's files."

"O'Malley fired us today. Other than that, I can't talk about it. It's privileged."

"Don't give me that. This is a murder investigation."

"Come on, Kelly. You went to law school. The privilege belongs to the client and lasts forever, even if he fires us."

"Except your firm is a target of a criminal investigation. Your defense requires you to disclose client confidences, so the privilege is waived. Talk to me, Counselor."

"The firm hasn't been charged with a crime yet.

Besides, the waiver may only apply to that case and not yours."

"Unless Sullivan's murder is related to the grand jury's investigation. There's a long history of witnesses who die on the eve of testifying," she countered.

"You're fishing, Kelly. Pamela is arrested this morning because the DA thinks she killed Sullivan because he exposed her to AIDS. Now you want me to violate my client's confidences to prove he killed Sullivan to prevent him from testifying before the grand jury! Tell me what's wrong with this picture, Sheriff?"

"I'll tell you what's wrong with it, Counselor. There's an idiot named Lou Mason in the middle of it who thinks this is either just another game of cops and robbers or a law school hypothetical."

Her interrogation lasted long enough to get them to the Tuscany restaurant. Jammin, a jazz bar, was in the basement and Blues played there on Monday nights.

They settled in at a table beneath the black painted ceiling, ringed by a violet neon ribbon. Mirrored columns, chrome railings, and a parquet dance floor gave the club a hard edge. Only the music was alive. There were no smells. Not smoke, not food, not coffee. People were packed around small tables and along the bar. A middle-aged, heavyset man was stuffed in a chair at one table, his chin on his chest, his fingers wrapped around an empty wineglass. The man was either dead or asleep. They would find out when the waiter brought the check. It was not a risky looking crowd.

Blues was finishing his first set. The man knew Oscar Peterson—heard his voice and spoke his music with his fingers. Mason always liked watching

him play. He could tell when Blues was playing for
the crowd. The music was there but he wasn't.
When he played for himself, he moved from top
to bottom. His shoe tapped and his face danced,
all in time to the music. He'd look at his hands,
eyes wide, eyebrows arched with surprise that they
could do what they were doing—as if they had a life
of their own. The sweet melancholy of "Autumn In
New York" faded softly to appreciative applause.
Blues brought three frosted long-necked bottles to
their table.

"Man, you look like shit!" Blues said.

"Kelly, say hello to Wilson Bluestone. He gave
up being a cop to play a mediocre piano."

"He's right, you know," she said. "You do look
like you'd have to feel better to die. When was the
last time you slept?"

Blues looked at Mason as if he were measuring
him for a pine box. "You're the one who found
Harlan Christenson? Newspaper said it was one of
his partners, but didn't say which one. Figured it
was you."

He listened like the cop he used to be as Mason
repeated the story, adding that they now knew that
Sullivan had been murdered as well.

"Lou, you've got a real unhealthy practice. If
I was you, I'd find another place to hang your
shingle."

"I can't prove anything, Blues, but I've got to
believe the murders are connected."

"Let the cops figure it out."

"She doesn't buy it," he said, nodding at Kelly.

"So what. I said let the cops figure it out."

"Sheriff, show Blues your badge and he'll be
more polite."

Kelly smiled and showed him her badge, and her gun, both of which she carried in her purse.

"Damn! What are you doing out with a cop instead of a nice Jewish girl?"

"Is this guy really a friend of yours?" Kelly asked in disbelief.

"Yeah. He's just intimidated by heavily armed women."

"Well, Sheriff, do you think it's just bad luck that Lou's partners get whacked on back-to-back Sundays?" Blues asked.

"So far, that's all there is to connect them. It would help if Lou would tell me what his clients have to do with this."

"He's not going to tell you. It's privileged and even though you've got his tongue dragging next to his shoes, you're on the other side."

"That's what he says—that it's privileged, I mean."

"Don't worry. He'll tell me, and I'll tell you."

"Why will he tell you?"

"Because I'm watching his back, and I can't do that if he doesn't tell me."

"But why will you tell me?"

"Because I'm likely to need help."

Mason was about to argue with both of them, when he realized that Blues was right. He would tell Blues. Blues would tell her and Mason was in heat. He finally understood what Blues meant about watching his back.

"So you're the one who searched the office for more bugs," she said to Blues as Mason drank his beer in silence and listened to them work the case.

Chapter Nineteen

By Tuesday morning, the thirty-first floor had become an obstacle course of copy machines, banker's boxes, and stacks of files. Phil Rosa was asleep in the conference room, stretched between two chairs, snoring softly under a Pizza Hut box planted like a teepee over his face. Mason picked up the box and wasn't surprised that pepperoni made lousy morning breath. The fresh air woke Rosa up.

"Any survivors, Phil?"

"Barely. Two of our copiers went down after midnight. We ran out of paper at three. Maggie and I tried to organize the leftovers. Everyone else went home."

"How far did you get?"

"About two-thirds of the way through. We'll have to send the rest out to be copied if we're going to get the files delivered to O'Malley today."

"I don't like it, but we don't have a choice," Mason said.

"Well, well, the prodigal partner returns. I hope you can find some new assignment to keep us challenged today," Diane Farrell said as she sauntered in. She was wearing black khakis, a washed-out gray polo shirt, and an oversize chip on her shoulder.

"Diane, I'm glad you're here. Phil—take the day off. Diane will finish up this project."

"And the horse you rode in on, Boss," she replied.

"I didn't know you were an animal lover, Diane," Mason said on his way out.

Sandra stood him up for their seven o'clock meeting. He hoped that meant they were even. At 9:00 A.M., Mason's secretary delivered a memo announcing that the partners' meeting had been moved to 1:30 P.M. Scot's secretary answered Mason's call to his office and told him that Scot wouldn't be in until noon.

"Do you know where he is?" Mason asked her.

"No, sir."

"Can you check with the other partners?"

"Sorry, Mr. Mason. You're the only partner here."

He should have seen it coming then, but he had been too busy to pay attention to the firm's radio traffic and troop movements.

Kelly was a welcome sight when she arrived at ten. She was wearing stonewashed jeans and a burgundy blouse that would have looked ordinary on anyone else but looked irresistible on her. Her sharply sweet perfume wrapped her in a heady scent. Mason didn't know much about fashion, but he knew when he had a crush on someone. In high school, he called it being in deep like. In his twenties, he called it magic. Now in his mid-thirties, he called it dumb luck and hoped it would last long enough to fill the crater left by Kate. Kelly could have worn a gunnysack, and he would have thought she belonged on the cover of *Cosmopolitan.*

"Wait here," Mason told her, motioning to a small, round conference table in one corner of his office. "Pamela and B. J. gave me permission to show you Sullivan's will. I'll be right back."

"Your office is too masculine," she told him when he returned. "You need some flowers."

"Since when is masculine a bad thing?"

"It's almost my favorite thing," she answered. "But you need more hormonal balance."

"I'll rent you space," he said and sat down, pulling his chair as close to her as possible.

"The will was signed on August 31, 1997," Kelly noted as she began reading.

"There's a trust agreement that runs twenty-five pages," Mason said, picking up a separate document from the file. "Fortunately, Scot included a summary."

Kelly asked, "What's the bottom line?"

"According to this, Sullivan's estate is worth about twenty million dollars, ten million of which is life insurance to pay estate taxes. He bought the policy in 1997, before he caught HIV. Pamela gets five million and the rest goes to charity."

"Unfortunately for Pamela, five million dollars is a hell of a motive for murder."

Mason started to put the will and trust back into the file when a sealed envelope he hadn't noticed before slipped out. Kelly grabbed it and tore it open before he could claim another privilege.

She said, "I don't get it," as she handed it to him.

Mason studied it for a few minutes. "I don't get it either. This is an amendment to Sullivan's will.

It's called a codicil. It's dated this February 17. Sullivan revoked his will."

"I can read too," she snapped. "What's it mean?"

"It means that Sullivan died without a will, which makes no sense. He might change his will. But he'd never revoke it. That would cost his estate a fortune in taxes. He'd spent his entire career making sure his clients avoided taxes. I wonder if Scot knew about this."

"What happens to the estate now?"

"In Kansas, if you die without a will, the entire estate, after taxes, goes to your heirs. Your spouse gets one-half and your kids share the rest equally. Pamela and Sullivan didn't have any children, so she gets it all."

Kelly said, "And the charities get screwed. Just in case five million bucks wasn't enough to see her through her golden years, now she gets ten million. I think the DA's case just got a little better."

"Not if Pamela didn't know that Sullivan canned his estate plan. In Kansas, a spouse has to give written consent to the terms of the other spouse's will, which Pamela did. She didn't have to consent to the codicil, and she didn't."

"Who witnessed the will?"

Mason flipped to the last page and read the names. "Maggie Boylan and Sullivan's secretary."

"And the codicil?"

"Diane Farrell and Angela Molina."

Kelly said, "I'll talk to them later. The hearing on Pamela's bail is this afternoon. Let's have dinner at J. J.'s. Blues told me he's playing there tonight. Meet me at seven-thirty?"

"Will there be dessert?"

Third kisses are answers, and Mason didn't have any more questions.

* * *

After Kelly left, Mason's secretary told him that Sandra was waiting for him in her office.

"Sorry about this morning, Lou. I had a late night," she said.

Sandra's desk was an oval shaped slab of blood-veined marble supported by shiny silver-colored pedestals at each end. The effect was simultaneously cold and passionate. *We are our furniture,* Mason thought as he sat down across from her. A bookcase beneath her windows held a collection of reference books. He noticed a copy of the PDR, the *Physicians Desk Reference,* that explained how drugs acted, how they should be used, and the risks of misuse. He used it frequently at his old firm when he handled personal injury cases. No one at Sullivan & Christenson had ever chased an ambulance.

"Do you have any medical cases, Sandra?"

"No, why?"

"I just wondered about your PDR. I didn't know anyone around here had one."

"I sold pharmaceuticals and medical equipment before I went to law school. It's just a leftover from those days."

Her long legs, crossed at the ankles, reached alongside his underneath the marble slab. She dropped one dangling shoe and brushed her toes against his pant leg. He couldn't tell if the contact was purposeful or accidental. Either way, the effect swam upstream against the lingering sensation of Kelly's kiss.

Mason decided to ignore her toes. "O'Malley fired us. I hope you had better luck with the son."

"Vic Junior isn't so bad if you keep his hands

busy. I think I'll know all his secrets by the end of the week."

"Sandra, that's not even a fair fight."

"I don't like fair fights, Lou. He's picking me up for lunch. I'll be back in time for the partners' meeting."

The receptionist called, announcing that Vic Jr. had arrived. Mason walked with Sandra to the front desk where Angela was pretending to be entertained by him. He left her hanging in midsentence when Sandra flashed her melting-point smile before taking him by the arm and heading for the elevator. Angela and Mason fought to contain themselves at Junior's transformation. He was grinning as if he'd just gotten a date with the homecoming queen.

"Don't tell me?" Angela said.

"Yep. Hard to believe, isn't it?"

"How can she stand the creep?"

"She put a leash on his dick and told him to heel."

Turning around, Mason saw Scot watching Sandra and Vic Jr.'s dating game from inside the conference room behind him. Scot shifted his gaze to Mason for a moment before turning away. His eyes were as cold as Sandra's marble.

Chapter Twenty

Diane Farrell was waiting for Mason in his office. "You want to talk about the fixtures deals or try and figure them out on your own?" She was sitting in the chair Kelly had occupied an hour earlier, holding a sandwich in one hand and a bottle of root beer in the other. "I brought you a sandwich. Consider it a peace offering," she said as she shoved a brown paper bag toward him.

"Do I need a food taster?"

"Don't be such a tight-ass, Mason. Try living on the edge. It's turkey and horseradish on rye. Same as me." Diane took a bite of her sandwich and washed it down with root beer.

Mason sat down, examined the sandwich, and resisted the temptation to sniff it before he bit into it. "Thanks," he managed to force out before the horseradish lit a fire in the back of his throat.

Diane laughed, reached beneath the table, and produced another bottle of root beer. She twisted the top off and handed it to Mason. "You don't like me, do you?" she asked him.

Mason wiped his mouth with the back of his hand. "Nope."

Diane laughed again. "Good. I don't like you either. Makes us even."

"Then why did you buy my lunch and offer to help me with the fixtures deals?"

"Sullivan was my boss. I still work here. It's my job. Take your pick."

"Works for me," Mason told her. "Tell me about the fixtures deals."

"Quintex started investing in these deals in 1998."

"How many deals?"

"Twenty. In each transaction, Quintex purchased fifty thousand to seventy-five thousand dollars' worth of fixtures."

"What kind of fixtures?"

"Retail store and entertainment fixtures. They could be used to display merchandise, serve food, or house televisions and stereos in bars and restaurants."

Mason asked her, "What were the economics?"

"Quintex leased the fixtures to other companies for thirty-five hundred to six thousand dollars a month on a ten-year lease with two ten-year options. Quintex usually got its money back in eighteen months. Ten of the deals have paid back the initial investment and just over half a million dollars in profit in the last year."

Mason finished his sandwich and his root beer and jotted some figures on a legal pad. "At an average of sixty thousand dollars per year per lease, Quintex will make twelve million dollars over ten years on an initial investment of around a million and a quarter. Who did Quintex buy the fixtures from?"

"I can tell you the names of the companies, but they won't mean anything. They're just shells. A parent corporation owns each one. Each parent owned five of the seller corporations. Two holding companies owned these four and a final holding company owned these two. All the companies were set up in Nevada."

"So what?"

"I forgot you don't do corporate work. Nevada doesn't require shareholders and directors to be identified in state records. It lets the companies keep their ownership secret. Kind of like a Swiss bank account."

"Somebody must have signed the papers?"

"Lawyers in Chicago had power of attorney. The firm is Caravello and Landusky. They represented the companies that sold the fixtures and the companies that leased them."

Mason tore off the page of figures, wadded it into a ball, and fired it at his wastebasket. "Somebody has gone to a lot of trouble to hide the ownership. If the Chicago lawyers are representing the sellers and the lessees, they could be one and the same. Otherwise, the lawyers would have a conflict of interest." Mason glanced at his watch and realized he was late for the partners' meeting. "Gotta go," he told Diane. "Thanks for the information and the sandwich."

Mason walked into the conference room in time to see Scot glare at Sandra from Sullivan's old chair while she smirked back from Harlan's former seat. The remaining partners wouldn't look at him. Scot fidgeted with a stack of papers in front of him.

Satisfied that everything was in order, he cleared his throat and began the meeting.

"I received a very disturbing call from Victor O'Malley, last night. He's fired us because of the way Lou handled the grand jury subpoena." Scot spoke with real regret, underscoring with understatement the gravity of their situation.

"Bullshit!" Mason said, slamming his palm on the table. "He fired us because he didn't want to tell me how he's hung us out to dry for St. John. We're better off without him anyway. Now we can concentrate on our own defense." He was the voice of impassioned reason.

"Lou, you're dead wrong," Scot said. "I trusted you with this job out of friendship. I tried to warn you—told you to leave O'Malley to me. But you wouldn't trust me. You had to do it your way. Now the firm's existence is in jeopardy."

"Come on, Scot, it's not that bad, " Mason said.

"You haven't been here long enough to understand the relationship with O'Malley. Everyone here except you and Sandra grew up with this firm. We've never had a problem like this."

"The two senior partners have never been killed in the same week either. O'Malley isn't blaming me for that too, is he?"

"That's part of your problem, Lou. You think that a few wisecracks will solve everything. The rest of us don't find any humor in losing our practice because the new kid on the block turned out to be a loose cannon."

"Look, Scot, we were going to have to dump O'Malley anyway. We've got a conflict of interest with him that even a Republican could recognize. Let's move on and figure out what we're going to do next."

"We've done that already, Lou. This wouldn't have happened if we were as close-knit as we used to be. We have to make changes if this firm is going to survive."

The picture Scot was painting was finally coming into focus. Sandra and Mason were the only outsiders—the only partners who weren't born into the firm after law school. They would be the sacrifices to O'Malley.

"Let me guess, Scot. You and the other partners had a meeting with O'Malley and he promised to keep the lights on for you if you canned Sandra and me. Don't you remember our discussion Sunday night when I told you that I had decided to quit before Sullivan was murdered and you begged me to stay and save your sorry ass? Or did you forget that when you were convincing our loyal partners here that Sandra and I were the real problem?"

"I met with Victor last night. He didn't promise anything. As for Sunday night—I should have let you quit then. Once you told me you'd lost your nerve in the courtroom, I should have known that there was no way you could handle something like this. I guess I thought I was doing you a favor—giving you another chance. But you blew it. I should have known you would."

Scot had told the worst kind of lie—one that had a kernel of truth in Mason's own admission that he had been ready to walk out on his partners; one that they were eager to believe; and one that he couldn't disprove. It was cruel and effective. Mason knew that his close relationship with Scot sealed it for the rest of the partners, ensuring their sympathy for Scot as the friend Mason had let down. Mason looked around the table. None of them even glanced at him, preferring the view of their laps. It was over. Sandra rose with Mason as he stood to leave.

"Leave your parking garage access cards on your desks," Scot continued. "We'll forward your final paychecks and refunded capital contributions as provided in the partnership agreement. Your personal belongings will be sent to your homes. I want you out of these offices now!"

Scot had tried to pull it off as Sullivan would have. The secret meeting to line up the votes. Appeal to old loyalties. All topped off with a ruthless finish. But he had one problem that Sullivan never had. Scot was scared. There was more desperation than anger in his voice and more fear than threat in his eyes. Sandra had been uncharacteristically silent throughout the coup, but her closing shot clearly hit the mark.

"It's too bad really, Scot," she began. "It was such a nice speech, and I'm certain you worked on it very hard. But you're too late. You can't stop what you've already started."

Mason didn't understand what she meant, but Scot clearly thought he did. He clenched the edge of the table in a white-knuckled vise. Before he could answer, Angela Molina opened the conference room door. A deputy sheriff walked in and asked for Scot Daniels.

"I'm Daniels. What do you want?"

"These papers are for you, Mr. Daniels."

He handed Scot an envelope with the seal of the Jackson County Circuit Court on it and left. Scot scanned the pages, losing color with each page before dropping them on the conference table. He walked out without another word. Sandra picked up the papers and Mason read them with her.

It was O'Malley's lawsuit against the firm seeking half a million dollars for work the firm charged him for but didn't do, plus fifty million dollars in punitive damages. The kicker was a court order appointing a temporary receiver to manage the firm's affairs until a hearing could be held on July 28 to consider the appointment of a permanent receiver.

They left the other partners to fight over the papers. Mason stopped in his office and filled his briefcase with the reports Diane Farrell had prepared and his copies of the O'Malley billing records. He tossed in Sullivan's X-rated DVDs and his Johnny Mathis CD as a reminder of happier times. They rode down the elevator together.

Sandra asked, "Was Scot telling the truth?"

"About me wanting to quit?"

"All of it."

"The truth is I did tell Scot that I had decided to quit. I didn't give him a reason, and I'm not certain I could explain it. That jury of our partners and peers wouldn't have believed any reason except the one Scot gave them. So the rest doesn't matter. What did you mean by your crack about Scot being too late?"

"Vic Junior told me about the lawsuit at lunch today. And a few other tidbits."

"All that over lunch? What did you order?"

"Room service." She didn't miss a beat.

"You didn't," Mason said, half pleadingly.

"Give me some credit, Lou. It was enough that Junior thought it possible."

"And the tidbits?"

"He bragged about all the money he was making that his old man didn't know about until he told him last week."

"Did he tell you where the money was coming from?"

"That was on the menu tonight. But it looks like I've been dumped."

Franklin St. John and his FBI attack dog, Gene McNamara, were waiting when the elevator opened.

St. John got in the first shot. "Well, Mr. Mason. You'll save me the trip upstairs. I'm sorry to hear about Harlan Christenson. He seemed one of the few decent people in your group."

"I'm touched that you came all the way over to express your condolences, Franklin."

"Actually, I've got more important business. The court has frozen your firm's assets to protect the taxpayers' interests."

He handed Mason an order issued an hour ago by the federal court freezing all of Sullivan & Christenson's assets pending a hearing on July 27. Mason gave it back to him with his most gracious smile.

"You are ever diligent, Franklin, but you'll still have to take a ride upstairs."

"Aren't you going to take it?"

"Sorry, Frankie. It's not my firm anymore. But I'll sleep better knowing that you're watching over my interests as a taxpayer."

Mason smiled and Sandra whistled "Hi-ho, Hi-ho, it's off to work we go!"

All in all, it wasn't a bad exit, Mason thought. "You know something, Sandra? I may actually enjoy unemployment," he told her when they reached the sidewalk.

* * *

Sandra invited herself to dinner with Kelly and Mason on the grounds that the newly fired should have their first meal together. She didn't give Mason the chance to tell her no. Under normal circumstances, Mason would have enjoyed the prospect of dinner with two attractive women, both of whom were showing more interest in him than he probably deserved.

Kelly wouldn't want the additional company. She had asked him to dinner to talk about the case, but there was more happening between them. Mason knew that Kelly wouldn't want Sandra tagging along for either part of the evening. Blues and Kelly were waiting at their table. He was between sets. Sandra struck first.

"Hello, Sheriff Holt," she said, extending her hand. "Lou invited me to join you for dinner. We both got fired today so we thought we could cheer each other up." Sandra had stopped at home and changed into a short white skirt and snug, deep-pink tube top. It was an outfit that would cheer up the fleet.

Kelly took her hand for an instant as she silently interrogated Mason with raised eyebrows. Mason coughed.

"It was a palace coup," Mason explained. "Scot lined up the votes in a secret meeting this morning after O'Malley fired the firm. He blamed everything on me. Sandra was guilty by association."

"Well, at least you've still got a job," Blues said to Kelly.

Sandra interrupted. "I'm Sandra Connelly," she said to Blues.

Blues looked up at her from the table. He was

dressed in black slacks and a black linen shirt, open at the collar. He had a thin sheen of sweat, more like a glow, from the energy of the set he'd just finished. "That's fine," he told her, giving her a long and appreciative look. "That's very fine."

She returned his stare with her own. "Who are you?"

"I'm Blues. I play the piano."

"That's very fine as well," she said and sat down next to him.

Mason was glad that Sandra had accepted Blues's offer to flirt. Kelly took advantage of Blues's diversion to motion Mason toward the crowded bar. Singles and couples were lined along the length of the bar. The buzz of mixed conversations covered theirs.

"I'm afraid that my day didn't turn out any better. The vial we found in Pamela's dresser drawer was saline solution, not insulin. The DA decided there weren't any votes left in the case and dropped the charges."

Mason asked her, "Does that take Pamela off your short list?"

"No. She lost a husband with HIV and picked up ten million dollars. That's a combination that will keep anybody on my short list. Did you really ask her to join us?"

Mason put his hand on the small of her back and pulled her toward him. "Not a chance," he said. "She just tries too hard."

Kelly put her hands on his chest, holding Mason back. "Don't make the same mistake."

They returned to their table and ate dinner. Blues finished his set and the four of them left together after deciding to regroup at Mason's house. Their cars were parked on a side street around the corner from the restaurant.

Mason never understood why he heard things before he felt them and felt them before he saw them. It was his built-in sensory priority system. Kelly's scream, the tire's squeal, and the roar of automatic fire mixed together in a piercing staccato wail as they turned the corner. Her shoulder smacked into the small of Mason's back, knocking him to the pavement and ripping the knees out of his pants. Mason's outstretched hands barely saved his face from permanent pavement lines. Looking up, he saw a man shooting at them from the front passenger window of a speeding black Ford Explorer. Even in that near-death moment, Mason could clearly see the slash on his face where his left eye should be.

Kelly was lying nearby on her stomach, propped up on her elbows and returning fire at the retreating car. She jumped to her feet and ran halfway down the block after them before returning to check Mason for damage. She found him sitting up, leaning against his car.

"You okay?" she asked, breathing hard.

He was shaking inside and hoping it didn't show on the outside. "Yeah. That car," he said as he stood up and brushed himself off. "I'd swear it's the same one from the highway on the way back from the lake."

Kelly surveyed the scene. Blues had tackled Sandra, covering her body with his own. She didn't complain, and they didn't seem to be in any hurry to get up. People were rushing into the street, sirens were wailing as the police raced to the scene. Mason watched Kelly, thinking she was looking for spent bullets or other clues to the identity of the assailants. She wandered in a wide circle, not focusing on anyone or anything. She finally stopped and leaned against a tree. Mason joined her.

"What is it?" he asked her.

She drew a deep breath, examined her gun, and slapped it back into the holster on her hip. "You recognized the car. I recognized the shooter. It was Jimmie Camaya."

"The guy gets around," Mason said. "Do you think he was after you or me?"

"Do you have a preference," she asked sarcastically.

"Yeah. Me." Mason stepped back from her.

"I'm sorry, Lou," she said, taking his hand. "I didn't mean that. This case is tough enough. If Camaya is involved, it's only going to get uglier."

A tall, beefy, barrel-chested man wearing an olive gabardine suit interrupted them. His face was large, round, and uneven, like a pumpkin. His shirt was damp around the collar. "Lou, what are you doing in this mess?"

Mason was relieved to see him. "It's a long story, Harry," he said. "Kelly, say hello to Harry Ryman."

"Kansas City Police Department, ma'am," Harry said. "Detective," he added, showing her his badge.

"Kelly Holt," she replied. "Pope County Sheriff." It was her turn to show her badge. She looked to Mason, waiting for him to complete the introductions.

"Harry's a good friend of my aunt Claire," Mason explained. "Harry, you read about my partner who was found dead at the lake last weekend. Kelly is investigating."

"From what I read, Lou, there's an epidemic of dead partners at your firm. Is this street shoot related to all that?"

Mason gave Harry a quick summary of what had happened over the last ten days, ending with the drive-by shooting. The only casualty was Mason's Saab. Even an indestructible Swedish machine could only take so much firepower. The body was peppered with bullets, the tires were shredded, and the windows were permanently rolled down. Harry told him he would have it towed and that he could get it back when the forensic people were done with it.

Blues and Sandra joined them. Harry and Blues barely acknowledged each other.

"Evening, Detective Ryman," Blues said.

"I should have known you'd be in the middle of this mess, Bluestone," Harry answered.

"I'm just the piano player, Ryman. Lou and his friends stopped in for dinner. That's all."

Harry said, "There's no such thing as 'that's all' with you." Turning to Mason, he added, "Your friend was trouble when he was on the force and nothing's changed. I'll get someone to take you home."

"Save it, Ryman," Blues told him. "We'll take my car."

Blues drove a silver Trans Am. He dropped Sandra off first at her apartment in the San Francisco towers near Union Station. He insisted on taking her up to her apartment to make certain everything was all right.

"What's the history between Detective Ryman and Blues?" Kelly asked while they waited for Blues to come back.

"A lot of bad blood. Blues blames Harry for getting him kicked out of the police department.

Harry thinks Blues should be in jail." Mason said. "It's not a good idea to invite them to the same party."

It took Blues ten minutes to tuck Sandra safely into her apartment and another ten to get back to Mason's house.

"That's funny," Mason said as he got out of the car. "My blue porch light burned out again. I just changed it last week."

Kelly and Blues gave each other a knowing look. Blues reached into the glove compartment and pulled out a .357 handgun. Kelly checked her own gun, making certain it was reloaded.

Blues told Mason, "Wait here."

"Not likely," Mason answered.

"I'll go around back," Kelly told him. Blues nodded his agreement. Mason followed behind him as they quickly approached the front door.

It was barely hanging on the hinge. Blues flattened Mason against the brick wall with one hand and slowly pushed the door open with his other. Weapon extended from his outstretched hands, Blues stepped inside, sweeping through each room with quick, purposeful strides, until they caught up with Kelly in the kitchen. Mason's dog, Tuffy, was at her side.

"I found the dog hiding behind the firewood on the patio," she said.

Mason scratched her behind the ears. "Your German shepherd ancestors would be very embarrassed."

They checked the bedrooms and the basement and found no one lurking behind shower curtains or behind closed doors. All they found was wreckage.

Everything soft was sliced open. Everything solid

was broken. Mason's answering machine and the phones worked, but that was about all. The wreckage was systematic, purposeful. The photographs of Tobiah and Hinda lay on the dining room floor amidst the shattered glass that had covered them. Tobiah had a scratch beneath his right eye. Hinda was fine. Their candlesticks lay close by, unharmed. Someone wanted something. Mason didn't have a clue what it was.

"Call it in," Kelly said to Blues.

Harry Ryman was there minutes later. "Your aunt isn't going to like this, Lou," he told him. "She loves this house. That's why she gave it to you. And she's more than partial to you. I'm going to assign a detective to keep an eye on you."

"That's okay, Harry," Mason told him. "I'll stay with Blues."

Harry shrugged. "If that's the way you want it, Lou."

They rode in silence to Blues's house. Once there, Kelly and Blues worked out the security details. Mason didn't interfere. He sat in Blues's easy chair with Tuffy curled up at his feet. He tried to make sense of a day in which he'd lost his job, his car, his home, and his possessions and nearly lost his life—all for reasons he couldn't fathom. He thought of his great-grandparents and their escape from the pogroms. They had lost everything they had held dear, except for a pair of candlesticks. Yet they recovered, starting a new life in a New World. He still had their candlesticks, but he wondered if he had their courage. His bodyguards talked softly in Blues's kitchen.

"What will he do now?" Kelly asked.

"Simple. What the man has to do—start over," Blues answered.

Chapter
Twenty-one

Mason spent the night flip-flopping between half-fetal and half-pretzel positions in Blues's easy chair. When he woke up, Kelly was asleep in the kitchen, folded onto the butcher-block table.

The sun made a cameo appearance on the eastern horizon before bowing out to the vagaries of a Kansas City summer where heat and humidity breed thunderstorms faster than time-lapse photography. By the time the three had gathered at the breakfast table, a fleet of towering thunderheads was forming in the distant southwest sky, readying for an assault on the city before day's end. The hum of the window-unit air conditioner bolted in above the kitchen sink added a strained chorus to an already tense morning.

Kelly said, "I still say one of us should be with him at all times. We'll take twelve-hour shifts."

Red-eyed and wrinkled, she slid a half-pint of milk across the table. Blues declined the milk and the suggestion as he stirred a tall glass of iced coffee.

"If Jimmie Camaya is hunting our boy, and he's half as good as you say, it isn't going to do any good to walk Lou across the street even if both of us hold his hands. Besides, you're a sheriff who's a long way from home." Blues returned her glare with the patient gaze of a man used to his own opinions.

Kelly pushed away from the table and threw the game plan back to Blues. "What do you suggest? Call Camaya and tell him to meet us on Main Street at high noon?"

"No. Not yet, anyway. Lou needs to take a trip."

Mason pulled an orange into two sections as juice squirted on the T-shirt and sweatpants he had borrowed from Blues, who was two inches taller and a size broader. The drawstring on the sweats kept them close to Mason's waist.

"Wrong," Mason said. "Drive-by shootings are the summer's top team sport. Besides, if this guy was Camaya, he was probably after Kelly to finish off his last job. I'm just an unemployed lawyer. Nobody's mad at me except MasterCard."

"I suppose your houseguests were just an overzealous cleaning crew?" Kelly asked.

"Random chance. Odds are the same as winning the Publisher's Clearinghouse Sweepstakes—just my lucky day."

Blues disagreed. "We'll put it on your tombstone. Somebody's decided to reestablish the pecking order with you at the bottom."

"Look, I've lost my job, my car, and my La-Z-Boy recliner. I'm not going to be run out of town." Mason was even beginning to believe it.

"So, Counselor, what are you going to do? Print

résumés and go door to door? Be sure and tell the receptionist that the guy who's shooting at you is really aiming for someone else," Kelly suggested.

"I'm going to go home, shower, and change. Then I'm going to the office and get some answers from Scot. You could do one thing for me that I would appreciate."

"Pick up your dry cleaning?" Kelly offered.

"That too. I left my briefcase in my car. Can you find out where the cops towed it?"

Kelly and Blues asked him in unison, "What's in the briefcase, Lou?"

"C'mon, guys. Pens, paper. Stuff from the office. Nobody would try to kill me for that."

"What's in the briefcase, Lou?" they repeated.

"Copies of the memos on O'Malley and his billing records. Nothing somebody couldn't get with a lot less trouble than shooting up a neighborhood and pillaging my house."

Blues said, "Buddy of mine handles impounded vehicles. I'll check it out. Kelly, take Clarence Darrow home, and I'll call you there." He slammed the front door behind him.

Even though Mason hadn't spent much on paint and plants around his house, it wasn't in as bad a shape as his neighbors seemed to think. Until yesterday. Not many houses can weather a full-scale assault. The yellow ribbon tied around the front porch was crime scene tape, courtesy of the police department, and not a welcome-home banner.

Kelly parked her car on the street since the driveway was occupied by two cars. One belonged to the cops who were guarding the house until the doors were repaired and the house could be secured. The other belonged to Nelson Sloane, Senior Casualty Adjuster for the American Casualty Insurance Co., according to the card he handed Mason as he got out of Kelly's car.

"Well, Mr. Mason, I've seen worse. Vandals can't hold a candle to a good old-fashioned hurricane."

He said it with the assurance of a man who knew his disasters. Small comfort. He looked up at Mason from thick black-framed glasses. A pencil rested above his right ear. A clipboard was clenched under his left armpit. His white dress shirt had a pocket protector full of number-two pencils. He wore a tan polyester raincoat even though the storm was still hours away.

Mason asked, "How'd you find out about this? I haven't turned in a claim yet."

Sloane twisted the end of his nose as he consulted his clipboard. "Telephone report of the claim came in last night about eleven. Source was a Mr. Bluestone. I looked at your car this morning in the city lot where the police left it. It's totaled. I think we'll be able to agree on a figure for the contents of your house."

Kelly gave strict instructions to the uniformed cops to give Mason a ride downtown to police head-quarters, where she would meet him. Then she left, explaining that she was going to the department of public health to review Sullivan's case history. The cops didn't mention that she was out of her jurisdiction and that her orders didn't mean squat. They just nodded the way subordinates do when they don't have any intention of doing what they'd been told.

Mason went inside and was floored by the wreckage even though he'd already seen it before. No piece of furniture was spared. Stereo equipment and TVs were smashed. Cabinets and drawers were emptied and upended. Even dishes had been broken.

Things were no better upstairs. The bedroom he'd converted to a study was a shambles. The only item untouched was his computer. The screen saver on the monitor displayed a dizzying psychedelic maze. Mason touched the keyboard to bring the screen back up. The icons for all the software were gone except for the one that was labeled *My Computer*. He clicked on the icon to check the status of the files stored on the hard disc drive. They had all been wiped out. On the floor beneath the printer stand he found the broken fragments of the floppy discs that had been his backup files.

The lining of his suit coats and sport jackets had been sliced open. The rest of his clothes were scattered all over the floor. It reminded him of when he was sixteen. Mason sifted through the piles until he found a pair of khaki Dockers and a polo shirt in good enough condition to wear. Thirty minutes later, he was showered, shaved, dressed, and ready for Nelson Sloane.

Mason was trying to make some sense of the last ten days. Bits and pieces were trying to come together, but before he could get a grip on them, Sloane handed him a claim evaluation report and a proof of loss form for him to sign. There was no place to sit inside, so they went out to Sloane's car and used the hood for a conference table.

Settling the claim on Mason's car was the easy part. Book value on his Saab was $8,000. Sloane handed Mason a check.

"That takes care of your car, Mr. Mason. I'm afraid things aren't as simple with the damage to your personal property." He wiped his glasses on his necktie as he said it.

Mason thought he sounded far too pleased to be afraid of what he was about to tell him. "Let me down gently. It's been a bad day already."

"Well, sir. It's classic good news and bad news." Sloane rocked back on the balls of his feet, a comedian dying for his straight man to deliver the setup.

Mason sighed. "Okay, Sloane. Give it to me. Both barrels."

Sloane pulled his clipboard from the protection of his armpit and held it up to Mason. The top piece of paper was a worksheet that listed the inventory Sloane had taken of the contents of Mason's house and his estimated value.

"I put your loss at fifty thousand dollars, Mr. Mason. But you're only covered for twenty-five thousand. You should have increased your policy limits instead of trying to skimp. Never pays to skimp on insurance, Mr. Mason. No, sir, it never pays."

Mason looked at him. The man was aglow with certitude. "That's it?"

Sloane stuttered. "Umm, well . . . actually, you are entitled to a hundred dollars a week for temporary living expenses for five weeks. Brings the total to twenty-five thousand five hundred. I can give you a check right now and we'll have everything picked up and sold for salvage. Gives the company a chance to get some of its money back, if you know what I mean." He winked at Mason, who resisted the urge to yank Sloane's eyelids down over his chin.

Instead, Mason asked, "Does that mean I get my premiums back too?" Sloane squinted at Mason, trying to decide if he was serious. "Never mind,"

Mason told him. "I'll keep my clothes, the pictures of my great-grandparents, their candlesticks, and my computer. You can have the rest."

"Splendid, Mr. Mason. Splendid indeed!" Sloane retreated to his car to do the paperwork.

Anna Karelson materialized across the street, waved, and came to visit.

"My goodness, Lou. What happened? Where's Tuffy?" She was wearing flowered Capri pants and a halter-top brimming over from a firmer time in her life. Her frosted hair was piled on top of her head. She'd been lying out in the sun, but was one of those people who splotched instead of tanned. Mason felt a sudden sympathy for Jack.

"It was some crazy kids, Anna. They trashed the place. Tuffy and I are staying with a friend of mine. Anything new with you and Jack?" he asked to change the subject.

"The SOB still wants me to take him back. He just wants that damn TR-6."

Mason lusted for the car as much as Jack, but she'd ignored his hints in their previous conversations that he'd be happy to take the car off her hands. "Why don't you sell it?" he asked.

"Can I do that?"

"The car is titled jointly in both of your names. You can do anything you want with it."

"But I wouldn't even know what to ask for it."

Mason knew what he was doing, and he was only mildly ashamed of himself. "Let my adjuster tell you."

Sloane was finishing his paperwork and didn't object when Mason asked him for the book value on a low-mileage, 1976 TR-6, which was the last year the cars were made. Mason silently blessed him when he said the figure was $8,000.

"Anna," Mason began in his most sincere, professional voice, "you've let this car come between you and your husband. If you have any hope at all of reconciliation, you have to find out if he wants you more than the car."

She looked at him with the pleading eyes of one who was lost and was about to be found.

Mason couldn't resist. "I need a car. Normally, I'd spend a lot of time researching in *Consumer Reports* and haggling with dealers. But I don't have time for all that. Anna, we can help each other."

Fifteen minutes later, Mason had the title, she had his check for $8,000, endorsed over to her, and Sloane had sold a policy on Mason's new car. He was halfway to the office, top down, wind in his hair, when he realized that he'd forgotten his police escort and that he hadn't heard from Blues.

Chapter
Twenty-two

Mason felt weirdly self-conscious riding the elevator up to the office he'd been thrown out of the day before. There weren't many places he had been thrown out of, especially ones that he wanted to leave anyway. Yesterday, he had been angry and embarrassed. Today, he was angry and scared. He half hoped to be met by a welcome-back committee of former partners, led by Scot saying it had all been a mistake. It reminded him of kids who fantasized about their divorced parents getting remarried. His fantasy dissolved when a security guard wouldn't let him off the elevator. He rode back down and walked outside looking for a can to kick.

Mason needed to talk to Scot. He still believed in the rule of reason, and he still trusted in the loyalty of friends. Even when the friend had cut him off at the knees. He'd been trained to be a creative problem solver, but his training was for a different game, and he was running out of patience. It was only eleven A.M. If Scot stuck to his routine, he'd spend the noon hour in the pool at the Mid-America Club, a couple of blocks from the office. Mason decided to wait for him there.

The Mid-America Club was one of those venerable Kansas City institutions, which means that it hadn't been decorated since Eisenhower was president and didn't accept Jews, blacks, and women as members until it didn't have a choice. He found an obscure conference room to wait in so that he wouldn't run into any of his former partners.

Scot was the lone lunch-hour swimmer. Mason used to swim with him occasionally. Scot's normal stroke was powerful, controlled, and precise. Today he was beating the water. Mason waited for him to surface at the shallow end. Five laps later, Scot stopped, pulled his goggles above his eyebrows, and shook his head at Mason.

"What do you want, Lou?" He sounded tired, as though he'd been worn down by something tougher than a mile swim.

"Answers. What's going on with you and O'Malley?"

"You're out of it, Lou. Keep it that way. It's for your own good."

"Okay. Let's try something else. Why did Sullivan revoke his will?"

The fog lifted. "What in the hell are you talking about?"

"Don't tell me you didn't know, Scot. I checked his file yesterday. He executed a codicil six months ago revoking all prior wills."

"He never said a word."

"Have it your way. Somebody shot up my car and ransacked my house last night. I'm starting to

take this personally, Scot. You owe it to me to tell
me what in the hell is going on!''

Water dripped from Scott's face, his eyes were
bloodshot. He pulled his goggles down and pushed
off, clawing at the water as he kicked away from
Mason.

Leaving the club, Mason grabbed a sandwich
at the food court in City Center Square, another
downtown office tower. He suppressed his fear of
a repeat of last night's drive-by shooting with the
myth that there was safety in a crowd. If Camaya
wanted to kill Mason, he didn't think the shooter
would try it at McDonald's.

Mason kept a watch for people shooting at him
from speeding cars while he walked to the county
courthouse. He checked the court file on O'Malley's case to see if anything new had been filed.
Nothing. It was the same story at the federal courthouse with St. John's lawsuit. He decided to pay
another unscheduled visit to St. John.

"Mr. Mason, you're going to have to learn to
make an appointment just like everybody else,''
St. John said wearily as Mason walked in past his
secretary.

McNamara was in his usual spot on the couch.
Mason was beginning to wonder if he slept in a
kennel at the foot of St. John's bed every night.

"Look, Frank, I don't feel much like everybody
else lately. I'd like some information.''

"Gee, Counselor, don't you like getting shot at?''
McNamara grinned, enjoying his keen wit.

"Frank, can't you housebreak this guy?'' McNamara started to get up, but St. John pointed to the
couch. He sat. "Good boy, Gene, that's a good
boy.''

"Mr. Mason, don't press your luck. You may not

have enough to go around, from what I understand," St. John said.

"I don't understand any of this, Frank. Maybe you can educate me."

"You've obviously aggravated the wrong person. Given your charming demeanor, I know you find that hard to believe."

"What do you know about Jimmie Camaya?"

McNamara's ears pricked up. Mason pictured him with his tongue out humping St. John's leg after he left.

St. John answered cautiously. "No one's ever been able to pin anything on him. He enjoys a rather celebrated reputation. If he's involved, you're in way over your head. We can give you protection if you'll tell us what you know."

"I'll tell you anything you want, except that I'm dumber than dirt. Kelly Holt thinks he's the guy who shot up my car last night."

"If Camaya was shooting, he most assuredly wasn't aiming at your car. My reports are that Holt returned fire. He's not used to that."

Mason asked, "Does he do floors and windows too?"

"I assume that the people who invaded your house and Camaya have the same employer. Why are you attracting all this attention?"

"I got into this mess when Scot Daniels asked me to check the firm's exposure from Sullivan's relationship with O'Malley. It's been downhill since then."

"Help us with that and maybe we can help you."

Mason considered the implications of the offer. St. John thought Mason could help him nail O'Malley and the firm. Mason had mixed emotions on the subject. He didn't like the idea of being a moving target. But he couldn't get excited about putting himself in St. John's hands. He told St. John he would think it over.

Mason tried the county courthouse again in the hopes that he might run into Kelly at the public health department. The clerk told him that he had missed her by an hour. He used a pay phone to call his answering machine, which had somehow survived the attack on his house. Blues had left word that he had Mason's briefcase. Kelly had found out that he left without the cops and was angry that he was running around unescorted. There were three hang-ups. Mason couldn't think of anyone who would call and not leave a message. Unless they just wanted to be certain he wasn't home.

Chapter
Twenty-three

Mason decided to try his luck with Angela. He was certain that he hadn't been restored to the office guest list, so he waited for her in the parking garage in the firm's office tower. Mason believed that people who designed underground garages had a twisted sense of reality. Mason never understood how parking levels could go up and down at the same time in opposite directions. This garage was one of the worst, a maze even a well-motivated rat couldn't figure out. Mason found a new appreciation for the design of the garage: It made a great hiding place. He waited in a dark corner, three stalls down from Angela's car. If the bad guys were after him, this was an unlikely place for them to look.

Angela showed up a little after five. Mason didn't want to startle her, but he didn't want her to get away before he could talk with her. He waited until she had her back to him before coming up behind her as she opened her car door.

"How's the radio traffic and troop movements, Angela?"

She jumped backward and he caught her elbows.

"Jesus Christ, Lou! You scared the shit out of me."

Maybe, but she wasn't shaking, unless you counted a subtle swivel of her backside against his belt buckle. The fabric of her lemon-yellow dress was thin, accenting the lines beneath. Her perfume was fragrant, even in the dank garage. Angela had a smoky allure that was more instinctive than calculating.

"Sorry, Angela. I'm just getting a little more careful in my efforts to reach old age. Can I buy you a drink?"

She finally turned around, but didn't back up.

"I don't think that's such a good idea. You've got official leprosy, and it may be contagious."

"Don't worry. I've had my shots. And we made a deal. I'll be straight with you if you'll be straight with me."

"Okay, get in. But I pick the bar."

Her choice was a place called The Limit near Quality Hill on downtown's West Side. Mason had never been there. Dim lighting left him almost blind until his eyes adjusted and then he realized why. The clientele was all women. Mason was one of those mainstream liberals who was comfortable supporting gay rights as long as he didn't have to leave the mainstream to do it. The chalkboard sign at the door didn't display the daily special. Instead it announced a seminar on alternative treatments for AIDS. The program was titled WHY THE FDA IS KILLING US.

Mason's "not that there's anything wrong with it" ambivalence must have shown, judging by the bemused and hostile looks he received as they sat in a booth across from one end of the bar. Then again, maybe it was because they were the only heterosexual couple in the bar. Or maybe it was just his imagination.

Angela didn't offer any explanation until after their drinks arrived. "Surprised, Lou?"

"I didn't think anything could surprise me after the last few days, Angela, but you are full of surprises."

"Because I brought you to a gay bar?"

"It's not something I would have thought—or thought about. You just seem so interested in men."

"I am. Exclusively. I come here sometimes when I don't want to be bothered by men. These women understand that and respect my privacy. Besides, there's not much chance of running into Scot here, is there?"

They both laughed, breaking the tension.

"What's happening at the office?"

"All hell broke loose after you and Sandra left. Scot and St. John had a real pissing match."

"We ran into St. John on our way out. He had a court order freezing the firm's assets," Mason told her.

"That's what was so funny," Angela said. A waitress interrupted long enough to take their refill orders. Mason asked for any beer on draft and Angela ordered a martini. "The two of them were fighting over whether the federal court order freezing the firm's assets trumped the state court order appointing a receiver to run the firm."

Mason smiled at the image. "Who won?"

Angela giggled. "I did. I told Scot we were screwed either way."

"Angela, you have the wisdom of Solomon."

"And very big ears. After St. John left, Vic Junior showed up again. He and Scot had their own screamer in the conference room."

Their waitress brought them their drinks. Mason sipped. Angela finished hers in two gulps.

"What was that one about?"

"I only caught bits and pieces, but it was mostly about the fees we charged his father for work we didn't do. In the meantime, half the staff has quit and the clients are panicked. Scot hired the security guard to keep out the press."

"And me." Mason signaled the waitress to bring Angela another round. Several women waved at Angela from across the bar. She caught their eyes and waved back, all smiles. The waitress set another martini on the table and wiped up the water ring left by the empty glass. "Angela, I need some answers."

"Don't ask me questions I can't answer."

"Can't or won't? Someone is trying to kill me, Angela, and it has something to do with the firm. You know more about what's going on there than anyone else. You've got to help me."

"You give me too much credit, Lou. All I know is what I read in the papers."

Mason waited a moment, not wanting to press too hard. The volume of the bar's background music had picked up, prompted by the arrival of the after-work crowd. Mason recognized the lyrics of a teen sensation singing about what a girl wants. He looked around. Context was everything.

He asked her, "Do you remember when Sullivan

changed his will last winter? You were one of the witnesses."

"Sure. Diane asked me to be a witness. What's that got to do with anything?"

"Did you know what changes he made in his will?"

"C'mon, Lou. That was six months ago. I don't remember what I had for lunch yesterday."

"I'm not interested in your diet. Just do your best. Was Sullivan in the conference room when you showed up?"

She hesitated, finally realizing that his questions were serious ones and that he expected serious answers.

"No. Diane was the only one there. We waited about ten minutes, but Sullivan didn't show up. Finally, she just gave me the document and told me to sign it, and she would take care of the rest later on."

"So you never actually saw Sullivan sign it?"

"I know that's against the rules, but we do it all the time with notary signatures."

Mason hoped she was loosening up so he decided to take the plunge. "Angela, do you remember our conversation the day after Sullivan's body was found—"

"—when you did your big-shot impression and told me you were in charge?"

She couldn't resist the chance to tease him. He smiled good-naturedly without taking his eyes off of her.

"Actually, that was old news by the time I got to your office. You already knew and I've been wondering how you got the word so quickly."

She reddened, swirled the ice cubes in her glass,

and drained it. She looked down the length of the bar as she answered.

"Like I told you, Lou, radio traffic and troop movements."

"I don't think so, Angela. Only Scot, Harlan, and I knew before the partners' meeting. I was the first one in your office after the meeting. Try me again."

No answer. Mason took the telephone bug out of his pocket and dropped it on the table. He'd kept it, waiting to confront her. Angela's death grip on her glass was answer enough.

"You had me going for a while, Angela. You followed the first rule of the con artist. Tell the truth you have to tell. A little honesty buys a lot of credibility and makes it easier to lie about the important stuff."

She wouldn't look at him, but she looked her age for the first time since he'd known her. He was learning to recognize the beaten look of Sullivan & Christenson.

Finally, she shrugged, as though it was no big deal. "All I wanted was something I could use to bargain with Sullivan. I knew that he'd hold my unauthorized loan from the firm over my head forever. There weren't enough blow jobs to pay that debt off."

Shakespeare was right, Mason realized. Neither a borrower nor a lender be. "So why bug Scot's phone and Harlan's phone too?"

"I didn't care where I got the information as long as I could use it."

"When did you find out about the subpoena?"

"After the retreat. I came to the office every Sunday night to check the tapes. Scot had called someone, and they talked about it."

"Who did he call?"

"It was a man's voice that I didn't recognize."

"Why did you remove the taps from their phones and not Sullivan's?"

"God knows I wanted to. I was afraid what Scot might do if he found out. I didn't want to deal with another partner who could blackmail me between the sheets or anyplace else. So I got rid of the ones in Scot's office and Harlan's office first. I was going to take out Sullivan's, but the cleaning crew showed up. I didn't want someone saying they'd seen me in Sullivan's office, so I left. I planned on getting rid of it on Monday, but you ordered his office sealed before I could."

"What did Scot and the other man talk about?"

"Scot told the other guy that Sullivan was dead. Then Scot told him that he'd convinced you to handle the grand jury subpoena. The guy got mad but Scot told him that he could control you. Then the guy told Scot to find some records and hung up."

"What records?"

"I don't know."

"Where are the tapes, Angela?"

"In a safe place."

"Does anyone else know they exist?"

"No. A FBI agent interviewed me last week. He asked about the wiretaps but I didn't confess."

"Did he interview you at the office?"

"At home. He said he didn't want to disturb me during the day because he knew how crazy things must be at the office."

"Why didn't you tell me?"

"He said the FBI's investigation was very confidential and that I should keep quiet. Otherwise, the suspects could be tipped off. Since I knew who had done the tapping, I wasn't about to open my mouth."

"What was the guy's name?"

"I don't remember, but he gave me his card." She fumbled in her purse and produced Gene McNamara's business card.

"Angela, I need the tapes. Someone tried to kill me. The tapes may help me figure out what's going on."

"Sorry, Lou, but I'm not sticking my neck out. They'll find out who did the tapping and then I'm finished."

"Just give me the tapes, Angela, or at least let me listen to them. I'll make certain your name stays out of it."

She stopped stirring her drink and looked at Mason as if about to answer. Her gaze went over his shoulder to the front of the bar and froze.

"Oh, shit," was all she managed to say. She looked down, but it was too late. They had company. Mason turned around.

Diane Farrell took a long drag on her cigarette, dropped it on the floor, and ground it out with her heel. She began a slow walk toward them, stopping along the way to kiss one woman and squeeze the butt of another.

"Well, Lou, are you coming out of the closet or are you just curious?"

Mason couldn't control his involuntary reactions and felt the flush creep into his cheeks. He clearly wasn't used to this place yet. She had a winner's satisfied smile. He'd been canned. She considered it one more notch in her belt, even if she hadn't helped him out the door. Now, he'd added icing to the cake by showing latent homophobia.

"Really, Angela, I thought you had better taste."

She dismissed Mason with a pathetic sigh and gave Angela a sympathetic pat on the shoulder before settling in at the bar.

"Let's get out of here," Angela said. She left a twenty-dollar bill on the table and he followed her out.

"Sorry, Lou," she said hurriedly, as he caught up to her. "You'll have to walk back to your car."

"I don't get it, Angela. It's no big deal when you take me into that bar. Then Diane shows up, and you can't wait to get rid of me."

"You're right, Lou, you don't get it."

"Then what is it?"

"You're the problem. Scot told the staff that we weren't supposed to talk to you or Sandra. I've got enough problems without losing my job. Don't do this again."

"Angela, we can help each other."

"I don't think so, Lou. Good-bye."

The air was thick and still. The peaks of the thunderheads were no longer visible as clouds settled in over the city. People quickened their pace. Mason marched in double time, watching the clouds and the cars.

Anna and her wayward husband were holding hands on their front porch when Mason pulled into his driveway. Any guilt he had about the TR-6 vanished with Jack's friendly wave. At least something was working out. The salvage crew had swept through his house. They'd left a card table and chairs in the kitchen and his computer and bed frame upstairs. A pile of underwear and socks was on the floor of his closet. The rest of his clothes were in one corner of the bedroom.

There were three messages on his machine. Blues said to meet him for dinner at eight at Constantine on Broadway. Kelly said she had to go back to Starlight and would call him tomorrow. The third call was from Sandra Connelly. He replayed her message twice.

"Lou, it's Sandra. I'm meeting Vic Junior at seven-thirty tonight at a bar in the West Bottoms. The address is 312 Front Street. Meet me there. I want a witness."

Mason wasn't crazy about the idea, but he figured it would still be light out, and Vic Jr. had never struck him as dangerous. Besides, even if Sandra did carry a big knife, he knew she was counting on him to be there. He'd only be a few minutes late for dinner with Blues. The first drops of rain were beginning to fall as Mason left.

Chapter
Twenty-four

Mason's grandfather, Mike, once was a butcher in a slaughterhouse in the West Bottoms. He was also a saloonkeeper and a ward healer and anything else that would put food on the table during the Depression. All of it in the West Bottoms, a flood-plain that drank in the overflow from the confluence of the Kansas and Missouri rivers.

His last career had been in the wrecking business. When Mason was a boy, his grandfather took him to work with him on Saturday mornings at MM Wrecking Company. The office was on the first floor of a warehouse that stored the leftover, cast-aside guts of buildings and businesses that Mike Mason somehow turned into cash. Mason spent the mornings hunting for magnets while his grandfather shuffled papers.

Mike Mason had got his start in the wrecking business through Tom Pendergast, the political boss who ran Kansas City and a good part of Missouri during the Depression. Bagnel Dam had just been finished, damming up three rivers and creating the Lake of the Ozarks. Pendergast's concrete company had provided the cement and Pendergast doled out the leftovers, one of which was the scrap that had been salvaged from the project. Mike Mason asked Pendergast if he could gather the scrap and sell it. Pendergast gave his blessing and waived his usual cut, as he often did for his boys who made sure the voters turned out and voted Democratic. MM Wrecking outlasted Pendergast. Mason played with his memories as he pulled his car alongside Sandra Connelly's BMW.

She had left it in the parking lot of a five-story, redbrick warehouse that was across the street from the bar and backed up to the Missouri River. The bar was a run-down watering hole with a half-lit neon sign in the front window promising cold draft beer.

A loading dock dominated the front of the warehouse that faced the bar. Steel-paneled garage doors closed off the dock's three bays. A walk-in entrance was just to the west of the dock. HAMLEIN FURNITURE was painted in faded yellow above the windows on the fifth floor. He wondered why Vic Jr. had arranged the meeting down here. Scot had given orders to the firm's staff to stay away from Sandra and Mason. O'Malley had probably told Junior the same thing. Only Junior apparently couldn't resist Sandra. Mason was not unsympathetic.

Sandra's car was empty, which gave Mason a fleeting panic attack until she called to him from the doorway of a nearby storage shed that faced the parking lot about a hundred feet south and east from the dock. Two large commercial trash containers flanked the shed.

"Where's our boy?" Mason asked as he joined her in the shed. It was a ten-foot-square aluminum can littered with discarded scrap metal and the lingering odor of tenants who'd been too careless for too long with food, booze, and tobacco.

"He's not due until eight o'clock. I wanted time to figure out what we're going to do."

"Does he know I'll be here?"

"No. He said he would only talk to me."

"In that case, I'll move my car." Mason parked the TR-6 in an alley half a block away.

"Say something," she said as he stepped back inside.

"This is a bad idea."

"Don't tell me you're afraid of Junior," Sandra taunted.

"After the last couple of days, I'm afraid of my socks. Whose idea was it to meet down here? What's wrong with Starbucks on the Plaza?"

"Vic Junior insisted. He said he wasn't supposed to talk to me and didn't want to meet where we might run into someone who knew him."

Sandra was wearing a hooded, navy nylon pullover, blue jeans, and running shoes. Her hair was pulled back tightly and held in place with a black band behind her head. She wasn't wearing makeup. Most women would have looked plain. It wasn't possible for her. She pulled a slender handheld Dictaphone from the front zipper pocket of her shell and replayed their brief conversation. Mason's voice was slightly muffled but understandable.

"I don't want any questions later on about who said what to whom," she said as she tucked the tape recorder back in its hiding place.

It wasn't too noticeable. Besides, Mason figured that Junior would have something else on his mind if he started talking to her chest.

Mason asked, "When did he call you?"

"He left a message on my machine at home late this afternoon."

They compared notes since last night. Sandra had also met the security guard at the office. She ran into Phil Rosa at the courthouse while reviewing the O'Malley lawsuit. His summary of office conditions matched Angela Molina's.

They decided that Sandra would try to keep the meeting outside in the warehouse parking lot. If Vic Jr. insisted on going inside the bar, Mason would just have to wait outside the bar. Otherwise, Vic Jr. would see him. Mason would observe her meeting from the shed and Sandra returned to her car. With the lights out, he had a clear view through the dirty venetian blinds on the front window. Sandra assured him that he was invisible if he stood back in the shadows.

The on-and-off rain was off again when a black Explorer pulled into the parking lot. Vic Jr. was driving but Mason couldn't see anyone else through the tinted windows. A wave of panic surged through Mason. It had to be the same Explorer, which meant that Camaya was inside or close by. Mason scanned the area and didn't see another car. He was desperate for a way to warn Sandra without forcing Camaya's hand. He ran out of time before he could think of anything.

Vic Jr. parked about ten feet from Sandra's car. She leaned against the hood, one foot on the fender, thumbs in her belt loops, welcoming him with her open stance as he walked toward her. If

Sandra recognized the Explorer from the night before, she gave no indication.

Vic Jr. took Sandra's arm and gestured toward the Ford. She stiffened as they walked to the passenger side, still in Mason's view. Junior stood behind her as he opened the passenger door. In an instant, barely visible hands jerked her inside. A thickly muscled, black-clad stranger appeared from the far side of the Explorer. In quick succession, he grabbed Junior by the belt, threw him inside, and slammed the door closed.

Mason suppressed a flashback to Harlan's kitchen as the stranger climbed into Sandra's BMW and followed the Explorer to the warehouse entrance. Two men emerged from the Explorer, one holding Sandra's right arm twisted behind her back, as they disappeared inside the building. Mason didn't see Junior get out of the Explorer, which was driven away, leaving Sandra's car behind.

It happened so fast that Mason had no chance to help her. From the looks of the competition, he knew he would have been outclassed in a straight-up confrontation anyway. Mason couldn't find a phone in the shed. He cursed himself for not replacing the cell phone that had been in his Saab. He considered driving to the nearest phone to call for help, but was afraid that they might leave while he was gone and he would have no way to find Sandra. Mason couldn't come up with anything better than self-help repossession of his partner, so he grabbed a foot-long piece of steel pipe from the floor of the shed and used the darkened sky to cover his approach to the warehouse as the rain returned in blistering sheets.

Hugging the exterior wall of the warehouse, he ran around to the back looking for another entrance. On the north side, overlooking the river, he found a narrow flight of concrete stairs that led down to a darkened landing. What had once been a door at the bottom of the stairs was now a brick wall. The heaving of his chest was punctuated by his rapid breathing echoing off the paved walls surrounding him. His skin was hot even as rain raced inside his shirt. He looked up, tracing the barely illuminated wall on its ascent, deceived by his perspective that made it seem to sway. It was time to go for help.

Mason started up the stairs. His head was barely above ground level when familiar hands lifted him by his collar and tossed him against the wall. His back absorbed the force of the throw as his steel pipe clattered uselessly back down the stairs. Mason crouched on the ground, promising himself that this time would be different.

Mason waited until the man was almost on him before launching himself at the bigger man's gut. The man didn't expect Mason to put up any more of a fight than he had the last time and Mason's lunge caught him by surprise. Mason shoved him with his shoulders and drove him backward with his legs. All Mason wanted was a little running room. What he got was a knee in his belly. Mason sucked in his breath and pulled the man's knee to his chin while still driving him backward. The man fell on his back and Mason rolled off, gasping for air. The man jumped lightly to his feet while Mason was still learning to crawl again. A boot in Mason's ribs put him in his place—back against the wall. The man won the round with a gun pointed at Mason's mouth. As heroes went, Mason conceded he was a bust.

Squinting through the rain, Mason looked up at

the man. He was dark complected with hair braided into shaggy cornrows. He wore jeans and a navy T-shirt that barely contained his chest and arms. He had a couple of inches on Mason and at least thirty pounds of muscle. It wasn't close to being a fair fight.

His escort prodded Mason inside the warehouse, where the only good news was that the roof didn't leak. The front of the warehouse was a long rectangle bathed in fluorescent light. A waist-high counter cut it off from rows of shelves rising to the ceiling. The aisles were too dark to make out their contents. Sandra sat on a wooden stool in the middle of the room, glaring at an invisible spot on the wall. She looked more angry than scared, which Mason figured was just about the opposite of how he looked.

The other two men Mason had seen earlier were standing in the far corner from the door he had entered. The one facing him was coal-black, strongly built, around Mason's height, his shaved head glistening from the rain. He studied the floor while giving close attention to the shorter, heavyset man with his back to Mason, who was obviously running the show. The taller man nodded his understanding and left.

The boss's head was a caramel-colored, clean-shaven dome with a crease in the back as if it had once been cleaved and healed with the painful memory intact. He wore a cream-colored tropical wool suit that hugged his stocky frame with a custom-made fit. He turned around as the door closed behind them.

Mason's bowels turned to liquid when he saw the boss's left eye. It was barely visible in the folds of an angry scar that ran from the upper lid in an ugly arc that ended at the corner of his mouth. When he smiled, the scar shuttered his eye to a narrow slit. Mason turned away toward Sandra, who looked up at him in the same instant. Mason could read her lips, and she wasn't glad to see him.

Jimmie Camaya said, "Mason, I'm glad you could join us. You've saved me a lot of trouble."

He was a killer and a natty dresser, Mason thought to himself. A pale blue silk shirt spotted with raindrops and accented by a hand-painted tie, stretched tightly across his ample belly. Gold rings flashed on both hands. One hand held Sandra's tape recorder while the other held a pistol. The contrast wasn't lost on Mason, who realized that a short, fat guy with a good suit and a big gun was one serious motherfucker.

Mason was afraid of Camaya and was certain that Camaya knew that. At the least, he certainly expected it. Mason had learned how to manage fear during a trial. When the opposing lawyer is hammering his client, sometimes the only way to regain control is to get in his face. Mason hoped the technique worked with killers.

"You could have just waited at my house last night, Camaya. I guess you just missed me again."

Camaya showed no surprise that Mason knew his name. "So you know I've been lookin' for you. So what? Julio will keep an eye on you and Miss Sweet Cheeks until I get done with some other business," he said, pointing to the man who'd brought Mason in out of the rain.

"If you want me, you don't need her. Let her go."

"Need got nothing to do with it. My customers place orders and I fill 'em. Customer says you two die. You die. Up to me how. That's all."

Supply and demand. Serving the marketplace. Jimmie Camaya was just a businessman, an entreprenuer. Mason felt Adam Smith's invisible hand at his throat. But he was determined to keep Camaya talking. Words were the weapons Mason was accustomed to. The longer their scrimmage lasted, the better Mason liked his chances.

"So who's your customer, Jimmie? Victor O'Malley?"

"Mason, you must think I'm a real dumb fuck, you know that? My business ain't your business."

"Cut the crap, Jimmie. You shot up my car and trashed my house. You want something you think I have. Tell me what it is, and it's yours."

Camaya's stomach shook as he laughed, a deep rumbling gurgle that reminded Mason of a satanic Santa Claus.

"Mason, you are a funny man," he said, wiping his good eye. "I wasn't shooting at your car. I was shooting at you."

"Don't give up your day job. You're a lousy shot."

Camaya stopped laughing. His bad eye disappeared into his scar as he walked toward Mason. He stopped a foot away, his head upturned slightly toward Mason's. Bay Rum cologne lay heavily on him. His breath was sweet. Death had many faces. Mason never thought his would look like this.

Mason couldn't help the tremor in his thighs. It crept upward, washing over his groin and twisting his gut. He looked at Sandra sitting on the stool behind him. Julio gripped her shoulder, clamping her to the seat. She struggled a moment, then quieted, whispering to him that she was sorry.

Mason's eye caught the movement of Camaya's arm as he raised his gun to Mason's face, brushing it across his cheek, probing his ear with the muzzle, then past his ear, under the base of his skull, then pulling the trigger. The bullet shattered the sheetrock, Mason's hearing, and his fear. Mason held his ground, depriving Camaya of the collapse he wanted.

Camaya's voice turned stone cold. "So you're a tough guy, Mason. Well, guess what, macho man. Tough guys die slow, real slow. You'll piss your pants and cry for your mama, and we'll just be getting started."

A cell phone rang, breaking the moment but not the sweat that dripped down Mason's neck. Julio answered and handed the phone to Camaya, who listened silently before hanging up.

"Julio, tie them up. I'll be back soon. When I'm done, you can play with them."

Mason took his first good look at Julio. He had a nose tackle's short, thigh-sized neck, powerful arms, and thick body. Mason couldn't believe he had taken on this freak outside. Julio bound their hands behind their backs and wrapped another length of rope around their waists, leaving them sitting on the floor, tied back-to-back. Camaya told Julio to check the other exits as he and the rest of his crew left. The rain increased to a pounding downpour.

"Help me tip us over on my right side," Sandra whispered as soon as Julio was out of sight. Mason didn't know what she had in mind, but he was open to suggestions. They rocked side-to-side until their momentum carried them over. Mason still wasn't sure if this was progress.

"Put your hand inside my jeans," Sandra instructed.

"Great idea, Sandra, but I hate getting aroused when I'm all tied up."

"Do what I tell you, and we might get out of this!"

It wasn't easy, but he was able to slip three fingers inside her jeans. No underwear. No surprise.

"Lower!" she said.

Her demand reminded him of an old joke he was about to repeat when he felt a slender object wrapped in tin foil pressed against her rump.

"Pull it out!" she commanded.

It was enough to make him forget that he was about to be killed. "It's coming, it's coming," he cried softly. Sandra dug her nails into his back, convincing him to shut up.

"It's a number-ten surgical knife blade," she explained. It was about an inch and a half long. Mason peeled the foil off and felt the razor-sharp edge.

He didn't need any more instructions. He sliced into the first rope he could feel. It was an awkward angle to wield a blade. Sandra flinched as he caught her skin with the tip. After cutting his thumb, Sandra's hands were free, then his own. Mason pulled his arms in front and cut the rope around their waists. They scrambled to their feet and headed for the door. Exploding thunder muffled the sound of Julio's return. He tackled Mason for the second time that night just as Sandra opened the door and disappeared into the storm.

Mason and Julio rolled across the floor and crashed into a workbench that fell over, showering tools onto them. Julio straddled Mason, hands clamped around his throat. Mason's lungs were searing and the fluorescent tubes in the ceiling were multiplying like rabbits. He grabbed a pipe wrench from the tools that had fallen on the floor, aimed for Julio's temple, and opened a gusher that showered blood on Mason's face. It took two swings, but Julio's fingers relaxed, and he fell off, stunned but still conscious.

Mason crawled to his feet before realizing that Julio was kneeling between him and the front door, blocking his escape. Mason took another swing with the wrench when Julio pulled a gun from his waistband. He adjusted his aim for Julio's hand instead of his head, knocking the gun to the floor. Julio dove for the gun and Mason threw the wrench at his head, missing as Julio grabbed the gun and scrambled up. Mason ran into the darkened aisles of the warehouse, praying for a way out. Julio found the right switch as light flooded the aisles. *Keep your head down,* Mason reminded himself. *Can't hit what you can't see.* He repeated the only things he'd ever learned about playing golf. He guessed the game had some practical use after all.

The shelves were crammed with boxes, pallets, and more scrap than his grandfather had ever kept lying around. The aisles were a slalom course of overflow junk. Mason ran down a middle aisle, zigzagging as bullets ricocheted around him, trying to pretend he was just dodging defenders on a rugby field. A bone-rattling blast of thunder shook the walls. The windows glowed from a lightning strike that was close enough to knock out the power. Mason tripped over a pallet of five-gallon cans in the sudden darkness, banging his head on the way down.

He blessed the dark as his first break of the night while his fingers checked his head for open wounds. Something warm and sticky was on his face. He couldn't tell if it was his blood or Julio's.

Mason knew that he couldn't hide from Julio forever in the rows of junk. He had to find a way out, which meant getting to the exterior wall and feeling his way toward an exit. The lightning's unpredictable strobe light guided him. The building was roughly square shaped. Support columns interrupted the even contour of the walls. Mason groped along, hunched over to shrink Julio's target. If he didn't find a way out, eventually he'd be back where he started. Julio would figure that out too.

Mason made it to a back corner and felt the wall jut out as his hand bumped into a doorknob. He drew a deep breath, quietly opening and closing the door. Stale, sour urine. He was hiding in the john.

The power returned, blinding him with the flash of the naked bulb dangling from the ceiling. In the moment before he turned it off, he saw the wooden partition that divided the sink and stool. Lights out. Mason stood astride the stool with his back pressed against the wall, his heart pounding against his ribs. He had trapped himself. Julio would check the exits to make certain they were still locked. He'd walk the aisles and not find him. The bathroom would be next.

Julio's footsteps slapped against the concrete floor and stopped outside the door. The smell of Mason's sweat disappeared in the bathroom's stench.

"Come on out, man. I won't hurt you." Julio's voice was surprisingly soft, almost feminine. Mason wasn't tempted. He turned sideways and lifted the porcelain tank lid off the back of the stool.

"Have it your way, man," Julio said with little regret. Five shots smashed through the door and into the opposite wall. Julio kicked the door open as Mason lowered the tank lid in a two-handed grip to his right side, praying that his timing was good while trying to remember his home-run swing. Mason counted off the two steps from the door to the partition and swung the toilet lid upward just as Julio's face appeared. He was swinging for the fences and hit Julio at the bottom of his nose with the edge of the lid.

Julio grunted and crumpled as Mason's swing carried them forward into a heap. This time Mason was on top but Julio didn't move. His eyes were wide open and fixed. His nose had almost vanished into his face. Blood trickled from his ears and the corners of his mouth.

Mason heard more footsteps running in his direction. He reached for Julio's gun, which had skidded beneath the sink, hoping that there were a couple of rounds left. Before he could reach it, two hands wrapped around a gun appeared in the doorway and a familiar voice yelled, "Freeze, shitbag!"

Mason forgot about Julio's gun when Blues stepped into the bathroom.

"I forgot to tell you. I'll be late for dinner," Mason said.

"Fuck you! What the fuck you think you're doing?" he screamed at Mason as Sandra pushed her way into the bathroom and knelt at Julio's body.

"He's dead," Sandra said when she couldn't find Julio's pulse. "How'd you do it?"

"I hit him with the tank lid," Mason said, finally getting up.

"I don't fucking believe it. You killed the son of

a bitch with a toilet!" Blues shook his head and walked out.

Sandra said, "Let's get out of here before Camaya comes back."

"They took Sandra's car. I've got my Trans Am. Where's your car?" Blues asked as they stepped outside into the driving rain.

"In an alley. What do we do about Julio?"

"Let Camaya clean up his own mess. Follow me back downtown. We'll leave your car in a tow zone," Blues said.

"Why do we have to leave it anywhere?" Mason asked.

"You're getting out of town. You can't go back to your place. The cops will tow your car and at least you'll know where to find it."

Mason parked the TR-6 in a handicapped spot in front of City Hall and got in Blues's car. Blues's friends at the police department had let him retrieve Mason's briefcase from the Saab, and he left it in the backseat of his Trans Am. He finally calmed down enough to explain that he waited fifteen minutes after Mason didn't show up for dinner before heading to Mason's house. He listened to Sandra's message on Mason's machine and raced to the warehouse. He was furious at both of them for being so stupid. As he lectured them, he wound through a maze of inner-city side streets, doubling back several times to make certain they weren't followed, before finally reaching the interstate.

Wiped out by the post-adrenaline letdown, Mason dozed off while thinking about the fraternity that he'd joined when he killed Julio. Camaya was a charter member. He'd just been initiated. When he woke up, they were at the intersection of Highways 50 and 65 in Sedalia, Missouri. Blues turned south on Highway 65 in front of a sign that pointed to the Lake of the Ozarks. Mason closed his eyes again.

Chapter
Twenty-five

Blues used his car phone to track down Kelly and tell her they were on their way to the lake. She met them at one A.M. on Highway 5 just after they had crossed the Camden County line south of Laurie, Missouri. Mason rode with her as she guided Blues through the last remnants of the storm, finally stopping at a cabin she owned. Her cabin was so isolated and hidden that Mason half expected it to be a bed-and-breakfast run by the seven dwarfs. Kelly was too furious to play the role of Snow White.

Her stony silence told Mason how she felt about what had happened at the warehouse. She crushed the one attempt he made at explaining with an attack on civilians who tried to play cops and robbers. He got the point. After handing out blankets, Kelly left, threatening more than promising to return in the morning.

They drew straws and Sandra won the only bedroom. Blues claimed the couch and Mason got the wooden floor. Aunt Claire had always claimed that sleeping on a board was good for a bad back. Mason decided that she probably cheated and used a mattress. He woke up at first light, heard Blues softly snoring, and quietly stepped outside.

Mason was getting used to waking up in strange places. This time it was a log cabin so deep in the Ozark woods that he expected a white-haired orphan boy to be playing "Dueling Banjos" out back.

The only log cabins he had ever seen before were on bottles of maple syrup. Studying this one was easier than thinking about Julio. It was obvious that strong and caring hands had built this cabin.

Rough-hewn logs, laid one on top of the other, rose from the ground. Both ends of the logs were sculpted to mate with the ends of the other logs that joined at ninety-degree angles to frame the cabin. The gaps between the logs were filled with mortar made from clay and mud. Windows and doors were cut from the logs with a precision that surprised him. The roof was made from split rails raised to a modest pitch that extended over the front porch. The limestone chimney on the north side neatly accented the rustic appearance.

Walking around the cabin, he saw that it was set on the side of a hill in a clearing ringed by trees. The untamed grass formed a green belt roughly a hundred feet wide between the trees and the cabin. Long-stemmed purple stalks, sunflowers, and deep blue pansies painted the grass in a natural palate. The morning air was rich with earthy scents.

A fifty-gallon propane tank on the north side fueled the hot water heater, kitchen appliances, and an electrical generator. Along with the bathroom, they were the only concessions to modern living.

A wooden love seat hung suspended from the roof overhanging the porch that faced east. Mason wiped the morning dew from the seat as the seasoned oak planks protested against his weight. The rising sun warmed him on its climb while he relived last night.

Hallmark has a card for almost every occasion. There's one for birthdays, remembered or forgotten, comings and goings of all kinds, friends and loved ones gained or lost. There's even one for mother-in-law's day. Mason was fairly certain there was no card for killing someone. After all, what would it say? *Congrats on hitting the big one!* Or maybe, *The bigger they are, the harder they fall!*

He was just tugging at the fringes. He didn't know how this was going to feel now or in the future. Somehow, he stuffed the experience into a drawer and closed it tightly. He wasn't ready to open it. He knew two things for certain: The first was that he had responded to the most basic instinct of survival. And the second was that killing came more easily than he would have ever imagined possible. He knew that the threat was still there. If he didn't deal with that, the rest of it would be academic.

Everything had begun with Sullivan's death. Harlan's murder and the latest efforts to add him to the obituary list connected events since then. Mason considered whether the same person had committed the murders.

Sullivan had been poisoned, which is a chancy way to kill someone. The killer can't be certain that the poison is going to be consumed or that the dose is sufficient for the size of the victim.

Unless the poison acts instantly, there is always the possibility the victim will fall ill and get to a hospital before it's too late. Sullivan had been poisoned with insulin. According to the autopsy report, the reaction time can vary from a few hours to a few days. Even if the killer was present when Sullivan took the fatal dose, he or she could not have known where he would be when the stuff hit him.

Poisoning was like drawing to an inside straight when compared to the pat hand used with Harlan. His neck had been snapped like a dried branch. Nothing left to chance. Poisoners and neck-snappers weren't cut from the same cloth. First conclusion—two killers. Probably.

Someone in a black Explorer tried to run him off the road. The next time he saw that car, Jimmie Camaya was shooting at him from the front passenger side. The last time he saw it, Vic Jr. was driving it but Camaya was in it. Second conclusion. There may be two killers but they are tied together somehow.

The short list of suspects he'd given Kelly didn't include a favorite. Pamela had enough motives for a miniseries and probable access to insulin. Mason didn't think she could find enough courage in her to kill her husband. Without his own clients, Scot's best chance of securing his future was to inherit Sullivan's practice. Angela was squirming enough under Sullivan's blackmail to risk bugging the offices. Either one—or both—could have rented a ski boat, met Sullivan at the condo, and poisoned him. As long as Sullivan agreed to sit still while they injected him with a fatal dose of insulin. With the feds closing in, O'Malley may have decided Sullivan was the weak link in his defense—or maybe he really didn't like paying for work that wasn't done. O'Malley wasn't at the lake, but he was the type who hired people to cut his grass, shovel his snow, and do his killing.

Even if one of them killed Sullivan, Mason couldn't guess at a reason to kill Harlan or—better yet—to hire Camaya to kill him. What did he have that was worth killing for?

Mason tried thinking about it as if he were preparing for trial. Putting a case together means building a puzzle, tearing it apart, and putting it back together again. You keep at it until any jury can understand and believe it. No matter how many times he prepared a case, he always worried that he'd forgotten something that would unravel his case faster than a loose thread on a cheap suit. This case was all loose threads—each one leaving a hole in the pattern when he pulled it out.

The rumbling growl of an engine in low gear scattered his thoughts. Mason resisted the urge to run for cover, barely convincing himself that he was safe. The engine belonged to Kelly's maroon, middle-aged Chevy pickup. She swung the truck in a tight arc, braking so that the Chevy's nose was pointed downhill. She climbed out, took four brisk strides to the porch, folded her arms across her chest, and glared at him. The dust hadn't settled around the truck tires. She was ready to pick up where she'd left off last night when Blues opened the cabin door. He was wearing a ratty T-shirt and boxer shorts and was engaged in the male morning scratching ritual when Kelly turned her high-intensity eyes on him.

"Morning, Sheriff," he said in a lazy drawl. "Glad you could join us for breakfast—hope you brought enough for everybody." With an easy stretch and a wide yawn, he pivoted half a turn and slid back inside.

Mason said, "Well, you can take the cop out of the country but you can't take the country—"

"Save it, Counselor! It's going to take a lot more than smart-ass punch lines to clean up this mess."

Kelly was back in uniform, body and soul. She had a real knack for spoiling magic moments. Mason pulled himself up from the love seat and followed her inside.

Blues had already found the coffee, and the aroma filtered into the bedroom, bringing Sandra back out with it. Mason had never developed a taste for coffee and still felt like a kid when he was the only one sucking on apple juice. Unfortunately, the cabin didn't have a fully stocked minibar so he settled for rinsing his mouth with tap water while the others drank their attitude adjustment.

They each stood their ground silently in the cramped kitchen, sorting their muddled feelings for each other and their circumstances. Kelly stood at parade rest, shoulders drawn back, fingers of both hands wrapped around her mug, eyes fixed on a watermark on the wall. Blues hunched over the sink, humming something unidentifiable under his breath, pausing only long enough to take an occasional sip. Sandra lounged against the refrigerator, drawing invisible circles on the hardwood floor with her bare toes. Mason filled the doorway between the kitchen and the den, bottling them up. Steam rose from coffee cups. Nothing else moved.

"Kelly—" Blues began softly, his back still to her. "Lou and Sandra were in a jam. We had to get them out of there before Camaya came back."

"Goddammit, Bluestone! You were a cop! How

could you be so stupid? You let him run around until he almost gets himself and Sandra killed and then you leave the scene of a homicide! And just for kicks, you drop the whole mess in my lap!"

Blues placed his cup on the Formica countertop and watched a pair of squirrels chase each other in the grass. "You called it in, didn't you?"

"The body, the one you called Julio? You knew I would the minute you told me what happened," she answered.

"Kansas City cops or the feds?" he asked in a flat monotone, one the shrinks would say lacked affect.

"Kansas City—it's their jurisdiction."

"They told you someone had already called it in." It was the answer, not the question.

"Yeah. How did you know?"

"Because I called it in from the car, Sheriff. You call them back this morning to find out what went down?"

"Yes." The edge was gone from her answer.

Blues turned around slowly, facing Kelly, and raised himself onto the counter. "And they told you they checked it out and didn't find a body." Not a question. Just the facts, ma'am.

Kelly's face softened as she nodded her reply.

"Wait a minute!" Mason said. "I killed that son of a bitch and his body disappears?" He sat down in the lone kitchen chair, a metal-backed model with torn, red vinyl upholstery.

"I told you Camaya would clean up his own mess," Blues said to him. Turning back to Kelly, he continued, "Camaya was coming back to finish up with Sandra and Lou. If the cops got there first, it was Jimmie's problem. If he cleaned house first, it stayed private. Either way, Sandra and Lou had to get out of town."

Satisfied for the moment, Kelly changed course. "Camaya isn't the only one looking for you, Lou. Gene McNamara called first thing this morning wanting to know if I knew where you were."

"What did Fido want with me?"

"Victor O'Malley's son is missing. McNamara wants to talk with you about it. I told him I would let you know the next time I saw you."

Mason knew that if he talked to McNamara, he would have to tell him all about last night. Body or no body, he'd killed a man. He knew it was self-defense, but he also knew that he wasn't ready to talk to McNamara about it. He'd probably end up on the receiving end of one of B. J. Moore's comforting chats. Trouble was, if he didn't tell him what he knew about Junior's disappearance, he could be in more trouble for obstructing justice. While that sounded fairly puny compared to homicide, it appealed to his lawyerly sense of duty. Since McNamara had sent his question through Kelly, he decided to use her for the reply.

"Tell him to look for a black Ford Explorer. Last time I saw Junior, one of Camaya's boys was loading him in the back like a sack of groceries."

"I don't suppose you noticed the tag number, Counselor?" Her sarcasm hung in the air, another layer of tension.

"It's an Illinois plate," Sandra said. "I caught the first three numbers—735—before they put me in the car."

Kelly looked at Sandra, unable to thank her for the information or fire a shot across her bow. She was saving her ammunition for Mason. She wrote the information down without a reply before stuffing her notepad into her shirt pocket.

"You'll have to talk to him eventually, you know that."

Anger takes a lot of energy to sustain, especially if the other side won't fight back. She'd had all night to work herself up. Mason hoped that her anger was partly out of concern for him. That, plus the realization that he'd screwed up big time and was lucky to be alive, kept him from firing back.

"Yeah, I know. Only not yet. You can tell him everything I know, which isn't much, and his investigation won't be stalled."

Mason didn't want to go home until he had a lot better idea who his friends were. The only way he knew to figure that out was to put this puzzle together from the beginning.

Kelly agreed not to arrest Mason for homicide, obstruction of justice, illegal parking, or any of the other offenses he'd committed in the last twenty-four hours. With a look that said she knew she would regret it, she went outside to call McNamara from her cellular phone. She returned a few minutes later carrying her briefcase, phone, and a sack of groceries. She tossed the briefcase and phone onto the sofa and headed for the kitchen. Mason followed.

"What did he say?"

She didn't answer until she had emptied the contents of the sack on the table. A dozen eggs, butter, a pound of bacon, a gallon of orange juice, a loaf of Ozark Homestyle Honey & Wheat Bread, and a jar of strawberry preserves.

"I like my eggs scrambled and the bacon crisp," she said. "Butter the toast lightly. I'll get my own orange juice."

Mason saluted and went to work.

Kelly continued. "McNamara accused me of harboring a potential suspect in a kidnapping investigation and threatened to have my badge. I told him he could have it if I got to pin it on." Her mouth opened in a half-moon smile, her first of the day.

Mason negotiated an "I'll cook and you clean" package with Blues and Sandra. Within minutes, the small cabin was brimming with the fragrance of Ozark smoked bacon snapping in the frying pan. Fresh air, hot food, and being alive—things could be worse.

Kelly and Mason sat on the sofa while the dishes were washed. The fabric was rough tartan wool. The springs had long ago given up. The ones that still had some punch were pointed at odd angles guaranteed to poke where the sun didn't shine. The floor was looking better to Mason all the time.

He retrieved his briefcase from Blues's car and started reviewing the O'Malley summaries, looking for a thread to tie everything together. Kelly opened a manila folder and began thumbing through her reports. Mason was seeing the words without reading them. They were too familiar to him. He glanced at Kelly. She was equally glazed over.

"Listen," he suggested, "we both need a fresh approach. Let's trade files. Maybe we'll see something the other has missed."

Kelly handed him her folder. Sullivan's medical records from Charlie Morgenstern's office were on top. The chart was organized chronologically with the most recent records on top. It was like reading Sullivan's life story in reverse. He already knew the ending. He just hoped there was something useful in the past.

The first entry was curiously impersonal. "Patient died in boating accident, Lake Of Ozarks, July 3—date estimated—await autopsy from coroner." No hint of a twenty-plus-year friendship. Mason hoped when his doctor made his final entry for him that he at least rated a "poor Lou" instead of the anonymous "patient died."

There were almost weekly entries since Sullivan's diagnosis of HIV. Regular blood work and prescriptions for AZT. Mason expected to find records of multiple injections but there weren't any. He assumed that the needle marks found at autopsy were treatment related, but the records didn't support that. He started writing a list of questions to be answered on a legal pad. *Needle marks?* was at the top.

Prior to the HIV diagnosis, Sullivan's records were routine and uninteresting. His weight fluctuated between 150 and 160 pounds. His blood pressure was generally around 120/80. He never showed any signs of masses or lumps. His chest X rays were clean. He rarely had a cold and had never been hospitalized in the twenty-two years that Morgenstern had been his doctor.

Mason started skimming the chart as he got nearer the beginning until he noticed an entry dated September 29, 1977: *Sample drawn and delivered to Comm. B. B.* The next entry was three days later and was written in physician shorthand that he could only partly decipher: *TC from Dr. Ashland, Comm. B. B.—pt's sample 95%+.*

"Kelly, what do you think this means?" Mason handed her the chart and pointed out the entries. She studied the entries, her brow knitted in concentration. Keen blue eyes flicked through other entries, double-checking for anything that would shed light on their meaning. The cabin resonated with the mixed scents of pine logs, remnants of breakfast, and musty upholstery. The potpourri couldn't hide her own fragrance. It was subtle, spicy, and elusive. He inhaled deeply and realized his last shower had been a day and a half ago. Not wanting to spoil the moment, he edged away from her.

"The records don't explain it," Kelly confirmed.

Sandra said, "Let me have a look. I used to spend half my time reading medical records. 'Comm. B. B.' is probably the community blood bank. My guess is they tested him for something and the results were ninety-five percent positive."

"Most doctors do their lab work in-house unless they need something sophisticated done at a specialty lab. What do you suppose the community blood bank tested for?" Mason asked.

"Could be a lot of things, I guess. Hepatitis, special blood counts, paternity. The easiest way to find out is to ask Charlie Morgenstern. I'll put in a call to him."

Mason decided that it was a good time to try out the shower. He coaxed a thin, lukewarm stream from the single-setting showerhead and moistened most of his body. Julio's boot had left an angry inkblot on his left side. Raising his arm above his head, he peered at his side, examining the yellow and purple tinges that were forming in the blood pooled beneath his skin. He fingered the area gingerly, afraid to discover what fractured ribs were supposed to feel like. He was encouraged when his palpations didn't produce shivers of pain. An odorless scrap of soap was stuck like a piece of gum on the underside of the soap dish. It yielded a pale film that was harder to rinse off than it was to scrub on. The total effect was like an economy car wash—one pass without the undercarriage blast. Putting yesterday's clothes back on made the entire effort a break-even proposition. He was half clean, uncombed and unshaven and starting to blend in with the logs.

When Mason came back into the front room, Kelly and Blues were deep into the O'Malley papers. They spread the summaries in front of them on the floor in a semicircle and were taking notes on legal pads resting in their laps. Sandra was rereading Sullivan's medical records. Kelly's cellular phone rang, interrupting the study group. She picked up the receiver, identified herself, and began taking notes. Thanking the caller, she hung up and smiled at the others. This one was wide, toothy, and satisfied.

"That was Dr. Morgenstern. Sullivan took a paternity test and passed. He's a daddy."

"So who's the lucky heir?" Mason asked as he prepared to add a name to his suspect list.

"He doesn't know. In 1977, some woman contacted Sullivan and claimed that he was the father of her ten-year-old child. Sullivan didn't deny it, but wanted a blood test to confirm it. Afterward, he never mentioned it again."

"Call the blood bank," said Blues. "They keep their records forever."

"Forget it," answered Sandra. "I've dealt with them on other cases. You won't get anything out of them voluntarily. They're too worried about confidentiality. You'll need a court order."

"That's what assistant prosecuting attorneys are for," said Kelly.

She dialed a number and asked for Tina DeVoy. Kelly told her what she wanted and that she wanted it yesterday. Even though they could only hear one end of the conversation, it was easy enough to piece it together. DeVoy was following standard rank-and-file procedure. She gave Kelly a lengthy explanation why she couldn't get the order before Monday and why it would take another week to get the records. Kelly wasted no time in explaining that she would get the order that very day, hand-deliver it to Kansas City, and return with certified copies of the records or spend the rest of her career serving subpoenas in child-support cases. She punched the end button, terminating the call.

"She'll get the order today, but we'll be lucky to get the records before Monday. But at least it's a start," Kelly said.

Sullivan's blood tests triggered a memory from Tommy Douchant's trial. Tommy's hip was lacerated by one of the I-beams he hit on his way down to the pavement. Mason had used his bloody clothes as trial exhibits.

"How long will dried blood last?" he asked.

"Are you planning to start a collection?" Sandra replied.

"Just trying to revive a lost cause. Any ideas, Kelly?"

"There are too many variables to generalize. Depends on the surface, the temperature—a lot of things."

"Who would you use in Kansas City to analyze a safety hook for dried blood?"

"Virginia Norville. She's the county medical examiner, and she does freelance forensic work if it's interesting enough."

Mason called Webb Chapman on Kelly's phone

and left a voice mail message instructing him to take the box of hooks to Dr. Norville for analysis. Mason reminded Chapman that Tommy's blood type was in the medical records Mason had given him when he first became involved in Tommy's case. Sandra grabbed the phone as Mason was about to hang up and told Chapman to also have the hooks checked for fingerprints.

"Good enough," Mason said, hanging up the phone. "Let's see if we can figure anything out in the O'Malley records. The fixtures deals are the key," he said. "Quintex invested in a series of sale and leasebacks of store fixtures. Scot did all the legal work," he added.

"Who signed the deals for the corporations?" Blues asked.

"A Chicago law firm with power of attorney for the corporations. The real players are anonymous."

"What's the name of the law firm?" Kelly asked.

"Caravello and Landusky," he answered.

The light drained out of Kelly's eyes as she grabbed Mason's file and tore through the pages. Dropping the file, she balled her fists under her arms and paced around the room.

"What's the matter? It's only a law firm. Did they turn you down for a job?" he asked.

She stopped with her back to the stone fireplace, her expression grim. "Caravello and Landusky is Carlo D'lessandro's personal law firm. They don't sharpen their pencils unless it's to cover for the mob. Jimmie Camaya has always been freelance, but D'Lessandro is one of his best customers."

"What else do we know?" Blues asked.

Mason answered. "Quintex invested fifty thousand to seventy-five thousand dollars in each deal.

Annual rent was around sixty thousand. The first group of deals have recouped the initial investment and threw off about a half million dollars in the last year.''

"Anything else?" Kelly demanded sharply.

"In the last twelve months, O'Malley paid Sullivan and Christenson a half million dollars for work it never did."

"Who controlled the billing?" Kelly was boring in.

"Angela Molina on the administrative side. She planted bugs in Sullivan's, Harlan's, and Scot's offices to try and get something she could use on them."

"Where in the hell does that news come from and when were you planning on telling me?"

Kelly strapped her arms down with her hands to keep from strangling Mason. Blues just grinned, enjoying the show.

Even Mason couldn't believe that he hadn't told them everything he'd found out. Then he remembered that he'd spent most of the time since he talked with Angela being beat up, shot at, hitting bad guys with toilets, and sneaking out of town in the back of a car. It was easy to forget petty stuff like blackmail, wiretapping, and fraud when he got caught up in the fun and excitement of dodging bullets. Mason felt a little sheepish—well, actually, stupid, but he thought he could sell sheepish easier than stupid.

"Okay, look. I've been kinda busy the last couple of days, what with being beat up, held prisoner, shot at, rescuing Sandra, and killing a guy. I know I should keep you guys more up to date, and I'll try to do better from here on out."

Blues grimaced as if he had gas. Sandra stuck

two fingers down her throat. Kelly wasn't buying any of it. It seemed like a good idea to finish the story.

"Okay. Here it is. Angela and I had a drink at a gay bar called The Limit. She admitted the bugging and said the tapes were in a safe place. I think she was about to tell me where they were when Diane Farrell showed up."

"Somebody is laundering money through Quintex and the law firm," Kelly concluded. "Somebody has dirty money, maybe from drugs—I don't know what. They've got to clean the cash so the government can't trace its origin. The only way to do that is to run the money through a series of legitimate transactions until it can't be traced back to its origin. That's what the fixtures deals are for. The lease payments on the fixtures are way above their fair market value. The deals make no sense otherwise."

"The money is coming from the companies doing the deals. They'll be hard to identify. Probably have better luck tracing the money after it leaves the firm," Blues said.

Mason asked, "How do we find out?"

"The first thing to do is examine the firm's expenses. Are there any new, large expenses that aren't easily explained? Do they match up in time with the receipt of the fees from O'Malley?" Kelly explained.

"We'll have to get into the firm's records to figure that out. I doubt if Scot will just turn the books over to us."

"That's assuming he's still running the show," Sandra added. "Last we heard, the firm was the prize in a dogfight between St. John, with his federal court order freezing the firm's assets, and

O'Malley with the receiver appointed by the state court."

"Don't leave anything else out, Counselor," Kelly said in a generously patronizing tone.

"There is one other thing. Diane Farrell had Angela witness Sullivan's codicil revoking his will. Except that Angela never saw Sullivan sign it."

"So we charge Angela with murder, wiretapping, and falsely witnessing a document!" Kelly said irritably.

She picked up Mason's file and started to return it to his briefcase when she hesitated, reached inside, and pulled out two blank CD cases and a Johnny Mathis CD. "I thought you said you told us everything, Lou. What are these?"

"Souvenirs," Mason told her. He took the CDs from her. "These two are DVDs. Sullivan watched dirty movies on his computer. We checked them and didn't find anything else," he said, holding up the two blank CD cases. "The Johnny Mathis CD was Sullivan's too. You gave me his briefcase when we searched his room at the lake. This was in it. Pamela didn't want it."

"So you kept it?" Kelly asked. "What? Do you listen to Johnny Mathis?"

"No, but my aunt Claire always told me his stuff was great make-out music. I left Sullivan's briefcase at the office and took the Johnny Mathis CD just in case my aunt was right."

"Where did you find the porno DVDs?" she asked.

"One of them was in his office and the other was at his house."

"Tell me again how you know that there isn't anything else on them."

"Diane Farrell looked at them for us."

Kelly's eyebrows rose with each word until Mason thought her forehead would vanish. He realized again how lame some things sounded when you tried to explain them to someone else.

"This is the same Diane Farrell who told Angela to witness Sullivan's codicil without Sullivan's signature and who showed up just in time to stop Angela from telling you where she was hiding her wiretap tapes?" Kelly asked.

Mason decided to treat this one as a rhetorical question.

"Yeah," Blues answered for him. "My money says these discs will get you more than a rise in your Levis."

Kelly picked up her phone again.

"Riley, it's Kelly. Meet me at the courthouse computer center as soon as you can and be prepared to do some hacking." She replaced the receiver and gave Mason some advice.

"Riley Brooks set up the county's new computer system. If Sullivan hid something on these discs, he'll find it. And, Lou, another shower wouldn't hurt."

Chapter
Twenty-six

"There's got to be something hidden on those DVDs that will unravel this whole thing," Kelly said over the wind whipping around the open windows of her pickup. She worked the stick shift as if it were a natural extension of her arm, engaging the four-wheel drive when they hit a particularly rutted stretch of road that rose and fell like a poor man's roller coaster. The road was barely wide enough for one vehicle.

"Something worth killing Sullivan, Harlan, and me?" Mason asked. He sat in the front seat as Kelly drove them out of the wilderness. Humid morning air, heated by the quickly rising sun, filled the cab and softened the stiffness in his back and neck. The rough ride loosened the tougher kinks that remained from sleeping on the cabin floor. Kelly was pushing the pickup at a fast clip that would have been suicidal for someone unfamiliar with the road. Blues and Sandra followed at a distance in his Trans Am.

Kelly answered. "Not Sullivan. Camaya doesn't poison people. He shoots them or breaks their neck or runs them off the road. Sullivan may have been on Camaya's hit list, but somebody beat him to it."

"Even if you're right about that, those DVDs are still pretty pricey," Mason said.

"Camaya is the only one who thinks about how much it's worth. That's how he makes payroll. Price didn't matter to whoever hired Camaya. If you have to ask how much it costs, you can't afford it. Whatever is on the DVDs could explain why. You and Harlan may have just gotten in the way, known too much."

Mason protested. "But I don't know anything."

"Yeah, but the bad guys think you're a lot smarter. The rest of us know better. You've got the DVDs and that's enough to make you a target."

Mason braced his hands against the dash as the pickup splashed through a washed-out patch of road and leaped over a hilltop. Kelly let out a whoop as she put the truck into a hard right onto smooth blacktop, where it fishtailed briefly before leveling out. She slowed until she caught sight of Blues turning onto the road.

"Your cabin isn't exactly on the AAA TripTik."

"That's the idea. I'm the only one who knows where it is. That makes it private for me and safe for you."

Mason said, "If there are two killers, maybe Sullivan's murder set off a chain reaction that's out of control. Sandra calls it chaos theory—the rule of unintended consequences."

"We can't rule out anything yet. We haven't even

accounted for Sullivan's movements during the time he was most likely poisoned," Kelly said.

"Angela has Scot on tape talking to someone about Sullivan's death and St. John's subpoena the same day Sullivan's body was found. Scot left the lake before you woke me on the beach. How did he know that Sullivan was dead?"

"You said that Angela didn't recognize the voice on the other end of Scot's call. That rules out anyone in the firm. So who was Scot talking to?"

"I don't know. All I do know is that Scot has been more worried about O'Malley than anything else. When O'Malley fired the firm, Scot lost more than a client—he lost Vic Junior and Quintex. I'd sure like to find out where that half million dollars in unearned fees ended up."

Kelly said, "That may be another link to Harlan's death. If he was getting laundered money, I doubt that he would have reported it on his Form 1040. He may have been willing to give up the whole scheme to stay out of jail. Somebody figured Harlan would deal and killed him to shut him up."

"That makes Angela a link between both murders. She knew about the fees. She bugged the phones. She witnessed the change to Sullivan's will."

Mason wondered whom Angela was covering for on the phony bills. He had assumed it was Sullivan because O'Malley was his client. He thought back to his conversation with Angela and realized that his questions assumed that it was Sullivan. Angela never said that. Mason had. He remembered the advice he always gave his clients before the other lawyer questioned them: "If he hasn't got the facts straight, that's his problem. We're not here to help the other side."

Scot and Harlan were the lawyers on the fixtures deals—not Sullivan. Angela could have been covering for them as easily as Sullivan. The dirty money that was being washed through Sullivan & Christenson's books may have financed her "loan" from the firm. Her story about Sullivan blackmailing her could have been just that—a story.

Angela had always been one to play every angle. She said the tapes were in a safe place. Mason hoped she had one picked out for herself.

Kelly interrupted his thoughts. "The paper trail on the fixtures deals leads to a Chicago law firm that fronts for the mob. Jimmie Camaya works for the mob. Scot and Harlan wouldn't know how to make those kinds of connections."

"So they were drawn into the fixtures scam with Vic Junior," Mason said. "He was the O'Malley involved in the fixtures deals, not his father. Camaya used him as bait to grab Sandra and now he's missing."

"Who knew you had the DVDs?" Kelly asked.

"Plenty of people. Pamela Sullivan, Sandra Connelly, Diane Farrell, Angela Molina, Maggie Boylan, and Phil Rosa. They'd all had seen me with the discs. I'm sure everyone else in the office had heard about them."

Mason finally understood the reason his house had been trashed—to find the discs. That's why they left his computer intact. It was a calling card— a message that they knew he had the discs and they wanted them. And they didn't know whether he had found what was hidden on them. When in doubt, kill first and ask questions later.

* * *

Riley Brooks was waiting for them in the basement of the courthouse that had been converted into the county's computerized nerve center. What was once a deteriorating, mildewed graveyard for closed files and ancient furniture was now a gleaming, climate-controlled tribute to high-tech government. A staff of computer technologists fed the information appetite of the county's operations from a bank of monitors and keyboards. Up to date with the most advanced ergonomic workstations, the room hummed with the efficient whir of miracle hardware.

Riley stood in the center of it all, beaming at the gadgetry spread around him. Kelly introduced Sandra and Blues. Each of them was greeted with an enthusiastic handshake and clap on the shoulder.

"All right," he said to Kelly. "What have you got that old Riley's supposed to break into?"

He rubbed his palms together and his face shone with excitement. Kelly handed him the DVDs and the Johnny Mathis CD. Mason laid out the essential pieces of the puzzle. Riley listened thoughtfully, tugging occasionally at one of the gray wisps above his ears.

"What do you think, Riley?" Kelly asked when Mason finished.

"I like Johnny Mathis. Always made the missus melt. Mind if I keep it?"

"Be my guest. What about the movies?" Mason asked.

"It's easy enough to hide data on a disc so that an amateur won't find it," he answered as he tapped one disc against the palm of his hand. "But I'm no amateur."

"Diane Farrell told us she checked the list function and didn't see anything else on them," Mason added.

"May not have been on the same program as the video," he answered in a distracted but patient voice. "I'll check it out through the utilities program. That should identify everything on the discs. If someone was really clever, they could hide the data from that too. It may take time, but I'll find it if it's there."

They left Riley, and Kelly took them to the shops ringing the courthouse square. An hour later, Blues, Sandra, and Mason had clean clothes. Their next stop was the showers in the county jail. It pays to have connections when traveling.

Mason found his way to Kelly's office on the first floor of the courthouse. She sat in front of her desk digging through six inches of in-basket, but shoved it aside when he pulled up a chair next to her. A faint breeze wandered in the open windows adding the smell of freshly cut grass.

"Blues and Sandra are checking in with Riley. Where do we go from here?" he asked.

"You don't go anywhere. Stay out of it. You don't know what you're doing, and I don't need any more bodies showing up on my doorstep."

She answered without looking up from her papers. Her message was clear. Take off.

Mason wasn't listening. "Why are you so angry with me?"

It wasn't an innocent question. He knew part of the reason. She had already made that plain. He hoped she would tell him that it was his body she didn't want dumped somewhere. She sat back in her chair, arms folded across her chest, lips pressed flat. She knew what he was asking her and the answer wasn't easy. She gave it in a tightly controlled voice.

"Lou, this is a murder investigation, not the *Dating Game*. You are attractive and fun to be with—in spite of your one-liner approach to life. If we'd met another time, maybe something good could happen. But you're screwing up this investigation."

"Which means that you're using your badge to keep me away. You're protecting yourself, Kelly, not me. I'm not your dead partner. I'm not a cop and I'm not dirty."

She flinched and became rigid as Mason spoke. He knew that he had hit home. She had become the one bright light in his suddenly chaotic life. He knew he couldn't hold her if she didn't want him. But he wasn't about to roll away into the darkness.

"You're way out of line, Counselor!"

She bit off each word and spat them at him. They traded hard stares until hers began to redden and glisten. "Damn you!" she snapped and swiveled her chair around, leaving him to argue with her back.

Mason got up slowly. "Blues can find his way back to the cabin even if it's supposed to be a secret. I'll wait for you there. Sandra can stay and work with Riley." No response. He walked to the door and turned, still talking to the back of her chair. "You might want to run Vic Junior through one of your crime computers, Sheriff. He's got to be the link to Chicago. Maybe you'll find something interesting."

Chapter
Twenty-seven

Mason found Blues loading three shotguns and
enough ammunition for a small army into the backseat of his Trans Am.

"Where in the hell did that come from?"

"Store across the street," he said pointing to
Smith's Hunting and Fishing Shop.

"Did you get a hunting license?" Mason asked,
ever the careful lawyer.

"We're not going hunting," he said as he slid in
behind the wheel. "Get in," he added impatiently.

Mason closed the door and looked again at the
armory in the back. "Well, I guess it's a nice day
for target practice, huh?"

"You ever shoot a gun, Lou?"

"No. Is that important?"

Blues smiled. "All depends on how you feel
about getting your ass shot off."

"I'm feeling very attached to it, actually."

"I'm not going to sit up in those woods waiting

for Camaya to come looking for us and not have anything to offer him except coffee."

"Camaya doesn't know where we are."

"You killed one of his boys. It would have been better to kill him. He's getting paid to kill you so he's got to find you. He'll find Kelly and figure you won't be far."

"Thanks a lot, Blues. You're the one who brought us here. If you knew Camaya would figure it out, why didn't we go somewhere else?"

"Because that won't solve your problem. He'd still find you."

"So I'm supposed to become a gunslinger overnight and call Jimmie out for a showdown?"

"You'll be lucky if you don't shoot your dick off. Shotgun's your best bet. Know why?"

"No, but I have a feeling you're about to educate me."

"A shotgun fires a pattern of shot that spreads out the farther it gets from the gun. It makes up for a lot of weak stomachs and shaky hands."

"So why does Camaya use an automatic weapon?"

"Ain't nothin weak or shaky about him. He's got a lot more experience killing folks. Although your toilet-tank-top attack may give him a run for his money. But, I'll take a shotgun every time for close work. The New York City Police Department did a study of shootings involving their officers. The average distance between the shooters was seven feet. At that distance, the cops only managed hits thirty-six percent of the time."

"Lousy shots."

"Nope. Just human. A man can stand on the firing range all day and put ten out of ten slugs in the center of the target. Trouble is, the target is standing still and isn't shooting back. When it's real, anyone with a full bladder can be a lousy shot. All I want you to learn is how to load, point, and shoot. The shotgun will do the rest."

They dragged a half dozen hay bales that had been lined against the back of the cabin over to the edge of the woods and stacked them two across and three high to create a makeshift shooting range. Blues positioned each layer so that there was a narrow ledge in front of the second and third bales. They scavenged through the cabin until they found an array of tin cans and other junk that didn't object to being shot to pieces. Blues arranged their targets on the ledges.

He picked up one shotgun and started class.

"This is a semiautomatic shotgun. Once it's loaded and the safety is off, you pump it and pull the trigger. Keep pulling the trigger and it keeps firing until the magazine is empty. Anybody who gets in the way will have a very bad day."

"That's it, just point and shoot?" Mason asked, reaching for the gun. "This is starting to sound fun."

"Not exactly, Wyatt Earp. The safety doesn't come off until you're ready to shoot. Don't point it at anybody or anything that you don't intend to shoot."

"Sounds reasonable. Let me have it." Mason could already feel the attraction of the weapon.

Blues made him practice loading and unloading the gun, using the safety, sighting, and firing without ammunition for an hour before letting him fire a live round. Then he handed Mason a pair of shooting glasses and earplugs.

Blues paced off firing lines at ten-foot intervals from the hay bales. Mason began at the closest mark, firing three rounds before backing up to the next station. The shot patterns on the bales vividly demonstrated the spread from each shell. As he backed up, the spread grew into an ever-widening killing field. A blue-gray cloud of acrid smoke hung in the air. Mason had learned how to load, pump, point, and shoot. He just hoped the bad guys were as cooperative as the hay bales.

Afterward they sat on the front steps of the cabin sipping cold beer they'd bought on the drive back. The sun was on the backside of the cabin, leaving the front in comfortable shade. The quiet of the woods had returned and it was hard to believe that they'd just finished their war games.

"So, what are you going to do?" Blues asked.

"Circle the wagons, make 'em pay for every inch of ground—what am I supposed to say?"

"No, man. When this is over, what are you going to do?"

"I'll treat the question as a vote of confidence. To tell you the truth, I haven't really thought about it. I guess I'll have to find a job or take up piano again."

"You'd be better off joining the foreign legion. Why do you want to keep practicing law anyway?"

"I'm not certain. I had the right motives when I went to law school. Fight the good fight. Protect the individual. But I lost the fire somewhere along the way."

"But you turned out to be pretty good at it."

"Sometimes. I lost my last case. It was one of those I couldn't really afford to lose. Maybe I lost my nerve."

"Fall off the horse, you're supposed to get right back on. Maybe you should go back to the kind of practice you started with."

"And maybe I should start doing what I should have done in the first place."

"What's that supposed to mean?"

"Listen to my aunt Claire. How about you? Are you going to spend the rest of your life as the Piano Man?"

"Nah. I've been making my changes all along."

"Somehow musician and scuffling PI doesn't sound like a grand strategy for fulfillment."

Blues laughed and agreed. "You're right about that, brother. I'm tired of bouncing from gig to gig. I'm buying my own place."

"Get out! What kind of place?"

"Used to be a restaurant on Broadway, north of Westport. I'm gonna call it 'Blues on Broadway.' It'll be a first-rate piano joint. I'll play when I feel like it and if I don't feel like it, I'll get somebody to sit in."

He said it with the satisfaction of a man who'd figured it all out.

"Have you closed the deal yet?"

"Supposed to close in three weeks. That's why I wanted to have dinner at Constantine last night. My place is across the street and I was going to ask you to look over the paperwork for me."

"How big is it?"

"The club is around a thousand square feet. But I'm buying the whole building. There's an office upstairs that I need to rent out. Make a nice place for some mouthpiece to hang his shingle. I'll make you a good deal."

Mason looked at Blues as he smiled and pulled on a long stem of grass he'd been chewing. Before Mason could answer, Blues stood up and said he was going for a walk. Mason watched him disappear into the woods, carrying a shotgun. He looked around for his, checked its load, made sure the safety was on, and climbed back into the love seat on the porch to consider Blues's offer.

Practicing law was the only way Mason knew how to make a living. He'd chosen the profession because he believed in the law—in its central role in society—in its capacity to heal and make whole. At first, representing injured people gave shape to those values. But the practice of law introduced a different human dimension to living those values. Partners he couldn't trust. Clients whose cases he couldn't win and who had nowhere else to turn. He had abandoned those values just to keep practicing when he joined Sullivan & Christenson. Some safe harbor. A desk above Blue's bar might be the right place to start over.

Kelly pulled into the clearing around five o'clock. Mason was inside trying to scrape more clues from the printouts on O'Malley. She came in carrying sacks of groceries for the night and no signs of baggage from their conversation in her office. Mason wasn't going anywhere and so far, she wasn't throwing him out.

Mason asked, "Any luck?"

"Not yet."

"Where's Sandra?"

"She's staying with Riley until they find something."

The sacks contained K.C. strip steaks, corn on the cob, charcoal, watermelon, and more cold beer. Mason was back in the barbecue business. He built a fire and put the steaks on when the coals turned white on the outside while still glowing red on the inside. Kelly joined him and they watched the flames lick the steaks until Mason decided to test the waters.

"Any news on Vic Junior?" he began.

"McNamara called again. He's really pushing me to bring you in."

"Bring me into what? He makes it sound like I'm a criminal."

"He isn't satisfied with the information I gave him. Says he has to talk to you personally. I told him I'd let you know."

"Great. What else?"

She hesitated to answer. When she did, Mason understood why. Amateurs aren't supposed to be right.

"Vic Junior attended the University of Chicago. His senior year, he was charged with drug trafficking and interstate transportation of a minor. Since he crossed state lines it became a federal case. And then it all went away."

"Daddy buy him out of it?"

"I don't know. But it puts him in the right place at the right time. Carlo D'lessandro runs the skin trade and the dope in and out of Chicago. He might have hooked up with someone in D'lessandro's organization and the contact followed him home to Kansas City."

"So now what?"

"I'm going to Chicago in the morning."

"Why? The money laundering isn't part of your case. Leave that to the feds. I thought you wanted to find Sullivan's killer."

"We both know they're tied together. I want to get a look at Junior's complete file."

"That's it?"

"No. I've still got sources in Chicago from when I was with the FBI. I may be able to find out if

D'lessandro is running this operation. If he is, I might come up with some way to pressure him to back off."

"How are you going to do that? Go see him and ask him nicely not to let Camaya kill the poor schmuck who wandered into this mess?"

"Lou, sometimes you make it hard to care about you."

"Well, that's just part of my charm."

"Really? If that's as good as it gets, I may bring him back here to meet you in person."

The grill was going up in flames and the steaks were sizzling on the edge of incineration. Mason rescued their dinner just in time. Later, she joined him in the love seat and surprised him by leaning her head against his shoulder. He put his arm around her, and she didn't resist when he pulled her closer. Blues came outside and wisely announced he was going for another walk.

"My dad and I built this cabin," she said wistfully. She nestled against him. They were a natural fit. "It was just before he died. He could build anything—do anything. I helped him trim the trees and notch them so they'd fit together. Making it together made it really special."

"It is special, Kelly."

"It's always been my hideout. I come here to lick my wounds."

The air was clear, the sky a starlit panorama. The love seat rocked them gently as he pulled her face to his. Finally, she breathed his name.

"Lou, do you want to see my trapdoor?"

Mason didn't know whether to swallow her face or his own. "Kelly, you're a hopeless romantic." He finished his answer by fumbling with her belt. She held her hands in check.

"No, you dope. I really do have a trapdoor. I made my dad build it in the cabin. I thought it would be fun to have a secret way out."

"Oh. Sure, I'd love to see it," Mason said with as much enthusiasm as he could fake. "Where is it?"

"In the bedroom."

She spun out of his grasp, clinging to his fingertips. They made it to the bedroom, but Mason never saw the trapdoor. They began to undress each other as the moonlight cast their shadows against the wall. The bed was soft and they rolled to the center as they became entangled. There is an exquisite sense of discovery when two people make love for the first time. Part shyness, part adventure. Mason traced the freckles on her chest with his fingertips, an abstract pattern caressing her breasts. She stroked the side of his face in a soft gesture that slid past his chest and ended with a grasp both firm and delicate. They paused for a moment, eavesdropping on the night sounds rolling through the woods.

Soft but certain footsteps, a discreet tap at the bedroom door, a cautious whisper as it opened a crack. "Lou, Kelly . . . we've got company."

Chapter
Twenty-eight

"How many?" Kelly asked, instantly alert. She dressed with an economy of movements, ignoring Blues's presence. He kept his back to her, but Mason couldn't. Watching her put her shirt back on was nearly as mesmerizing as taking it off. The sound of shells rattling into shotgun magazines finally got him moving.

"Three coming up the drive from the road. A short heavy guy is waiting in an SUV cutting off traffic. Can't tell for sure, but I'll bet it's a black Explorer. I was watching the road from the woods and saw their headlights when they turned off. The three guys are muscle and act like they don't care if anyone knows they're coming. I figure we've got a couple of minutes."

Blues tossed Kelly her holstered service revolver, which she snapped around her waist. Mason watched Blues dump extra shells into three ammunition bags, clipping one around his middle and laying the other two alongside the shotguns. The woods came alive with animal sounds telegraphing news of the advancing party. The air in the cabin thickened with their sweat. Beads of water dripped from the back of Blues's neck. Kelly's hair was matted along the edge of her cheeks. Blues and Kelly were wired but under control. That made Mason feel better about the acid churning in his stomach as he picked up his shotgun and ammo pouch.

Kelly slipped into the front room and peered out the edge of a window. The moonlight illuminated the clearing enough to make out shapes but not faces.

"I'll bet that's Camaya with the SUV. I don't recognize the others," she whispered over her shoulder. "They're at the edge of the clearing. There's about a hundred feet of open space between them and the cabin." She crouched below the window line and scooted back into the bedroom. "They'll see us if we climb out the windows. We'll go out the back way, boys," she said, opening the closet door. Blues started to roll his eyes until Mason explained.

"Trapdoor. Every high-class cabin has one."

Kelly knelt and pressed down on a plank in the center of the closet floor with her right hand. The other end rose, revealing a steel ring that she grasped with her left and pulled up. A two-foot-square lid swung open on hidden hinges. She rested it against the wall of the closet. Holding her shotgun and ammo bag, she dropped into the crawl space below the cabin and disappeared. Blues went next, followed by Mason. He stood in the trapdoor opening using the barrel of his shotgun against the edge of the closet door to pull it toward him until he could grab the handle and close it. He pulled the trapdoor shut behind them and got down on the ground on all fours beneath the cabin.

Kelly was already crouched against the base of the rear wall, running her hands along the stones that formed the foundation for the cabin.

"Got it," she said, pushing open a square section of rock that swung. She slipped through the opening and, an instant later, stuck her head back in and motioned them to follow.

Mason and Blues crawled on the hard dry dirt beneath the cabin until they emerged into the night. Running closely to the ground, Kelly led Blues and Mason across the open field behind the cabin, not stopping until the woods camouflaged them. They turned around in time to hear automatic fire ripping through the inside of the cabin.

"Bastards!" Kelly spit, as they listened to the assault.

Mason asked, "What now?"

Blues answered. "My Trans Am and Kelly's pickup are out front. They know we're here somewhere. They'll come looking for us."

Blues said it calmly, somehow satisfied with their predicament. Mason looked at him more closely. His eyes shone intensely. He shifted his weight lightly from right to left, like a boxer keeping loose before the first bell. Sweat trickled off his face. But it wasn't from fear. It was adrenaline, pumped from a primal well.

Kelly acknowledged his coiled tension with a soothing hand cradled around his arm as she drew both men near her. She had muffled her anger to focus on the fight they were about to have.

"Lou and I will circle around to the north. Blues, you take the south side. They won't find the back door, so they've got to come out the front. If we can catch them in the open, we can take them. Don't shoot unless they don't give us a choice.''

Moving slowly to make as little noise as possible, Mason and Kelly threaded their way through the trees, watching the open space around the cabin for signs of company. There was no path to follow. The moonlight barely penetrated to the ground in the woods, leaving tangled vines and thorny bushes hidden in the dark, grabbing at their legs and feet. The few minutes it took to reach the front of the cabin could have been an hour on Mason's clock.

Through the trees, Mason could see the yard in front of the cabin and imagined its oval shape to be a clock. The cabin was at twelve o'clock. He and Kelly were hiding at three o'clock. The Explorer was parked in the mouth of the drive at the six o'clock mark, engine still running. Camaya leaned against the back, taillights lighting his face with a red glow. Blues's Trans Am and Kelly's pickup were parallel parked at the edge of the grass clockwise from the Explorer. Mason tried to imagine Blues stalking his prey between nine o'clock and midnight.

From inside the cabin came the sounds of reckless searching. Cursing followed the crash of furniture upended and glass broken. Mason knew they were looking for both him and the discs. He was glad that he was outside and that the discs were safe with Riley and Sandra.

"The angrier they get, the better off we are. It'll make them careless," Kelly whispered.

They announced their exit from the cabin by kicking the front door off its hinges. Mason and

Kelly eased to within a few feet of the clearing and crouched behind a mound of limestone boulders.

Kelly whispered again. "Dad dug these up when he cleared the foundation for the cabin. The ground around here is full of them."

"I wish I could have met him. Do you plan to invite them to surrender?"

"I doubt if they'll RSVP. If they start shooting, let me return fire before you do. That way, I can reload while you're shooting." She really meant that this was no time for amateurs. He understood.

Mason's throat was dry and tight, but his hands felt slippery and wet around his shotgun. He marveled at the odds that he would be waiting to kill someone who was waiting to kill him for the second time in two nights. He felt no more skilled with a shotgun than he did with a toilet tank lid. Only this time, he felt more ready, more willing to level the gun, squeeze the trigger, and watch a man die. That was the true marvel, he realized. The night before, he hadn't thought about killing, only surviving. Now, he thought about killing.

Three dark shapes stood on the porch. Camaya raised his arms, directing one of them to return to the Explorer and the other two toward the woods on either side of the cabin. Mason heard the safety on Kelly's shotgun click off as she steadied the barrel on the rocks. He matched her movements from his spot two feet away.

"Shit!" Mason hissed as one of the killers started toward them.

"Shut up and watch the other side of the woods. I'll watch this one," Kelly hissed back.

Despite Kelly's order, Mason couldn't take his eyes off the killer moving toward them. He didn't make any effort to move quietly. As he got closer,

Mason could see his gun. It had a triangle-shaped frame stock, a pistol handle, and a short barrel. It reminded Mason of the guns favored by bad guys in every action movie. They fired a lot of rounds before the victims could hit the ground.

Mason's eyes had adjusted to the dark and, with the moonlight, he could make out the killer's facial features. Wide forehead, mushy nose, hard-set mouth. Most of all, there was no emotion, no fear, no nerves, no regret. Kelly jabbed Mason in the side, pointing to the south side and reminding him with the gesture of her order. The cabin was closer to the south side of the clearing than to theirs on the north. Mason watched Blues's target take his first steps into the trees before stopping and crumbling to the ground. Blues was good, but not good enough to smother the sound of the man's startled cry.

Mason glanced to his left to see if Camaya had heard his man go down. Camaya took a cautious step forward, now flanked by the third gunman. Kelly spoke in a voice loud enough for her man to hear but not loud enough for Camaya.

"Freeze, shithead, or I'll blow you in half!"

"Fuck you, bitch!"

The killer fired first. An instant later Kelly made good on her promise and Blues proved right about shotguns. Two blasts tore into him, twisting his body as the buckshot shredded his chest. His finger clung to the trigger of his gun as he fell, exhausting his clip.

One of the rounds found the propane tank mounted ten feet from the north side of the cabin. Mason and Kelly froze, blinded by the ball of fire that erupted until the shock wave knocked them to the ground. Their limestone wall shielded them from the molten shrapnel. Kelly was sprawled on the ground beyond the rocks. Mason crawled to her and pulled her to him, though her hands dug into the dirt and resisted. Tears ran down her soiled cheeks as the flames consumed the dry kindling of the cabin.

Above the roaring blaze, Mason heard more automatic fire. He looked in the direction of the shots and saw Camaya riddle the tires on the Trans Am and the pickup from the open window of the Explorer. The third killer had given up the fight for the safer job of driving the getaway car. Camaya must have figured the odds had turned and he'd get another chance. As his driver sped away, Blues ran into the yard and emptied his magazine at them. The shattered rear window of the Explorer littered the ground.

Kelly stiffened, clotting off her tears. She and Mason were stunned by the power of the blast, but otherwise in one piece. The searing heat from the fire drove them from their rock pile. Kelly used her cellular phone to call out the rest of the Pope County Sheriff's Department, the fire department, and Doc Eddy. Blues and Mason walked the quarter mile to the county road to await the arrival of the cavalry. Kelly stayed, a lone silhouette framed by the inferno devouring her hiding place. Incandescent shadows swarmed through the trees like extras in a low-budget horror movie before evaporating into the black sky.

The rescuers and the rescued worked through the night stamping out the few burning embers that had drifted into the trees. By daylight, the fire had consumed itself. There had been no breeze to carry it to the surrounding woods. Brilliant tracers of pink and orange crept into the morning sky as the last tendrils of black smoke drifted away. Soot-stained and weary, Blues, Mason, and Kelly poured themselves into a deputy's car and joined the procession back to town. Tow trucks dragging the Trans Am and the pickup bounced along, bringing up the rear.

Riley and Sandra, their faces pinched with fatigue, were sprawled in front of the courthouse when they pulled in. Sandra was stretched out on the wide stone handrail using her arms for a pillow. Riley lay across the stairs like the hypotenuse of a triangle. Mason had the feeling that the morning wasn't going to get any better.

"Hi, honey, I'm home!" he called out with more good cheer than was fair. He figured the one who answered was probably still alive.

Sandra rolled off her perch and reeled Riley to his feet.

"You folks okay? The deputy told us what happened when you called in," Riley explained.

Kelly walked into Riley's waiting arms and he held her, patting her gently on the back. She pulled away a moment later.

"A little shell-shocked, Riley, that's all," she said. "Any luck?"

"Well, Kelly, I've got an answer but it's not the one you expected," Riley said. "There's nothing else on the porno discs."

"What do you mean?" Mason demanded.

"The only thing on those DVDs is people doing the horizontal mambo and switching partners faster than you can say swing your partner do-si-do," Riley answered.

"That doesn't make any sense," Mason lectured

him. "Something has to be on the discs. You'll just have to keep looking until you figure it out. It's been a long night. We'll all get some rest and start fresh this afternoon."

"I'm sorry, son. There's no point in it. I spent half the night looking and there just isn't anything else there."

Mason took a deep breath and shoved his hands in his pockets to keep him from shaking Riley until he made some sense.

"Riley, what in the hell are you talking about? People are getting killed for those damn discs, and you're trying to tell me it's all a big mistake? What the fuck is that supposed to mean?"

"Son, no one's getting killed for the skin flicks. Now Johnny Mathis—that's a different story entirely," he said with a grin that lifted their spirits.

"Johnny Mathis?" Kelly asked.

"Yup. It's not a commercial CD, like an album you'd buy. Somebody copied the songs onto a blank CD."

"They put it in a CD case from a Johnny Mathis album to make it look like the real deal," Sandra added.

"I was playing it on a boom box while I was fiddling with these other discs," Riley continued. "Right smack in the middle of my wife's favorite tune, he hit that high note—kinda like a warble— then it cut out. Nothing. So I got to wondering about Mr. Mathis and I decided to run some tests on his CD."

Sandra joined in. "Riley found two documents that had been imaged onto the CD. We printed them out," she added and distributed copies to Blues, Kelly, and Mason.

Each document consisted of a single page. The

first listed the shell companies O'Malley had set up to borrow money from his bank and identified the owners. Sullivan owned half of each of the companies. O'Malley owned the other half. The document would have made St. John's case against him.

"This must be the document Sullivan wanted you to destroy," Kelly said to Mason.

"I don't think he wanted me to destroy anything. I think he was just testing me to find out which side of the line I walked on. There was no way he could know if every copy of this had been destroyed. Especially if it had been imaged onto a CD. Besides, he wasn't the only one who knew about this. O'Malley knew. They were partners. What's on the other page?"

Sandra said, "It's another list. I recognize the names of some of the companies involved in the fixtures deals. But there's also a list labeled 'accounts.' Each account is a combination of letters and numbers. I don't know what they mean."

Kelly scanned the second document. "It's a combination of bank account numbers and passwords. Offshore banks in the Cayman Islands use the codes to identify account holders and give them access to their accounts without using names. When I was with the FBI, we spent a lot of time breaking these codes down so we could trace laundered money."

"So break them down," Mason told her. "It's the key to the fixtures deals. We'll follow the money and find out who started all of this."

"It's not that simple, Lou. You just can't hold the numbers up to a mirror and read them backward. But this is another reason for me to go to

Chicago. I've got friends there who can break them down."

Kelly led the way to the Home Style Café on the west side of the square for breakfast. It was 7:30 and the restaurant was filled with the regular customers who made it part of their daily ritual. The men in denim shirts and blue jeans were stretching their last cup of coffee before starting their day. The storefront was dusky brick, unchanged for the last forty years. Kelly and Mason slid side by side into a booth while Sandra, Blues, and Riley chose the counter. They were too wrung out to deal with one another.

"Why do you think Sullivan imaged those documents onto a CD with Johnny Mathis?" Kelly asked.

"He was hiding them in plain sight. Anyone who found the CD case would see the Johnny Mathis label and think it was nothing important. If they opened the case and saw a disc without a Johnny Mathis label, they might get suspicious and listen to it. There was enough music on the CD to make most people assume there wasn't anything else on it. It took a true fan like Riley to listen long enough to find the documents."

"I respect the man and his music," Riley intoned from his seat at the counter.

Mason continued. "Sullivan knew that St. John had him cold when St. John served the subpoena on him. The fixtures document was his trump card. Sullivan was going to offer a trade to St. John. Somebody else found out. They must have been looking for the documents when they broke into Sullivan's house last month."

"Harlan was going to try his own version of let's make a deal. Now they're both dead," Kelly said.

The sun flattened out against the water-spotted

window. Kelly rested her elbow on the ledge, chin cupped in her hand, her eyes set on some distant place. The sad weariness Mason had first sensed in her had spread in the hours since her cabin burned. She hadn't talked about it and didn't have to. It was the last link to her father. He'd died long ago but now he was truly gone. Mason tried to comfort them both by holding her close. She pulled away, a melancholy smile gently telling him that he was not what she needed right now.

Breakfast passed quietly. She explained that her chief deputy would handle the investigation while she was away. Another deputy would drive her home to clean up and pack and then take her to Jefferson City, sixty miles away. She'd take a charter flight to St. Louis and catch a Southwest flight to Chicago in time for lunch.

There was a Holiday Inn two blocks away with a vacancy and Mason's plastic was still good. He showered and slept past noon, too tired for nightmares. It was Friday and he counted on the latest set of clothes he'd just purchased to last through the weekend or his insurance settlement wouldn't see him past Labor Day. By two o'clock, he was all dressed up with no place to go. He drifted back to the courthouse and Kelly's office, figuring that Blues and Sandra would turn up eventually. Nobody told him not to, so he camped out in Kelly's chair. He was about to go looking for Blues when a file clerk walked in with a fax from the community blood bank. Like all faxes, it had a bold *Confidential* stamp across the cover sheet. Like all people who were tired of getting shot at, Mason ignored it.

The second sheet was a copy of the blood bank's laboratory test from September 1977 for Richard Sullivan. The lab data were medical hieroglyphics to him, but the narrative report couldn't have been clearer. It was 95 percent certain that Richard Sullivan was the natural father of an unnamed child, then aged ten. The mother was Meredith Phillips. The report was addressed to Dr. Kenton Newberry of Rogersville, Kansas.

Mason finished writing the information on a yellow pad just as Blues and Sandra came through the door. Judging from the creases in their jeans, they'd been on the same schedule as he.

"Trans Am's got new wheels and is running fine," Blues reported.

"Well, Chief, got any bright ideas for the rest of our summer vacation?" Sandra asked.

"Yep. We're going home."

"Pardon me, Lou. But unless I'm missing something, we came down here to hide from Camaya and now we're going back to Kansas City! Should we just paint a target on our backs or would a 'Shoot here, Stupid' sign be better?" Sandra was back in form.

"We haven't done a bang-up job of hiding. Besides, he won't look for us there if he thinks we're still down here. We're the only ones who'll know where we're going and we won't tell anybody, now, will we?"

The mildly accusing tone came out without premeditation.

"No, we won't!" Sandra said, bristling at the implication in Mason's voice. She turned and walked out.

"Hey, where are you going?" he called to her.

"To the bathroom. Do I need an escort?" she replied over her shoulder.

"What's that all about, man?" Blues asked when she was out of range.

"I don't really know. I didn't intend for it to sound that way. But she sure took it personally. It just seems kind of odd that Camaya found us so easily."

"I told you he'd come looking for us, and he'd figure you were with Kelly."

"Yeah, but how did he know where Kelly was?"

"She's the sheriff, for crissakes! You look for her at the sheriff's office."

"Well, unless he keeps tabs on ex-FBI agents, how did he know she was the sheriff down here? St. John didn't even know that."

The more Mason talked, the more he warmed up to this latest thread. "Even if he knew Kelly was in the Ozarks, the location of her cabin was practically a state secret. Somebody sure as hell had to tell him how to get to it. And, back at the warehouse, Sandra didn't bat an eye when that black Explorer pulled up."

Blues got his clenched-jaw cop look as he chewed on the possibilities. "And, she didn't complain about being stuck down in that basement all night with Riley."

"Maybe I'm just grabbing at shadows. But we don't know where Camaya is or how much help he's got. If he stayed in the area, chances are he'll watch the likely roads back to KC. I've got a different route in mind."

Mason told Blues about the blood bank results before showing him a road map he'd dug out of Kelly's desk. They were about 180 miles south and east of Kansas City. They would take Highway 54 west across the state line into Kansas to Highway 169, then head north on 169 to Rogersville, a little town about sixty miles south of Kansas City. It was roughly the same distance to Rogersville from the lake as from the lake to Kansas City. It would take three to four hours to get there. Mason didn't know what they would find there on a Friday night, but he doubted anyone would be watching for them along those roads. He and Blues agreed to say nothing to Sandra about their route. They would stop in Rogersville for dinner. Mason hadn't gotten any further in his thinking when Sandra reappeared.

"Okay, guys. I'm ready," she said brightly, all trace of hostility gone. "I hope your moms told you to go to the john before going on the highway."

"You betcha!" Mason said. "Come on, Blues, I'm not stopping every ten minutes for you."

As they were walking out of the bathroom, Mason noticed a pay phone tucked in an alcove between the sinks and the urinals. He told Blues to take Sandra to the car and he would meet them in a minute. He pretended to have forgotten something in Kelly's office and on the way back out, stopped to talk to the sheriff's dispatcher, a greasy-haired kid, probably not yet twenty-one and barely winning the war on acne.

"Were you on duty last night when Kelly called in from the cabin?"

"Sure was! That must have been one hell of a fire!"

"Lucky thing the troops knew how to get there. I never could've found the way on my own."

"Shit, man!" he said laughing. "Nobody knew how to get to that cabin. Kelly had to damn near talk the lead deputy all the way in. We all knew she had the cabin, but she was mighty private about where it was."

"No kidding?" Mason's stomach tightened with a cold shiver and he changed the subject. "How do you keep in touch with Kelly when she's on the road?"

"Age of the beeper, man. Just dial her in and punch in the return number. Works all over the country."

"Mind giving me the number? I may need to get in touch with her."

"No problem," he said as he scratched it on a piece of paper and handed it to Mason.

Mason started to leave and stopped. "Just one last thing. I was wondering, do you have any pay phones around here?"

"Yeah. There's one in each john."

"Thanks," Mason said and headed for the car. Sandra was in front, ready to ride shotgun.

Chapter
Twenty-nine

Sandra showed no surprise or interest in their roundabout course. An uncomfortable silence filled the car, squeezing out any small talk. Mason couldn't explain his sudden suspicion of Sandra, yet he couldn't shake it. It didn't help that she didn't confront him. That's what he would have expected her to do. His doubts must have begun subliminally when she told him about her medical background. She knew enough to poison Sullivan. And Camaya couldn't have found them without somebody telling him where to look. But she had been in as much danger at the warehouse as he had been. He wondered if paranoia made him a clear thinker or just paranoid.

They chased the afternoon sun through the rolling, wooded Ozark hills, across the state line, and into the gentle, grassy knolls of eastern Kansas. Highway 54 beckoned westward to the broad, endless plains. Mason had once driven that road all the way to Liberal, Kansas. Eight hours of seamless prairie. He always wondered at the pioneers who had dared to cross that land. There must have been moments when they looked in every direction finding nothing to reveal where they were, where they'd been, or where they were going. Swallowed by their surroundings, they had to press on or go mad where they were. Mason felt on the edge. He couldn't go back, and he wasn't certain if he was headed the right way. They finally turned north on Highway 169.

An hour and a half later, Blues pulled into the parking lot of a Kentucky Fried Chicken restaurant. After his diet the last few days, those red and white stripes and tantalizing choices of original or extra crispy were Mason's little slice of heaven.

A weather-beaten phone book dangled on a steel cable from beneath a pay phone planted in a corner of the asphalt parking lot. While Blues and Sandra went inside, Mason lingered at the phone so he could check the local listings. There was no listing for Dr. Kenton Newberry. Meredith wasn't listed either. She may have married, died, or moved away. There were ten different listings under *Phillips*. One of these Phillipses might be her family. He furtively tore out the page, joining the fraternity of phone book vandals, and went inside.

Blues and Sandra sat opposite each other in a booth. He was eating and she was watching. Mason slid in next to Blues and reached for a chicken thigh. That was as close to dinner as he got.

"Okay, Boy Scouts. I've been good and kept my mouth shut. But I've had enough. Either I get some answers, or I'm out of here." She didn't have to raise her voice. Sandra had one of those tones that sliced right through you.

"We just thought it would be a good idea to take a different route home in case anybody was watching for us," Mason offered, hoping it was the question she wanted answered. Wrong again.

"I'm not stupid, Louis, so don't patronize me. We're having this wonderful bonding-in-the-midst-of-danger experience and you all but accuse me of tipping Camaya off about the cabin. Now what is this bullshit all about?"

The mound of chicken, gravy, and mashed potatoes on Blues's plate was turning to a pasty gray as it disappeared on his fork. He was not going to bail Mason out. The teenage cashier, not burdened by any other customers, gave up wiping the counter next to the cash register ten feet away. Mason heard the snap of boiling oil and smelled the sizzling chicken fat in the kitchen. He thought of every witness who'd blown his or her credibility by stalling an answer to the tough question and felt his own draining away.

"I don't know, Sandra," he said without looking at her. Bad start, getting worse. "Somebody had to have tipped him off and you weren't at the cabin. I didn't mean to imply anything. It just came out that way. I was out of line. I'm sorry." Vintage wimp-out.

"So, since we're all friends again, tell me what was so interesting in the phone book."

Mason glanced out the window and saw the pay phone directly in Sandra's line of sight. Blues had moved on to the biscuits, the cashier wasn't moving, and Sandra wasn't buying. He wasn't fast enough with a response. Fact was, he didn't have one that wasn't a lie she wouldn't see through.

"Listen, Sandra . . ." he stalled.

"No, you listen, Louis! I saved your ass at the

warehouse. Or did you forget how we got untied? Blues, Kelly, and me. We're saving you—not the other way around. And now you treat me like a suspect! You don't even have the nerve to accuse me."

She shoved the bucket of chicken in his lap and stormed out. Mason knocked it onto the floor as he followed her outside.

"Wait a minute!" he yelled. "Where are you going? What are you going to do?"

"I'm going to do what I should have done in the first place, Louis. Handle this on my own."

She walked across the street to a truck stop. Two minutes later she was riding in the passenger seat of an eighteen-wheeler, heading north on Highway 169. Blues was standing next to Mason.

"Man, you sure know how to handle women!"

"Fuck you! Did you leave me any chicken?"

"Nope. But, I'm surprised you still have an appetite."

On the way home, Mason scanned every tractor-trailer rig they passed, looking for Sandra, alternating between feeling guilty for goading her into leaving and relieved that she was gone. When he felt guilty, he kept his eyes open for rape victims lying abandoned on the shoulder of the highway. When he felt relieved, he concentrated on their next move.

Blues left him to his thoughts until they reached the southern edge of Overland Park, the biggest of Kansas City's suburban bedrooms.

Blues asked Mason, "You make up your mind yet?"

"About what?"

"Whether you want to let trouble keep finding you or whether you want to start running the show."

"I'm tired of running—that's why we came back. I've got a short list—Pamela Sullivan, Scot Daniels, and Angela Molina. You got any preferences?"

Blues pulled into the crowded parking lot of the Wal-Mart at 119th and Metcalf and they headed inside.

"You've been set up. Scot picked you to investigate the firm because he figured he could control you. When you picked Sandra to help you, he knew that he'd screwed up."

"There's a big difference between trying to control the investigation and committing a murder."

"One's the beginning and the other's the end. Scot knew you had the discs and told the wrong people. After that, it was out of his hands. Maybe he knew what he was doing and maybe he didn't. Either way, you'd have been just as dead."

They made their way past the permanently smiling Wal-Mart greeter. The store was crowded with people pushing grocery carts, some leisurely, some hurriedly. It was a normal trip to the store for them. Normalcy had become a forgotten luxury for Mason.

Mason didn't want to confront the possibility that Scot would let him be killed. He could live with the O'Malleys being crooks. He could handle some unknown bad guy sending a slimeball like Camaya to punch his clock. These were people he didn't know or care about. They presented problems that he would find a way to solve. But betrayal by a friend was another story. He was loyal to his friends and expected no less of a commitment in return. It seemed a modest standard in a world too often covered with shifting sands. They stopped in the sporting goods department and Blues bought two boxes of .45-caliber shells.

"Scot has a lot of questions to answer," Mason began as they dodged shoppers darting between daily specials. "He was in on the fixtures deals from the beginning. But he wouldn't know what rock to turn over to find Camaya, so he's got to be reporting to someone higher up. He's not equipped for this."

"If he's scared enough, he might talk to us," Blues suggested.

"Then we'll give him a chance."

Mason dialed Scot's home number on Blues's car phone. They were in the Wal-Mart parking lot. It was nearly eight o'clock. Time to find Scot. His wife answered.

"Gloria, it's Lou Mason. Is Scot around?"

She didn't answer at first. When she did, she struggled to keep her composure. "No—Lou. He's been working late—every night."

"Friday nights too? You think he's still downtown?"

"He called a little while ago—and said he was going to swim and grab a bite at the club before he came home."

"I'll try him there. If I miss him, tell him I called, okay?"

"Lou—what's happening? Will we be all right?"

She started to cry. Mason tried to imagine what their home had become. He remembered the dead, flat look in Scot's eyes the last time he'd seen him and thought again about what Scot had done to him. Mason owed Scot nothing and he wouldn't lie to her.

"I don't know, Gloria," he answered softly and hung up.

"Any luck?"

"Not home. His wife is on the edge."

"They have any kids?"

"Yeah. Three."

Then Mason felt sick as he remembered one of those loose threads, the elusive piece of the puzzle. Scot's oldest child was diabetic.

Mason tried Scot's direct dial phone number at the office. His voice mail message said he was gone for the day.

"Let's try the Mid-America Club. It should take us about twenty minutes to get downtown," Mason said.

"You got a plan? Or you just going to ask him to write it out nice and neat for you?" Blues asked.

"I'll ask nicely, but he doesn't have to write it down."

Blues opened the glove compartment and removed a blue-steel revolver. "It's a Sig Sauer .45 caliber," he explained as he loaded the clip and showed Mason the safety. Handing Mason the gun, he added, "Just in case he doesn't understand nice."

Mason looked at Blues and the gun, afraid to take it. A freak blow to a stranger trying to shoot him was one thing. Hiding in the woods with a shotgun to protect himself against a killer was doable. Pointing a gun at a friend, even one who'd betrayed him, was in a different league.

"It's not a game, Lou. Nobody is who you thought they were—at least not anymore. Blood changes everybody—there aren't any rules. Don't use it if you don't have to. But don't take the chance you won't need it. I'll drop you off at the club, park the car, and catch up to you."

Twenty minutes later, Mason stood in front of the revolving door entrance to the club, shirt untucked, the gun stuck in his waist, pressed flat against his belly and pointed at his crotch. He was more afraid of tripping than anything else.

As the door spun around depositing him inside, Mason began to fear something else—his own anger. Knowing that someone wanted him dead scared him at first and still did. But his anger balanced his fear, giving him a chance to do what he had to if he was going to live. And that made him afraid of who he would be if he did survive. The gun was fast becoming an easy answer. Mason's growing sense of the inevitability of that answer— and his acceptance of it—was terrifying. Blues was right, nobody was who he thought they were anymore, including himself.

Scot was alone in the pool, doing the backstroke. His head was cocked slightly upward and cradled by the water. His long arms were looping around rhythmically, like twin paddle wheels shoved along by a powerful kick. Mason stood at the shallow end as Scot swam away from him, content to wait for the return lap. He watched Mason without any sign of recognition. When he approached Mason's end again, he rolled over, tucked, and spun underwater, emerging in a crawl back to the deep end. Patience was no longer a virtue.

When Scot reached the deep end, Mason was waiting. Before he could tuck and turn, Mason grabbed his hair and slammed his forehead onto the edge of the deck. Scot grunted and slid backward into the water, trailing blood from the cut

Mason had opened. Mason held on while he gagged on the water before slipping his hands under Scot's arms and pulling him out. Scot lay on the deck, coughing and bleeding.

"Jesus Christ, Lou! Are you out of your goddamn mind?"

"Awfully fucking close, buddy. Swimming is a dangerous sport. You need to get out of the water before you get hurt." Scot was sitting up, holding his head in his hands. Blood trickled through his fingers, pooling on the floor. Mason tossed him a towel, yanked him to his feet, and shoved him into the locker room.

"Come on, let's check the damage," Mason said.

Wooden lockers lined three walls and filled a half dozen aisles furnished with benches. One wall was all mirrors and sinks split by a doorway to the toilets and showers.

Scot leaned on Mason, woozy from the blow. He kept muttering that Mason was crazy as Mason leaned him up against the wall by the sink and cleaned the cut. Mason wrapped the large towel around his neck and gave him a hand towel to hold against his forehead. When the bleeding slowed, Mason sat him on a bench and propped him against a locker near one corner of the room. He pulled up another bench parallel to Scot's and sat with his back to a locker on the adjoining wall. They were in a corner of the locker room with the sinks straight ahead of Mason, Scot on his right and another aisle extending to his left. The air was close, humid, and rank with the familiar pungent scent of sweat and aftershave. It was time to begin.

"So, Scot, how long have you and Vic Junior been using the firm to launder money?"

"You really are crazy, Lou. You're out of your fucking mind."

"No, Scot, I just want to get out of this alive. And I don't much care if you do. Help yourself and answer my questions."

Scot laughed weakly. "You don't have it in you, Lou. Give it up and go away while you still can."

Mason stood up, facing him, and grabbed the ends of the towel around his neck, choking him. Scot dropped the hand towel and clawed at the one around his neck. Mason yanked his head forward and then backward against the locker, reopening the cut over his eyes. Mason's gun was suddenly pressed against Scot's nostrils. Mason didn't realize that he'd pulled the gun until his finger tightened around the trigger. Scot blinked as blood ran into the corners of his eyes.

"Now, Scot, I'm not having a very good day. Frankly, I'm more than a little edgy. Been doing some really weird shit. Help me out, will you? Talk to me. It calms me down. Okay?"

"Okay, sure, just put the gun down, please."

Mason sat down, keeping the gun in his right hand and lowered it to his right side, resting the butt on the bench.

"It was Vic Junior's idea. He got hooked up with some mob guys while he was in college in Chicago. They bailed him out of a jam and he agreed to help them out."

"How, Scot?"

"Laundering their money."

"So why did you get into it?"

"Money. They let Junior take a cut. Junior needed Harlan and me to cover the deals, so we got a piece of it too."

Mason wasn't surprised that Harlan had been

involved. The fixtures deals must have been the source of the unreported income that caught the attention of the IRS. "That's what the fixtures deals were for?"

"Yeah. Quintex bought the fixtures and leased them back. The lease payments were the dirty money."

"What were the fixtures for?"

"Strip joints and porno shops. The rent on the fixtures was pumped way up to provide the cash flow."

"And the fees for work that was never performed?"

"We had to get the money out of Quintex and the firm was the easiest place."

"But how did you get it out of the firm?"

"Consulting fees paid on behalf of Quintex."

"To whom? Who's behind the whole thing?"

"I don't know who got the fees and I don't know who was running the show."

Mason grabbed the towel again.

"Okay! I knew but I didn't know. Sure, it had to be the mob but I never heard any names. Please, Lou! I'm telling you the truth!"

Mason let go. "Tell me what you did know."

"We always dealt with a Chicago law firm. They had power of attorney. The principals were never identified."

"Who got the consulting fees?"

"Don't know. We just made out the checks to corporations and mailed them. Everything went to a post office box."

"Angela had to cover the billings for you. You had to cut her in. And you had to pay the money back out. Seems like a lot of trouble for the amounts involved."

Scot laughed weakly. "The firm was only a piece of it. We set up separate corporations to contract with Quintex for phony services. Ran a lot of the money through them. Harlan thought it would be fun to run some through the firm since O'Malley was Sullivan's client."

"Harlan?" Mason thought of that gentle man getting a kick out of setting up Sullivan's biggest client. Every partner has his secrets, Mason realized. Harlan's secret must have been that he hated Sullivan.

"Oh yeah, Harlan," Scot said, reading his friend's thoughts. "He hated Sullivan as much as the rest of us. The more you needed him, the more you hated him."

"Enough to kill him?"

Scot's shocked expression was genuine. "No way! That was just a lucky break."

"Where were you before the poker game?"

"I don't know. I mean, I don't remember."

Mason slapped him hard across the face with the back of his hand.

"Lying violates your oath as a lawyer, Scot. You don't want me to report you to the bar association, do you? Now tell me where you were before the poker game started."

He looked away, letting out a resigned sigh. "Angela and I had a thing going. We rented a ski boat and went for a ride." He laughed softly. "Not easy to screw in one of those boats. But Angela's something else."

"Why didn't you use O'Malley and Sullivan's condo? You had to know about it."

"Sure, but I didn't want to run into Sullivan. Angela and I didn't need the publicity."

"How's the family, Scot? Have you introduced Angela to them?"

"You really are a prick, Lou."

"And how's your oldest—the one with diabetes? Must be tough, all those injections."

He gave Mason another bewildered look. "He's fine. We control it with diet. He doesn't have to take insulin."

It was Mason's turn to backpedal. Mason sat on the bench, the gun at his side, studying Scot's face. The bleeding on his forehead had slowed to an ooze. His nose was pink and runny from Mason's slap. Scot was limp against the lockers. Not much fight left in him.

Mason asked, "Did Sullivan know about Quintex?"

"Not until St. John's subpoena. Sullivan started digging into the files. Harlan and I were supposed to meet with him Sunday night after the retreat."

"Did Sullivan tell you that he knew?"

"He didn't have to. He showed us the subpoena and St. John's target letter and said we needed to talk about the work we'd been doing for Vic Junior. That was enough."

"How could you have kept it from Sullivan and O'Malley?"

"Sullivan only cared about his own work. He gave me Quintex and forgot about it. Junior convinced his old man to do the same thing. Said he needed to prove himself."

"If Sullivan was on to your scam, that's a good motive for murder."

"Yeah, but I didn't do it and I don't know who did," he said weakly.

"Why did you and Harlan leave so early Sunday

morning? And don't tell me it was to get ready for your closing."

"We wanted to search Sullivan's office to find out how much he knew. I got there before Harlan. He called me when he found out that Sullivan was dead."

"Who did you call from the office that afternoon to talk about Sullivan's death?"

"How do you know about that?"

"Angela bugged your office, you schmuck. You were screwing her, but she was fucking you."

Scot shook his head. "I trusted her."

"Imagine that. Who did you call?"

"It was just a number and a voice. No names."

"And you didn't find the discs?"

"Didn't know about the discs on Sunday."

"When did you find out about them?"

"At Sullivan's funeral. Angela told me she walked into Sullivan's office the week before. He was talking to O'Malley about having the records they needed on a CD. Angela was worried that some of our legitimate work for O'Malley would get screwed up and, with Sullivan gone, he'd fire us. None of us could afford to lose O'Malley's business."

"You mean she didn't know what was on the CD?"

"If she did, she didn't say anything about it. She was just looking after the firm's biggest client."

"So how did you know there was anything on the CD?"

"I didn't know for certain. But it was the only thing that made sense. I knew Sullivan had the information and I couldn't find it anywhere else. Everyone in the office knew you had the discs."

"So you told your anonymous business partners

I had the discs even though you knew it could get me killed?"

"I didn't know!" he protested.

A husky voice interrupted. "Sure you did, Scot."

It was Camaya, standing at the opposite end of the row of benches. Mason never heard him come in. Camaya was pointing a pistol at them. A silencer was screwed into the barrel. Scot turned whiter than the towels. Mason tightened his grip on his gun, holding it next to his thigh out of Camaya's view.

"How do you do it, Jimmie? You always show up just when I'm getting to the good part."

Camaya flashed his serpentine smile. "You just got bad luck, Mason. I came here to tell Scot about his retirement. Looks like you both can have a going-away party now. Too bad I didn't get here before Scot got so talkative. But it doesn't really matter since you're both dead."

"If it doesn't matter, then let me hear the rest of it, maybe you'll learn something." Mason forced himself to look back at Scot, half expecting Camaya to shoot him. He had to distract Camaya a little longer, hoping that he'd hesitate an instant. Mason eased his gun up slightly, keeping it below the top of his thigh. "Your boy Jimmie says you're lying, Scot. Says you knew they'd kill me? Is that right, Scot?"

"I don't know which one of you is crazier!" Scot shouted. "I didn't want you to get hurt, Lou," he continued. "I was in too deep. They told me to get the discs back—"

"Or else?" Mason added.

"Or else Scot would end up like Harlan Christenson," Camaya said.

Scot's face froze. The unspeakable meaning of what Camaya said hit Mason head-on.

"You told them about Harlan's audit and they killed him?" Mason accused Scot with the question.

Camaya delivered the verdict. "That's right. Julio snapped that old man's neck like it was a chicken's leg." Camaya said. "You should have gotten there early, like Scot did. He had a front row seat."

Mason listened in disbelief. The tears rolling off Scot's face and the retreating look in his eyes said it was true.

"He made me watch—" Scot whimpered. "So I wouldn't forget to do what I was told."

"And then you take Julio out with a goddamn toilet! Great story, huh, Mason? Scot, you want to watch another one of your friends die?"

Mason turned back to Camaya, who was pointing his gun at Scot. He estimated the distance between them to be about ten feet.

"Jimmie, do me a favor, come a little closer, will you?"

"Why?" he asked.

"Better odds at seven feet," Mason explained as he raised his gun over his thigh and fired three quick rounds.

Mason didn't know which one hit him, but only one round did. Camaya fell over as the mirror behind him shattered. Scot toppled onto Mason, who landed on the floor.

Mason looked up to see Blues standing over Camaya. "He ain't dead, but he sure bleeds a lot. They're going to need a new carpet in here."

"I guess Scot's dues will go up. Better call the cops."

Chapter Thirty

Mason listened to Blues call in a "10-71," the cop code for a shooting, while he watched Camaya wheezing and bleeding from the round that caught him in the right side of his chest. Blues covered the wound with a towel that Camaya pressed against his body to slow the bleeding. He was conscious and in a better mood than Mason was.

"Hey, Mason," he whispered in a feathery voice. "Why'd you shoot me, man?"

"Gee, Jimmie, I don't know. Seemed like a better idea than letting you shoot me."

"Aw, man! I was gonna shoot Scot—I hadn't made up my mind about you."

"Yeah, how come?"

"Friend of mine wants to talk to you—besides, you was gettin' to be good company."

"Who's your friend, Jimmie?"

"Man—you wouldn't believe me if I told you."

"Try me."

"No way—it's all I got to deal with—" He started to cough blood and gag just as the paramedics arrived. Mason went to look for Scot when they started talking about establishing an airway.

Camaya did get a shot off that had grazed Scot's shoulder. One of the paramedics was cleaning a crimson furrow along his upper back when Mason found him. He sat mannequinlike on a bench, expressionless as an EMT tended him.

"Scot," Mason said to him.

"Forget it, buddy," the EMT said. "The guy is zoned out."

"What do you mean? Is he in shock?"

"Way past that. The shrinks got a name for it. I call it 'zoned.' Sometimes they come back. Sometimes they don't."

He finished bandaging Scot and unfolded him onto a stretcher. Scot never blinked as they rolled him out to the elevator.

Harry Ryman questioned Mason in one corner of the locker room while another detective quizzed Blues in a different corner. A forensics team methodically gathered evidence, taking photographs and measurements to preserve the scene. An hour later, they were ushered downstairs through a gauntlet of reporters. Their police scanners had picked up the report of the "Mid-America Club Shoot-out," as one overheated journalist dubbed it. Mason managed a tight-lipped "no comment" before their police car pulled away.

The homicide squad room was a collection of grimy steel desks, gunmetal gray chairs, and matching filing cabinets overstuffed with the statistical residue of the city's violence. Mason sat in a chair next to Harry Ryman's desk while Ryman banged away on his keyboard, entering his report on his desktop computer.

"You leave out any details you want me to know about, Lou?" Harry asked him when he finished typing.

Mason had told Harry almost everything. He didn't tell Harry that he'd killed one of Camaya's henchmen with a toilet. Mason couldn't think of any reason to possibly incriminate himself. "I think I hit the high points, Harry. When can I get out of here?"

"Pretty soon. It'll be up to the prosecutor to decide whether to charge you with anything but I don't think he will. It's a pretty clear case of self-defense. You might get some heat for carrying a weapon without a license, but that won't play too good. You'll come out of this a hero."

Mason shook his head. "That I don't need."

"There is one other thing, Lou. Couple of nights ago, we got a call about a dead body in a warehouse down in the West Bottoms. Only thing was, there was no dead body. We found some blood on the floor at the front of the warehouse and some more in a bathroom in the back. Turns out the warehouse is owned by this Victor O'Malley you been telling me so much about. You got any clues for me on this situation?"

"Sorry, Harry. I can't help you with that."

Harry studied him closely. "Lou, your aunt Claire and me got something nice going. She cares a lot for you. Talks about you all the time. Don't do anything that might mess that up for any of the three of us. Are we clear, Lou?"

Mason nodded. "We're clear, Harry."

"Try that sofa over there. They'll be done with Bluestone pretty soon."

Mason moved over to a faded, dust-soaked couch and closed his eyes while he waited for Blues. He didn't expect to sleep. He just wanted to hide for a few minutes. The hardened footsteps of cops and perps played an uneven cadence on the linoleum floor. Tired questions and angry answers swirled around him in a smoky haze of fading aftershave and streetworn smells. A door slammed but Mason didn't peek until he heard a familiar voice.

"No-good pencil-necked son of a bitch!" she said to no one in particular.

It was Sandra Connelly. She tripped over Mason's outstretched legs, unable to catch herself before landing on the sofa next to him. Mason decided she was too good-looking a woman to be a bad guy.

"Bad day?" he asked. Have to start somewhere.

"Are you the victim or the suspect?" she asked. "Never mind, I don't care." She started to get up, but he grabbed her arm.

"Hold on, Sandra. What the hell are you doing here?"

She yanked her arm free and stood up. "Touch me again, Louis, and I'll perform your second circumcision."

"Just a little off the sides, please." Mason was scrambling, but she hadn't left yet. It was progress. "I plead temporary insanity. I don't blame you for walking out. I won't blame you for leaving again. And, I'm sorry and I'm glad you're all right. Sullivan's illegitimate kid was born in Rogersville. The mother was named Meredith Phillips. She's not in the phone book but her relatives might be. I'm here because I shot Camaya. What are you in for?"

"Depends. Burn any of your friends at the stake today?"

She eyed Mason suspiciously. It's not easy to accuse someone of trying to set you up and then regain her trust all in one day. Mason may have been wrong about Sandra. But Scot's betrayal was real.

"Angela is dead," she said finally as she sat back down.

Mason couldn't respond. For a minute, he thought he would join Scot in his twilight zone.

"The cops think she committed suicide, but I don't buy it," she continued.

Images of Angela flashed in Mason's mind. Lover to Sullivan and Scot, amateur spy, embezzler, manipulator. Whatever she was, she was a risk-taker, not a quitter. He couldn't picture her taking her own life.

"How did she die?"

"Some kind of overdose. They won't know for certain until they do the autopsy. It just happened tonight."

"How did you find out about it?"

"I found her." Sandra's anger softened with the telling of the story. "I told you I would figure this out myself and I decided to start with Angela. I went to The Limit and waited. She showed up around eight."

Mason glanced at the classroom clock on the opposite wall. It was one A.M.

"She was alone," Sandra explained. "I told her that if you figured out the wiretaps, the wrong people could too."

"Thanks for the endorsement."

"She was really shaken when she heard what happened to you at the lake, and she started to talk. She knew from the wiretaps that Sullivan had the goods on Scot and Harlan and that he was keeping the information on a CD. She wanted the disc for blackmail and guessed that the information was on one of the CDs you had. So she copied them."

"Then the bad guys would chase me, never knowing she had a copy. She could blackmail them, and they'd never know what her sources were."

"Exactly," Sandra said.

"Then Scot told Camaya's boss that I had the discs, knowing he'd send somebody to get them and kill me."

"How did you know?" she asked.

"Scot found religion tonight too." He told her what happened at the Mid-America Club. Sandra gave him a sympathetic look that showed more compassion than he gave her credit for. "Did Angela tell you anything else?"

"She said there was something else that she didn't want to talk about in public. She said she was meeting someone else at nine, so we agreed to meet at her place at eleven. When I got there, she was dead."

"So why do the cops think it was suicide?"

"No signs of forced entry, no visible signs of violence. I found her slumped over her PC with a suicide note on the screen. The cops found a syringe in her bathroom that they think she used to overdose."

"What did the note say?"

"Something about Sullivan exposing her to AIDS and not wanting to die that way. I tried to tell the cops that she wouldn't have killed herself, but they like the easy way out."

Before Mason could ask another question, Blues

joined them, nodding a noncommittal hello to Sandra.

"You done?" he asked Mason, who nodded his reply. "Then let's get the hell out of here," Blues said.

Mason asked, "Any news on Camaya?"

"Yeah, he's gonna make it. Scot's been admitted to Western Missouri Mental Health."

Blues didn't say a word when Sandra walked out with them. Mason was relieved that Camaya would survive. He preferred the threat of Camaya to more blood on his hands.

A weak storm front had coasted through the city while they were inside. The air smelled wet, and tepid steam rose from the pavement beneath the streetlights. Ghostly clouds draped the moon as they walked to the cars.

"Mine's this way," Sandra said to Mason, motioning to a parking lot catty-corner from police headquarters. "We've had a rough ride, Lou. We both could use some company."

Mason needed some company, but not Sandra's. "I can't, Sandra. But thanks."

She forced a bright smile. "That's okay, Lou. Say hi to the sheriff for me."

Blues dropped Mason at home, where he found his TR-6 in the driveway.

"Did you arrange that?" Mason asked.

"I been too busy to worry about your damn car. There's a note on the windshield."

Mason got out of Blues's car and pulled the note from beneath the windshield wiper.

"It's from Harry Ryman," Mason said. "It says 'We traced this car to your neighbor, who says she sold it to you. Claire made me get it back for you. Be glad she don't ask for too many favors.' "

Blues shook his head. "You should have been dead at least three times in the last two weeks, man. Somebody is looking out for you. I'm outta here."

Mason watched him drive away before going inside. His empty, forlorn house couldn't slow the spring in his step as he bounded inside, bouyed by the return of his TR-6. The message light was blinking on his answering machine. He realized he hadn't been home in days. The first ten messages were from reporters promising a flattering exclusive. Mason was in the fast lane of his fifteen minutes of fame. The last was a message from Kelly. She left a number for him to call and ended by saying she missed him.

He called the number Kelly had left but there was no answer. He dug the pager number given to him by the sheriff's dispatcher from his wallet, dialed in, and waited. Ten minutes later, the phone rang. Guessing it was she, he picked it up and spoke first.

"Hi, Kelly, it's Lou."

"I know who it is, you dope," she said softly. "I recognized your number when it flashed on my pager."

Mason warmed at the sound of her voice. "What's the latest?"

"You made CNN. Are you all right?"

He filled her in on the details of the shoot-out, answering her pointed and professional questions. "Now it's your turn," he told her.

"I've still got some friends in the Bureau's Chicago office. They let me have a look at Vic Junior's file. He was busted in 1996, just like the computer records said."

"Could you tie him to D'lessandro?"

"He was represented by Caravello and Landusky. That's the same firm that represents D'lessandro and that signed off on the fixtures deals."

Mason said, "Seems like too much of a coincidence."

"The FBI got involved because he was transporting across state lines."

"Drugs or girls?"

"Both. And you don't do that in Chicago without D'lessandro's permission."

"So, that's it? There's nothing else to tie Vic Junior to the mob?"

"Maybe—not exactly—I don't know for certain."

"What aren't you telling me, Kelly?"

The line was lifeless for a moment and then she answered, raising more questions.

"Nick busted Vic Junior. I was off that weekend and he was working alone. He claimed that he got a tip, thought it might be a link to D'lessandro, and ended up with Junior."

Her voice was heavy with sadness and uncertainty. Her partner—and dead lover—had arrested the son of Sullivan & Christenson's biggest client. Then he ends up gut shot on a sidewalk in Kansas City, Junior disappears, and Mason becomes a moving target. No matter how he arranged these pieces, he couldn't make them fit.

"Did D'lessandro make Nick dump the case against Vic Junior?"

"I don't know. But a week after the bust, McNamara took him off the case and reassigned it to himself."

"McNamara? St. John's lapdog?"

"The same. I told you, we were all in Chicago at the same time."

Sandra's chaos theory was in full bloom. These bumper cars were in a major pileup. "What about the bank accounts and passwords?"

"I'm still working on it. I'm on the Southwest flight that gets in at five fifty-five Sunday night. Will you pick me up?"

"No problem," he said.

"Lou, be careful. This isn't over yet," she said, and hung up.

Mason got up with the dawn, still too wired to sleep. After a run and a shower, he decided it was a great top-down day. After changing into faded jeans, a navy T-shirt, and sneakers, he took the TR-6 for a drive. Without meaning to, he headed south, through the suburbs and into the country, following the same route he'd taken six days earlier to Harlan Christenson's farm. He shut out everything except the sun and the breeze until he pulled into Harlan's gravel drive.

Mason had missed Harlan's funeral. He realized that he'd come to Harlan's farm to pay his respects and to find an explanation for what had gone so wrong in Harlan's life. Harlan was the one partner who had truly reached out to him, whose friendship seemed genuine. He was the one who had come to Mason for help when there was no way out. Mason didn't turn Harlan away. He just didn't pay enough attention.

Mason left the car in the drive and went for a walk through the pasture that surrounded the farmhouse. The pond he and Harlan had fished in was a quarter of a mile away, surrounded by cottonwoods. There was a break in the trees at one end of the pond and a small dock that hung over the water. Mason found Harlan's fishing rod lying on the dock. It wasn't baited but he cast the line into the water anyway.

At least three of the people connected to Harlan's murder had been accounted for. Julio was dead, Camaya was in the hospital, and Scot was somewhere over the rainbow. None of that meant that Harlan's murder was solved. Whoever had given the order, whoever had set Vic Jr., Scot, and Harlan up in a money-laundering scam, whoever had ordered Mason's death—was still in business.

Camaya was the best bet to nail Harlan's real killer. Camaya would use the identity of his boss to make a deal with the U.S. attorney, a fact that wouldn't escape his boss and would, for the moment, make Camaya a bigger target than Mason. Still, Mason hoped Camaya's nurses were good with a gun.

But none of that explained Sullivan's death or Angela's. Angela's confession to Sandra fit with his theory that the two murders were only indirectly related. Whoever killed Sullivan had set in motion everything else. Angela bugged the offices to get something on Sullivan. After his death, she hit pay dirt with the CDs and decided to set Mason up as the fall guy and watch what happened. Only she never got the chance to cash in. Suicide made no sense for her. She'd already taken all the big risks. She may have been scared when Sandra told her about the shoot-out at the lake, but Mason couldn't believe Angela was frightened enough to kill herself.

He wondered whether Angela's death was connected to Sullivan's or Christenson's. Death by lethal injection was not part of Camaya's repertoire. In any case, he was digesting a .45-caliber slug when Angela died. Sullivan died by lethal injection. Mason caught himself humming "Will The Circle Be UnBroken?" as he walked back to his car.

A short time later, he stopped in front of Pamela Sullivan's house. He was going back over ground he'd already covered but he didn't know what else to do. A FOR SALE sign had been recently planted in the front yard.

Pamela greeted Mason dressed in a purple and yellow tennis warm-up suit. Judging from the boozy fragrance that hung over her, Mason doubted she would be hitting the courts any time soon. Her face was puffy, her hair barely brushed. She wasn't wearing makeup. Her eyes were slightly glassy. She was racing her demons to the bottom.

"What can I do for you, Lou? Did you come back for something else?"

"I just wanted to talk, that's all."

"Well, come on in, then. I've got plenty of conversation."

She took him through the front hall, past Sullivan's study, and into the kitchen. There was a bottle of wine on the kitchen table next to the morning paper. She fumbled in a cabinet for two glasses.

"Nothing for me, Pamela. It's a little early."

"Well, in my case, it's a little late," she answered and poured herself a full glass. "My husband left one hell of a mess," she said, pointing to the headline in the morning paper.

The front-page headline read SHOOT-OUT WIDENS LAW FIRM SCANDAL. A picture of the shattered locker room mirror with Camaya sprawled on the

floor promised more gory details on the inside
pages. Mason quickly scanned the article and took
small comfort in the correct spelling of his name.
A companion story related Angela's death. The
investigating officer tempered his preliminary conclusion of suicide by commenting that a final decision would depend on autopsy results not yet
available.

"I've been in the middle of the whole thing,
Pamela, and I still don't believe what's happened.
I hope it's about over."

"So do I," she said as she joined him at the table.
The wine fed her melancholy. "I'm heartbroken
about Scot. Mostly for Gloria and their kids."

"He probably didn't intend for it to go this far—
it just got out of control. Actually, I think Sullivan
was on to Scot and Harlan and was going to confront them," Mason replied.

"And probably demand his cut! Oh, don't look
at me that way, Lou," she said as he picked up his
jaw. "The man was a shit. I don't think he would
have cleaned house."

"Did he ever talk with you about what was going
on?"

"No. He made it clear early in our marriage that
business was off-limits. I never made an issue of
it."

"Pamela, I don't mean to pry but there are some
questions I need to ask you."

"You won't offend me, Lou. I'm past that."

"Why didn't you have children?"

She sighed and looked over his shoulder,
through the window, and back to another time.
"We tried. I got pregnant twice and lost both babies
with miscarriages. The doctors said I shouldn't try
again. Richard said it wasn't my fault, but he never

forgave me. He started cheating and I pretended not to notice."

"Had Richard been married previously?"

"No. What are you getting at?"

"Richard fathered a child back in the late sixties by a woman named Meredith Phillips. I've seen the results of the paternity test."

What little color she had drained from her cheeks. Mason saw the ache for her own babies in her moist eyes. "I didn't know," she said softly.

Mason believed her. If she'd been a client, he would have stopped and come back another day. But he didn't know if there would be another day, so he pressed on.

"You knew that Richard was HIV-positive?"

"Yes."

"Did you discuss that with him."

"I screamed and he listened. Nobody deserves to die like that."

"Weren't you concerned about being exposed?"

"We quit having sex years ago." She hesitated and then added, "Richard didn't want me, but I needed to be wanted. You don't always find that where you think you will, Lou."

Mason thought about the woman that he'd seen Pamela with after the funeral. "I hope you found it, Pamela. Did Richard tell anybody else that he was HIV-positive?"

"I don't know. We never spoke of it again."

"Did you tell anyone?"

"Diane dropped some papers off a few days after that. I just started bawling like a baby—about everything. I made her promise not to repeat anything."

"Was Sullivan taking medications on his own—injecting himself?"

She nodded her head with a dry, humorless

laugh. "I told him he could live a normal life for years and begged him not to try black-market drugs."

"But he did anyway?"

"At least he thought so, but he was being taken. It was saline solution. Someone must have been selling it to him as an experimental drug. I found a vial of it. It's the one the police found when they searched the house."

"Do you know who he was getting it from?"

"I have no idea."

Mason thanked her for her time and she walked him to the door. This time, as they passed Sullivan's study, he noticed the computer on his desk.

"By the way, did Sullivan do much work on his computer?"

This time, her laugh held genuine amusement. "Are you kidding? He had to have that damn PC and every other new gadget that came out. He never learned to use it. Besides, he couldn't type."

The doorbell rang just as Mason turned the knob. It was Diane Farrell. A new Diane, wearing makeup, hair washed and styled, and wearing a lively blue-and-yellow floral-print dress.

"Diane, darling! You look marvelous." Pamela sang out with newly found vigor. "Diane just turned thirty something. We don't keep an exact count. I gave her a day of beauty and a new dress. Doesn't she look fantastic? Happy birthday, dear."

"And many more," Mason added as he walked out.

Chapter
Thirty-one

Ten names: Anson, C. J., Donald, Harry, Keenan, Martin, Missey, Opal, Vernon, and Wyatt. Tangled branches of the Phillips family tree. Mason sat in his car in Pamela's driveway and studied the names on the page he had ripped from the Rogersville phone book. He hadn't had time to search for Meredith Phillips when they stopped in Rogersville on the way back from Kelly's cabin. It was ten o'clock. He could make Rogersville by eleven.

The addresses were a crisscross of numbered streets and dead presidents. Anson lived at 227 Jefferson and Wyatt at 1634 Roosevelt. The others were evenly distributed between Republicans and Democrats. Once he figured out where the party lines were, he would be able to find them all by early afternoon.

Mason stopped for gas and a phone call to Blues. He thanked Blues for dropping him off at home, and Blues grunted in return. When Mason asked him to check out the preliminary autopsy results on Angela, he answered with two grunts. Sensing that Blues's baby-sitting reserves were running low, Mason said he would call back later and hung up.

Most small towns are laid out with Main and First as the north-south and east-west dividers. If you can count and tell your right from your left, you can't get lost. Rogersville was no different except that the presidents weren't in chronological order. Filmore and Hoover were back-to-back. Maybe the city fathers just had a wry sense of humor.

Anson Phillips's house was the third from the corner, west side of the street, on a block lined with heavy-limbed oaks leaning over the center of the street in a green canopy. Well-tended lawns, one-car garages, and sturdy wooden front stoops were reminders of the longevity of the neighborhood. Mason parked in the driveway behind a late-model, white Buick Electra 225, a car the size of Brazil. His TR-6 looked like a mutant exhaust pipe protruding from its tail end.

Anson was as round a man as Mason had ever seen. He filled the width of the glider on his porch, work boots not quite touching the ground. His head perched like a paperweight on his shoulders with no visible support from a neck. Eyes, nose, mouth, and ears melted into a pie-pan face. He was a denim-wrapped doughboy given too long to rise. Mason bet he hadn't seen his feet in years.

"Morning," Mason called out from the driveway. "You Mr. Phillips?"

"What you want, boy?" No one had called Mason a boy in years. He liked this guy already.

"Help. I'm looking for a woman named Meredith Phillips. Last I knew, she lived in Rogersville. You're the first one in the book."

"What d'ya want with her?"

"I'm a lawyer from Kansas City. She may have a child who's inherited some money."

"Don't know her. Might try Vernon Phillips. That family's been around here a long time."

No one was home at Vernon's, so Mason spent the next hour running down the rest of the Phillips clan. Only a few were home and none of them as helpful as Anson. He decided to try Vernon again.

This time there was a car in the driveway, a lime-green, road-worn Chevy Nova with a BABY ON BOARD sign hung in the rear window. It was littered with Happy Meal bags, two car seats, and a scattering of diapers and baby wipes. Not a good sign.

A chorus of bleating kids sang their demands from the other side of the screen door. A loose-jointed girl no more than twenty, her right hip jutting out to hold the rheumy-eyed infant glued to her side, answered Mason's knocks. Stringy maize-colored hair hung carelessly over her narrow forehead as she examined him with defeated, washed-out eyes ringed by dark circles. She ran her tongue over chapped lips, while another toddler clung to her T-shirt, dragging it off one bony shoulder. The sour stench of soiled diapers followed them to the door.

"Ma'am, I'm looking for Vernon Phillips. Is this his house?"

"Yeah," she said timidly, pushing the older child behind her and tugging her shirt back over her exposed dull gray bra strap.

"May I speak to him please?"

"He don't live here no more. I'm renting from him."

"Do you know where I can find him?"

She disappeared for a minute and returned with

a scrap of paper on which she'd written an address, 1860 Lincoln.

"Do you know Mr. Phillips?" Mason asked her.

"Sure, known him all my life. We moved in across the street when I was five."

"Did he have children?"

"A girl, Meredith."

"She's the one I really need to talk to. Do you know where she lives?"

"No place. She's dead. Killed in a car wreck 'fore my folks moved in."

From in the back, Mason heard another wailing voice cry out. The toddler bolted while the baby spit up. She didn't have to say good-bye.

1860 Lincoln was the address of the Loving Hands Convalescent Center, a low-slung, U-shaped building made of sandblasted brick. Heat waves radiated off a playground on the south side. Overgrown weeds had erupted through the asphalt, wrapping around the legs of a steel jungle gym. It was the only landscaping. A faded tire hung from a chain in the center of an otherwise empty swing set.

Mason parked in the circle drive next to a barren flagpole. The plaque embedded at its base declared that it had been donated by the alumnae of Lincoln Elementary School in 1953. Oversize, pale pink hands cupped together were painted over the entry beneath the gracious claim CARING FOR YOUR LOVED ONES SINCE 1985. He wondered if any of the alumnae had reenrolled at their alma mater. Life is a circle.

Airplane-sized fans stood in the lobby blowing antiseptically flavored air down each stuffy hallway. Mason could feel the decaying lives of the patients as he passed each room. It reminded him of the time Aunt Claire dragged him to a nursing home to visit her mother. He was six. His grandmother was ancient. She lay in bed, near death, her hair fanned out around her head. Aunt Claire patiently brushed her hair, working out the tangles. He looked into her cloudy black eyes sunk deeply into her face. Her skin was brittle and translucent, like looking through tissue paper into her skull. Parched lips shut over a mouth that would no longer sing him to sleep. Gnarled hands lay uselessly at her sides. She smelled like the stuff that the cleaning lady used to clean the toilets. Neither of them ever went back.

Vernon Phillips lived in room 12 on the north wing. So did three other people, each cordoned off by a peach-colored vinyl curtain suspended from a track along the ceiling. Four to a classroom. Each bed with a view. Probably a lot less crowded than the days when third graders roamed the halls. A clipboard with an erasable surface hung on each classroom door listing the occupants and their bed numbers. Vernon was number three. Each patient's space was furnished with a chair for visitors. One and two were empty. Sandra Connelly sat in Vernon's.

"About time you got here, lover boy. I almost gave up on you," she said as she stood.

Sandra had an inexhaustible capacity for the unexpected. She had made it plain that she was doing her own investigation. Still, he was surprised to see her.

"Sorry to keep you waiting. I had some other stops to make."

"Tell me all about it."

"Later. How's Vernon?"

"Like all vegetables. Not good company."

His chart hung from a hook at the end of the bed. The top page contained the admitting information. He'd been there five weeks following a stroke. Mason put the chart back and looked at the figure lying in bed.

He was propped up, placing them in his line of sight. His gaze passed through them, through the walls, and kept going. Ragged gray stubble covered his chin and peppered his mottled cheeks. A loose-fitting hospital tunic lay over his chest and upper arms. His Adam's apple bobbed rhythmically, the only sure sign part of him was still with the living. Mason couldn't take his eyes off of him. Vernon knew the answers to Mason's questions but they were locked inside him. Mason sat at the foot of his bed, staring at him, weary at another dead end.

"Let's go," Sandra said. "Maybe you'll come up with another bright idea." Mason didn't move. "Come on, it's not your fault. We'll come back on Monday and check the city's birth records."

"Good idea. But I think I'll stay awhile. He might come around."

"Yeah, and the first thing he'll say is 'Lou, good to see you. Let me tell you about my daughter.'"

Mason looked at Sandra, feeling the harshness in her, trying to figure out why she was risking her life to solve this case. He decided that she thrived on the combat. It was all about winning.

"Stranger things have happened. I'll call you," Mason said neutrally as he settled in the guest chair.

"Don't count on it," Sandra replied.

She waited for him to say something. He ignored her, seemingly content to watch the old man breathe. Sandra waited in silence for five minutes.

"You damn well better call, Louis," she finally said in exasperation and left.

Twice over the next hour, an aide came in to turn Vernon so that he wouldn't develop bedsores. She was a copper-colored Hispanic woman, jet-black hair, broad, flat features, and strong hands. Vernon had eight inches and a hundred pounds on her in his prime. Even now, he retained most of his bulk. Yet she rolled him effortlessly from side to side, massaging his flanks to encourage his circulation. She spoke no English. He hoped for Vernon's sake that Medicare didn't ask for her green card.

At three o'clock, she returned with a portable IV cart and a bag of clear liquid suspended from it. A spare bag was snapped around the center pole of the cart. Vernon was on his back again. She rolled up his right sleeve, cleaned his arm with alcohol, and neatly slid the IV into place. Smiling at Mason, she moved on to her next patient.

He stood to keep the circulation moving in his own legs and took a close look at the medicine bag. It took a couple of seconds for the print to register and when it did, Mason grabbed Vernon's chart and tore through it. Vernon was diabetic. His physician had ordered insulin by IV each day since his admission. He ran down the hall to the pay phone in the lobby and called Blues.

"What'd you find out about Angela's death?" Mason demanded, skipping the chitchat.

"Insulin overdose, just like Sullivan. Cops canceled the suicide."

"Thanks. Stay near the phone. I'll be back soon."

Mason had to see Vernon one last time before he left. Now he knew how Sullivan and Angela had been murdered. Vernon could tell him who and why but he wasn't talking. Mason sat on the edge of his bed, looking intently at him, feeling like an idiot. What did he expect Vernon to do? Listen to a list of suspects and blink once for innocent, twice for guilty? Mason stood up, strung taut with frustration.

The Loving Hands people provided a nightstand for each patient's personal items. A copy of a *Kansas City Star* newspaper lay on Vernon's. Mason picked up the newspaper to check for the date. It was two days old. Vernon had had a recent visitor. Mason dropped the newspaper in the trash can next to the bed and saw a Bible that had been hidden beneath it. The Bible was bound in black leather, frayed at the top of the binding with *Phillips Family Bible* embossed in small gold filigree letters on the side. Mason had never read the Bible. Aunt Claire had not been religious. But he remembered seeing a big one at Tommy Douchant's house when they were kids. Tommy had showed him the family tree on the inside cover that traced his clan back five generations. *Be there, baby,* Mason prayed as he picked up Vernon's Bible.

And so it was written. Vernon and his wife had been married in 1946. Four years later, a daughter, Meredith, was born. She died in 1980. Beneath her name was the inscription *Alice, born to Meredith July 3, 1967.* Alice made no sense. There was no Alice. Mason went back to the beginning, to Vernon and his wife. He read her maiden name. Then he knew.

He said good-bye to Vernon and tucked the Bible under his arm. Promising himself that he'd return it when everything was over, he drove straight to Blues's house. On the way, he struggled with the last hurdle in solving Sullivan's and Angela's murders. How to prove it. A brilliant trial lawyer once told him not to bother him with the facts, just tell him what the evidence was. Now he knew what the evidence was, but he wasn't certain that he could prove the facts.

He flashed back to the chalkboard at The Limit announcing the symposium on alternative AIDS therapies. The title was *Why The FDA Is Killing Us.* His mind conjured the haunting image of Sullivan injecting himself, thinking it was some experimental AIDS treatment, not realizing he was killing himself. The killer stood at a safe distance, not wanting to betray any undue interest, content in the knowledge that Sullivan would die by his own hand.

And that would be the story. He killed himself. The killer would claim not to have known. There must have been a mistake, a terrible mistake. The source for the drugs had made the error. Good intentions would be the defense. He remembered another of Aunt Claire's brutal truths. The road to hell is paved with good intentions.

There would be no confession. Too much was at stake. The killer knew that, at best, the circumstantial evidence was as thin as yesterday's soup. Mason would prepare the same way he prepared for trial. And that meant tying up a few more loose ends.

Tuffy's barking announced Mason's arrival at Blues's house before Mason could knock on the door. The dog was staying there until Mason figured out what to do with his house. Blues was standing at his kitchen sink, cutting slices from a fresh peach, not caring that the juice was mixing with the sweat on his weight-lifting gloves. Blues was wearing black shorts and a tank top. A pair of thirty-five-pound weights sat on the floor. Tuffy pawed happily at Mason's side until he scratched her ears.

"Peach?" Blues offered.

"Pass," Mason answered. "Here's how I think Sullivan was murdered."

Blues listened, probing, picking, and ripping at any weakness. When Mason finished, Blues dropped the peach pit in the sink and wiped his gloved hands on his shorts.

"I believe you. But you can't make it stick."

"Why not? It's all there."

"On Sullivan, maybe. But where does Angela fit in?"

"Murdered the same way. Insulin overdose," Mason said. It was clear to him, why not to Blues?

"People get shot every day. Don't mean it's the same gun. If you're right about the killer, why take out Angela?"

Mason sagged under the weight of the question. "Angela told Sandra she had something else to tell her besides the money laundering. Something she could only tell her in private. It must have implicated the killer. Did the cops find anything at Angela's apartment?"

"Harry told me they turned the place upside down. Nothing."

"I thought you guys didn't talk to each other."

"Normally, we don't. The guy's a real tight-ass. He's helping you, not me."

The phone rang, cutting off Mason's next question. Blues answered, hung up, and looked at Mason, shaking his head. "That was the hospital. Man, I think you got your first new client."

"Who?"

"Jimmie Camaya. He's out of intensive care, and

he's asking for you. Says he won't talk to anybody until he talks to you."

"Where is he?"

"County General, fourth floor."

"Gee, suppose he's got a private room?"

"More like a private floor with heavy security. You better take something just in case Camaya is feeling frisky," Blues said. He disappeared for a moment before coming back carrying a handgun.

"What is it?" Mason asked as he held the gun.

"Thirty-eight caliber. Good enough for close range."

"Camaya can't be dangerous. I already shot him once. Plus, the cops will be there."

"Somebody might be hanging around the parking lot waiting for you to come visit. Better keep the safety on so you don't shoot your dick off."

Mason stuck the gun under his shirt in the small of his back. Curiosity was the itch that made Mason decide to see Jimmie. He doubted that he would agree to plead for justice and mercy on Camaya's behalf. Then again, principles don't pay the rent and Mason was on his own.

Blues followed Mason out to the driveway and tossed Vernon's Bible onto the passenger seat of the TR-6.

"Don't leave the Good Book lying around," Blues said as Mason drove away.

On the way to the hospital, Mason used his cell phone to check his messages at home, hoping that Kelly had traced down the owners of the Cayman Island bank accounts. She had left him a disturbing message.

"Lou, one of my old informants tells me that D'lessandro owns Vic Junior. I won't be surprised if he sends someone to clean up after Camaya. Be careful.''

Mason didn't consider going home and locking his doors. Camaya was under armed guard in a hospital.

A single uniformed officer sat outside the door to Camaya's hospital room. So much for heavy security. He nodded silently when Mason identified himself and motioned him into the room.

The head of Camaya's bed had been adjusted slightly upward so that he could see the TV mounted in the corner of the ceiling. The remote speaker lay on the pillow next to his ear. It was a repeat of the *Daily Show*. He never figured Camaya for a *Comedy Central* fan.

When Mason walked in, Camaya turned off the set and pushed the control on the bed, raising himself almost upright. A drain ran out of a bandaged hole in his chest. An IV dripped nourishment into his veins while an oxygen tube pumped air through his nose. His head and his cheeks were clean-shaven.

"Hey, Mason, how do I look, man? It ain't much, but it's all I got."

This was the new Jimmie Camaya. Repackaged and user friendly. A better approach for a guy in his kind of trouble.

"You don't look bad for a guy with a hole in him who's looking at the death penalty."

Camaya's laugh caught in his throat as he winced in pain. "Don't make me laugh, man. It's killin' me."

"What do you want, Jimmie?"

"To talk. That's all, Mason, just talk. Thought you might help me do some business with the boys out in the hall."

"I don't handle death penalty cases."

"Got to be a first time. Besides, we can help each other."

Mason walked to the window, looking at nothing in particular. Camaya laughed again and Mason turned around.

"What's so funny, Jimmie?"

"You're packin', aren't you?"

"I'm what?"

"Packin', man. Carryin' a gun. Man, you kill me!"

Mason flushed at the absurdity of it all. Camaya was fresh out of intensive care, still peeing in a bag, and Mason had a gun to protect himself from him. He laughed too.

"Yeah, Jimmie. I've got a gun. So don't get out of bed. How'd you know?"

Camaya's good eye narrowed, matching the other, as he drew his lips back, baring his teeth, almost hissing his words. "You walk the walk, man. It changes you."

Mason nodded without realizing it.

"Feels good, don't it, Mason? Real good."

Before Mason could answer, the door swung open. No knock. Just company.

Chapter Thirty-two

St. John and McNamara could darken a room like a solar eclipse. They cast the biggest shadow on Camaya, who flipped from snake eyes to wide eyes. Mason assumed that Camaya was a coward at the core, like all bullies. But he didn't expect him to fold before the interrogation started. Particularly since he was holding a great trump card, the identity of his boss. Mason didn't have anything to say so he waited for somebody else to kick things off.

McNamara must have pulled St. John off the golf course. He was wearing a straw fedora, Hawaiian flowered shirt, electric-lime SansaBelt trousers with matching white belt, and bucks. He looked like the punch line to a joke that began "What do you get if you cross Don Ho and Chi Chi Rodriguez?" McNamara was his straight man, decked out in Bureau-issue brown suit, cream shirt, brown tie, and brown brogues. Mason didn't get nervous until he saw the large veins in McNamara's neck start to pulsate.

"What are you doing here, Mason?" McNamara demanded.

"Jimmie invited me over to watch *Comedy Central.* He's not sure he gets all the jokes."

"Showtime's over, wiseass. Take a walk."

"No thanks. Jimmie and I were just about to compare our video collections."

Mason couldn't help but do the opposite of what McNamara wanted to him to do. It was a petty way of showing him up—and probably not too bright—but he couldn't help himself. To make the point, he sat on the edge of the bed, facing McNamara with his back to Camaya.

"Mr. Mason," St. John began in a conciliatory tone, "we have to question Camaya. You can come back during visiting hours."

"Frank, you forget that Jimmie is entitled to have his lawyer present for any questioning."

St. John smiled broadly and answered. "And you're his lawyer. How convenient. Do you really want him to represent you, Jimmie?" he asked.

"Nothin' but the best for me. Lou's my main man."

"I'm truly sorry to hear you say that, Jimmie. I thought you had better judgment," St. John said.

"I'll make you guys a deal," Mason offered. "I'll tell you what you want to know and you'll tell me what I want to know."

St. John answered. "Mr. Mason, you know what we want from your client. We want to know who hired him."

"Come on, Frankie. You already know that. It was Carlo D'lessandro. Mr. Chicago Mob. No, what you want is for Jimmie to roll over and testify against

D'lessandro. And, if he agrees, you'll give him a nice new identity flipping burgers in Bumfuck, Montana. How's that sound to you, Jimmie?"

"I ain't flipping no fucking burgers, man. No way."

St. John let out an exasperated sigh. "Mr. Mason, you are more than an inconvenience. What do you want?"

"A history lesson."

"On what subject that wouldn't exceed your limited grasp?" St. John asked.

"Chicago mobsters and their migratory habits."

St. John looked at McNamara, who nodded slightly. "Begin, Mr. Mason."

"Why did you take Nick Theonis off Vic Junior's case after Theonis busted him?"

McNamara lost his snarl as if he'd just been hit across the nose with a newspaper. St. John's eyes fluttered in a momentary panic. Neither had expected Mason to bring up their dirty laundry.

"Sorry, time's up," Mason said. "No answer? I get to go again. Vic Junior was strictly small time. How does he hook up with a mob mouthpiece like Caravello and Landusky?"

The corners of St. John's mouth began to quiver as he and McNamara exchanged glances. Mason was getting warmer. He loved body language. Still no answer.

"Somebody had to refer Junior to Caravello," Mason continued. "Somebody who could be certain that the case against Vic Junior would evaporate and that Vic Junior would show the proper appreciation. Nick Theonis could have done that. Screw up the bust just enough to get Vic Junior off. Then Vic Junior's lawyer tells him that Mr.

D'lessandro has a small favor to ask. He wants to use Daddy's bank to launder money."

Both faces went blank, eyes narrowed, focusing in on Mason. McNamara's arms hung at his sides, his hands balling up into fists. St. John crossed his arms, hiding his hands in his armpits.

Mason said, "You guys must have known that Theonis was dirty but you kept him in play. Then Theonis gets whacked and you lose control. Bet that was a tough one to explain to the organized crime boys in the Justice Department."

"You're full of shit, Mason," McNamara replied. St. John stepped back, pressing himself against the wall.

"That's an artful response, Gene. Your ass was on the line. What did you think you were doing with Theonis? Turning him into a double agent? Like on *Hogan's Heros*? St. John was Colonel Klink and you were Sergeant Schultz. Next you'll tell me that you know nothing."

Mason let the silence fill the room. He felt as if he had released the brakes on several of Sandra's bumper cars. He was anxious to see what would come from the chaos. St. John composed himself and sat down in a hardback chair on the opposite side of the room. McNamara held his ground.

"You're to be congratulated for doing your homework, Mr. Mason. Or perhaps it was Sheriff Holt and you just copied off her paper." St. John smiled indulgently while McNamara snickered. "No matter. Nick Theonis arrested young O'Malley. The case involved drugs. We suspected that Theonis was dirty, and we removed him from all drug cases while we continued to investigate him. Quite simple," he said as he brushed his hands together.

"Then why bring Theonis and Kelly to Kansas City?" Mason asked. They didn't answer.

Mason looked at Camaya over his shoulder. Camaya's oxygen tube was foggy and moisture trickled beneath his nostrils.

"Theonis had compromised both of you. You didn't know which side of the street he was really working. You had to hold on to him in the hope he'd help you nail D'lessandro without giving the bureau a black eye."

McNamara answered. "We take care of our own problems. Privately."

"Except D'lessandro took care of it first. He had Jimmie hit Theonis. I guess he didn't want Theonis working for two bosses. Or maybe it was just a salary cap problem."

"Are you admitting that your client murdered an FBI agent?" St. John asked.

"Not me. I'm just thinking out loud. You guys interrupted us before Jimmie could tell me a thing. Here's the way I see it. You lose Theonis but you've still got Vic Junior's old man. He's already under the microscope for his own banking problems. You figure he's also in on the money-laundering scheme. You pressure him to roll over or his son takes the fall."

"An investigation has its own life, Mr. Mason," St. John said. "We just follow it."

"But you screwed up. O'Malley wouldn't cave. So you tried to squeeze his lawyer. Then somebody kills Richard Sullivan and you're fucked again."

"If you mean by that, that we ended up dealing with you, I would quite agree," St. John said.

"And everyone says you have no sense of humor, Frankie," Mason said. "Sullivan's murder knocked everything off track. You threatened to prosecute

Sullivan so that he would put pressure on O'Malley to cooperate. If O'Malley wouldn't give up his son to save himself, did you really think he'd do it to save his lawyer?''

"I didn't care," St. John answered. "Richard Sullivan was involved in the senior O'Malley's bank fraud and he knew about the money laundering. We were negotiating a plea bargain when he was killed.''

"So you must have known that Vic Junior was washing the mob's money through the law firm with the help of Scot Daniels and Harlan Christenson. O'Malley had nothing to do with it.''

"Apparently so. Sullivan had proposed giving us the evidence on his partners and Vic Junior in return for a free pass for himself and O'Malley.''

Mason said, "So that's why Sullivan didn't tell anyone about the subpoena for the firm's records. He was going to give you the records, claim ignorance of the money laundering, and let Scot and Harlan take the fall along with Vic Junior. Did O'Malley know what Sullivan was doing?''

"A detail in which I had no interest," St. John said.

"With Sullivan dead, you were back to Vic Junior, to make the case against D'lessandro, but he's disappeared. Harlan Christenson is dead and Scot Daniels is going to be the next poster boy for electroshock therapy. Camaya is your last chance.''

"It pains me to admit that you're right," St. John said.

"There's one thing I still don't get," Mason said. "How did Jimmie find Kelly's cabin?" Mason asked the question, almost forgetting that Camaya was lying in bed behind him.

Camaya answered. "I found a map in Theonis's apartment after—"

"That's enough," Mason interrupted. "Don't confess to anything yet."

Before Mason could ask another question, the door to Camaya's hospital room flew open. The police officer that had been on guard was shoved inside and onto the floor, his hands cuffed behind his back. Two men dressed in black, silenced pistols drawn, followed. One was tall, the other about Mason's height, only broader. Both had the slack appearance of men who aren't impressed by much and who care about less.

"Hey, Jimmie," the taller man said. "You don't look so good."

Camaya sat up, using Mason as a partial shield. "Feel better than I look, Tony." Mason could feel Camaya's labored breath on the back of his neck.

"Carlo said we should come down. Check on you. If you was feeling bad, he said we should put you out of your misery. So, how you feelin', man?"

Mason realized that Kelly's informant had been right. Carlo D'lessandro was cleaning house. McNamara made a poorly disguised move for his gun.

"Hey, fat boy," Tony warned. "Don't be stupid. Gino," he said to his companion, "get this dickhead's piece."

Gino shoved McNamara against the wall, grabbing his gun. McNamara offered no resistance. He also took McNamara's wallet. St. John's face twisted with disgust, though he remained silent.

Mason felt Camaya's hand slide under the back of his shirt onto the butt of his gun. Mason couldn't move without giving Camaya away. He hoped Camaya knew which side he was on.

"This guy's fucking FBI," Gino said after opening McNamara's wallet.

Tony turned to St. John. "And who are you, J. Edgar Hoover?"

"You should see him in a dress," Mason said.

"Shut the fuck up," Tony told Mason. "Jimmie, you got all these visitors. Carlo don't like that. He's worried you might talk to the wrong people. Maybe say the wrong thing."

St. John couldn't keep his mouth shut. "My name is Franklin St. John and I'm the United States attorney. Put your guns down. You're under arrest."

Tony laughed. "Jimmie, where did you get these guys? And who are you?" he asked Mason.

"I'm Jimmie's lawyer."

Tony said, "So, that's the way it is, Jimmie? You got your lawyer, the FBI, and the U.S. attorney in your room all at the same time. Smells like you're selling out. I guess we got here just in time."

Gino pulled St. John from his chair and shoved him against McNamara, leaving them huddled in a corner next to the window. Gino took a step back, keeping out of McNamara's reach and keeping his pistol pointed at the two of them.

Camaya lifted the gun from behind Mason's back and nudged Mason with the barrel. Mason edged forward until he was barely on the bed and the balls of his feet were pressed to the floor like loaded springs. He braced his hands against the edge of the bed for added leverage.

The tall man Jimmie called Tony stood at the door, about five feet directly in front of Mason. The second man was closer to Mason, but at an angle to Mason's left. Mason knew that Tony would shoot him before he got close to him, but he'd have a chance with Gino if Camaya took care of Tony.

"Listen, Tony," Mason began. "This isn't working out like you expected. You probably counted on the cop outside the door. You didn't figure on an FBI agent and the U.S. attorney. You kill everyone in this room and your boss is going to catch so much heat you'll never be able to go home again."

Tony considered Mason's comments. "It is the way it is, pal. Lots of people end up in the wrong place at the wrong time. I guess this is just your time."

"Last chance," Mason told him. "Put your guns down and give up or Jimmie will shoot you." Both gunmen laughed. "Don't say I didn't give you a chance."

Mason stood up, stepping toward Gino and drawing Tony's attention away from Camaya. Tony froze in astonishment at the gun in Camaya's hand long enough for Camaya to shoot him in the face. He was dead before he hit the floor.

Mason leapt at Gino but not before Gino shot McNamara. Gino had weight on his side. Mason had surprise and desperation on his. And he fought dirty. Mason grabbed Gino's gun with his left hand and Gino's testicles with his right, squeezing both while he drove his head into Gino's neck.

The gun flew out of their grasp as they toppled onto the floor. Gino slammed his knee upward, breaking Mason's grip on his crotch and wrapped his hands around Mason's throat. His fingers were crushing Mason's windpipe and cutting off his breath. Mason straddled Gino as the bigger man held Mason at arm's length, strangling him. Raising his right hand from Gino's chest, Mason jammed his forefinger into Gino's eye, puncturing the outer surface until he felt the hard socket against his knuckle. Gino's piercing scream nearly shattered Mason's eardrum as his grip on Mason's throat gave way. Mason withdrew his bloody hand, leaving Gino's eye dangling alongside his nose.

Mason staggered to his feet. McNamara lay on the floor, moaning but alive. St. John had wet himself and assumed the fetal position on the floor next to McNamara.

"My man! My main man!" Camaya crowed, waving Mason's gun in the air.

Mason knew that Camaya had saved his life. But only to save his own. Mason snatched the gun from him and grabbed him by the throat.

"I'm not your man, you miserable piece of shit. Now call the nurse!"

Chapter Thirty-three

Sunday started with a steady rain pinging against Mason's windows as he lay in bed long after the cops' last questions stopped reverberating in his ears. It was welcome white noise, something to concentrate on when he felt Gino's blood trickling down his arm again. Bright flashes of light sparkled against his eyelids when he clenched them tightly against the jarring array of mortal images he had collected. Snapshots of Sullivan's bloated corpse, Harlan's gargoyle death mask, Julio's pulverized face, and Gino's mutilated eye dotted his mental landscape like unholy billboards. He had slipped so easily from a world of rules where uncivil conduct toward an adversary was grounds for sanction to one in which blood ruled and the only sanction that mattered was death. He doubted whether he wanted to return to his old world and he was equally uncertain he would ever fully depart his new one.

Dawn, gray and misty, found him pounding the

jogging path around Loose Park, two blocks from home. Breathing raggedly, he tried to outrun the demons that had become his new best friends until he dropped facedown in the grass, cool and wet. The rain ran off him as he rolled onto his back, squinting skyward, looking for an opening in the clouds. With no epiphany in sight, he trudged home to find Anna Karelson camped on his doorstep, dry and nosey under her umbrella.

"For pity's sake, Lou, you'd have to look better to die!" she said.

"Early morning isn't your best time of day either, Anna," he said, returning the compliment good-naturedly.

The right side of her hair was still flattened by her pillow. Crow's-feet threatened to overrun laugh lines, and she hadn't found her bottle of Scope yet. She was wearing a candy-striped housecoat, loosely tied at the waist, over an aqua-colored nightgown that was playing peek-a-boo with her heavy bosom.

Mason insisted, "It's just the rain. I'm fine."

"In a pig's eye! My two-week-old bananas have better color than you do."

"Look, Anna. I appreciate your concern, but I'm really okay. I promise to look better after I clean up and get some rest," Mason replied as he unlocked his front door.

"Well, Mr. Celebrity Lawyer, I wouldn't plan on getting any rest today if I was you," she announced, following him inside.

"Meaning?"

"TV trucks and reporters have been banging on your door since you left this morning. I told them you took a cab to the airport. But they'll be back, that's for sure."

Mason had one more rock to turn over before he was ready to go to the cops on Sullivan's and Angela's killer. It wasn't Camaya. He'd never take the time to poison someone. If the media started shining their light on him now, he'd lose the privacy he needed.

"Anna, mind if I shower at your house?"

"Lou!" she said as she blushed and clutched her gown to her chest. "Jack's still asleep!"

"Don't worry, I'm a quiet scrubber." He ran upstairs and grabbed clean clothes, a black windbreaker, a Beaver Creek cap, and Vernon's Bible.

"Drive my car around the block behind your house," Mason said as he handed her the keys to the TR-6. "I'll be in the shower."

Anna came in through her back door, dripping and cursing Mason as water ran off her neck and between her breasts. "Honestly, Lou, I don't know why I let you talk me into these things."

He was sitting at her kitchen table, tying his shoes while scanning the front page of the morning paper. McNamara would live. St. John announced that his investigation into organized crime would continue.

"That's what neighbors are for, Anna. I owe you one."

Mason glanced out her living room window across the street. Camera crews for the local affiliates of the major networks were setting up shop in his front yard, their logos emblazoned on the rain ponchos of each crew. The clock was running on his fifteen minutes of fame.

Mason kissed Anna on the cheek and went out the back door, cutting across lawns to the next block and his car. It was eight o'clock. Early for house calls. Mason hoped he wasn't too late.

* * *

Pamela's newspaper was still in the driveway and there were no lights on in the house. Mason doubted she was an early riser. It felt as though more than twenty-four hours had passed since he'd last knocked on Pamela's door. Vernon's Bible lay heavily against his side, protected from the rain by his jacket, as he leaned on the doorbell. Five minutes of chimes brought protesting footsteps that stopped on the other side of the peephole in the door.

"Lou, what are you doing here at this hour?" Pamela asked in a voice muffled by the thick oak door.

"I've got to talk with you. It's very important."

"I had a late night. Can't it wait until later, or tomorrow?"

"Pamela, please open the door. I can hardly hear you."

Mason hoped that it would be harder to send him away face-to-face than separated by the heavy door. The dead bolt slid back reluctantly. Pamela pulled the door open enough to peer around the edge. Mason stepped sideways through the narrow opening before she could protest.

She had the same puffy-eyed, just-rousted-from-bed look as Anna. He stood close enough to taste the stale smoky aroma that hung on her. He could smell the booze in her sweat. Pamela hunched her shoulders inside her velour red robe zipped to the neck, magnifying her pallid complexion. She was close enough to rock bottom to touch it with her tongue.

"I'm sorry to barge in on you like this. I know

who killed your husband. I thought you would want to know.''

She slumped against the door, pushing it closed, as she covered her mouth with one hand, her eyes asking questions that she refused to speak.

"I don't want to go to the police until I'm certain," Mason continued. "There are a few details about Richard's past that I need to clear up. Let's talk in the study.''

Mason led the way, Pamela following silently. He hoped that taking charge in her own house would keep her off her guard. The study reeked of Pamela's long night. She didn't smoke. Mason wondered who did.

The cushions on the sofa had been left in casual disarray with two of them piled at one end. Pamela planted herself next to them and grabbed another to wrap her arms around. Mason settled into the wingbacked chair opposite the sofa, setting his jacket next to the ornamental letter opener on the small table next to the chair. He had wrapped the Bible inside the jacket. They were separated by a dark walnut butler's table water stained by a now empty wine bottle. Two streaked glasses, one with lipstick on the rim, lay on their sides. He pretended not to notice. It wasn't any of his business if Pamela skipped the grieving widow stage and jumped into friendly arms.

Pamela squeezed the pillow in her lap as if she were trying to pull herself inside it. She hadn't uttered a sound since he'd told her why he was there. Not even a monosyllabic "Who?" The silence was so puzzling that he decided to wait her out—make her ask him who did it.

Smiling neutrally at Pamela, Mason stood and began a quiet survey of the study. The bookshelves behind Sullivan's desk were filled. Mason had a theory that you could learn a lot about a person by the books they kept. Some people kept them for show. Others because they intended to read them someday though they never would. Still others read them, loved them, and took comfort in being around them. He had some of all three. Most of Sullivan's, the bindings crisp and virginal, belonged in categories one and two. Having them was what counted. Not knowing them.

Wandering into the far corner from the windows overlooking the front lawn, Mason pulled up short in front of a volume half hidden by the vertical molding on the end of the shelves. The top half of the letters in the title was visible enough along the book's spine that he could read *Rogersville H.S. 1963 Yearbook*. He sat down in Sullivan's desk chair and began leafing through the book. Pamela was still mute. So much for clever psychological ploys.

"Did you and Richard get back to Rogersville very often?" Mason asked, looking at Pamela rocking slightly on the sofa. Her eyes bore down on the intricate pattern in the Persian rug as if the answer could be divined in the weave.

"Pamela, over here," he said, breaking her spell. She jerked her head up and raised her lids halfway in his direction. "Did you and Richard get back to Rogersville very often?"

"Not in years."

Mason found Sullivan's senior class picture and index of achievements. Flattop, shiny cheeks, cocked arrogant smile, head tilted at a jaunty angle. Look out, world, here he comes. Lettered in track and cross-country. Choir. Junior Achievement.

"Why not?" he asked.

Flipping backward through the pages, Mason ran

his finger under the names beneath the pictures, stopping at Meredith Phillips's photograph. Page boy, wide nose, wider face, crooked smile, square chin. Unremarkable, yet vaguely familiar. Home Ec Club.

"No reason to," she said to the floor. "We wanted out."

The girl in the photograph next to Meredith's had long dark hair tucked behind her ears, bangs pulled across her forehead, oval face with perfectly aligned teeth, dimpled cheeks. Cheerleader, Homecoming Queen. Pamela Phinney. Mason looked up. There was no doubt. Pamela Phinney Sullivan lay back against the couch, her eyes raised to the ceiling.

"You knew Meredith Phillips?"

"We were best friends," she said softly.

"And you didn't know about the baby?" Some best friend.

"Best friends in high school—not later."

"What happened?"

"She and Richard dated all through school. No one could figure it out. Great looking guy and the homely girl."

"No competition," Mason explained.

"Maybe. Anyway, she was a small-town girl. Richard and I couldn't wait to escape."

"And you ended up with Richard."

"Chased him for four years in high school. That's why Meredith and I were best friends. She kept me close to Richard. Back then, he was loyal. But I got him in the end."

"But not before he and Meredith had one last stroll around the park."

"No—not before."

"And you didn't know about the baby until I told you yesterday?"

She hesitated an instant before answering. "Not before—"

"Not before what?" Diane Farrell asked, one hand on her hip, the other on the entry to the study. She was wearing a half-buttoned man's pajama top that fell to midthigh and, nearly as Mason could tell, nothing else.

Mason hadn't felt the same mixture of shock and embarrassment since his aunt Claire had caught him in the bathroom with a copy of *Playboy* when he was thirteen. Pamela paled at Diane's appearance, growing smaller behind her pillow.

"Diane—please don't do this to me," she pleaded.

Smiling voraciously, Diane walked toward her. A tremor shook Pamela.

"Pamela dear, I told you last night that I wasn't like the society lesbians you cheated on Richard with," she said, standing in front of her, stroking her hair. "You didn't tell me we were having company for breakfast," she added with a predatory look at Mason.

Mason said, "I was in the neighborhood." It was the snappiest explanation he could manage until he regained his footing.

"Pamela, you're ruining my new dress under those pillows." She reached down and extracted the wrinkled dress Pamela had given her on her birthday.

"Please, Diane—no," Pamela managed, her lips barely moving, her face downcast.

"But, Pamela, it's all I've got to put on. After all," she giggled, "I didn't pack my overnight bag."

She shook the wrinkles out of the dress and

looked at Mason again. "If you don't mind, Mason.
I'm a little modest around men."

Nodding automatically, he stood and turned his
back, placing the yearbook on the credenza behind
Sullivan's desk. A dictating machine, no doubt one
of the firm's frozen assets, sat next to the book.
Trusting that Diane had her eyes on Pamela, he
picked up the handset from the cradle, put it in the
record mode, and set it down next to the recording
unit. With any luck, it would pick up whatever
happened next.

"Okay, Mason, you can turn around. I'm decent."

"Not by half," he said as he pushed Sullivan's
desk chair back, blocking her view of the credenza.

"Mason," she said, sticking out her lower lip
in a mock pout, "I sense your disapproval. How
provincial. This is the new millennium."

"Leaving someone their dignity never goes out
of style."

"Noble horseshit. Now tell me what you and
Pamela were talking about. She seems to have lost
her spark. She probably needs a drink."

"I was asking her if she knew where you worked
before you came to the firm."

"You came here at eight o'clock on Sunday
morning to ask Pamela about my work history? You
can do better than that."

"I've taken up genealogy. I'm trying to figure out
if pathological behavior is a generation-skipping
phenomenon."

Mason returned to the wingback chair, picking
up his jacket. She held her ground by the sofa,
warily appraising his comments, calculating her
response. Pamela's muted sobs were buried in her

pillow, the undercard to the main event about to begin.

"In that case, my family wouldn't interest you."

"Why not?"

"Every generation has been pathological," she said without a trace of humor.

"Tell me about them. Maybe I'll change my approach."

"Oh, Mason, you're being so coy. Why don't you ask me what you really want to know?" she suggested.

Diane sat down next to Pamela and placed her arm around her. Pamela froze at the gesture, then shook her off. She stood, smoothing her robe and glaring at Diane, who smiled serenely in reply. Pamela moved to the windows, looking for answers in the rain. Mason wanted to tell her that she'd have to find them inside. Pamela turned to look at Mason, reading his thoughts. She looked around the room as if to find someplace else to go. Diane smiled at her like a mother silently encouraging her shy child. Pamela sighed and she slowly made her way back to the sofa, accepting Diane's outstretched hand.

Mason ignored Diane's triumphant grin. "What did you do before you came to the firm?"

"Really?"

"Really."

"I went to school. Penn Valley Community College. Paralegal degree with distinction."

"And before that—where's home?"

"No place special. A little town you've probably never heard of."

"Family?"

"None anymore."

"So your first job was with Sullivan?"

"You are a quick study, Mason. I'll bet you're terrifying on cross-examination."

"I like to let things build. What did you think of Sullivan?"

"He treated people like dirt, but I didn't have a problem with him."

"The two of you must have had a special relationship."

Her eyes flickered for an instant with uncertainty. She leaned forward, legs crossed, her chin cupped in one hand, elbow resting on her knee. She was studying Mason closely. Diane was no fool and wouldn't allow him to trap her easily. But Mason knew more than she could suspect and he was better at this than she was. And she was living on lies, which made for a foundation with deep faults. Not the kind that would withstand much stress. Her outrageous treatment of Pamela told Mason that she felt safe—beyond his reach. Now doubt was creeping in, filling the faults and pushing them into wider cracks.

"I knew what he wanted and I did it."

"Including figuring out what Scot and Harlan were doing with Quintex and the phony fees?"

She sat back, leaving her legs crossed at the ankles, arms extended across the back of the sofa. "Including Quintex. Sullivan asked me to check into it. I put it all together for him. Including the Cayman Island accounts. It wasn't difficult. Scot and Harlan weren't very clever crooks."

"But why hide it on the Johnny Mathis CD?"

"That was my idea. Nobody listens to Johnny Mathis. It was the perfect hiding place. All I needed was a scanner and a CD burner. Sullivan didn't want anyone to know he had the information. Except for the U.S. attorney. But I guess he didn't get the chance to rat out his partners and poor Vic Junior," she added with a quick laugh.

Mason connected the last dot. "You knew Sullivan was going to make a deal with St. John?"

"I figured it out. It was the only way he could avoid going to jail," she said with a thin-lipped smile.

Pamela drew herself up, focusing clearly enough on Diane to shrink further into the sofa. Diane clamped her hand on Pamela's thigh, keeping her close.

Mason asked her, "Why did Sullivan revoke his will?"

She shifted her weight uneasily. "He changed his mind about the charities. The codicil gave him time to decide what to do with the money."

It was a practiced reply. The kind that is believed if repeated often enough, but doesn't make sense to anyone else.

"Then why not keep the will and change the beneficiaries? Revoking the will means he dies intestate, the estate pays huge taxes, and the heirs get screwed."

"There would still be plenty for Pamela," she said.

"And for any other heirs," Mason added.

"They never had children. You should do your homework, Mason."

"Oh, I have, Diane. I have. *They* never had children, but Sullivan did."

"So the kid gets a share," she said with forced nonchalance.

Diane avoided looking at Mason as she released her grip on Pamela and toyed with the frayed corner of a cushion. Pamela quickly got up and moved silently behind Mason's chair, peering over his head at Diane.

"How did you know there's only one kid, Diane?"

She reddened slightly, stood, and walked toward the bookshelves. Mason gripped the arms of his chair to keep from cutting her off before she discovered the tape recorder. She stopped at Sullivan's desk and took his seat.

"He said something about it once, a long time ago," she offered.

"What did he tell you?"

Her eyes filled with the memory. "That he'd gotten some girl pregnant a long time ago but didn't find out until years later. Once he found out, he paid support but never saw the child." She couldn't keep the bitterness out of her voice.

"That must have been torture for you, Diane. To be right there in front of him and realize he didn't know you."

"You don't know what you're talking about! Pamela, get him out of here. We don't have to listen to this!"

Mason glanced up at Pamela, whose face was a furious mask. Diane pushed the desk chair back against the credenza. Her eyes were wild.

Mason reached in his jacket and opened the Bible in his lap.

"Pamela, there's an old man lying in a nursing home in Rogersville. He's in a coma. His name is Vernon Phillips. This is his Bible. His family tree makes interesting reading," he said.

"Where did you get that?" Diane hissed, her body taut, ready to spring at him.

"Homework, Alice. When did you take your grandmother Diane Farrell's name? Were you just being clever or did you want Sullivan to figure it out on his own?"

"My mother loved him, gave herself to him, and he pissed on her—on both of us!" she screamed. A lifetime of venom contorted her face.

"He paid child support," Mason said.

"Money!" she spat. "She didn't want his money! She wanted him! But Pamela, beautiful Pamela, got him. And we got nothing."

"You couldn't stand that he didn't want you— didn't even want to see you," Mason said, driving each nail slowly. "When did Meredith tell you about him?"

She was startled at his use of her mother's name. It was another invasion of her life. Mason was Sherman marching through Georgia, and he was just warming up.

"Did she tell you Daddy was dead or that she didn't know who your daddy was? Or maybe she didn't tell you anything at all. Then one day, you found a check from a man you'd never heard of before."

Diane/Alice bolted from her chair, leaning hard on the desk. Mason had scored a direct hit. The words poured out of her in a torrent.

"When I was thirteen, she wrote him a letter begging him to acknowledge me. He sent it back unopened with a check. My mother left it out. That's how she told me!"

"And working for him was your way of getting even? Wasn't it worse when he didn't recognize you or your name? Surely he must have remembered Meredith's mother?"

"My grandmother died when my mother was young. He'd have never known her."

"But still, not to recognize you at all. There had to be some family resemblance."

Mason shook his head sympathetically. Pamela stood as still as Lot's wife as he moved from his chair to the arm of the sofa. He couldn't predict what Diane would do if he kept pushing her, and he wanted more mobility. "When did you finally tell him?"

"Last January."

"Just before he revoked his will. What was his reaction?"

"He told me to keep my mouth shut and my billable hours up."

"That's it?"

"We made a deal. I told him all I wanted was my inheritance. I didn't care if anyone knew so long as I got my share."

"Why not make you a beneficiary in the will?"

"That was too public an acknowledgment. This way, if Pamela died first, I'd get everything as the only heir."

"How were you going to prove paternity?"

"He took a blood test when I was ten. That's when he started paying child support. And I made him sign something."

"Where is it?"

"It doesn't matter."

Mason remembered that Angela had told Sandra that there was something else she wanted to talk with her about. "Angela found it, didn't she?"

Diane's face softened and then hardened again as she sensed where he was headed. "Mason, I'm getting tired of this." She stepped away from the desk. He stood as she reached behind the Carl Sandburg biography of Lincoln and turned around, holding Pamela's gun.

"Oh shit," Mason said involuntarily.

"How thoughtful," she responded.

"You don't need the gun, Diane," Pamela said pleadingly.

"Don't tell me what I need, Pamela. If you'd have left my mother and father alone, none of this would have happened."

"Richard chose me—that's not my fault!" Pamela cried.

"Not your fault! Ha! Mother told me how you seduced him. How did it feel to be seduced by his daughter, sweet Pamela?"

"I've been a greater fool before and no doubt will be again. But there's no need for a gun."

"Tell him that," Diane said, waving the gun at Mason.

"What is she talking about, Lou?"

"She killed Sullivan. Now she's trying to decide whether to kill us."

Pamela stepped toward her. "Diane?" she asked in renewed disbelief.

"You're a pathetic whore. You stole my father. Over there, on the couch where I can see both of you," Diane commanded, directing them with the gun.

Pamela complied, clutching a pillow in her lap.

"How did you know about the gun?" Mason asked.

"Pamela told me. She told me everything."

"Including that Sullivan was HIV-positive?"

"That was rich. It renewed my faith in God."

"But threatened your inheritance. AIDS is a very expensive way to die. But if you killed Sullivan, you'd get your money and your revenge." Mason couldn't think of anything else to do except to keep her talking.

"It was a good deal for both of us. We'd both stop suffering."

"So you told Sullivan that you had access to experimental drugs through the gay community and, as the loving daughter, you wanted to help him."

"I told you he trusted me."

"And you let him shoot himself up with saline until you were ready to give him the fatal dose of insulin."

"My, my. You have done your job, Mason."

"The nursing home doesn't seem real careful about its drugs. Lucky break that your grandfather ended up there."

"It didn't matter. I would have found something to give him."

"How did you get him to inject himself?"

"The day before the retreat, I told him I had something new, very powerful. He begged me for it. I made him wait until Saturday night at the lake," she said with delight.

"And you just watched him kill himself."

"It was a dream come true."

"You might have gotten away with it if you hadn't killed Angela too. How did Angela find out about you?"

"The wiretap on Sullivan's phone. She tried to blackmail me for a share of my inheritance."

"So you went to her apartment. But how did you do it?"

"It was easy. I stabbed her in the neck with a dose of insulin. It's very quick that way."

"And left the suicide note on the computer."

"I thought it was a nice touch," she said.

"Actually, it was stupid. Angela didn't know Sullivan was HIV-positive. Other than his doctor, you and Pamela were the only ones who knew. Too many bodies, Diane. You can't cover all your tracks."

"I can try. After I shoot you, I'm going to help sweet Pamela put the gun in her mouth. A messy murder-suicide should at least muddy the waters."

Diane began walking toward them as Mason stood up.

"Sit down!" she screamed.

There was no way out. She was too far away to try and disarm her, but she was close enough to shoot them both. Mason decided to at least put some distance between him and Pamela.

"Sit down!" she screamed again as he moved toward the desk.

"Diane," Pamela replied wearily, "the gun isn't loaded."

Diane and Mason stopped in their tracks. "What?" he yelled at Pamela. "Were you waiting for a sign from God to tell me?"

"I wanted to know everything," Pamela said. "There have been too many lies. She wouldn't tell the truth if she thought the gun wasn't loaded."

Diane threw the gun at Pamela, striking her on the shoulder and charged her, screaming. They rolled on the floor in a tangle of arms and legs, knocking over the butler's table. Mason pulled them apart, but not before Diane raked Pamela's face with her nails, opening ugly wounds. Mason held Diane with her arm twisted behind her back until her breathing steadied, while Pamela called 911.

Diane sat in the wingbacked chair while they waited for the police. The doorbell rang and Pamela left to answer it. Mason had his back to Diane as he rewound the Dictaphone tape. He turned around just as Pamela and the cops came in the room. They all stared at Diane. She was holding the ornamental letter opener that had fallen on the floor during her wrestling match with Pamela. Diane stared back before plunging the letter opener into her neck.

Chapter Thirty-four

Diane sliced her jugular vein. The cops did what they could and the paramedics did more. Diane lived long enough to be pronounced dead in the emergency room.

The clouds were breaking up when Pamela and Mason left the hospital. It had been two weeks since he had identified Sullivan's body at the lake. For the first time, the air seemed to clear.

Pamela thanked him for the ride, for everything, she said. Mason promised to check in on her but it was a promise neither of them wanted him to keep. It's too hard to become friends after you've been stripped naked.

Mason believed that Pamela must have suspected Diane. At least that she was Sullivan's daughter. Yet she allowed their relationship to become dangerously intimate. Perhaps had even encouraged it. He'd read that some people stay in abusive relationships because they think they deserve it. Maybe

Pamela knew what she was doing with Diane—punishing herself for taking Sullivan from Diane and her mother. Jerry Springer would probably do a show on women who sleep with their stepdaughters who kill their husbands to get even with their fathers for abandoning them.

Sunday evening, Mason met Kelly at the airport. Other friends and lovers streamed past them, embracing one another, grabbing luggage, moving on. Mason and Kelly stood for a moment, holding hands, measuring where they were. She clutched him briefly, brushed his lips, and said she was glad he was all right. The intensity of the last two weeks had locked them together. Both sensed that the grip of those days was loosening.

They had a quiet dinner at Constantine, dancing small steps around the future.

"Blues is buying the bar across the street," he told her. "It comes complete with office space upstairs. I'm thinking about becoming his first tenant."

"That's great," she said. "Really, great. You'll be happier on your own."

Mason knew that she was talking as much about herself as about him. She'd buried her partner, exhumed his memory, and had to bury him again. Another part of her had been lost when her cabin burned.

After dinner, they drove to the plaza and parked in front of their fountain. The top was down on the TR-6. The air was close, thick with humidity. Bugs danced in the fountain's spray. Cars filled with teenagers sauntered past, rap and rock bellowing from open windows. Mason and Kelly smiled ru fully at each other, realizing that the magic had been in the moment, not the fountain, and the moment had passed.

Mason read her thoughts. "Nick was dirty, Kelly. That was about him, not about you."

She sighed deeply, rubbed her hands in her lap, and nodded. "I didn't see it," she said. "That is about me." A thin tear leaked from the corner of her eye. Mason reached to wipe it away. She took his hand. "The cabin was my hiding place, Lou. I hid everything there, including my feelings for Nick, for you, and for myself. I've got to rebuild before I can decide what I want."

Mason dropped her at her hotel. Kelly stepped from the car, leaned back in, and kissed him. He watched her walk away until she disappeared through the revolving door.

The next day, Mason returned Vernon's Bible to him. He was unchanged. A new nurse was caring for him and told Mason that he could last for years in that condition. He almost promised that he'd come back to visit, but he was tired of making promises meant to be broken.

When he got home, he called Webb Chapman. "Any news on the safety hooks?" Mason asked him.

"I was getting ready to call you. The test results came back today. Several of the hooks have blood on them. One of the blood samples matches Tommy's blood type. You need DNA tests to prove it was Tommy's blood and that's not cheap to do."

Mason quickly calculated how much money he ⸢ ⸥ left from his insurance settlement. "Do it," ⸢ ⸥d Chapman.

"Have you told Tommy?"

"No. I want to be certain first."

Blues On Broadway opened the week after Labor Day. It was a straight-ahead joint. No cutesy memorabilia from funkier times. A rectangular-shaped mahogany bar dominated the center. Glasses hung in racks from the ceiling. Single malt scotch got premier billing on the shelves behind the bar. Black leather booths lined the walls and a handful of matching round tables dotted the floor. Blues's Steinway grand piano, its ebony wood buffed to a high sheen, sat a foot off the floor on a stage barely big enough for it and the big man who played it. Mason had an office upstairs and a part-time job, tending bar.

Sandra Connelly dropped in one afternoon as he was wiping glasses. Her auburn hair was shaped, shortened and highlighted for fall. She was wearing a deep burgundy suit, open at the throat. A glistening diamond hung from the center of a gold necklace. She stood in the doorway, silhouetted by the sunshine.

"Come on in," Mason told her. "You can sign up to be a charter regular."

"What do I get? My own chair at the bar?"

"Any seat that isn't taken."

"Suits me," she said and settled in on a bar stool. "Give me a glass of your best house wine. And don't open a fresh gallon on my account."

Sandra had been at the center of a fierce recruiting battle among the major law firms in town. She didn't discourage the soft exaggerations of her exploits by the media and leveraged her high profile into a corner office and a fat paycheck. Mason admired her ambition but didn't envy her. He poured and she sipped.

"Victor O'Malley just wrote my firm a check for a hundred thousand dollars."

"Still paying for work his lawyers didn't do," Mason teased.

"Cute, for a bartender. This one is the real deal, Lou. I'm his lawyer. St. John is still going after him."

"Any word on Vic Junior?" Mason asked.

Sandra turned serious. "No. The cops assumed that Camaya killed him. His father wants me to keep looking. I came by to tell you something else."

"What's that?"

"Camaya escaped from the prison hospital last night. It looks like he had outside help."

"I'm not worried," Mason lied. "Jimmie and I have an understanding."

"All the same, watch your back. Are you going to spend the rest of your life tending bar?"

"Nope. I'm just helping Blues. The DNA tests on one of the Philpott safety hooks turned up Tommy's blood. I'm going to file a motion for a new trial next week. Then I'm going to hang my shingle out in an office upstairs and see what comes through the door."

"Just remember, Lou. My door's always open." She left him a nice tip.

Mason wandered upstairs to his office. Tuffy was curled comfortably on a rug next to his desk chair, waiting for her ears to be scratched. Kate demanded he return the dog when she came back from her road show. He told her to tell it to the ︱dge. Tuffy perked up at his return and followed ︱ to his desk.

︱n settled into his chair, swiveled around to

look out his windows onto Broadway, and reached for the back of Tuffy's head. His office was in a part of town the mayor described as "in transition." He felt the same way. There was nothing fancy about the office—just the basics. Blues had given him an office-warming gift. It was a metronome. He told Mason to just listen to the beat. It was good advice.

"Book 'em!"
Legal Thrillers from Kensington